T0196492

THE LEGEND OF ESTRELLA

The Legend of Estrella

Brenna McVay

THE LEGEND OF ESTRELLA

iUniverse books may be ordered through booksellers or by contacting:

iUniverse
1663 Liberty Drive
Bloomington, IN 47403
www.iuniverse.com
1-800-Authors (1-800-288-4677)

Because of the dynamic nature of the Internet, any web addresses or links contained in this book may have changed since publication and may no longer be valid. The views expressed in this work are solely those of the author and do not necessarily reflect the views of the publisher, and the publisher hereby disclaims any responsibility for them.

Any people depicted in stock imagery provided by Thinkstock are models, and such images are being used for illustrative purposes only. Certain stock imagery © Thinkstock.

ISBN: 978-1-5320-1703-2 (sc)
ISBN: 978-1-5320-1702-5 (e)

Library of Congress Control Number: 2017901866

Print information available on the last page.

iUniverse rev. date: 02/22/2017

This is book is dedicated to the memory of my grandfather Benjamin "Archie" McVay. May his love and memory live on in the hearts of those who loved him, and in the hearts of everyone who reads this book.

I love you, Grandpa.

TABLE OF CONTENTS

PREFACE

The Legend of Estrella has been a long time in the making. Writing it has been my passion and my labor of love. I hope that it finds you well and you treat it kindly. It started out as the story of my life written in the genre of fairy tale, but over time it became an epic fairy tale inspired by my own thoughts.

The Legend of Estrella is a work of fiction set in medieval times. Some things may not be historically accurate for the time period, but that does not trouble me, as I do not write to please historians or picky critics. I write for my own pleasure. And if the reader enjoys my work, then that will make it even more pleasurable for me.

As you follow Estrella through her first quest and meet her new friends and new enemies, you are drawn to her character and into her world. You will notice that the animals who appear in this tale talk not only to their owners but also to Estrella. (The animals' dialogue appears in curly brackets). As an added bonus, you will find hidden among the pages little stars, just like Estrella will find that her fate and path lies hidden among the stars.

Acknowledgment

Scripture quotations are taken from the *Holy Bible: New International Version*. *NIV*. Copyright © 1973, 1978, 1984 by International Bible Society. Used by permission of Zondervan. All rights reserved.

PROLOGUE

The Problem with Magic

Queen Althea, awaking in the middle of the night to the sound of Estrella gasping for breath, jumped out of bed and rushed to the bassinet. The queen lifted up her child, who was weak and burning up with a racing pulse. Holding her baby close, Althea took her to the bed. Once there, she shook Indra awake.

"Indra! Indra, wake up!"

"What is it, my queen?" Indra asked groggily, sitting up.

"It's Estrella! She can't breathe and she is burning up. I don't know what's wrong with her. You have to do something! Please?" The queen was sobbing.

"I will summon the staff and a physician. I will do whatever I can. We will get help for her. Don't worry, my love." Indra swung the bedchamber door open, grabbed the guard by the collar, and ordered him, "Go wake the staff! My daughter is sick; we need the physician!"

Althea paced the room with the infant in her arms, rocking her back and forth in an effort to calm her. The first to rush in were the nursemaids, who finally coaxed the queen into handing over the baby so they could check her nappy. Upon discovering that the child had diarrhea, they changed her, but she still fussy. On top of that, she was wheezing. The rest of the staff worked to comfort the king and queen, saying things such as, "Your Majesty, you must sit down and relax. She is going to be okay. You won't make her any better by being in such a state," and "Your Highness, you must sit down. The physician is on his way, but you have to calm down first, and sit. Please, sire."

Then the kitchen staff came in with cups of tea and something light for the royal pair to eat. Meanwhile, the nursemaids tried to get Estrella to feed, but she wouldn't latch onto a breast. They thought it was their milk that the baby didn't want, so they handed her to the queen to see if her mother's milk would make her eat. But she still refused to eat, which broke Althea's heart.

When the physician finally arrived, Estrella was in a worse condition. He took her from the nursemaids, felt her head, pricked her finger to test her blood, and then wrapped the finger. He looked in her nose and listened to her chest. Then he said, "I am sorry, Your Majesties. She seems to be phlegmatic, that is, she has fluid in her lungs, which is making her sick. She has a low fever, which will get hotter over time, as well as chills. She has breathing problems from the fluid. She is weak and in a lot of pain. I don't know what else to do for her."

Once the physician was excused and had left the castle, Althea broke down in sobs, clutching the limp and weak infant to her chest. Indra's heart sank. How could this be happening to his baby girl?

Estrella only got worse. She coughed and wheezed the whole night. Indra sat by the fireplace, his face in his hands. Althea tried everything she could to calm Estrella, but nothing was helping.

"Please, my child, you have to breathe for Maia. Come on, take big slow breaths. Please, Princess?" she begged. But Estrella's breathing didn't slow down; it only got faster. "Indra, will you please hold her? You haven't even touched her since the physician left. Please, she needs her father too." Althea held the baby out to him.

"If the physician can't help her, how can I?"

"At least put her back to bed for me? Maybe the love of her father will ease her enough to sleep," Althea said, trying to persuade him.

Indra hesitantly took the small, weak baby in his arms and hummed to her. As he rocked her, her coughing slowed down, but she was still wheezing.

He put her back in the bassinette and joined Althea, who was now in bed. They tried to fall asleep, but Estrella's wheezing kept them awake. At one point, Althea curled up and cried.

The next day, Estrella was even worse. Her breathing was shallow, her fever was hotter, and her coughing wouldn't stop. Indra had the staff come in and move the baby and her things into the nursery. Althea came to the door in time to see them take Estrella and the bassinette out of the room.

"What are you doing?! You can't take her away. She needs me; she needs us. Indra, do something!"

"Althea, I told them to. She needs isolation. They can care for her and we can sleep. We need our health; we can't afford to get sick," Indra replied, trying to calm his wife.

"How could you? She needs us, the love of her parents, even if we get sick!" She sobbed and followed after the nursemaids.

It wasn't that Indra didn't care about his child. In fact, he cared so much that he sent out messengers to all towns searching for a magic cure. Magic had to have the answer. If anything could heal his child, it had to be magic.

The first to arrive with the magic cure was a shaman from the next town over. An old man with long gray hair, he wore a long brown robe.

"Your Highness, thank you graciously for the invitation." He bowed. "When do I get my reward, as you promised?"

"You get the reward if you succeed in curing my daughter," Indra said coolly.

"As you wish, sire. Where is the child?"

"I will call for her nurses," Indra replied. Then he sent a servant to tell a nurse to bring Estrella. A nurse came into the room with Estrella loosely wrapped in a thin blanket. The baby was shaking and coughing, and her wheezing was now wet and raspy. The airways in her nose were apparently blocked; she was working harder to breathe.

"What seems to be the problem with the child?" asked the old man.

"She is phlegmatic," replied the nurse.

"Can you help her?" asked Indra.

"I will do my best, my lord," he replied. Then he started mixing herbs and making a paste. When he finished, he carefully took the baby and started chanting words and rocking her around. Simultaneously, he rubbed the paste on her head and chest. But all that did was give her a rash.

Indra was upset. This man was clearly a fraud. The king's suspicion was confirmed when he ordered the guards to escort the charlatan out of the castle and the shaman had the audacity to ask again about the reward.

The nurse took Estrella back to the nursery. As they passed by Indra, he caught a look at his tiny frail daughter in so much pain. It strengthened his resolve to find her a cure.

The next day and the days following, the same sort of things occurred. Some charlatan claiming to have a miracle cure for the princess arrived, only to fail and demand the reward. After the shaman, it was the magician, then the druid priest, then the psychic, and then the illusionist—all frauds hoping to profit from the king's desperation for a cure.

By the end of the week, Estrella had gotten a lot worse. She wasn't eating and was vomiting. She was gauntly thin from starvation. If she did eat, she just vomited it back up. Her cough was worse—raspy and constant. Her fever was extremely high, but her body was taken by chills, so those attending to her kept her loosely wrapped in the hopes of bringing down the fever but stopping the chills. And at this point, the child's little lips and fingernails had turned blue because oxygen was not getting to them.

At midday on Friday, a wise old gypsy medicine woman arrived at the castle. When Indra heard of her arrival, his hopes rose, as this woman had a reputation for her miracles and cures, which reportedly could cure anything you had.

"Hello. My name is Madame Arrosa. Where is the child?" she asked, bowing in front of Indra.

"She is in the nursery. Shall I send for her nurse to bring her?" he asked.

"Yes, that will be fine."

Indra called for a nurse to bring Estrella out. Within moments, the nurse appeared, holding the tiny baby.

Upon seeing the baby, Madame Arrosa said, "Let me hold her, sire. I can help her."

Indra nodded, and the nurse handed Estrella to the gypsy. Madame Arrosa held the baby close in one arm and rocked her. Using the other arm to pull out creams, she rubbed some on Estrella's chest. Then she pulled out an amulet.

"Mermaids' tears always pulls the sickness out." She waved the amulet over the baby, circled it above her chest, chanted foreign words, and then placed it on her chest. But something unexpected happened. Instead of pulling out just the fluid from the child's lungs, it pulled out all the fluids and water from her whole body. Her mouth became dry and sticky; her eyes became dry, red, and sunken in; and the soft spot on top of her head had sunken in. She was very irritable.

The nurse, in shock, grabbed Estrella from the gypsy. She held her close, rushing off to the nursery to attend to the baby's needs.

Indra was furious. "How could you, you witch?! I trusted you. You said you could help her! You were supposed to be the miracle worker. Where is her miracle?! You cursed her worse. You did something awful to her!" He snatched the amulet and smashed it on the ground. Looking at the guards, he demanded, "Throw this witch out of my castle and out of my kingdom!"

The guards seized the gypsy and escorted her out of the castle. Once she was off the property, they closed the gates behind her.

Indra was enraged. This couldn't be happening! Magic had the answers; magic was the cure. How could everything he believed in fail him, and curse his daughter? Magic was not the cure; it was a curse. It had no answers; it just created the problems.

Six hours after she had become dehydrated, Estrella's nappy was still dry. She remained unable to wet in it. She finally was able to cry, but it was a dry cry—no tears.

A week passed. Estrella's phlegmatic humor had cleared, but she became choleric. She cried and screamed all day, her fever was higher, and she was fussy and irritable. Her nurses had to wear cotton fluff in their ears to block out the noise. Queen Althea sunk down in a depression. At night she cried herself to sleep, and she spent her days just sitting outside the nursery to be close to her baby. Indra was withdrawn, distracting himself with work and drinking. He was spending less time with his family and more time trying to drown out the guilt he felt from failing to cure his daughter.

Besides the nurses, the only visitor Estrella had in the nursery was her brother, Gideon. Only two years old, he was Estrella's best friend. He would come in and sing to her, holding her hand and rubbing her tummy, refusing to leave until she fell asleep.

One day, the mood and the hopes of everyone in the castle utterly dropped. They thought all hope was lost. But then something happened that afternoon. Around two o'clock, there was a knock at the door. The staff was shocked. After the king had banned all magic and had issued warrants for anyone showing up at the door for a reward, they didn't think anyone would dare risk imprisonment and show up.

The door was opened to reveal a young woman standing there. Judging from her stature, she was a young adult, maybe nineteen years of age. She wore a modest frock that was faded and frayed. Her sleeves were dirtied and tattered. She was obviously middle class. Her hands were petite yet calloused, showing that she was used to working with her hands. Her hair was raven black, shoulder length, and tied back in a braid, and her eyes shone like emeralds, those with these traits were common in the neighboring town. The dust on her shoes made it plain that she had traveled for quite a ways.

The doorman glowered at the young woman. "Go away! The king is not seeing any more visitors. Please leave."

"Please, sir, I am here to see the babe."

"The king refuses to let anyone else see her. Please go away!"

"Sir, please just let in to see her. I only wish to help."

"If I get in trouble for letting you in, the king will have my head."

"I promise, sir, that if you get in trouble, I will take the blame for you."

"All right." The doorman agreed and opened the door. The young woman walked into the castle and looked around.

"Where might I find the king and his family?" she asked.

"The king is in the study, and not to be disturbed if you wish to live. He has been in a terrible temper since the last person to claim to make the princess better, failed yesterday. The queen is outside the nursery; she has been very sad since the princess got sick."

"Where is the princess?"

"As I have told you, miss, no one sees the princess."

"Listen to me. You have to let me see the baby. I can heal her. If you don't let me see her, she might die, and the death of the princess could be on your hands. And the king would have your head."

"All right, I will take you to her," agreed the doorman, leading her to the nursery.

He opened the door and the young woman went in and walked over to where Estrella lay, yelling and thrashing around in her bassinette. She picked up the frail little baby and began to rock her gently and sing to her, Estrella was crying, fussing and yelling, but the young woman just held her close and rocked her.

One of the servants saw the young woman go into the nursery, and ran to report it to Indra.

Indra was drowning himself in business affairs and plans of war campaigns, when the servant whispered the news in his ear.

"What?! Who allowed her in?" he bellowed, standing up from his seat and storming out of the room.

"The doorman, sire. He let the girl into the castle. And worse yet, he let her into the nursery to the baby."

"He what?!" he bellowed, storming down to the nursery. Arriving, he pushed the door open. "Put my daughter down!"

"Hush. Please lower your voice, Your Highness," she whispered.

"I am the king. You don't tell me what to do, you whelp," he growled.

"I mean no disrespect, Your Highness, but I finally got the babe to sleep and your tone will wake her. You don't want her to wake up and start screaming again, do you?" she asked.

"No, of course not."

Queen Althea stumbled into the room, disheveled and pale. "I can't hear her. Is she okay? Is my baby okay? I can't hear her crying. I can't hear her crying! Have I lost my hearing? Have I gone deaf? Please, Lord, say it's not so." She started to cry.

"Get ahold of yourself, Althea. You're a disgrace to your station," Indra snarled.

"It's all right, Your Majesty. You have not lost your hearing. I just got her to sleep. She is sleeping now."

"You got her to sleep? How?" Althea questioned.

The young woman replied, "I comforted her with contact, gentle rocking motions, and a soothing voice singing to her. She is an infant with discomfort, not a disease-carrying leper. She needs to feel loved."

"That's what I have been saying!" Althea sobbed.

"But comfort alone can't cure her. If you don't let me try," the young woman said to the king, "your daughter will die. She is very sick. Any time we have is precious. Sire, I know a cure that will heal her and bring back her back to health."

"Indra, please, I can't lose her. She is my baby," Althea begged.

"Silence! I'm thinking. She is my baby too. Don't you think I love her too? I tried everything I could to find her a miracle," the king said to his wife. Turning to the young woman, he said, "If the physician couldn't help her and magic couldn't heal her, what makes you think that you can?"

"You have to trust me; I know how to heal her," the young woman reassured him.

"Fine, but if you fail like the others and she dies, then you die too," he threatened.

"I understand," she answered. She began walking around and rocking Estrella, with one hand over her while muttering something in the Gaelic tongue. She did this for an hour.

Finally, when the royal couple thought they had lost their daughter, Estrella stirred. Then her color returned. She started fussing, making suckling sounds, and reaching up with grasping fingers.

"Your Majesty, I think your princess wants to eat. Why don't you see if she wants some of your milk now?" The young woman smiled as she handed Estrella over to her mother. Althea sat down to the feed the baby. Estrella latched on for dear life and started eating heartily. Althea was so excited that she started crying tears of joy and calling all the nurses over to see that Estrella was feeding. Indra was confused, wondering how could this young woman could heal his daughter when no one else could.

"What is your name, young lady?" he asked her.

"Erynne Macrae, Your Highness." She smiled and curtsied.

"Miss Macrae, what magic did you use to bring her back? All the magic the others used failed, but whatever you did brought her back. How did you do it?"

"I used no magic, sire. I used faith and prayer. I prayed and had faith that the Lord God of miracles would heal her."

"Please accept a reward of anything you want. Wealth, jewels, fame, land, station—name it and it's yours," he offered.

"Sire, I didn't do it for a reward. I did it to save the princess. I heard about her illness and knew I had to try to use my faith to heal her."

"Erynne, please, you have to stay with us. You could be Estrella's official nursemaid," Althea offered.

"And I will gift your family with land and money to provide for and support them well," Indra added.

"Very well, I accept," Erynne agreed. Then she gathered the whole family together and prayed over them. Thereafter, with the king's permission, she left to go back home, share the news with her family, and pack her things.

That night, Indra swore against all magic, vowing to keep Estrella away from it and to protect her.

* * *

When Estrella was two years old, Indra discovered that some good friends of the queen were elves, and that the elves' daughter was becoming friends with Estrella. The king banished the family from his home and then moved his family away to a new kingdom in England, When king Arthur offered him a small kingdom as payment for his loyalty. He built big walls around the kingdom to keep Estrella in and the world out.

CHAPTER 1

Reunited

The sun had just started to ascend over Castle Faylin. Already the castle was buzzing with the hum of activity as the servants were cleaning and setting things up, and the kitchen staff were shuffling around, starting the fires, and prepping for breakfast. Above the soft sounds of the castle waking up, one sound rang out clear: that of footsteps running through the halls, accompanied by giggling. Estrella ran through the hallways, jumping over buckets, dodging staff, throwing sheets over her head and behind her, and pounding on bedroom doors. Her maidservant, Erynne, chased her from behind. "Princess, slow down! I'm not as young and fast as I used to be."

"Oh, come on, Erynne. You still have a spring in your step! You're not that old yet." Estrella giggled.

"Why are you up so early, anyway? I have to wrestle you out of your bed on good days." Erynne huffed behind her.

"Because Gideon comes home today! Father said in his letter he would send Gideon home early. And he has gifts for us!"

"All this over a gift?"

"Of course not. It's because Gideon is coming home. He is my best friend—and he promised he would give me more sword lessons."

"You really shouldn't be playing with swords. Those are lessons young men learn, not young ladies."

"Ugh, Erynne. You sound like my mother: 'Princesses don't fight'; 'Get down from that tree. You will ruin your new dress'; 'Get out of that mud puddle'; 'Slow down. You will bring up your condition'; 'You can't ride that big horse. Start on your pony.'"

"She only says those things because she is concerned. She just wants you to be safe and doesn't want to lose you again. She almost lost—" Erynne began to explain, only to be interrupted by her charge.

"Oh, not again with that story. You and Mother tell me that baby story every time I do anything more than sit around and needlepoint. That's dangerous too, you know. I prick my fingers many times in one day."

"Let me look at it. I will make it better."

"No! I don't want to be babied anymore. I am seventeen years old. I like playing outside and getting hurt. It means I'm learning to do things better in the hopes of one day not getting hurt."

"If you wish, Princess, but these practices are dulling and blunting the swords in the armory."

Jumping on the banister and sliding down to the first floor, Estrella called back, "Don't worry, I will sharpen them later." Then she threw open the door to see that no one was there.

Estrella was disappointed. Gideon wasn't home yet, but then again it was just barely dawn. She spent her time waiting by tossing stones at the wall and pestering the sentry.

"Is he here?"

"No, Princess. He has not appeared here in the past two minutes, since the last time you asked."

She sighed and waited five more minutes before asking again. "Can you see him now?"

The sentry groaned and teased her, saying, "Oh yes, now. Now I see him. I wasn't sure if you meant now or the other twenty times you asked. But now that you made it twenty and one times, I do see him."

"Really, you see him?"

"No. It was just a bird on the horizon. Sorry."

"You're a fiend."

"Yes, I know. But I'm a fiend trying to do his job with the princess pestering him."

Estrella stuck her tongue out at him, thinking he couldn't see her.

"I saw that."

Estrella grumbled at the sentry and then stomped off. She spent the rest of the morning wandering around the town and getting into trouble. When Erynne finally caught up to her, she grabbed her by the ear, pulled her through the town, took her to the home of her teacher, Kasim, and sat her in front of him. Kasim, just six years older than she, had been her friend for years. She shared everything with him. At only six years of age, he lost his parents to ignorant murderous people. Then he lived with Tibetan monks for two years. When he was twelve, he became an ordained minister.

"Can you calm her and keep her out of trouble?"

"I think I might know how." Kasim smiled. Erynne, rolling her eyes, left the house. "Estrella?"

Avoiding eye contact, she answered, "Yes?"

"What are you here for this time?"

"Nothing."

"Estrella Sela, your handmaiden wouldn't drag you in here for nothing. Now what has you all excited, so much so that you're causing trouble again—and this early?" Kasim sighed.

"I can't help it. Gideon is coming home! I miss him when he is gone."

"I understand how much he means to you, but you should put some of that energy to better use. Now give me the list. What did you do this time?"

"I pestered the sentry, stole cookies from the baker, hid the tailor's ribbons, and stole meat from the butcher and gave it to the stray dogs."

Kasim, sighing, rubbed his forehead. "Is that all?"

"Well, it is only morning. No one is awake to play with me." She pouted.

"That wasn't a real question, Estrella."

"Then why did you ask, silly?" She giggled.

"Well, while I have you here, I might as well give you your lesson to keep you busy. Where did we leave off?"

Estrella sighed. "We were reading the book of Esther; Queen Vashti had just disobeyed the king's order."

"Yes, of course. 'Then Memucan replied in the presence of the king and his nobles, "Queen Vashti has done wrong, not only against the king but also against all the nobles and the people of the all the provinces of King Xerxes,"'" Kasim said, starting the lesson. They read through the rest of the verses, stopping for discussions.

They had reached the next chapter in the book of Esther when they heard, "The prince is here! The prince is here! Prince Gideon has arrived! Prince Gideon has returned!"

Estrella jumped from her seat and rushed to the door, calling, "Bye, Kasim! Gideon is back!"

"Stay out of trouble, Princess!" he called after her. But he knew it was useless. Trouble followed that girl like flies to honey. Estrella ran out of the house, grabbed the hidden sword she kept by the gate, and climbed onto the roof of the nearest house, and waited.

Prince Gideon rode up to the gate of his father's small kingdom and called up to the sentry, "Good morning, Joshua. By any chance, have you seen my sister?"

"Unfortunately, I have. She was here at dawn pestering me, asking if I had seen you yet."

Gideon chuckled. "That sounds like my Estrella."

"I teased her a little, and then she stomped off to cause trouble somewhere else."

"Yes, that sounds just like her. No doubt she heard you announce my arrival and is waiting to ambush me once I'm inside."

"Sire, if you know what she is going to do, why do you always act so surprised when she attacks you?"

"Because she enjoys it so much." He smiled and rode through the gates.

Estrella lay in wait, keeping perfectly still and quiet, as she watched Gideon approached right underneath her position. She leapt off the roof, sword raised, and yelled like a crazy girl, "Ahh!"

Gideon smiled and raised his sword, blocked her attack. He arched his back and used her own weight in the momentum and threw her to the ground. and threw her to the ground. He dismounted and pinned her down.

"Ha! Nice try, Princess, but you need to work on a silent attack." He laughed.

"Aw, but Giddey, it's more fun to yell at you when I attack."

"Other than its being fun, it serves no purpose and it gives away your attack. Do you surrender, Princess?"

"Never. You will have to do more than just pin me and gross me out with your stinky fish breath," she taunted, sticking her tongue out at him.

"Be careful with that thing, Esy. I might just grab it next time," he teased her, pushing his sword harder against her, trying to get her to yield.

"Try it, I dare you!" She laughed, and then stuck out her tongue and quickly retracted it. "How do you expect to train me with you on top of me, you oaf?"

"Tough talk for a little princess." He laughed and stepped back, getting into a fighting stance. "Are you ready to back those words up with some fighting moves?"

Estrella laughed as she somersaulted backwards, hopped up on her feet, and stood ready. "Ready!"

"Who taught you that move?"

"Oh, just some old guy. I think his name started with a *G* or a *J*. I can't remember," she replied, teasing him.

"Hey now. I am only two years older than you, nowhere near old enough to be called old. And you remember my name perfectly well."

"I know. I wanted to see your reaction." She laughed, and then lunged, thrusting her sword. He jumped out of the way, perfectly parried her jab, and flicked it away. They practiced their fighting until noon, when they collapsed in the grass.

"How long are you staying home this time, Gideon?"

"Well, the thing is, Father wants me to take over as the new ruler in his place. He finds himself too busy to go back and forth, so he is focusing more on outer kingdom affairs," he told her. But he knew there was something else keeping his father away from the castle.

"Yay! I'm glad to have you home more." Estrella sighed. Without her father around to be her male figure, Gideon took up the role and taught her things that she wasn't taught in her princess lessons. She learned to ride horses, care for her weapons, defend herself, escape captors, and fight back. Gideon wanted her to be prepared if she ever found herself in trouble or danger and he wasn't around to protect her. He wanted her to be independent and take care of herself. She had insisted on learning to ride a horse at six years old. At nine years of age, she had learned how to fence, to use a sword, and to shoot arrows. At ten years old, she had learned how to escape being tied up, how to survive being confined, and how to get out of chains. Queen Althea was less then than thrilled that Gideon was teaching Estrella these lessons. The prince and princess would serve their punishments but then get right back to business the next day. Estrella had almost mastered archery at fourteen. She learned from failures and pushed herself to perfection.

＊ ＊ ＊

The day was warm and the afternoon sun was beating down on the two figures in the open field. Arrows were flying through the air. Estrella wiped the sweat from her brow as she reached behind her for another arrow to shoot.

"You are doing better, but you keep missing the mark," Gideon called to her.

"I would be able to hit the mark if you came closer and held it still!" she shouted in frustration.

"Come on, Estrella, you are not nine years old anymore. You can shoot further than five feet, and you don't expect your enemy to hold still for you to hit him. Let's try again," he called back, picking up the shield again.

A messenger arrived at the kingdom, asking for the ruler. The sentry directed him to the training field. When the messenger reached the area where Estrella was practicing archery, he was confused to see the guards all covered under their shields. One of them pulled him under a shield for safety.

"What is going on? Is your kingdom under attack? Why are you all under your shields?"

"We are not under attack. The princess is in archery practice; the shields are for our own safety," said the guard.

"Do you know where I might find the king?"

"He has not been home for months."

"What of the prince?"

"He is on the field with the princess. He is giving the lesson."

"I have an urgent message for him."

"Here, take this shield." The guard handed the messenger the extra shield. "And run fast. She is learning to shoot moving targets."

The messenger took the shield and ran clumsily across the field to the prince. When Gideon saw the messenger moving toward his position with a shield, he called, "Hold!" He kept his shield up until messenger reached him. An arrow hit the shield dead center, with a thud.

"Yes!" Estrella exclaimed.

"Doesn't count," Gideon called.

"Ugh! Why not? I hit it!" she shouted.

"The target was not moving, and you fired after I called, 'Hold.' The hit is disqualified."

"Argh!" Estrella yelled. She threw her bow into the air.

"Bow!" called the guards.

"Go pick that up," Gideon called back after opening the letter the messenger had given him.

"Ahh!" Estrella yelled, stomping off after her bow.

After reading the letter, Gideon whispered to the messenger, "How long do I have?"

"You must come immediately, I'm afraid—today."

"Very well. Give the high king my reply."

"Very well," the messenger said. Then he headed off the field.

Estrella found her bow and called back, "Found my bow! I'm ready to try again."

"That's enough, Estrella. We are done for today."

"Come on, Gideon. I know I messed up that last one, but I know I can do better this time."

"Estrella, we are done. I have to leave. King Arthur has summoned me." Gideon immediately ran into the castle to begin packing. Estrella followed him in.

"You're leaving me?" she asked.

"I have to. This is a summons, not a request or an invitation. You can't ignore it, or else there are penalties," he explained.

"But the kingdom needs you. We need you. I need you!" she said pleadingly.

"And now Arthur needs me. I can't say no. I'm the representative for our kingdom at the Round Table."

"Gideon, wait. Who is going to watch over our castle and kingdom when you are away? It's your job in Father's absence. Who's going to do it?" she argued, sitting on his trunk to stop him from packing. He pushed her off.

"You are. It's your job now," he replied, opening the trunk to fill his sack. Estrella fell backwards onto the bed in shock.

"Gideon, I can't watch the kingdom! That's a male's job. Females take care of running the household and the servants, not the whole kingdom's affairs."

"Estrella, you can do it. I know you can. It's only until I return. You have to do this. You know Mother can't handle it on her own. You're the best one for the job. I have faith in you."

Shortly, Gideon bid his family good-bye. After kissing Estrella on the forehead, he headed out.

CHAPTER 2

The Gift

The next day, Estrella took on her first job as part-time ruler. Her job was to hear from her people and see to their problems. At first the issues were petty problems, easy things to fix, but soon after the problems got bigger and people were fighting. Estrella was getting overwhelmed and frustrated. She excused herself to her room to cool down.

It was a lot of pressure to put on a princess. She started pacing around her room, muttering to herself, and fidgeting. Very frustrated, she tore the blankets off her bed, threw her papers around, and pulled off her clothes. Now she was only in her shrift. She was having a meltdown, something she hadn't done since she was six, as she was overwhelmed without Gideon there to tell her what to do. If she couldn't handle the responsibilities after the first day, how could she handle them the whole time Gideon was gone? She started to break down and cry, tears rolling down her cheeks, her eyes becoming bloodshot.

Estrella was losing control of her emotions. She grabbed her favorite doll, Bonnie, sat down on her rug, and started to pray. "Dear Heavenly Father, I am so lost. I don't know how to do this on my own. It's far too much for me to handle. What do I do? What's my next move? Please, I need your help. In Jesus's name I pray, amen." After finishing, she listened in the silence until she heard a small voice.

"My child, you are not alone. I am with you; I will lead you. Call out to me and I will hear you and answer. Go to the Enchanted Forest.

The help you seek will come from Bronwyn, Queen of the Fairies," the Lord answered her.

"But I can't leave the kingdom. It's not safe out there. My father doesn't want me to leave the walls. He says it's dangerous," she said out loud.

"I am your Heavenly Father; I will protect you. If you wish for help, you have to follow my directions."

"Lord, you lead and I will follow," she answered. She looked around her room at the mess she had made. Sighing, put her dress back on and then straightened up her room. After that, she went back to her duties.

Although Estrella had her answer, she didn't like it. She didn't like the idea of leaving the comfort of her walls, but she would go.

The next day, she set out to follow the Lord's will. She walked out of the kingdom gates and uneasily crept through the Enchanted Forest. She had heard stories about the fey to keep people out of the Enchanted Forest, stories about a terrible banshee and an evil wild horse called Nightmare. She'd heard about sprites, goblins, and mean little pixies. Worry snaked through her as she looked around her, her imagination running wild as she saw things that weren't there.

Coming to a small lake and looking around, Estrella wondered what to do next. Then she heard the voice of the Lord again. "Remove your slippers and get in the water. This is your test of patience."

"You have got to be kidding me. You want me to wade in there?" she asked to the air. When there was no answer, she took that to mean yes. She took off her slippers and waded waist deep into the water. "Now what do I do?"

"You must call out her name and announce who you are. Acknowledge her power and declare your belief in magic."

"I can't do that. Father told me that magic is bad and I shouldn't have anything to do with it," she argued to the wind.

"Do you trust your Heavenly Father?"

"Yes, but..." She tried to find an excuse to use and reply to the trees.

"Then do what I say. This is your test of trust."

Estrella sighed and called out, "My lady? Queen Bronwyn? I am Princess Estrella of Faylin. I, uh, acknowledge your power, and I believe in your magic."

Nothing happened. So she waited and waited for anything to happen. It felt like hours. She started to catch a chill from the water; she was turning pale, her skin was covered in little bumps, her teeth were chattering fast, and she started shaking. She was so cold that she had forgotten what her request was. All she was thinking about was how cold she was getting. Having given up hope on hearing a reply, she turned to walk out of the forest before getting pneumonia. That is when she heard the Lord's voice whisper, "Stay."

She stayed put. Soon a warm, inviting light shone down on her through the trees. It enveloped her like the sun and warmed the water around her. The color returned to her skin. She felt like she was back home playing in the sunshine. Suddenly the air around her was alive with sparks of lights that twinkled like stars in the sky. As she looked closer, she was surprised to discover they were tiny fairies. The fairies were surrounding her and lifting her out of the water and onto the land. To add to her disbelief, Estrella discovered that her clothes were clean and dry, as if they had come right off the clothesline. It was as if she had never walked through the forest or stood in the water. The fairies even brought her slippers over to her.

Estrella stood there looking around, wondering what would happen next. Then she saw a tall beautiful figure approaching her. She dropped to her knees and bowed her head in fear and respect.

"Are you frightened, young princess?" asked the stranger.

"Y-yes and n-no. I mean, well, my father taught me that all magic is bad and should be feared. If you are the banshee, please don't hurt me. If you are Queen Bronwyn, then my father also taught me not to make eye contact with those of higher stature than me," Estrella managed to explain.

"You are wise for your age, young princess. Yes, I am Queen Bronwyn. You have my permission to rise and lift your head," said Bronwyn.

Estrella stood up on shaky legs and lifted her head to look at the beautiful queen of the fairies in front of her. Bronwyn was tall and slender with ivory skin, kind silver eyes, white hair, and beautiful yellow butterfly wings.

"Did I hear you right? You said you believe in magic, but you said that your father told you that magic is bad and should be feared. How did you learn about magic, and what led you here?" asked Bronwyn.

"I have heard stories about the fey that live here, and I have read about magic creatures in the books that my father tried to keep from me. I came here because the Lord God told me that you could help me."

"And what do you need my help with?" asked Bronwyn.

"Queen Bronwyn, I was given the responsibility of watching over my kingdom while my brother is away. I am but one girl. If I may ask for one thing, I ask for help to accomplish my duties. In your power, would you see it fit to bestow on me the skills to do such a task?" requested Estrella.

Bronwyn smiled. "Yes, my dear girl, I will give you what you need and more. For, you see, the almighty God also spoke to me. He sent me a vision that you were coming. Princess Estrella of Faylin, you have proven yourself to be of pure heart and true intentions. I bless you with the sword of truth, the dagger of justice, and the crystal ball of future sight. I also bless you with a forgiving heart. You will also have a warrior spirit, to defend yourself and those in distress. This spirit must be kept at bay. She thirsts for justice and hungers for adventure. She is released from inside you and takes control when she hears the word *weak*. When that word is uttered, you will change into a fierce warrior. To send the warrior spirit back inside you and gain control over yourself, you must say the word *peace*; then you will go back to being a princess." Bronwyn enchanted Estrella as the fairies bestowed her tools upon her.

"I thank you, my lady." Estrella smiled. When she looked back up at Bronwyn, there was a silver glint in her own eye, the glint of the warrior.

Estrella returned to the kingdom after receiving her gift. She was excited about receiving such a gift, but she was also very cautious not to let others know. Since magic was outlawed in the kingdom, what would that say about her having deliberately gone outside the kingdom and into a forbidden fairy forest where she was given magical powers? Surely they would look down on her, or call her a witch or something terrible, so she kept it to herself until she arrived at her trustworthy friend Kasim's house. Then she told him.

"That was awfully brave of you, my friend," said Kasim.

"I had to. There was no way I could do it without some kind of help."

"Well, it's a good thing you came back. Your mother is swamped. A dispute broke out. She is trying to handle that and the household."

"Oh no. Let's pray first before I go back."

"Yes, let's," agreed Kasim. "Heavenly Father, we come together to ask you to bless Estrella with the wisdom she needs to know how to rule over this kingdom. We know that anything we ask in your Son's name will be given to us, so we ask for wisdom. In your Son Jesus's holy precious name, amen."

Estrella heard the voice of the Lord again, but this time it filled the room. "It is given!" And like that, Estrella was filled with the wisdom of Solomon.

"Thank you," she said, not only to Kasim for praying but also to the Lord for granting his prayer.

Estrella hurried out of Kasim's house and ran to the castle to find the throne room in complete chaos, and her poor mother in a dither, with a terrible migraine. She stepped up, took a big breath, and let out a sharp ear-splitting whistle. Everyone stopped what they were doing and looked in the direction of the sound.

"Thank you! Now, everyone with neighbor disputes, please move to the left and wait behind the velvet rope. Everyone with property damage and livestock issues, wait on the right. Everyone with financial issues, please line up in an orderly single-file line in front of my throne. I will be with you in a moment," she ordered. Everyone complied.

"Thank you, my dear. I don't know what happened. One minute I was organizing some papers in the throne room, and the next minute the doors opened up and these people flooded in. I thought I would hear some of their problems, but they wouldn't listen to me. As a result, I got one of my migraines. Without your father home, and with Gideon gone, I don't who is going to help me rule this kingdom. There is just too much to take care of," Queen Althea explained.

"Maia, I will take care of the kingdom. You have too much to take care of already. Let me handle this," Estrella said.

"Oh, darling, that's nice of you to offer, but this a big job. And it's a job for a man, not a lovely young lady like you," Althea said, coddling Estrella.

Estrella felt the blood rise in her cheeks. Her own mother was telling her what she could and could not do just because she was a girl. She wanted to shout, to scream, but shouting at her mother right now wouldn't help anything. Knowing that it would only upset her mother and make her cry, she instead took a deep breath and calmly stated, "Maia, Gideon put me in charge of the kingdom in his absence. I can do this. I can take care of the kingdom just as well as Father and Gideon can. I have the Lord on my side. This is my job. Please let me take this responsibility off your mind. You have so much to take care of already. Let me do this for you."

Althea saw the plea in her daughter's eyes, heard the sincerity in her voice, and knew how much she wanted to prove herself and help. But it was the queen's job, or a job for a man. Looking around at all the people, she remembered all the yelling. Her migraine returned. Taking a sigh of relief, she smiled.

"All right, my lovely girl. Thank you very much for helping me. I am handing you the reins. God bless you with the knowledge. You can do this." Althea left the throne room and walked to the kitchen to take care of the shopping list for the meals.

Estrella's chest swelled with pride knowing that her mother trusted her. She smiled and sat down in the big throne, looked over all the people, took a deep breath, and said, "The regent princess, and acting ruler, will now hear your problems. Those in the middle line may come forward in an orderly fashion and one at a time."

And from then on she took care of the kingdom justly.

Chapter 3

Pirates!

A week after she had taken over for her mother, Estrella decided to take a trip to the coastal port of commerce to check on the kingdom's imports coming into the harbor. She agreed to her mother's wishes and brought along two armed guards for her protection. They rode the half hour to the port, where they dismounted their horses and walked into the town. It was crowded in the market today, as it was trade day and the ships were coming in. Estrella was making her way through the crowds of busy, pushy people in order to reach her favorite vendor. In the process, she had lost her escorts in the crowd. An uneasiness came over her. She couldn't put her finger on why, but she didn't like the fact that she had been separated from her guards.

Making her way to the storehouse, Estrella felt rough hands bind her arms behind her, and a rough calloused hand cover her mouth. She was being dragged away, away from the crowds of onlookers, away from the protection of her escorts. She tried to struggle and fight, but she felt a sharp pinch in her neck. The world around her faded to black. When she awoke, her hands were bound behind her body with a thick coarse rope and there was a bitter taste of fabric in her mouth. Her vision was blurry, but she could make out the shapes of about two dozen men. They all reeked of body odor, salt air, and pungent rum. It made her stomach flip.

"She wakes. Good day, bonny lass," said one of them smugly. He was dressed in nicer clothes than the others, a puffy white shirt tied at the waist with a black sash and navy blue pants. His blond hair was combed back nicely. He had a moustache, and five-o'clock shadow on his jaw and chin. Estrella figured he must be either the captain or the first mate. She tried to plead with him to let her go but it came out as incoherent mumblings.

"What was that? I can't understand you," mocked another of her captors. This one was obviously just a deckhand. He had maybe sixth teeth, soiled clothing, and greasy hair, and reeked of rum and bile.

The one who had spoken first pushed the smelly pirate away and introduced himself. "Never mind him, miss. Charlie means no harm. My name is Rogers; I am the one in charge of these sea rats. Is there any way we can accommodate you, lass, as you will be with us for a while?" Rogers had come on the ship as a young man, having been the sole survivor of an attack on the ship he was aboard. His father was a royal prince on board a Royal Navy ship headed home. After the ship was attacked, it went down in flames and everyone aboard died, except Rogers. He was found adrift at sea barely alive, with amnesia. He was named after the pirate flag, the Jolly Roger, and was taken as a slave. Eventually he worked his way up to the position of first mate.

Estrella mumbled again and looked down at her gag.

"Oh, get that gag out of her mouth," Rogers ordered. The one called Charlie stepped forward and pulled it down.

"Parley! I demand a parley," she called.

The crew groaned. Just once they hoped they could capture a hostage who wouldn't involve the captain. Rogers ordered one of the crew members to fetch the captain from his office.

These men weren't the smartest captors, as they had forgotten to search Estrella for weapons. If they had, they would have found her dagger secured to her left bicep and her sword in its scabbard strapped to her back between her shoulder blades. She used the time it took for the captain to be summoned, while the men were distracted, to get hold of her dagger. She wiggled her arms around, moved the dagger up and out of its strap, and wiggled it to slide down her arm.

The captain burst out of his quarters, indignant and raging. He was dressed in a rich dark purple coat, a crimson silk shirt, a purple sash, black pants, and a big hat with a bright plume sticking out of it. He obviously thought highly of himself. Judging from his wardrobe, it was apparent that he was driven by both ego and greed. He wanted to be feared, and he sought wealth. He stood arrogantly with his hands on his hips, so as to prove his power.

"There better be a good reason you brought me out my office!" he bellowed, his anger causing the vein to pop out on his forehead.

"I demand—" Estrella yelled.

"Who are you to be making demands on my ship?!" he blustered, stomping over to her. "If you haven't noticed yet, dearie, you are tied to the mast and we are the ones with weapons," he said gloatingly, spitting in her face as he spoke.

"Captain, she is the princess you wanted us to ransom," said Charlie.

"This?" He laughed. "Can't you tell? She isn't even from a wealthy kingdom. She is too small and scrawny; she is barely decorated. I wanted a wealthy princess for a lofty ransom, not the low-ranked milkmaid nobody-type princess you just picked up." He sneered.

"I request you release me at once. If my lord, King Indra—" she said in protest.

"And which one of you Nancies gave her permission to speak?" he snarled.

"Rogers told us to."

"Rogers!"

The first mate reluctantly stepped forward.

"Captain, I—" Rogers said, beginning to explain.

"Rogers, I am the captain of this ship! I give the crew their orders. You are a lousy first mate. She is a hostage." He flashed Estrella a menacing smile. "Her comfort is no concern of ours. All we care about is keeping her alive. Now stuff that rag back in her mouth," the captain barked, rubbing his temples in impatience.

"Yes, Captain Roberts!" the crew called back.

All their talking allowed Estrella time to work through the ropes. The rope was thick, but she was already through two strands when Rogers reluctantly approached her, mouthed the words "I'm sorry," and shoved the terrible rag back into her mouth. This time she could taste the bitter rum and sour sweat. Her head swam, her eyes watered, and the rocking of the ship, combined with the smells of urine, feces, rotting meat, vinegar, sweat, and body odor, made the bile rise up in her throat. The bile burned as she choked it back down, making her even more uneasy. The captain barked more orders at his crew before turning his attention back to his prey and flashing a mocking grin.

"As for you, whelp, you are nothing but a rat aboard this ship—that is, until we hear from your rich daddy who will pay your ransom to get you back. Maybe then we will decide whether to send you back in one piece or not," he threatened.

Rogers gave Estrella a genuinely sympathetic look. She then heard a voice in her head ask, "Are you going to let him talk to us that way?" It snapped at her.

She answered back in her thoughts, *Who are you?*

The captain was laughing at her with his crew, poking at her in the ribs, pinching her cheeks, and pulling at her hair. He was mocking her size, saying she was even too small to feed to the sharks.

"I'm the warrior spirit Bronwyn gave you. Remember me? Yeah? Now let me loose!"

"No! Not yet. You know the trigger word; I still have control!"

Estrella was shaking her head back and forth, debating with the voice in her head. The captain and crew kept laughing at her and called her crazy.

"He called you a rat! That's close enough. Let me play!"

"No!" Estrella demanded.

As she was fighting with the voice in her head, the spectacle gave the crew the distraction she needed to work through most of the rope's strands. She stopped just short of the last strand to make them believe they still had her tied. All it would take to free herself would be one swift cut. She was just giving the captain time to trigger her. He was just stupid enough to insult her.

"She is no threat; she is a weak little girl," he said, taunting her.

The silver glint appeared in Estrella's eye. The warrior was released. Estrella couldn't control her anymore. With a last swipe of her blade, she was freed from the bonds. Now she stood in front of the pirates with her weapons in hand and a wicked grin spreading across her face.

Jumping atop a barrel, she said, "Weak, am I? Just a little girl? A rat aboard this ship? Oh, Captain, how wrong you are. I will soon make you choke on those very words," she snarled.

"Seize her! Who tied her knots?! Where did she get the weapons?! Didn't you check her before bringing her aboard?! You are all a bunch of idiots! Don't just stand there; seize her!" bellowed the captain, glaring at her. The veins in his neck and forehead were bulging and throbbing as he looked around frantically, waving his arms. His blood boiled with rage. The crew rushed her, and she laughed. She jumped off the barrel and watched them as they crashed into each other. Pulling out her sword, she whipped her enemies as they came at her. She dived out of their grasp, ducked out of their reach, evaded their traps, and tricked them into falling in those traps themselves. She hacked at their clothes, slashed at them, and laughed at their attempts to stop her and capture her. They may have been more accustomed to the ship with their sea legs, but she was smaller, quicker, and lighter. She evaded and ditched, dodged and reeled, rolled and jumped, crouched and pounced, and laughed as they scrambled and mangled. In a whirlwind of colors and blades, Estrella had shredded their clothes, left welts on their backsides, made cuts and slices everywhere else, and tied some of them to the mast themselves. Others she threw overboard.

"Give me one good reason why I should not paint the Jolly Roger red with the blood of this crew?" she growled at them.

"Peace, please, Princess," begged the one called Rogers.

"Why should I spare you?" She sneered.

"Because I showed you kindness and I know there is still mercy in you. I promise you on my life that if I am captain, you shall never see our faces again."

"In exchange for your lives, I demand half of your plunder. As I am the one with the upper hand and the weapons, and as you are the ones tied up at my mercy, I believe I am in the position to make demands," she snarled.

"I won't be giving half of anything to no females on my ship," growled Captain Roberts.

"And I don't negotiate well with pirates. The more you refuse, the fewer men you will have. The less you give me, the more men I will kill," she snapped.

"No, my lady, don't do this. You are better than that, to take lives. Men, if you want to keep your lives, I say make me captain. All in favor, say aye," pleaded Rogers.

"Aye!" yelled the crew.

"My lady, as the new captain of this ship, I hereby grant your requests in exchange for our lives and peace," declared the new captain, Rogers.

"You will have your lives. I will leave with half your plunder and leave you in *peace*." Estrella smiled, phasing from warrior spirit back to princess. She stood up on the bulwark, called to her escorts, who finally found her at docks, after searching every vendor stand, to attention, and instructed them to take from the pirates half of their plunder. When her guards had taken the allotment, Estrella left a knife at the feet of Captain Rogers so that he could use it to cut himself loose once she was gone.

It was reported a few months later that the crew of the *Scorned Mistress* spread the word of the princess who attacked them. And the captain changed the name of the vessel to the *Vengeful Princess*.

After having freed herself, Estrella carried on with her duty of picking up the kingdom's imports. Once she and her escorts returned home, she instructed them to hand out a quarter of the plunder to the needy and poor, to give a quarter to the church, and to place a quarter into the treasury. The last quarter of the booty she kept for herself.

Since that episode, Estrella thought that fighting under her own name was too dangerous, so she determined she needed a different name. She couldn't let her enemies know her true identity; it was too much of a risk for her loved ones. Deciding to ask the warrior if she had a name, she sat down one day in meditation to talk with the spirit.

"You almost went too far with those pirates the other day."

"They deserved it."

"No one deserves to die. We, meaning you and I, do not kill people."

"I was only threatening them, hoping to scare them into meeting my demands. You should work on our restraints."

"That I will. What should I call myself when you're in control?"

"I am called Alyia the Defender, or plainly, Alyia."

"Very well. Alyia I will be, to protect my identity."

The day after that, Estrella wrote a letter to her brother informing him of what she had accomplished. She rolled it up, sealed it, then gave it to her faithful falcon, Merlin, and told him to fly it Gideon.

Merlin was a specially trained falcon. He had a unique bond with Estrella. Even though no else could understand him, Estrella could. It was as if they had their own secret language. Among Merlin's other traits was that he could find anyone and he responded to whistles.

Two days after Merlin had heard the whistle and flew off to find Gideon, he reached his destination. He handed Gideon the letter, and Gideon opened it and began reading it. When Gideon finished with the letter, he began to write his response. Upon finishing writing, he set the letter aside and told Merlin that he should rest for the night. Merlin accepted the gracious favor and roosted next to Gideon for the night.

The next morning, Merlin awoke to the sound of Estrella's whistle, which he heard from many miles away. He took Gideon's letter and flew back home.

Estrella had whistled for Merlin while she was tending to her horse. He hadn't returned home after she sent him off with the letter, so she had started to worry. She was relieved when Merlin flew back to her and landed on her arm, the letter from Gideon in his beak. After asking him to open his beak so she could retrieve the letter, she took the letter and began to read. It read as follows:

> Dear Estrella,
>
> I have been waiting to hear from you. I am very glad that things are going so smoothly. I hope you are well. Getting help from your fairy friends was a

good idea; I knew you would make the right choice. I really like your new name; I think it was very wise to change it for the sake of the family's safety. I can't believe you took on a whole crew of pirates. I am so proud of the young woman you are becoming.

Things out here on the front are getting a little rough and kind of bumpy. We lost three knights but are getting to Camelot okay. It was very funny when yesterday Basil of Talons told Crispin of Claws that the latter's wife made such terrible liverwurst that even the dog refused to eat it. When the dog wouldn't eat it, Crispin gave it to the pigs. When the pigs wouldn't eat it, Crispin had to bury it. Two weeks after he buried it, the ground become so soft that he planted an apple tree on that spot. The tree eventually produced one hundred ninety-two apples, which Crispin's wife made into sixty-four delicious pies, tarts, and breads that fed the whole village. It was so funny that Edmund from Gorgy laughed so hard that he fell off his horse.

*Well, I really must go. We're going off to fight the dragon of Vladimir tomorrow. I need my rest in order to be in tip-top fighting condition. Wish me luck.

Love,

Your beloved brother, Gideon

That letter made Estrella so happy that she almost dumped the feed bucket on her poor horse's head. She was lost in the joy of knowing that her brother was still alive and was proud of her.

CHAPTER 4

The Call

The next week, Estrella was picking out her wardrobe for her mother's next party. Her crystal ball was blinking the warning color, so she put down the lovely jade-green gown, walked over to her crystal ball, and saw that the witches of Lamire were hypnotizing three innocent little girls to turn them into witches. Estrella pulled on her commoner's gown and ran out to stop them.

"Who do you think you are, stealing these young ladies from their homes?" she asked the witches once she arrived on the scene.

"Go away, young whelp. Coming into our territory and talking to us like that is a very bad and foolish thing to do, not to mention dangerous," said one old hag.

"If I were you, weakling, I would turn around and run back to your lovely little home before we turned you into a toad," said another, with a sneer.

And that's when the glint appeared in Estrella's eye. Alyia freed the three young girls from the trance. She was about to kill the old witches, when she heard something that she thought she would never hear. She heard them beg for mercy.

"Please spare us, O powerful warrior. We're just lonely old witches who are looking for someone to teach," one of them begged.

"Fine, I'll spare you, but you must promise me that you won't harm anyone else," she said.

"We won't. We won't. Oh, thank you, miss. Thank you," one of them said.

"Now no groveling. You will go with me in peace to my fairy friends, who are going to give you a new image and a new lifestyle," Alyia told the witches.

"Okay," they said.

So she took them into the Enchanted Forest and called out to her fairy friends, who were too afraid to come out. She tried to persuade them by saying, "It's okay. I brought them here for a new image and a new lifestyle, so come on out and work your magic."*

The fairies emerged and said they would do what Alyia asked. They remove some of the witches' warts, straightened their hair, put in some highlights, and brought back their youth. She then told them they could pick only two children from the closest village to visit and teach. They had to give up their black magic and learn and teach only white magic, for example, useful spells for instance instant meals, beauty potions, good-luck charms, blessings, and healing powers. In renouncing their dark magic, they also had to accept the Lord Jesus Christ as their Savior and their source of power.

Once the witches agreed to accept Christ, a heavenly light shone down from the sky. The dark veils were lifted from their faces, the scales on their eyes were peeled away, and they wept bitter tears upon seeing the error of their ways. They were healed and cured of their evil ways. No longer called witches, they were now called priestesses and prophetesses. When they were done sobbing and had gained control of their senses, they picked two girls by the names of Violet and Iris. Alyia went to the girls' parents' house to explained that the witches would never again harm their daughters and that they had surrendered their evil ways and were now divine teachers and healers. Alyia then asked the parents if it was okay for the witches to teach Violet and Iris how to exercise special talents and make use of blessing powers from the Lord—sort of like charm school. The parents were a little concerned at first, but then Alyia explained that it would only be on the weekends and the girls would still be able to complete their chores. The parents then warmed to the idea and ultimately agreed. Violet and Iris eventually came to call the two witches Aunt Aurora and Aunt Flora. ✱

Soon after that, Estrella returned home. Seeing all the rips, tears, and snags in her plain commoner's shrift, she decided it was time for a new outfit. She went down to the seamstress and asked her to create a certain outfit for her—a pair of dark blue pants, a long-tailed blue shirt with tan sleeves, a belted skirt, and leather gloves. Next she went to the cobbler and ordered a pair of tall brown leather boots. The next week, she picked up her orders and hid them in her chest. Deciding that she would only use the outfit for great adventures and to hide her identity, she then went to bed.

The next morning, Estrella awoke at eleven o'clock. She got up and got dressed. As she was about to put on her favorite ruby earrings, the crystal ball began flashing the warning color again. When she looked into it, it made her heart sink and her stomach lurch. What she saw was the image of a hunter taking aim at her beloved pet, Merlin. She changed into her warrior's outfit and rushed out to meet the challenge. Running outside, she jumped onto the hunter's back right when he was about to let go of the arrow, which flew in the air and landed in a tree. The hunter wrestled Estrella off his back and was about to take aim at her when Merlin dive-bombed him. Alyia jumped to her feet and pulled out her sword. She watched as Merlin safely flew in through her bedroom window.

"What did you think you were doing, young maiden? You made me miss," the hunter bellowed at her.

"Do you even know whom that bird belongs to? That bird is Princess Estrella's pet falcon, Merlin. He's probably flying a letter back to her from her brother, Gideon. Poor dear, she's been so sad since he left," Alyia said.

"I had no idea. Please give the princess my deepest apologies. I was only trying to provide for my family. I did not know the bird belonged to the princess. I just assumed it was a wild raptor, with a fish." The hunter replied.

"Well, if your family is hungry, then I shall ask the princess if she will make arrangements for a roasted wild goose to be served to your family this evening," said Alyia.

"Thank you very much, miss," he said. And then he left to tell his family.

Estrella went back into the castle and ran all the way up to her room, where Merlin was waiting impatiently for her. When he saw her, he started screeching up a storm. Estrella understood every word he was screeching as if he were using her language. Their conversation went as follows:

{"What did you think you were doing?!"}

"I was saving your sorry tail feathers. What did it look like I was doing, needlepoint?" she protested.

{"I can save myself. You, on the other hand, could have been killed."}

"Oh yeah, right. I can handle myself," she said.

{"You're not off the hook with me, girly."}

"I know, I know. Do you happen to have a letter for me from Gideon?"

He nodded and handed her the letter. She began to read its words:

> Dear Estrella,
>
> How are you? What is happening at the castle? It's pretty dull out here. Yesterday we slayed two dragons, five ogres, and three cyclopes. All these battles with strange beasts, has become monotonous. We only have a little more distance to go until we get

to Camelot. As soon as I get knighted, I will come straight home.

Love,

Your beloved brother, Gideon

Right after Estrella read the last sentence, she was overwhelmed with joy and started smiling.

My brother's going to be a knight. Whoa! she thought. *This is a big deal. It's not every day that your brother gets accepted into King Arthur's court.*

Then she started to write a letter back. When she was done, she rolled it up, sealed it, and put it her drawer. Coming out of her daze and daydreaming, she heard a screech and knew that Merlin was waiting.

{"Wait a minute?! I thought that right after you write the letter, you give it to me and I take it to Gideon!"}

"I know, I know. I just want to wait a while before I send this one," Estrella said. Then she went to eat lunch.

Estrella returned to her room with a lot on her mind. *I need a friend, a companion. No, what I really need is some help, somebody whom I can talk to, who will be there for me when I need assistance. Let's face it: Gideon won't be around forever. He'll be off fighting with King Arthur. I need to find someone fast.*

The next month, while Estrella was in the throne room going over plans, permits, ledgers, and budgets with her advisors, she heard the still small voice of the Lord call to her again. "Estrella."

She ignored it, thinking that she couldn't answer it now, as she was busy with her new job as ruler.

"Estrella! Listen to me."

She sighed. It probably wasn't best to ignore a call from the Lord and push it aside. She dismissed her advisors, telling them she would return to the matters at hand when she could. And once they were gone, she left to the quiet of her room, where she answered him, "Yes, Lord, I am here."

"I have a quest for you, for the glory of my kingdom. You have to leave your home again."

"Lord, not now. I have too much to take care of here. And you already took me out of my home once. I can't leave it again."

"If you stay, then I will send someone else. You will miss out on the destiny and plan I have set for you. You have been called for such a time a this."

"But when I leave, who is going to take care of my kingdom? I was put in charge. You gave me the wisdom to rule here. Who will watch it while I am away?"

"Do not worry about it. I will fill your place with someone qualified."

"But, Lord, how will I know where to go and what to do? I will be lost out there on my own."

"I will be with you, and the Holy Spirit will be your guide."

"All right. When do I leave?"

"In a month, which will give you some time to prepare yourself. Thank you, my daughter."

Estrella planned to set off on her journey that first weekend. A week before her journey, she ran down the stairs and out into the village to find Kasim at his hut.

Today he was teaching a group of young ones stories from the Bible.

Estrella snuck up behind him and whispered in the secret language they had made up when they were younger, "Freend, I nide ta spek ta falu" (Friend, I need to speak to you).

"I haven't heard that in a long time, friend," came his reply. "Class, we will pick this up tomorrow." There came some murmurs from the class, and some giggles as Kasim and Estrella scurried off. One of the little girls said something about the teacher, the princess, and a tree. "Little girls these days, so silly." Kasim sighed.

"Estrella, it's been a long time. What brings you down to my little hut?"

"I'm leaving."

"The castle?"

"Yes."

"May I ask why, Princess?"

"The Lord called me."

"Yes. A call from the Lord is an honor to follow."

"That's why I must go."

"I see. When do you leave?"

"In a week."

"How long will you be gone?"

"I don't know."

"When will you get back?"

"'I don't know that either."

"I will greatly miss you. You know I will always be your friend."

33

"Yes, I know. I would love it if before I leave you will say a blessing over my trip. It would mean so much to me for you to ask for the blessing, and to see you one last time before I leave."

"It would be my honor."

"Thank you. I love you, my dear friend."

"I love you too, my dear friend." With that, the two hugged, and then Estrella departed.

The last weekend of the month arrived. Estrella didn't want to tell her mother in advance about her quest, knowing that her mother would not let her leave, so Estrella wrote a letter to her mother explaining what she was doing. She also wrote words of comfort to her mother, asking her not to worry. Sealing the envelope, she placed it next to her crystal ball inside a drawer. Then she handed Merlin a letter for Gideon.

"Merlin, fly this to Gideon and then come straight back. Tomorrow night we embark on our quest." He nodded and took the letter. Then Estrella lay down and went to sleep.

CHAPTER 5

The Quest Begins

The next morning, Estrella awoke to Merlin squawking at her, saying, {"Good morning, my princess."}

"Good morning, my dear friend."

{"Is today the day?"}

"Yes. Tonight we depart on our quest."

{"I will never leave you."}

"I know."

Estrella began laying out what she would need for the trip. She picked out two dresses and a light blanket, setting them next to a thick wool blanket. Once her things were ready to be packed, she went down to breakfast—the last one she would have in the palace before she left. She sat down at the table next to Kylia. Kylia is Estrella's younger sister by five years. Estrella had been her best friend since Kylia was born, she has the kindest heart, infectious smile, shimmering green eyes, and fiery red hair. Estrella was a little nervous. This was going to be her first time away from the only home she ever knew without anyone else with her. Kylia knew that something was on her mind.

"Esy, are you okay? You don't look okay."

"I'm fine, Ky. Just tired, is all."

"All right," she said. They went back to eating their breakfast.

Estrella was so nervous that she barely had an appetite. After breakfast, she skipped her lessons, thinking, *What is the point? I'm not she going to use needlepoint on my quest, and I don't know how long I will be gone.*

That afternoon, Estrella stopped by the kitchen and took some bread, some jerky, a waterskin, and a food basket. She then stopped by the livery and got two strong skeins of twine to carry her stuff with. Then she stopped by the armory and grabbed a shield, her bow, a quiver of arrows, and her enchanted sword and dagger. After that, she stopped by the laundry maid's quarters to pick up some lye, some soap, and a washing stone. After gathering these supplies, she went back to the palace and up to her room. Taking the outfits she had set out and the washing materials, she put them in the light blanket and rolled it up. Then she set the light blanket, along with her her little treasure chest, atop the thick wool blanket, which she rolled up and then tied with twine. Next, she put her food in the basket, covered it with a handkerchief, and placed it under her bed, along with her weapons. All was ready for the next time she would come to her room, at which point she would grab her things and go.

When the day was done and everyone headed to their chambers, Althea stayed up to go over royal plans and say prayers for her family. Estrella slipped inside her room, changed into her warrior outfit, climbed into bed, and covered herself with the blankets to hide her clothes. A few minutes later, her mother came into the room to check in on her and kiss her good night. After her mother left the room, Estrella climbed out of bed, made it nice and tidy, took out her crystal ball, and left it on a velvet pillow on her bed. Then she took out the letter she had written to her mother and left it next to the crystal ball. Next, she grabbed her stuff, including her coin purse, and whistled quietly for Merlin. Having decided to carry her boots so her feet wouldn't make as much noise on the staircase, she quietly headed down the stairs and went out of the palace.

Estrella walked past the guards. Once she was beyond the palace grounds, she slipped her boots on, went into the city, and made her way to Kasim's house. She quietly knocked on the door. Kasim emerged. "Evening, dear friend."

"Evening, Kasim."

"You are sure about this?"

"I am."

"Then I give you not only my blessing but also the Lord's," he declared. Then he prayed for the Lord's protection over her.

"Thank you," she said as she curtsied.

"Be safe, dear friend," he said, bowing his head to kiss her forehead as his blessing, as she came up.

"I will. Good-bye, dear friend," she said as she walked off toward the enchanted woods.

That night, Estrella just made into the woods. She was nervous, but deciding to be brave for the Lord, she soldiered on. She kept walking until her feet hurt and her eyes grew heavy. The Lord led her to the trunk of a tree, and eased her to rest there.

When Estrella awoke the next morning, she was face-to-face with a wild girl and the sharp point of an animal's horn. Overcome with fear, she recognized the pair as the terrible banshee and nightmare horse told of in the ghost stories.

"Please, spare my life, banshee. I am too young to die. I did not mean to trespass into your domain of the forest," Estrella pleaded.

"I am not a banshee," the girl grumbled. "If you did not mean to trespass here, why are you here?" she asked.

"I'm on a quest. The Lord sent me on a quest for his kingdom. I became tired last night and stopped here to rest."

The Lord whispered to Estrella, inside her head, "She is your first."

"My first what?" Estrella asked out loud.

"Who are you talking to?" asked the girl.

"No one," Estrella replied.

"I am sending you to those who need you. She needs you," the Lord answered.

Estrella started to reply and answer the Lord out loud.

The girl and the horse exchanged confused looks.

{"She is crazy; she was clearly cast out of her kingdom,"} neighed the horse.

"I will admit, she does seem strange. But so are we, a girl living in the woods called a banshee and talking to a unicorn. She can't be more strange than we are. She could even be our rescuer," the girl said.

Estella sighed, looked up, and said the following words: "My name is Princess Estrella. The Lord God sent me to rescue you from your situation and to invite you into his family—and into my family as my sister in faith."

The girl was shocked. How did this stranger in her woods know the deepest longing of her heart, namely, to know the Lord, accept his salvation for her life, and have a family again.

"Who did you say you were?" the girl asked.

"My name is Princess Estrella of Faylin," Estrella answered.

"My name is Karmina. I have been longing for God and a family for many years. How did you know?"

"The Lord told me. He has been longing for you to come to him. He has been watching you, and his heart has been longing for you as you have longed for him. Karmina, do you want to know him?"

Karmina broke down in tears and fell at Estrella's feet. "Yes! With all my heart."

"You need to invite Jesus into your heart. I will pray over you as you say these words: 'Dear Lord God, I know I am a sinner. I confess with my mouth that I believe Jesus Christ shed his blood on the cross and died for my sins. Forgive me now, and fill me with your Holy Spirit. I accept Jesus Christ as Lord and Savior of my life. I turn my life over to you, dear Lord, and thank you for the gift of salvation. Help me to lead a life that is pleasing to you from this day onwards. In Jesus's name I pray, amen.'"

Karmina spoke those words as Estrella prayed over her. The sun streaked through the trees and fell on the girls. When the girls finished, Karmina looked up with tears in her eyes. She felt the Lord fill her soul. She smiled at Estrella as their eyes met. The two knew that they would be friends forever and sisters always. Tears of joy rolled down their cheeks, smiles appeared on their faces, and laughter bubbled up from their bellies.

"I'm sorry I called you a banshee." Estrella laughed.

"I'm sorry I called you crazy." Karmina giggled.

"You... hic... called me... hic... crazy?" Estrella asked through hiccups, which she'd gotten from laughing so much, which fact made her laugh more.

"Technically, no. I didn't call you crazy. Juniper did," Karmina replied, getting ahold of herself, yet still giggling on account of Estrella's hiccups.

"Who is Juniper?" asked Estrella.

"Oh, she is my companion, the one everyone refers to as the nightmare horse. But she is actually just a very protective unicorn. I will introduce you. Estrella, this is Juniper; Juniper, this is Princess Estrella," Karmina said.

"It's very nice to meet you, Juniper. You are a very beautiful girl with a very shiny horn." Estrella smiled and cooed at the unicorn as she petted her mane.

The unicorn tossed her head and nuzzled Estrella's head.

"I think she likes you," observed Karmina.

"I know she does." Estrella, smiling, invited Karmina to join her. Karmina agreed enthusiastically and followed her out of the forest.

When they had traveled for a day and stopped for the night, Estrella set up a small camp and cooked dinner for the two of them.

"All right, let's play a game called secret for secret; you tell me a secret and I will tell you one," Estrella suggested.

"All right, I'll play." Karmina smiled. "They call me a banshee because I am a songstress. I have been blessed with the gift of song. I sing louder to scare intruders off. Your turn, Princess."

"Well, it is my turn. You should know that I have another side."

"What do you mean, another side?"

"You see, I have been blessed with a gift as well. I have a warrior spirit. It's like another personality. She has a different name so as to protect my identity. Her name is Alyia."

"How will I know if it's you or the warrior at any given moment?"

"Alyia is triggered by the word *weak*, or she takes over when I let her. You will know that it's her when you see a silver glint in my eye." Estrella smiled.

"Good to know. One more question. You've met my companion. Who is yours? You've got to have one. I wouldn't think you would come out here on your own," Karmina reasoned.

"You are right again. I do have a companion, like your Juniper. However, my companion has two legs and feathers." Estrella smiled, and whistled out low. A silver streak flashed across the orange and purple sky of the setting sun, and came to perch on her outstretched arm. "Karmina, this is my closest companion, Merlin."

"He is beautiful, Estrella."

"Thank you. He definitely thinks so." Estrella laughed.

The girls finished their meal and then settled in for the night.

The next morning, as they were packing up and eating breakfast, Estrella asked Karmina another question.

"Kar, let's play secret for secret again. Tell me, how did you and Juniper meet?"

"I'll tell you, but it's not a very happy story. ✳ It all started about two years ago. I was a slave to a greedy king. Every night I was forced to sing for him and his greedy family. One day I was dragged along by the king and his hunting party as entertainment. One night, one of his men mentioned the legend of the unicorn and remarked that one is supposed to use a maiden, or a virgin, as bait to catch a unicorn. Well, the king thought that the idea of using me as the bait sounded like a smashing good idea, and that hunting a unicorn sounded like a splendid sport. So the next day they dragged me out to a field, where they tied me to a birch tree. Then they went into the woods to watch and wait. About four long hours went by, and then finally this magnificent black-and-white unicorn appeared almost out of nowhere. She saw me tied helplessly to the tree. I tried to warn her, to let her know she was walking into a trap. But she approached and lay down beside me, putting her head in my lap. At that moment there was an instant bond between us. But then reality set in as the king and his men came running toward us. I tried to get the unicorn to run away and save herself, but she stayed by my side, and even tried to fight off the men and protect me. They overpowered her and captured her, throwing ropes and nets over her, and then cut me loose. They dragged us both to the castle. When we arrived, they presented the unicorn as a gift to the king's oldest daughter, who weighed as much as a pig and had the face of a horse. It broke my heart. They threw me in my cage and raised it above the ground, and then they took the unicorn out to the stables. That night I was released from my cage and chained up in the king and queen's bedchamber to sing them to sleep. When they were fast asleep, I picked the lock on my chains, slipped out, and ran to the stable. When I got to the unicorn's stall, I untied her. We ran away into the night, for as long as we could. By morning, when the king and his men realized that we were gone, it was too late; we were already in the enchanted wood. Once there, I gave the unicorn the name Juniper. And we have stayed here ever since, until now. See, I told you it wasn't a happy story."

"Oh my gosh, that's so sad. I'm so sorry," Estrella said.

{"That story really touched me. Of all the stories that I've heard, this one has to be the saddest of all,"} Merlin added.

"It's okay, Merlin," Karmina said. "I'm happy now. I have Juniper and my freedom, and now I have you and Estrella. But, Estrella, tell me, how did you and Merlin meet?".

"Oh, our story is not that exciting. It all started a couple of years ago. The great and famous wizard Merlyn Emrys was staying in our castle for a few months. He had a pet falcon, who had laid her eggs while they were with us. The eggs hatched on my birthday. As a gift, the wizard gave one of the eyases to me. I thought it was only fitting to name him after the wizard himself. Five days after my birthday, everyone said that Merlin and I were made for each other. Since then, we've been inseparable," Estrella told her.

"Wow, that's very interesting. You two really do make a good couple," Karmina said.

{"I agree,"} Juniper neighed.

"Thanks, you guys. I'm just glad he hasn't left me yet."

"What do you mean?" Karmina quipped.

"Well, we do get into a lot of arguments," Estrella told them.

"Well, that is only natural. Companions are protectors. They worry over us when we get in trouble. Juniper and I don't always agree, but we still love each other and stay together. I'm sure Merlin means well and won't ever leave you. A companion's bond is forever. Now that all that is cleared up, we should get going before it gets too late to travel, or too hot."

"You're right, let's get going." Estrella smiled. The girls packed up camp and started walking where the Holy Spirit was leading them.

"Estrella, do you want to rest your feet? I am sure Juniper would let you ride her for some ways," Karmina offered.

"No, I am fine for now, but thank you. She is your horse; you should ride her, at least for now. If my feet start to get too tired, we can both ride her."

"All right. Estrella, do you even know where we are going?"

"No, not exactly. This is my first time outside my kingdom on my own."

"This is your first time out, and you have no idea where we are going?! How do you even know we are going the right direction?"

"Listen, this the Lord's quest for me. The Holy Spirit is leading me."

"You're right. Sorry for getting upset like that."

"No, it's okay. I understand where you are coming from. You have been on your own for a long time. I'm the who hasn't, and I'm supposed to be leading."

CHAPTER 6

Sloan

Estrella and Karmina traveled for days, stopping only to rest and eat before traveling some more. Estrella's feet were killing her, and her boots were wearing thin. At one point, the two girls finally wandered into a small town. They were walking down the main road when Estrella felt pulled to a small blacksmith shop. So she decided to go in. Karmina and Estrella told Juniper and Merlin to wait outside. Once the girls walked inside and looked around, they were amazed by the craftsmanship of the tools and weapons. They heard a voice from behind them, which almost made them jump.

"Those are quality hand-forged tools," said the girl behind them. They turned to see who was talking to them.

When Estrella first saw the girl in the leather apron, her spirit stirred. Then she smiled as she heard the Lord whisper again. "Here is your second. She needs hope and fellowship," he said.

"I made all of that myself. My name is Sloan, by the way."

"Hi, Sloan. My name is Princess Estrella, and this is Karmina," Estrella said by way of introduction. "It's a pleasure to make your acquaintance."

"Princess, it's nice to meet you, as well as you, Karmina. So you two appreciate my work?"

"Oh yes, the tools are remarkable," replied Estrella.

"And you made them all yourself?" asked Karmina.

"Yes, my father taught me at an early age how to become a blacksmith."

"That is amazing," remarked Estrella.

"I was wondering, do you have any pets, or are you alone?" asked Karmina.

"Oh, I am not alone. My furry companion is my otter Odell," answered Sloan.

"Cool. Can we meet her?" Estrella asked.

"Sure. I'll get her out here right away," Sloan said. "Oh, Odell, come here and bring my arrows," Sloan called. A large brown thing the size of a cat scurried out from the back with a large quiver of the most beautifully crafted arrows Estrella and Karmina had ever seen.

"Odell, meet the girls. Girls, meet Odell," Sloan said as she introduced her pet otter.

"Aw, she's so cute, Sloan," Estrella said.

"What's that she has on her back?" Karmina asked.

"Oh, those are my custom-made arrows. I made them myself. You see those tips? They're made with" Sloan explained.

"Whoa," Estrella and Karmina said in unison.

"That's so cool," Estrella exclaimed.

"Do you girls have any pets of your own?" asked Sloan.

"As a matter of fact, we do. I have a pet unicorn named Juniper, and Estrella here has a pet falcon named Merlin. We told them to wait outside, though," Karmina answered. Then she asked, "Hey, do you want to come with us on Estrella's quest?"

"Sure," Sloan replied. "Where are you guys headed?"

"We're headed anywhere this journey take us. I'm looking for new friends. I'll tell you the whole story on the way to our next destination, but first I would like you and Odell to meet someone," Estrella said.

"One sec, I'm going to put my brother in charge. When I was little, it was just my Mother and Father, myself and three brothers and baby sister. My mother handled the finances and business end, while my Father crafted the products. Our father taught my twin brother, Skylar and I everything we needed to know about minding the store, like making change and bringing out the good stuff for the best customers. When he died Skylar and I took on the family business and used everything he taught us. I'll bring him out here to meet you and tell her of my decision," Sloan explained. "Skylar, come out here, please. I have someone for you to meet." And from behind the curtain a young boy, about 17 years old. He was slender with auburn hair and a little goatee stubble, and a crooked smile in a blacksmith apron, polishing a small dagger.

"Oh, hello there," Skylar said with a smirk,

"Skylar, this is Princess Estrella and her friend Karmina," Sloan explained.

"Oh, Your Majesty, I'm very pleased to meet you." Skylar said.

"Skylar, Estrella and Karmina have asked me and Odell to join them on their quest. I am joining them on their quest and leaving you in charge. Don't burn down the shop, don't let the others make a mess of it, you know how much I have worked to keep this place in the order father left it to us. I'll write you every month" Sloan told her brother, slugging him in the shoulder playfully. Much like Karmina and Estrella, Sloan was leaving the only home she had ever known.

"Don't worry I will keep everything in order. Stay safe and don't get into too much trouble without me. If you do I want to know everything." Skylar chuckled, he smiled as he watched them leave the shop.

The playful moment between two siblings brought back memories of how she used to play around with Gideon, it made he smile as she wondered what he was doing right now.

"Sloan and Odell, I would like you two to meet Merlin and Juniper, our pets," Karmina said. Then she and Estrella called their pets to them.

{"I am very pleased to meet you, Sloan. I am also pleased to meet you, Odell,"} Merlin said in two squawks.

"Merlin said he's pleased to meet the two of you," Estrella translated.

{"I, likewise, am happy to meet you guys,"} Juniper added.

"Juniper says she's happy to meet you too," Karmina said, translating for Juniper.

"Well, I speak for the both of us when I say we're very glad to meet you too," Sloan said.

CHAPTER 7

Avalon

"So, Estrella, where are we going next?" Karmina asked.

"Well, I thought we would stop by Avalon and stay the night there. Then in the morning we will travel some more," Estrella suggested.

"That's a great idea. I could go for a nice cushy bed and a good meal. No offense, but I'm kind of getting tired of your jerky and sourdough," Karmina said.

"No offense taken. I think a little rest and some hearty food will be good for us," Estrella said.

So with that said, they continued on, traveling on their way to the kingdom of Avalon, not saying a word until Sloan had something on her mind and thought she just had to speak.

"Hey, Estrella, what's it like to be a princess?"

"I bet it's great having big fancy meals, sleeping in a nice soft bed, and having your maids and ladies-in-waiting serving you and waiting on your every word," Karmina said.

"You know, for me it's not all that great. Yeah, there's the big bed and the nice food, but it gets sort of annoying having the maids wait on me all the time. And I never have time for fun. It's always needlepoint, lessons, and jousting, and having all my days planned for me: go here, do that, place this there, and blah, blah, blah. It gets so irritating that sometimes I just want to escape the palace and do something fun," Estrella concluded. *

"Wow, now that you put it that way, being a princess does sound really boring. Oh man, you know, my life doesn't seem that bad now. I'm sorry that I was jealous of you," Karmina said.

"That's okay. I've had lots of people come up to me and, evidently assuming that I live a comfy, pampered life, say they wish they were me," Estrella said.

The three girls walked for what seemed like forever until they came to a large gate.

"Hark! Who dares approach the kingdom of Avalon?" the gatekeeper bellowed down at the girls, who were standing in front of the gates.

"It is I, Princess Estrella of the kingdom of Faylin, and my friends Karmina, the songstress of the Enchanted Forest, and Sloan, the blacksmith of the town of Travelers Way. We have been traveling for many days and many nights, sleeping on piles of leaves and sticks. We would be most pleased if you would grant us entry," Estrella pleaded.

"I must confirm this with my king first. I will return soon with his decision," said the gatekeeper, who then left to alert the king of the visitors and ask for his decision about letting them in or not.

While the gatekeeper was gone, the girls got to chatting.

"So, Estrella, why did you pick Avalon, other than its being the closest kingdom?" asked Sloan.

"Well, if you must know, the king and queen are good friends of mine," Estrella replied.

"Wow, I guess it pays to be friends with royalty. I will tell you this: it will feel very good to sleep in a real bed," said Karmina.

While the girls were discussing sleeping conditions and frivolous things, the gatekeeper entered the castle and approached the king and queen's thrones, kneeled in front of them, and addressed them, saying, "My lieges, the princess Estrella of Faylin, with her friends, asks for entry into our kingdom. Shall I let them in?"

"Of course. The Princess of Faylin is a dear friend of ours, and any friends of hers are friends of ours. They are always welcome in our kingdom," replied the king.

"Yes, Your Highness."

"Well, go on, man. Don't leave them waiting outside all day. Let them in," said the king as he dismissed the gatekeeper.

The gatekeeper left, and the queen turned to her king.

"I do say, it has been quite a while since we have seen her, hasn't it?"

"Yes, I do believe it has. If I remember correctly, it has been seven years since her father brought her along on one of his journeys," replied the king.

"Poor thing, moving around so often and not getting to be seen as often because of those ridiculous campaigns," added his queen.

"I wonder how she is holding up, and what she is doing this far from home," the king said.

The gatekeeper approached the girls and called out, "My liege has granted you entry into our kingdom. I hope the three of you enjoy yourselves here."

"Thank you very much, kind sir," Estrella said.

As they entered the kingdom gates and walked up to the castle, the girls took in all the scenery and beauty of the kingdom. Karmina and Sloan had never been inside a kingdom before; they had only seen glimpses from the other side of the walls. The little shops looked very inviting, and the little houses and cottages looked comfy and warm. When they finally reached the castle, all Karmina and Sloan could do was stare at its splendor and majesty. It was huge, with stone walls, pillars, and turrets. Estrella decided that it was time to break the trance the girls were in.

"Hey, guys, you know, the inside of the castle is better, and probably warmer than the outside."

They all giggled and then entered the castle through the massive oak doors.

As they approached the king and queen, they bowed. The king and queen stood up to greet them.

"Rise. Welcome, Estrella. It has been quite a few years since we last saw you," said the king.

Estrella rose and answered, "Yes, it has. I would like to introduce you to my two newest friends, Karmina, who has her unicorn Juniper with her, from the Enchanted Forest, and Sloan, with her otter Odell, from the little village of Travelers Way." Once the girls rose, Estrella continued. "Girls, these are my close friends, the handsome and noble King Liam and the always beautiful Queen Irinia."

The girls bowed once more and addressed the king and queen.

"Your Majesties, it is an honor to meet you," said Karmina.

"It is a great privilege and honor to make your acquaintance," said Sloan ever so humbly.

King Liam and his queen turned to the girls. "It is always a pleasure meeting friends of Estrella's. Any friends of hers are friends of ours," said Queen Irinia.

"I concur most definitely. It is not every day that our dear friend Estrella stops by to grace us with her presence. But tell me, what brings you by on this glorious day?" remarked King Liam.

"Oh, just passing by. I thought it would be nice to pay my old friends a visit. And I was hoping that with your permission, my girls and I might stay the night in some comfy beds."

"Of course you have our permission to stay here. You know that you and your friends are always welcome here, anytime you like," said Queen Irinia.

"You girls may stay in the guest rooms upstairs. Your unicorn friend, Juniper, may stay in our royal stables, and your otter, Odell, may stay in your room with you, Sloan. Or if she'd like, there are little dens for otters out by the pond."

"Thank you very much, but I believe that she will stay with me," said Sloan.

"Very well," said Queen Irinia.

Estrella looked around and then asked, "Where are Lucian and Nolani? Running around and causing their nannies grief?"

"No, they are in the nursery," Irinia explained.

"Would you like me to call them for you?" asked Liam.

"Oh, please, would you? I have missed them so," Estrella replied.

Liam turned his head toward the back of the castle and bellowed out, "Lucy, would you please send Lucian and Nolani here? There is someone here who would like to see them."

Within a few minutes, the kids came running out. Seeing their friend Estrella, they ran at full tilt into her embrace.

"Lucian, Nolani, how are you, my dear little friends? I have missed you so. It has been too long. How old are you now?" asked Estrella, hugging her little friends.

"I am five years and one month," replied Lucian.

"I'm two years," replied Nolani.

"So you are," Estrella remarked.

"We missed you too, Esy," said Lucian.

"You are going to stay for longer this time, Sela?" asked Nolani.

"Only for one night, I'm afraid, my little friends. I'm on a big quest, you see."

"Really? A big quest?" asked Nolani.

"Children, let the girls get settled into their rooms first. Then I am sure Estrella would be more than pleased to share her story about this quest of hers with us—after dinner," said Liam.

Once the kids left, the King and Queen summoned the servants to carry the girls things to their things to their rooms, the girls followed behind. They really didn't have much, since the only one who knew that they were going to do much traveling was Estrella.

The next thing that Karmina did was to get Juniper settled in the stables. Then she went back to her room and threw herself onto the big straw bed. To a girl who had spent many nights in the past sleeping chained up, or outside in the dirt, the bed felt like heaven. Sloan and Odell were shocked by the space of their chambers. For many years, Sloan and Odell had shared the tiny back room of the shop and a bed with Skyla and her otter. This room was at least three times the size of Sloan's room at home.

After getting settled into their chambers, the girls went downstairs for dinner. Once they saw the spread of food on the table, they began to drool. Let's face it: when all you eat for days is sourdough bread and jerky, you get really hungry. Laid out on the table was roast pig, duck, pheasant, and stag. There was also plum pudding and fig pudding. Many other things graced the table as well.

Everyone took their seats. Nolani said grace, and then the girls ate their fill. When dinner was finished, the servants brought out dessert, the richest and loveliest chocolate cake with cream the girls had ever seen.

CHAPTER 8

Letters from Home

After dinner, Estrella sat down in the parlor room with her friends and the children, and told the family the story of her quest. When she finished, the little ones were sent off to bed, and everyone else retired to their bedchambers. Estrella entered her room and found that Merlin was waiting for her with four letters, the first of which was from Gideon. The second was from her mother, Queen Althea; the third, from her sister Kylia; and the last, from an old friend of hers. Estrella thanked Merlin with a scratch under his beak. She also gave him some pork she had saved in a napkin. Then she took the first letter, opened the seal, unrolled the scroll, and read as follows:

Dear Estrella,

How is everything going on your friend quest? I pray for your safety, and I know that you will be very successful. We just reached the gates of Camelot. The trip was long and tiresome but well worth it. The city is just as it was described in the stories that Father used to tell us.

When we reached the castle, we saw many banners among the high king's banners. We found out that they belonged to visiting royals. Many of the visiting kings and queens had brought along their beautiful daughters. As we approached the inner courtyard of the king's royal keep, we were met by many beautiful courtiers, but my heart was stolen when my eyes met the beautiful visiting princess Bliss. From that day on, there has been no other maiden in the whole world for me but Bliss. Her beauty knows no bounds; her kindness knows no limits. Her hair is golden like sun, and her smile is as bright as the moon. Her voice sounds melodious, like that of the birds in springtime. The sound of the nightingales, the larks, and the other songbirds cannot compare to her voice. Her smile brightens my day, and her laughter brings joy to my soul.

We were escorted into the king's royal throne room. * Once we all kneeled before the high king's great throne, we were knighted as knights of the Round Table and accepted into the king's court. I spent the whole next day following Bliss around. I have fallen in love! I can think of no other young woman; I have no interest in any courtiers. She swims through my thoughts and intoxicates my soul. After a few days, I had finally won her attention and favor. I asked her parents for permission to court their daughter. I promised that I would stay loyal and faithful, and that I would always return to her after my battles. They granted me permission to see her. I'm in love and wish to shout it to the heavens! I wish you luck and happiness.

Love,

Your devoted brother, Gideon

After Estrella finished reading the letter, she fell backwards on her bed, filled with joy. Her brother was not only safe, and now a renowned knight of the coveted Round Table, but also had found love, the kind of love that is felt with the soul. Estrella was lost in her world of thought about Gideon's news when Merlin broke through her trance, saying, {"Excuse me, my princess, but you have forgotten the other three letters."}

"Oh, I am so sorry, my friend. Thank you for reminding me," she said. She smiled as she opened the next letter, this one from her mother.

> My Dear Daughter,
>
> I have found your letter; I can't believe that you are gone. Your room is so empty and the castle is so cold without your warmth and happiness. I miss you dearly; I love you with all my heart. I pray for your safety and know that you will find what you are looking for. I know that the Lord is with you and that you are in his protection and care. I also know that you are doing what you do best, being yourself and making friends in remarkable ways.
>
> Love,
>
> Your caring and proud mother, Raine Maia Althea

Once Estrella had finished reading the second letter, she began to cry. O how she missed her mother. This was the first time she had been far away from home by herself. Drying her tears, she opened the third letter.

Dear Esy,

Why did you leave? It's so lonely without you at home. Maia told me that she found your letter and that you left to find more friends. What I don't understand is why you had to go so far away from home. Why couldn't you find more friends in the village or from a nearby kingdom? I miss you so much. It's not the same with you gone. Please be safe. I will be praying for you.

Love,

Your concerned sister and friend, Kylia

It hurt her heart to know that her little sister was so concerned about her. They were always close as sisters, but they were even closer as friends, having spent a great deal of time together and sharing many happy memories. Estrella held the letter close to her heart. Then she glanced at the last letter out of the corner of her eye. With a slight hesitation, she took the letter from Merlin and opened it.

Dear Estrella,

I was just practicing my spells and potions when I saw Merlin fly overhead toward your home kingdom, Faylin. That can only mean that Gideon is sending you a letter or that you have left home. I decided that I too would write you a letter. Not a day goes by that I don't miss the days of old, when we were just little girls playing games, driving your nannies crazy, and running amok throughout the castle. But then we grew up and chose different paths. You spent your days studying, and in training sessions with Gideon. And I chose to spend my days studying plants and their powers, and potion skills. I spent many lonely nights thinking about us and how we used to be. I was so consumed by my trade and loneliness that I tried many charms to gain the affection of young men, but they never lasted and I was left alone again.

I hope that wherever you are, and whatever you are doing, you are safe.

Yours truly,

Biana

PS: I sent you a little gift I acquired from a wizard in exchange for my potions. Be careful with it. It is the ruby of power; it grants the user power beyond her wildest dreams.

Estrella put down the letter and looked quizzically at Merlin. The falcon, meeting her gaze with a sheepish look, reluctantly handed over a small velvet pouch. She took the pouch from his talon and scolded him for withholding it. Opening the pouch, she let the ruby drop into the palm of her opened hand. She looked deep into the surface of the ruby and saw it glow, and pulse, and shine. Feeling the dark mystical powers of the ruby, she put it back into the pouch, threw the pouch in the back of the wardrobe, and said, "Merlin, we can't let that jewel fall into the wrong hands. This thing, it corrupts the holder. No one can have this jewel."

{"Why do you think I kept it from you? What should we do with it?"}

"Well, early tomorrow morning I'm going to take it to a blacksmith and have him destroy it. That thing is too powerful. As long as it exists, it threatens the peace. It must be destroyed." With that, Estrella lay down on her bed. It felt good to lie down in a bed again. Her feet hurt and her back ached from traveling for so long. It had been a long time since she had slept in a bed. It wasn't that she didn't like sleeping on the ground—she didn't mind it at all—but there was no feeling like lying down to sleep on a straw bed. She fell asleep as soon as her head hit the pillow.

CHAPTER 9

The Destruction of the Cursed Ruby

Around three o'clock in the morning, Estrella woke herself up, slipped on the robe that her hosts had provided for her, grabbed the velvet pouch containing the ruby, and silently snuck out of the castle to seek out the blacksmith. She ran through the town, reading all the signs on the shops. At 3:30, she came to the shop of the blacksmith, one Master Doyle, and knocked on the door.

The blacksmith was just waking up to get ready for work when he heard the gentle knock on the door. He thought, *Now who could that be knocking on my door at this ungodly hour?* Putting on his apron, he walked toward to the door, saying to the person on the other side, "I'm coming, I'm coming. Hold on a second." Then he undid the bolt on the door, looked out, and saw the young princess at his door. She was standing there shivering in nothing but her dress and robe, clutching a small velvet pouch. He said, "Your Highness, Princess Estrella, what is one such as you doing up at this hour, at my door?"

"I am dreadfully sorry if I have wakened you, Master Doyle, but I have a small favor to ask of you."

"You did not awaken me, Princess. I always wake up early to start work. What is this favor you ask of?"

"Well, if it isn't much trouble, may I come in first? It is rather nippy out here at this hour."

"A thousand pardons, Princess.✻ Where are my manners? By all means, please come in and warm yourself by the furnace."

Once she came in, he offered her the best chair there was and placed it by the furnace. Then he began to stoke it to warm up the room as he asked her to sit down. She graciously took the seat and thanked him wholeheartedly. Then Master Doyle asked her again, "Now, what is this favor you speak of, Your Highness? I would gladly do anything asked of me, to the best of my abilities."

"You see, I have this old friend whom I haven't spoken to in many a year. She has chosen the path of those who use the gifts of nature and other elements for their own gain. She sent me the cursed Ruby of Power. And I can't let this ruby exist. If it were to fall into the wrong hands, it could threaten the peace and bring disaster and corruption."

"I see. And what would you have me do to it?"

"Destroy it, by any means."

"Your Highness, how would one go about destroying a gem?"

"I have a few ideas. First of all, I need you to crush it, smash it into many little pieces. Take your hammer and chisel, and chip it into small chunks. Then grind it into miniscule pieces. When you have ground them into tiny bits, I want you to throw the bits into the furnace and melt them down until they mix with the ashes. Finally, scoop out the ashes and bury them deep within the earth. But most important of all, do not look into the ruby at any point, for the power will corrupt you," she instructed the blacksmith.

"I will do my best to follow your instructions accordingly," he said. She handed the velvet pouch to him, and he took it from her.

An hour into the destruction of the ruby, the blacksmith's wife came downstairs to make breakfast. She started fussing and going on about her husband. "Jeremy, what have I told you about making such a racket this hour of the morning? You will surely wake up the whole town, never mind the little ones."

"Helen, my dear, we have company," said Master Doyle through his visor as he was crushing up the stone. His wife, Helen, looking up from the work she had begun at the counter, saw Princess Estrella sitting down in front of the furnace.

"My humblest apologies, Your Highness. Had I known you were coming to our shop, I would have made a fresh loaf of bread. And here I was ranting and raving at my husband in front of you. And shame on you, Jeremy, for letting me go on and on, and not telling me know the princess was here," Maid Helen said.

"I tried to tell you, dear, but you kept talking. And if my work doesn't wake the children, your ranting certainly will."

"Please, don't argue with each other. And you're forgiven. Your husband has shown great hospitality to me by letting me come in and warm myself by the furnace."

"Well, he is a good man, a good husband, and a good father."

"And you, my dear Helen, are a wonderful and loving mother and wife."

"See, it is far better to compliment each other than to argue over petty differences and problems."

They both smiled at each other. Then Helen remembered their royal guest and remembered her manners.

"Oh, my goodness gracious, where are my manners? Forgive me, Your Highness, but would you like something to eat? To have been up before the sun and not having eaten a thing, you must be very hungry. We may not have much, but I can make you a fried egg and a slice of toast, and I can warm up a pot of coffee."

Jeremy, as he took the ground-up dust from the jewel to the furnace, whispered to their guest, "My Helen is the best cook in Avalon."

Estrella smiled. Maid Helen said, "I heard that. I am only a humble cook. The palace chefs are far better than I."

"Please do not think less of yourself. Your humility and your humbleness are refreshing. In the world I come from and with the life I live, everyone thinks too highly of themselves and each other. This happens when you are of a higher rank." Maid Helen smiled, offered a plate to Estrella, then handed a plate to her husband, who put down his tools just long enough to share the meal with them. Maid Helen then fixed herself a plate of breakfast. She managed to carry it and three mugs of coffee over to the table, where they all sat down.

Maid Helen set down her plate and the three mugs of coffee. When she sat down, Estrella noticed that she and her husband both bowed their heads and began to say grace. Estrella joined in and said grace. When Master Jeremy ended the prayer with "Amen," they began to eat. Estrella took a bite of her fried egg and instantly thought it was the best thing she had ever tasted. Of all the delicacies she had ever eaten at all the banquets, this was far better. It was remarkable how a simple dish made so humbly, with humility and love, could taste so delicious. She also noticed how the simple hardworking folk shared their lives with each other at the table and had an interest in what each other had to say. Back home, there was no discussion at the table; meals were eaten in silence. And the royals never had to work and do things for themselves, as was the case for the simple folk of the kingdom. At the palace, there were at least a dozen servants to wait on you hand and foot, doing everything for you.

Estrella enjoyed every aspect of this meal, and then she wondered what time it was getting to be. "I don't mean to interrupt, but what time is it?"

"It's a quarter till five, Your Highness," replied Maid Helen.

"Thank you both for your hospitality and the delicious meal, but I must get back to the castle, and get ready for the day, before they start to worry about me."

"Thank you, Princess, for gracing us with your presence. And don't worry, I remember your instructions. God be with you, Your Highness," said Master Jeremy.

"Thank you, Master Jeremy. The Lord will greatly bless you for showing such kindness to me."

"I am already blessed, but I welcome any more blessings the Lord chooses to pour out on my family."

And with that, Estrella left the shop and hurried back to the castle.

CHAPTER 10

Lena

Estrella made it up to her room. In time to enjoy a hot bath waiting for her and get herself ready and packed with time to spare. The girls slept in till the sun rose and enjoyed every minute of the comfy beds, the hot luxurious baths and the clean clothes. These were girls who had spent most of their lives without having the pleasure of a warm bath. Sloan was a daughter of a blacksmith. She spent her days working, and when she bathed it was in a washtub. Karmina had spent most of her life as a slave, and once she escaped, she lived in the woods. The chance to take a hot bath, clean up, and wear a beautiful gown was an opportunity too great for the girls to have missed.

Once she was downstairs, she saw that her girls were looking lovelier than ever. Then again, their inner beauty was what Estrella saw most of us. Even without all the fuss and frills, Sloan and Karmina were lovelier than the fairest flowers. This morning their outer beauty matched their inner beauty, and their outer beauty was surpassed only by their hostess queen.

"My word, Estrella. Why on earth are you not wearing the lovely gown we provided for you in your room?" exclaimed Queen Irinia.

"Yes, Estrella, why are you not dressed in the gown? You are the only princess between us three," said Karmina.

"Okay, okay. First of all, I packed the lovely gown, Irinia. I am not wearing it right now because we are leaving soon and I wished not to ruin my lovely dress by walking around outside in it. And, Karmina,

I am a princess, but that doesn't mean I have to dress like one all the time. Back at home, I had to dress up for breakfast every morning. I am on my own now, and I choose not to dress up every morning," said Estrella.

"All right, that makes sense, I guess. Well, enough talk. Let's all sit down to breakfast. The cooks worked really hard to whip up your going-away feast," said King Liam.

And what a feast it was. The whole table was filled with every kind of food imaginable. There were pancakes, waffles, and crêpes. There were omelets, scrambled eggs, eggs Benedict, fried eggs, and poached eggs. There were sweetbreads, ham, sausage, bacon, and pork. There were flatbreads, rolls, and baguettes. There were scones, doughnuts, and bagels. There was every kind of fruit imaginable, and so much more.

Karmina and Sloan loaded up their plates with all sorts of good things and then filled their cups almost to overflowing with delicious juices. Estrella, knowing that she would have to eat healthy and in moderation if she didn't want to have a stomachache, loaded up her plate with proteins, carbs, fruits, vegetables. She filled her cup halfway full with milk, and then she took out her napkin and filled it with breads and bacon, to save for the trip.

After they finished their food, Sloan and Karmina had stomachaches and were too full to go anywhere, so they waited an hour before pressing on. While the girls were letting their stomachs settle, Queen Irinia and King Liam saw to it that they received pack mules and carts to carry their belongings. Queen Irinia saw to it that that any leftover food was preserved and packed in picnic baskets, and that the beautiful gowns and jewelry were wrapped up and strapped onto the pack mules.

Once the girls were feeling well enough to go on, they packed up their things. Karmina and Sloan changed their clothes for traveling. Then all three said their good-byes and set off on the next part of their quest.

They left the wonderful city and the kingdom of Avalon by way of the main road. The Holy Spirit was their guide. Without him, they would have been truly lost. He was within them, leading them, pulling them, and pushing them toward the right path that would continue them on their journey.

Estrella, Karmina, and Sloan had gone about two miles from the city when they heard what sounded like a young girl in distress. *

"Ouch, you're hurting me. Please let me go, please. These ropes are hurting my wrists. Please, can't we just stop for a short break? My feet hurt and I'm very thirsty." The young girl was begging.

As the girl and her captors came into view, Estrella and the girls could tell she was about their age, and truly lovely. On the other hand, when it came to looks, the thugs who were kidnapping her had gotten the short end of the stick.

As the girls watched the scene before them, the Lord whispered to them, "She is your third. She needs your friendship and help."

Seeing this scene greatly troubled Sloan and Karmina. Estrella, however, recognized the kindred spirit and saw that this girl wasn't so much a damsel in distress as her two companions thought she was. Estrella could hear it in the girl's voice and see a brief glimpse of it in her eyes. She had a plan, but if she, Karmina, and Sloan rushed in now, they would put themselves at risk and spoil the captive girl's chance of putting Estrella's plan into action and getting away from the kidnappers.

Sloan and Karmina were already getting into fighting positions. Appearing gung-ho, they obviously had no plan and no foresight, so Estrella interjected, "Hold on a minute there, girls."

"What do you mean, hold on? Can't you see that the girl is in trouble?" asked Sloan.

"Yeah, come on, Estrella. If we don't step in now and do something, those thugs are going to succeed at capturing her," came Karmina's response.

"Have you girls thought this through? Tor one thing, we may have them outnumbered three to two, but they have us beat in muscles. We probably have them outsmarted in brains, but did it occur to you that this beautiful young girl might have a plan of escape? And another thing, we could risk getting captured ourselves. Then what good would be to her? Let's just see where this goes. And if the time comes for us to step in, we will by all means charge in full tilt," reasoned Estrella.

Sloan and Karmina agreed to sit back and watch for their opportunity to take matters into their own hands.

As the three watched the scene, they heard one of the captors yell back at the girl, "Silence back there. You're going to be fine." This came from the first ugly brute, who had messy black hair under his cap and what looked like a nasty scar across his face.

"No. No, I am not going to be fine. My feet are sore, my wrists are chafing, and I'm filthy," said the girl.

"Quit your nagging and whining, whelp," demanded the first brute.

"Where are you taking me?" she asked.

"You're going to make the perfect bride for our prince Sheridan. He told us to search the land for the most beautiful girl to make his bride. As soon as we saw you in the tavern, we knew you would be the right one for our prince. He is going to be very pleased with us for bringing him a pretty young woman," answered the second brute. He was clearly not the brains of this operation.

The girl appeared to think this through, and then she came back with her rebuttal. "I don't think your prince is going to be so pleased to have a bride covered in dirt and dust, with bloody wrists and blistered and bloody feet. Plus, judging from the distance we have to walk, I could pass out from dehydration if you don't give me a drink of water every so often. So to save you from the harassment, and to give my feet a break, why don't you just hop off your horse, untie me from the horse, and carry me its back?"

"Wow, she is really good," whispered Sloan.

"Shh, let's see how far this goes," said Estrella, as they were watching the scene unfold.

The second brute took a minute to seriously consider what his captive had said. He evidently didn't want to get in trouble with the prince by bringing back a damaged bride, so he halted his horse and walked back to the girl to give her a drink from his waterskin. Once he finished giving her a drink, he was about to untie the lead rope, but then the other brute spoke up. "Boris, you moron, can't you see that you're playing right into her trap? As soon as you untie that rope, she is going to run away."

But it was too late. The lead rope was already loose enough for the girl to slip out. She was now running away. While she was on her way to the other horse to untie something that the girls couldn't see, the first brute threw a looped rope toward her. It wrapped around her ankles. As he was pulling her back, he began to mock her.

"You may have been able to outsmart my slow-witted friend Boris here, but you forget that if you get away, we will turn your *weak* little fox friend here into a nice animal skin to hang on the prince's wall."

"No! Please don't hurt her," the girl said as she was struggling. As the poor girl was getting closer to the horse, the girls saw the second brute raise a club to her knock out.

The silver glint appeared in Estrella's eye. Alyia spoke: "Let's play!" And the three girls charged.

Sloan had already nocked an arrow onto her bow when she saw the brute throw the rope and catch the girl around the ankles. When the second brute raised his hand, the club suddenly flew out of his hand with great force. He was shocked when he looked down to see an arrow lodged firmly into the club. As soon as the brutes saw the arrow, they knew they were not alone and began to draw their weapons.

The girls grabbed their weapons and charged the scene. Karmina rode Juniper while Sloan and Alyia, weapons wielded, ran toward the brutes. It was quite a sight to see for the girl. Once these three strange warriors reached the scene, they fought valiantly. The warrior with the long brown hair was rushing the brute who was pulling the girl back. The girl still couldn't get away, as the brute had tied her to his horse. The warrior slid under the brute as he rushed her. She began swinging her sword and cutting away at the brute's clothes, which began to fall off of him. The girl found the fight pretty hilarious to watch as the men were stripped of their pride, their dignity, and their clothes. They were bested by three female warriors. It was humiliating for them.

Alyia cut the poor girl free and then went back to fighting the brutes. When the brutes were down to their undergarments, Karmina rode in, tied them up, and sung them into a trance. Then Alyia whispered her message into their ears as they hovered in a semiconscious state: "We will send you back to your cowardly prince, but you will give him this message. You will tell him that you couldn't find a beautiful girl anywhere, and that you were beaten and robbed by the warrior Alyia and her feisty companions. And now your price must find his own princess and leave these people in peace."

Before the warrior girls sent the men off on their way, Karmina went behind the other horse to untie the girl's companion, which turned out to be a striking silver fox. Karmina soothed it with her calm voice as she untied it. Then Sloan gave a whistle and the brutes were snapped out of their trance, at which point Alyia sent them on their way.

After the brutes were gone, it was time for introductions. Estrella presented herself to the girl.

"Allow me to introduce myself. My name is Princess Estrella, but I am also known as Alyia the Warrior. And these are my colleagues, Karmina the songstress and Sloan the blacksmith."

"It's an honor to make your acquaintance, Your Majesty, and I am pleased to meet your friends as well. My name is Lena. This is my companion Tokala. We thank you greatly for rescuing us from those brutes."

"Tell me, Lena, where do you live? Where did they take you from?" asked Sloan.

"My home village is back that way," Lena replied, pointing toward the west, which happened to be the way the girls were heading. "It's called Willow Creek. I will tell you all more as soon as we get there."

The group of four traveled for a distance until they reached a small peaceful town beside a small creek. There was a beautifully blossoming willow tree in the center of the town. Estrella, Karmina, and Sloan followed Lena to a quaint little inn called Napping Willow, right next door to the bustling little tavern called Roselai. They all went into the inn. Lena, after being greeted with a warm and welcoming hug by an elderly gentleman, turned to her new friends and introduced the man to them.

"Girls, this is my father, Vincent. My family owns the inn and the tavern. I am the innkeeper and also a dancer at the tavern." Then she turned to her father. "Father, these are my friends, Princess Estrella and her companions, Karmina and Sloan." The girls bowed to the gentleman.

"It is a pleasure to make your acquaintance," Estrella greeted.

"It is a lovely little inn you have here," added Karmina.

"It is an honor not only to meet you, Your Highness, but also to have three beautiful young women such as you in my inn. On behalf of the whole family, I thank you for returning my daughter to us," Vincent said.

The girls straightened up. Vincent gave them each a hug.

"Please, have a seat at a table. You must be exhausted from your journey. Please feel free to order whatever you like to eat. It's on the house," he offered.

"Thank you kindly, sir," said Estrella as she and her companions took a seat.

Once the girls were settled at their table, a tray of food was brought to them. They began eating. Estrella asked, "So, Lena, tell us what happened. How did you end up with those brutes?"

"Oh, and tell us also about this town and your inn. We want to know to more about you," added Karmina.

"Well, first I will tell you about my town. As you can see, it's clear why it is called Willow Creek. The town has been here for many years, and the inn is named after the willow tree in the town square. In days of yore, when travelers would pass through, they would stop to rest under the big willow. The tavern is called Roselai, which means 'heavenly rose.' You have met my father, Vincent. My mother's name is Lucinda. She runs the tavern. I have two siblings: a little brother named Marco, who works in the tavern, and an older sister named Lorelei, who dances there. We have several cousins who also work in the tavern and at the inn."

"Will you please tell us how you ended up being kidnapped by those brutes," Estrella pushed. She really was interested in knowing what had happened.

"Well, it all started this morning. Those goons came to the tavern. We just assumed they were normal customers. They sat down and ordered two drinks, so Marco brought them two mugs of ale. While they sat there with their drinks, they were eyeing all the beautiful girls who were serving the other patrons. When I came on the stage to do my routine dance, they stared at me the whole time and whispered to each other. After my first number, I went backstage to change my costume for the next song. They came backstage and told me a lie about my father not paying his taxes, mentioning that as a result they had to take me as collateral. They took me out the back door and tied me up. When Tokala heard that I was in danger, she rushed to my side, and they tied her up as well. That is what happened," Lena replied.

"It's terrible that some men think they can just take what they want," Sloan said in response to Lena's story.

"Tell me about it. That's the story of my life. I lived as a slave for many years all because some king got greedy and wanted me as his own personal entertainment," Karmina said.

"Oh, that is terrible. I am so sorry to hear that, Karmina," said Lena.

Estrella smiled. She knew that only the Lord could bring these three individuals together by using her. Standing up, she said, "If you will please excuse me for a minute or so, I'm going to look around the town for a bit."

"Of course, Estrella. When you are done, just come back to the inn. The three of you can stay the here for the night. You can continue your journey in the morning," said Lena.

Estrella went to the door and looked around. She let out a whistle and Merlin flew to her shoulder. Then she walked to her pack mule and unwrapped her small treasure chest. She smiled to herself, thinking of all the amazing things she had never gotten to see before because she had never been outside the kingdom walls. Every time she had gone somewhere with her father, they saw only other kingdoms. The only villages she got to see were either within the kingdom walls or outside her carriage windows.

Estrella walked to the stable and looked around. There she saw a beautiful bay Hispano horse. Later she would learn it was named Sage and was owned by Lena. She then walked to the livery to see about purchasing some horses. Lena already had a horse and Karmina had Juniper, so she had to buy a horse for herself and one for Sloan. Indeed, something told her she would have to buy four horses. She walked in and purchased six saddles, five carts, and five more pack mules. Then she looked at all the beautiful horses. She bought a black Friesian, a chestnut Arabian, a palomino Belgian Warmblood, a gray Lustiano, a white and black Knabstrup, and a white Lipizzaner. When she was finished making her purchases, She walked back to the Inn, and invited the girls to follow her to the stable for a surprise. They came outside and followed her into the stable were shocked to see all the horses, pack mules, and carts she had bought for them.

"Oh my, Estrella, you did this for us?" Sloan asked in shock.

"For us, and for the other girls we might meet along the way, as well. I knew our feet were getting sore, so I decided it would be best for us to ride the rest of the way." Estrella beamed with pride. "Now go ahead and pick your favorite horse. It's yours to keep."

Sloan ran down the stairs of the inn toward the horses. Her eyes lit up, as she had never had her own horse before. Growing up as a blacksmith's daughter, she had never been able to afford one. Her family had only enough to pay taxes and buy the things they needed. For any gift-giving occasion, they had always handmade their presents to each other. Sloan looked over all the horses and found them to be very beautiful. The chestnut Arabian was pretty, as was the palomino Belgian Warmblood, the black Friesian, the gray Lusitano, the white and black Knabstrup, and the white Lipizzaner. They were all wonderful. After considering all of the choices, she picked the palomino Belgian Warmblood, which she named Fletcher. Estrella chose the chestnut Arabian, naming it Chesnutt.

"We will keep them in the stable for now. We can continue in the morning," said Estrella. "Lena before you go back in could you stay here for a minute I have something to ask you?"

"Of course, Estrella," Lena replied.

"Lena, I have left my home and journeyed on this quest to find friends. I am finding that the Lord is placing these friends in my path, as I go along. So I was wondering, would you like to be my friend and come along with me on this quest as we find more friends? It would mean that you would have to leave your home and follow me, and then go back to my home with me."

"Wow, Estrella, I'm honored. I would love to be your friend after what you did for me. I owe you my life. So yes, I would like to be your friend and come along with you," Lena replied. She kneeled down before Estrella.

"Thank you, my new friend. Let's get the mules to the stables, and then we can go back and get things ready for the night. You can straighten things out with your family, and I can get some letters written home," Estrella said. Once Lena rose, the two girls walked the mules into the barn. After fastening the mules to their stalls, Estrella retrieved her night bag and her saddle bag, the saddle bag contained her parchment, quill and ink bottle, then followed Lena back to the inn.

When they arrived at the Inn, Lena went to tell her family the news, and Estrella received the key to her room and walked up the stairs. She went into her room and set her things out for the night. When she was finished, she sat down at the little desk and wrote out her return letters, starting out with one to her mother, following that with one to Gideon, and finishing with one to Kasim. Then she sealed the letters, rolled them up, and placed them in the carrier. Figuring that was enough letters for the night, she sent Merlin off, and then joined the others downstairs for dinner.

Lena had told her family the news and had made the preparations to leave. Her brother, Marco, was put in charge of the inn, and her sister was assigned to take over her shows in the tavern.

All the girls went into the dining room of the inn to have dinner together. The food was brought to the table. They all enjoyed the great meal. Once their stomachs were full and their heads were sleepy, they adjourned and went to their respective rooms to sleep for the night. Before turning in, Estrella knelt by her bedside and said a prayer: "Dear Heavenly Father, thank you abundantly for the many blessings, including the places to rest, the food to keep us nourished, the Holy Spirit to guide us, and your angels all around to protect us. I thank you greatly for the friends that I have now, and I look forward to meeting the other friends that you will place in my path. I also anticipate the many adventures we will have in the future. In your Son's precious name, amen."

Restless, she tried to sleep. She was anxious about what tomorrow, or the next week, would hold, and she was nervous without her trusted falcon by her side. Instead, he was out there flying to deliver her letters to her family and Kasim. It could be days, weeks, or even longer before he would fly back with a response.

The next morning, the girls packed up their things, loaded them onto their pack mules and carts and then mounted their horses. Lena bid farewell to her family and her home, mounted her horse, and rode up to Estrella to await her leader's command. Estrella looked back to her hosts, saying, "Thank you both for your lovely hospitality. I promise I shall look after your daughter and protect her." Then she turned to her girls. "Let's head out, girls." And with that she spurred on her horse and they all rode off, leaving the town of Willow Creek behind. They were now headed off to the next town that the Holy Spirit would guide them to.

CHAPTER 11

Stories of Home

For quite a long span of time, the girls traveled by day, stopping only to eat and drink, and let the animals drink. At night, they would camp out under the stars. Every day as they rode on, Estrella would watch the skies, and every night she would whistle a tune in hopes of any sign of her feathered companion.

"Estrella, what are you looking for, signs of rain or smoke signals?" asked Lena one day during their travels. Estrella kept looking to the skies.

Karmina responded, "She is watching the skies for any sign of her falcon, Merlin; she must have sent him off with letters for home and is waiting for his return, to hear back from home. Estella, how long ago did you send him off?"

Still looking up in the skies, Estrella replied, "Back at the inn in Willow Creek, before our dinner, I sent him off with three letters, two for home and one for Gideon. I think he is still in Camelot."

"Estrella, that was at least three weeks ago. He could be anywhere. Anything could have—" said Lena.

Karmina cut Lena off, saying, "Shush, don't say it. Merlin is more than her pet. He is her closest friend. They have been together for years. She saved his life from a hunter. The last thing she needs is to think that the same thing could have happened again. It would crush her."

"I am sorry, Estrella, for suggesting that something bad could have happened to Merlin. I'm sure he is still finding his way back to you."

"Thank you, Lena. I know he is out there," said Estrella.

Later, they set up camp for the night. It was Sloan's turn to catch dinner. They had roast rabbit with dried herbs and fresh wild vegetables. After eating their meager dinner, three of the girls went into their tents. Estrella sat out under the stars, listening for Merlin, singing to herself, and hoping that Merlin would hear her and recognize his old lullaby: "Always know, my love, that wherever you are, that is where my heart is. No matter where the wind takes you, always find your way home to me. No matter where you are, my love, know that the love that we have will bring you home to me." She stopped singing and started whistling the song. In the middle of the tune, she heard the same melody whistled back to her. And instantly her spirits were lifted as if she were flying along with Merlin on wings. The winged messenger flew down whistling the tune with the letters in his carrier. He chirped, {"I'm back. Did you miss me, Estrella?"}

"Only every day you were away, my friend. I didn't know I had the strength to keep going without you. Come, I have set up a perch for you. I shall read the letters tomorrow. Tonight I shall tie your tresses, and then we can go to sleep," said Estella. She took the letters from Merlin and placed them in her saddlebag. Merlin flew up to the perch. Estrella took the falcon tresses out of her saddlebag and used them to tie Merlin to his perch. Then they both fell asleep under the stars.

The next morning, while the girls were straightening up their campsite and Lena was cooking breakfast, Estrella opened her letters from home.

Dear Estrella,

I am so very proud of you, my beloved daughter. Remember, dear one, that you can do all things through Jesus Christ, who strengthens you. The Lord is with you every step of the way. Abide in him and he will grant you the desires of your heart. Meditate on his word and speak to him daily through your prayers, and he will give you all that you need and more. Keep in mind, my love, that he has plans for you and that he will never leave you or forsake you. Stay strong, and when things get hard, pray. He will be there to help. I am so very proud of the brave and independent young woman you are becoming. Remember, I am always with you in your heart.

Love,

Your proud mother, Raine Maia Althea

O not only to hear from her mother, but also to hear that she was proud of her! It was the one thing that Estrella wanted most right now. She held the letter close to her heart. Then she rolled it back up, tied it with a piece of twine, and set it aside. Then she picked up her second letter, carefully peeled off the seal, unrolled the parchment, and began to read.

Dear Estrella,

Thank you for your thoughts. I cannot wait to see you again. Bliss is looking forward to meeting you. I have told her much about you. I am very proud of you, Sister. Not only are you brave enough to set out on your own, but also you do so with the Lord's courage guiding you. I never doubted you for a second. I have known since you were young that once you set your mind to something, there is no stopping you. The fifteen nannies and handmaids would agree. Remember when you decided you wanted to learn how to ride a horse? The riding instructor, the stable hands, the horse handler, and half the palace staff tried to convince you to start off on a pony. They picked out a pretty brown one, tied a big pink bow on it, and even had the saddle on it. But you refused to ride a pony; you said that it felt like they were treating you like a baby. You were so stubborn that you insisted on riding a full-grown horse. I convinced the staff that I could talk you out of it. When I was done talking to you, I had finally coaxed you into settling for a colt. You grew up with that little horse, Blackie. You, Merlin, and Blackie were as thick as thieves; the three of you were inseparable.

Please be careful out there, Estrella. Remember to keep your weapons close, and be careful in whom you put your trust.

Love,

Your proud and protective brother, Gideon

A smile stretched out across Estrella's face. She lit up, glowing a rosy red, when thinking about all the adventures she'd had with Merlin and Blackie. Remembering the day she had gotten Blackie made her very happy. And the days she spent with Gideon were golden memories. Gideon meant everything to Estrella. His happiness was her happiness. When he hurt, she hurt. They were as close as brothers and sisters could get. With their father gone most of the time, Gideon had taken on the responsibilities of taking care of and protecting his family.

Now that she had finished reading her second letter, Estrella rolled it back up, tied it with twine, and then reached for the third letter, which she unrolled and started to read.

Dear Estrella,

I miss you terribly, my friend. The kingdom is just
not the same without your glowing smile to brighten
the days and outshine the sun. But I know that this
is a mission you must do for yourself. I am so glad
to hear that you are no longer lonesome and forlorn.
The Lord will always provide for you no matter what
your needs may be. Just like our Lord Jesus Christ
had to leave his home in order to find disciples, so
must you find your companions away from where
you are comfortable. Know that no matter what, and
through any circumstances, I will always be your
friend. God be with you, my friend.

Your dear friend,

Kasim

Reading that Kasim missed her that much made Estrella's former glow
dim. His letter reminded her of how her heart had broken upon leaving
him behind. But he was right: she had to do this on her own. This was
her quest, not his. If she had brought him along and something went
wrong to put him in danger, she would never have been able to live
with herself. She wiped away a stray tear, rolled the letter back up, tied
it with twine, and put it away.

The girls had just finished tearing down the camp and were now
all sitting down to rest before eating. Lena was just about finished
preparing the small meal when she noticed that Estrella was very
quiet. She decided that now would be a good time for everyone to
get to know each other better.

"Since we have some time before we eat, I think this is a good chance
for us to share about ourselves. I think Estrella should go first and
tell us about herself."

"Oh yes, please do tell us, Estrella. Tell us about Faylin. Tell us about your home," said Sloan.

"Faylin has always been my home. It's a beautiful kingdom, with orchards and flowers and farms and farmhouses. A giant stone wall surrounds the whole kingdom to protect everyone from invaders. And then there is the castle right in the middle of it. It's a beautiful castle. I lived there with my family: my mother, Raine Maia Althea; my older brother, Crown Prince Gideon; and my two younger sisters, Princess Kylia and Princess Keena." Estrella would have continued if she had not noticed the girls looking puzzled. "What is the matter?" she asked.

Karmina replied, "Well, it's just that we noticed that you didn't mention your father."

"Yes, surely you have one? I mean, everyone has a father," Sloan said.

"Ah, very true, very true. And good point; everyone does have a father. But, you see, King Indra was only my father in the technical sense of the word *father*, meaning someone who gives you life. In the emotional sense of the word, meaning a male figure who is present in your life and encourages you and loves you, he was not my father. You see, King Indra was never home. He was always away from home, either attending wizard councils or engaging in war campaigns. He missed most of my life and birthdays. So I grew accustomed to living my life without my father. Everything a princess needed to learn, I learned from my tutors. And the things a princess doesn't need to learn were taught to me by my brother, Gideon." By this point in Estrella's story the girls were really interested. They'd had no idea about their leader's past. They'd just followed her.

"Oh, please go on, Estrella," urged Lena.

"Yes, please do. We want to know more," said Sloan.

"Well, all that I can tell you is that as far back as I can remember, I have always lived in Faylin, but I feel somewhere deep in my heart that there was somewhere else I once lived with my father, Maia, and Gideon. But those are very distant memories. I can barely remember them. And yet there is something deep in my spirit that tells me that way back in the past, there was a place I once lived, a place of peace, joy, and light."

"Whoa!" said all the girls at once.

"That place sounds very beautiful. I would love to see it someday," said Karmina.

"I wonder where it is?" asked Sloan.

"I don't know; I can't even remember how I know of this place," came the princess's quizzical response.

"Well, no offense, Your Majesty, but I think that is enough about you. I say, before we go on with the next backstory, we should eat. I cooked each of you a poached egg with some dried seasonings. Let's eat them now before they get cold. When we are finished eating, Karmina should tell us her story," said Lena.

"Good idea. Telling a story does make a person hungry. Lena, if you wouldn't mind, please say grace before we eat. And then I will serve," Estrella said.

"Of course. Dear Heavenly Father, we come before you today to thank you for all the blessings you have bestowed upon us. Thank you for the little meal that we share at the start of our day and for the company of these lovely ladies around me. We ask that you please bless this journey and everyone seated here today, and that you please bless this food before us so that it may be used to give us strength and energy. May it be used to help us and not to harm us. Amen."

"Thank you, Lena. Now I will serve the food," said Estrella. She ladled out the poached eggs, placed them onto the girls' plates, and passed around the dried herbs. Then the traveling companions ate their little meal in silence, each one savoring what she had, hoping to save energy for the ride ahead. When Estrella finished eating, she put her plate aside, got up from her place at the fire, walked over to her horse, reached into her saddlebag, and then held out some dried fish in her hand for Merlin to eat. He graciously took the fish in his beak and tossed it into his mouth. Estrella laughed to see her friend perform like that. Then she grabbed an apple and some oats, walked over to her horse and pack mule, and fed them.

She then proceeded to heft a large sack of apples and fill the feedbags full of oats for the other pack mules. As she passed the other girls' horses, she gave each one of them an apple. She also placed the feedbags on the pack mules. After feeding each horse, she would whisper sweet words, gave a pat on the neck, and stroked the mane. Each horse neighed quietly and then tossed his or her head into the air playfully, making Estrella laugh, almost like they had shared a secret joke.

When Estrella finished feeding the horses and the mules, she picked up the girls' dirty dishes.

"Whoa, whoa, whoa there! Estrella, what do you think you are doing?" said the dismayed Sloan.

"I'm taking care of the dirty dishes."

"Yes, we can see that, but why are *you* doing it?" asked Lena.

"Yeah, you are a princess. You don't need to do dishes. Let us take care of them."

"My status doesn't change the fact that these chores need to be done. I was the first one finished eating, so I should do the dishes. On top of that, the Lord Jesus Christ said, 'For even the Son of Man did not come to be served but to serve.' So I am going to do the dishes." Then she turned to Odell and Tokala. "Come on, you guys. Why don't the two of you come with me down to the little stream I saw back some ways? The two of you can catch your breakfast before we head out." Estrella turned and headed for the stream. She was closely followed by the fox and the otter. While they were gone, the remaining girls talked among themselves.

"Did you happen to notice that while Estrella was reading her letters, she seemed to glow?" asked Lena.

"I'm sure it was just from the sun behind her," replied Sloan.

"You know, I'm not so sure, Sloan. There seems to be this quality about her."

"Yeah, and she seems to have a really good way with animals. They all love her, even the horses and pack mules," said Lena.

"You're right."

"I'm glad we chose to follow her. She makes a really good leader."

As Estrella made her return from washing the dishes, Odell and Tokala were following behind her, licking their lips.

"Well, the dishes are all washed, and the kids each caught a fish for their breakfast. I say that Karmina tells us her story while we ride to the nearest town for lunch. And once we find a place to rest for the night, Sloan can tell us her story. In the morning, Lena can share. And if by tomorrow we have a new companion, she can share her tale as well," said Estrella. Then the group began loading up the rest of their things. Once they were all packed up, they swung up into their saddles and started riding.

Karmina said to the group, "I agree with what Estrella said earlier. I already told this to Estrella, but what you two, Sloan and Lena, don't know about me is that I was a slave to a selfish king who would force me to sing for him all the time. Also, I was used as bait to lure in a unicorn for him and his friends to hunt. They did not kill it but gave it as gift to the king's daughter. I saved the unicorn, and we ran away together. That unicorn is now my faithful and loyal friend Juniper. But what you don't know, Estrella, is how I became the king's slave. ✳

"I lived as a princess in a small province. My family and I were happy. My people lived in peace and harmony. Just like my mother, I was blessed as a songstress. She and I would sing for each other every day. Our people loved to hear us sing. One day, a king from a far-off kingdom came to visit, saying he heard my singing. He gave my father a choice: either surrender the province to him, or give me as a gift to him. My father refused both options, saying that our little province belonged to our people and would never belong to any outsider, and that he would never, ever give me away. This upset the outsider. He killed my father and ordered his men to seize me and set fire to our province. I watched as they slaughtered my family, my people, and my fiancé. They burned down the village—the houses, huts, and crops. They killed all of the livestock. As this king rode away with me, I watched as my home was turned into a pile of rubble. This king wiped my father's blood from his sword right in front of me, and then he had the nerve to call my father a heathen, and my mother a harlot. He also called my people savages. He said that he had rescued me from squalor and from those savages, and that he would try to fix me and make me a more proper lady of his household.

"Over time, he tried to brainwash me into thinking that I was a heathen and savage, and that I needed to change to be accepted. When that didn't work, he tried beating my old ways out of me. When I still persisted in refusing to change my ways, he gave in and said that if wasn't going to act like a lady, then I would be treated as a slave and a savage. After that, he kept me chained up in a cage. The people of his kingdom didn't trust me around anyone or anything; they spread rumors about me, saying that I would kill them all in their sleep and steal their wealth out of hatred and vengeance.

"Then one night, like I told you, I rescued Juniper, and we stole back our freedom. We ran away into the night and have lived free ever since.

"One morning long after that, I got a visit from a lonely princess who asked me to join her on a quest. Juniper and I accepted, and we will stay with the princess forevermore. Estrella has become our new family."

The girls were in shock. Sloan and Lena were too stunned to speak, and Estrella was on the brink of tears.

"Oh my word, Karmina, that's such a sad backstory," Sloan said.

"I can't believe it. That's terrible," Lena added.

Estrella was still too stunned to speak. She was crying so hard that she almost lost her balance and fell off her horse, but she soon regained her composure. "So, Karmina," she said, but then she stopped speaking, as her voice was cracking from her emotions. After a moment, she picked up the thread again. "So, Karmina, tell us about this fiancé you had, or at least what you remember of him before that terrible day."

"Well, my people were not focused on looks, but I must say that he was one of the cutest young men in our village. His name was Kabari. He was intelligent, kind, and compassionate. At the time of my capture, we were to have been wed in two months. Our marriage was arranged, but our relationship was better than many. He treated me like the queen I was born to be. Every day during his courtship of me, he would have flowers delivered to my door. The night before the outsider came, Kabari came into my room and kissed my cheek.

"Then the outsider came and our lives went up in smoke. They killed Kabari. He had fought against them and tried to free me, but he failed. Some nights, I can still hear him call out to me. I relive and replay that terrible day in my dreams, and sometimes while I sleep I can still feel his kiss upon my cheek. He was my first love. We were to be wed, but all that was destroyed."

"Wow, that sounds really romantic—and sad. I am sorry to hear about Kabari," said Lena.

"I do miss him still, but that was in the past. I'm living for my future now. And my future is with my new family: Estrella and Merlin; Sloan and Odell; you, Lena, and Tokala; and whoever else we meet on this quest," said Karmina.

CHAPTER 12

Nori

When Karmina had finished telling everyone her story, the group of girls arrived in a village by the name of Aveline. As they entered the town, Estrella felt the pull of the Spirit leading her toward a small bakery. She smiled, deciding that this was a good place to stop for the day. Once they all dismounted, Estrella gave each of the girls a small purse of gold coins and her instructions.

"All right, girls, this seems like a good place to stay. Sloan, I want you to find an inn with four rooms available. If there are not enough rooms for everyone, then see if they at least have two rooms available with at least two beds in them. If we have to, we can share beds. Lena, see if you can find a stable with enough room for all the horses. If we need to, we can put them up for the night in the barn with the pack mules. Karmina, I want you to get us some food. Please go to the butcher and the grocer. We need some fresh salted meat—get some ham, some other type of pork, and maybe some salted venison. We also need some vegetables and fruits. Fresh would be best, but if you can't get any, then we can make do with dried fruits. I am going to look around to see what else there is in this town. When you are done, we will meet up—" she looked around and spotted a cute little bakery—"there. We will meet back up at that little bakery."

"All right," replied the girls. Then they went where they had been instructed to go.

Estrella walked around the town looking at the shops. She started off just getting the lay of the land, but then she decided she should look for a doctor. Since her arm was pretty scratched up from Merlin's talons, she needed an herb or a balm to soothe it. Maybe she could find a healer/herbalist in Aveline. Actually, her shoulder and her arm had started to throb from pain. Finding the shop of a healer, she pushed open the door and then stood inside clutching her right arm.

"Please, can someone help me? My arm is in a lot of pain. Please, can someone at least give me something to soothe the pain?" she pleaded.

The healer came out of the back room wiping off his hands; obviously he had been in the middle of something.

"Oh dear, what seems to be the problem?"

"My name is Princess Estrella from the kingdom of Faylin. My arm is in a lot of pain from the talons of my pet falcon, Merlin. I was hoping you would be able to help me with some salve or balm to soothe it."

"Of course. May I have your permission to untie your sleeve to look at the wounds?"

"You have my permission to untie my sleeve."

He untied the sleeve, pulled it down, and saw all the scratches and scabs. Estrella's shoulder and forearm were covered with wounds.

"My dear, these are pretty deep wounds. Before I give you the balm, let me first dress the wounds. Then I suggest you go over and see the tanner. Ask for a leather tunic to wear underneath your clothes to prevent further wounds."

Estrella smirked a little and then responded, "That was kind of my plan."

The doctor poured a bit of alcohol on the wounds to clean them up. Then he applied a salve to draw out any infection. After adding a thin layer of soothing balm, he wrapped the wounds up in bandages, tied Estrella's sleeve back on, and gave her the balm. "Rub this on your wounds every night before you go to sleep, and keep the tunic on all day while you have your falcon on your arm."

"Thank you, Doctor; it feels better already." With that, she gave the man some money for his troubles, picked up the balm, went out of the clinic, walked along the road, and looked for the tanner. She searched and searched until she found the small tannery. Walking in, she addressed the tanner, saying, "Excuse me, sir. I was wondering if you could help me?"

He turned around, gave her the once-over, and replied, "The tailor is two shops down, miss; they can make you a pretty new gown."

"Well, that would be very helpful if I were looking for a new gown. I was looking for the tanner. I was hoping he could sell me a small leather tunic to protect my arm from my falcon's talons. But if he is too busy to help a visiting princess and make the sale, I will have to look somewhere else. Oh well," she said. Then she turned around and smirked. If there was one thing she had learned from those business trips with her father, it was how to make a deal. Sellers hate to lose sales. If there is an opportunity to make a lot of money, say, from visiting royalty, then they have to snatch at it while they can.

Estrella's comment had clearly caught the tanner's attention. He spun around and, evidently trying to get her to come back, said, "Wait, miss. Miss, please do not leave. Please, I'm sure I can find something for your troubles. Did you say you were a princess? Please come back."

Estrella smiled and thought, *I've got him hooked now.* "Oh, I guess I mentioned something like that. But I don't think you can help me, as you are far too busy. Besides, I don't think you have anything to help me." If there was another thing she had learned, it was that shopkeepers hated to be told that there was something they couldn't do. Telling them as much was to use a tactic called reverse reasoning. If someone was not doing something you wanted them to do, you could trick them into doing it by saying that they could not do it, and then they would want to prove themselves by doing it.

"Oh, please, miss, let me take your measurements and make something to fit your size. And I will give it to you for half price," he pleaded with her.

"All right. I guess it's the least I could do since you are taking time away from your very important work."

So the tanner took her measurements and found a small tunic, he made for falconers. He handed it to her, and she inspected it. The material seemed strong and durable, and the stitches were clean and uniform. Not too shabby for a tanner. Estrella went into the back room and tried on the tunic. It fit rather well. She stepped out and called Merlin to her. He flew in and perched on her outstretched forearm. She didn't feel the talons, only his weight. She smiled and turned to the tanner.

"Well, my dear tanner, you are very good at your craft. The tunic fits well, and it holds up very well beneath his talons. So how much do I owe you for your fine craftsmanship?"

"For Your Highness, a special price of twenty marks" he replied.

Estrella pulled out her coin purse, produced the coins—all while holding Merlin on her other arm—and handed them to the tanner. Then she left the shop. Once outside, she looked at her feathered companion and said, "You know, you are getting a little heavy. I think you even look a little chubby."

Merlin, shocked and indignant, squawked back in retaliation, {"Excuse me? I am not chubby, thank you very much."}

"I am only saying you have gotten a little heavier. Maybe you should cut back on the soda crackers, and maybe eat fewer field mice."

{"Hey, you are the one who feeds me. Besides, it's all muscle. I fly around everywhere."}

"All right, all right, then let's head to the bakery to wait for the rest of the girls," she said as she was drawing closer to the meeting spot. "Maybe you should wait out here in a nearby tree until it is time to go."

{"All right."} Merlin flew up into a tree.

Then Estrella walked into the bakery and looked around while waiting for the rest of the girls. While she was waiting, she thought back to all those business trips her father had made her go on. She had learned how to get a store owner's attention, how to make them wait on you, how to bargain and barter, and how to talk them into giving her a lower price than intended. Other than that, there was nothing that she enjoyed about those trips.

Snapping herself out of her daydream, Estrella looked around. The bakery was a quaint little shop with little tables and chairs and a glass case full of delicious-looking food. She made a mental note to purchase some baked goods for the trip. The girls didn't have many loaves of bread among their supplies, and the ones they did have were starting to get stale.

Within ten to fifteen minutes, the girls showed up at the bakery.

"All right, girls, what's the status update? Are all the preparations ready for tonight and for our trip?" asked Estrella.

"Your Majesty, all the animals are in the stable, aside from smaller pets, which are waiting patiently outside the bakery," reported Lena.

"Very good. Sloan, have you secured any rooms for us to sleep in tonight?"

"Yes, Estrella, I have found a close enough inn that has rooms available for us to sleep in tonight. I already purchased rooms for us." Sloan replied.

"All right, good job, Sloan. How about you, Karmina? Did you get us some more meats and veggies?"

"Yes, Estrella, we have enough for a couple more days of meals. It should suffice," replied Karmina.

"Very good. I think we deserve a treat. Come with me to the food display case and pick out a treat for yourselves. I will select a baguette for our lunch today and breakfast tomorrow."

"All right," they replied as they followed her to the display.

Estrella looked at all the baguette choices and decided to buy one made of millet. The girls looked over all the treats. When they had made their decisions, they walked over to the counter. Estrella rang a bell for assistance. Then they heard a girl's voice coming from the back room.

"I will be with you in just a minute. Please be patient."

"Well, she sounds pleasant enough," said Lena.

✳ Soon the girl stepped out, wiping her flour-covered hands onto her apron. She was a slender girl with beautiful long brown hair and dazzling brown eyes that sparkled like a citrine gemstone. She was wearing a simple brown dress beneath her white apron.

"Welcome to Cassia Honey Bakery. I am the owner and solo baker. My name is Nori. How may I help you today?"

"You make all these things?" asked Karmina.

"Why, yes. Yes, I do. Everyone says I make the best cakes in town. At least that is what I hope everyone says," said Nori, giggling. "Now what can I get for you girls?"

Estrella spoke up. "Well, first of all, we would like to buy the wheat baguette, please. I would like to purchase one of your cinnamon rolls, and my friends here would like to purchase one of your delicious-looking treats as well."

"All right, girls, what would you like?" asked Nori.

"I would like one of your cupcakes, please, with vanilla icing on it, please," replied Karmina.

"And I would like a blackberry muffin, please," said Lena.

"I would also like a cinnamon roll, please," replied Sloan.

"All right, that's one wheat baguette, two cinnamon rolls, one cupcake with vanilla icing, and one blueberry muffin. I will get those right away for you while my assistant rings up your purchases," Nori said. Then she called out toward the back room, "Mika, we have costumers at the counter. I need you out here to ring them up while I get their baked goods together, please."

The girls all thought that another girl would be coming out of the back room. They never thought they would see a raccoon in a tiny apron come out whipping her paws and chattering at Nori. {"The bread has ten minutes left. What did they get?"}

"Thank you for keeping your eye on it for me. They ordered a wheat baguette, two cinnamon rolls, a cupcake with vanilla icing, and a blueberry muffin. You can find the prices in the order register."

Mika pulled a chair over and stood at the counter. Then she pulled out the register and looked up the prices. Adding them up, she wrote down, "Fifty-five gold marks."

"All right. That seems to be reasonable enough," said Estrella as she pulled out the coins. She placed her stack of fifty-five shekels on the counter. By this time, Nori had appeared with the goods all wrapped up. Mika took the coins, jingled them on the counter, visually examined them, bit them, and then began sorting them. Estrella made the mistake of interrupting her while counting.

"I assure you, they are all real coins and are all there."

{"I know what I am doing, thank you. Please do not interrupt me."}

"She knows what she is doing. This is her routine. This is one of her only jobs. She used to bag up the goods, until one of my costumers got offended by it. Now she checks on the food and handles the money."

{"I don't like that story, remember."}

"She doesn't like that story. I made the mistake of asking her if she needed help adding things up. She got mad at me. She is actually quite bright and insists on doing things on her own," explained Nori.

{"All here; all accounted for."}

"Thank you for your purchase. Have a good day. God bless."

It was then that something inside Estrella spoke to her. Something just clicked. There was something she liked about this girl. She knew that this was another one God had placed in their path. Estrella smiled. Then she and her three companions sat down. Before they started eating their treats, Estrella said, "Girls, let's pray first." So they all joined hands and bowed their heads. "Dear Heavenly Father, we thank you for providing for all our needs. We ask that you please bless these treats to our bodies, so that they may be used to help us and not harm us. We also ask that you bless our new friend, Nori." She whispered, "And place it on her heart to join us on our quest if she is to be our new traveling companion. If not, bless her abundantly. I ask you that if she is not the one, you make the one known." She finished by saying, "Amen."

When the girl appeared again behind the counter, Estrella smiled. The Lord whispered in her ear, "She is your fourth. Her faith will greatly add to yours. She needs your protection, as she is in danger, but she will come to you in her own time. And it will be a while before she shares her story with you."

Before the girls started eating, Sloan turned to Estrella and asked, "Do you think she is the one we were meant to meet, the one to continue the quest with us? Aren't there some kind of criteria you use to pick your friends?"

Estrella turned to Sloan with a quizzical glance. "If I were that picky and had criteria, do you think I would have chosen a runaway slave, a blacksmith's daughter, and an innkeeper and tavern dancer? No offense." Estrella smirked.

Sloan said in response, "You do have a point."

"Do you think that our Savior, Jesus Christ, was picky when he chose his disciples? Have you read about the people he hung out with—prostitutes, tax collectors, and some of the most unworthy and unclean people? Most of his disciples were smelly fishermen. There was also a tax collector and a physician. Besides, I did not pick you guys. The Lord picked you for me. He puts my 'followers' in my path. When I know that someone is to join us, it's because he's told me so."

"You know, I hate it when you mention things that happened in the Bible, because there is no arguing with you after that," said Sloan.

"It's because it is the truth. You can't argue with the Word of the Lord."

"So is she the one?" asked Lena.

"Yes, the Lord told me so, but she has to come to us in her own time. The thing we can do is offer the invitation, and hope that the Lord moves her to follow us."

After their discussion, they ate their delicious treats. Estrella walked up to the counter and rang the bell, and once again she heard Nori's voice come from the back room. "I will be with you in just a minute; I have to put the finishing touches on this bread."

"That must be some great bread they are making. They have been talking about it since we arrived," said Karmina.

Then Nori came back to the counter. "Oh, it's you again. How were the treats?"

"They were excellent, thank you, but I have a question for you," said Estrella.

"Oh? And what's that?"

The girls all smiled at each other. Estrella replied, "I was wondering if you would be willing to become one of my new traveling companions, follow me on my quest, and join in on my adventures and travels?"

"And what quest are you on?" she asked with a quizzical arched eyebrow.

"Well—" began Estrella, but then Karmina interrupted, hopping up from the table to join her at the counter.

"Oh, Estrella, can I tell it please? Please, can I tell her the story? Please, please?"

"All right, Karmina, you can tell her the story."

"Okay, so this is Princess Estrella from the kingdom of Faylin. Her brother, Gideon, was summoned to come before King Arthur to become a knight of the Round Table. And since their father is hardly ever home to watch the castle and keep it and the family safe, that became her brother's job. But since he was summoned, he left that job up to Estrella. She realized that the task was too big and lonely, so she set off on this quest to find friends and companions to follow her home and help her take care of the kingdom. Did I get it right, Estrella?"

"Yes, you did," replied a very impressed Estrella.

"Well, that seems like a very noble and adventurous quest," said Nori.

"You don't have to decide right away. Give it some thought, meditate on it, pray on it. When you have come to a decision, come find us at the inn down the road. We hope to hear of your decision at dinnertime," said Estrella with a smile. Then the girls picked up their things and left the shop to head to the inn.

Later that day, while the girls were enjoying their lunch at the inn, Nori was thinking over their offer, which seemed to her to be a wonderful one. While she was thinking it over, she saw two very unsavory-looking men walking up the road toward her shop, and recognized them as men who had come to visit her father's church to collect taxes. She remembered what they did when her father, the minister, couldn't come up with all the money to pay the collection. They knocked over the pews, defaced the altar, and burned the hymnals.

The men were about five shops away from Nori's shop. She had just enough time to pack away some of her goods, including the fresh loaf of bread, for her journey with the girls. After that, she packed up all her belongings, including her clothes, and stored the parcels under the floorboards. If the men found out that she was planning on skipping town, they might kill her.

The two tax collectors entered the shop. One of them was carrying a club, and the other one had a large knife and a burlap sack. They approached the counter.

"All right, baker, time to collect the taxes. Hand over the dough, and I don't mean the kind you bake with."

"That's a good one, boss," remarked the less intelligent of the two.

Then Nori said, "I haven't had too many sales. Please give me a little more time. I can come up with the money. Please, just a little more time."

"The money is due today. You owe us nine hundred and fifty shillings of revenue," said the brains.

"Hey, boss, isn't that the preachy guy's daughter, the one we threw in jail?" asked the muscle.

"Oh yeah, you're right, George." To Nori, he said, "You know what we did to the minister? We threw him in prison and we burned down his precious little church. So unless you want to end up like dear old Daddy, I suggest you pay up."

Nori was shocked. She thought it had been bad enough when they defaced the church, but now she learned that they'd arrested her father and burned down their precious church.

"Please, I need more time. I can raise the money in a month or so. Please let my father go. He is a good man, but he hasn't had enough time to collect the tithes to pay what he owes you. Please, I beg you."

"We can give you one day's notice. Come up with the money tomorrow or face the penalty."

"I can't come up with nine hundred and fifty shillings in a day! Please, I need more time."

"Too bad. George, take care of this place."

And with that, George, the muscle, started doing damage to Nori's shop. He smashed the tables, broke the chairs, smashed the windows, broke the glass case, and smashed all of her goods. Then the one in command, whose name was Juda, stepped behind the counter, pushed Nori out of the way, grabbed the coin box, and dumped its contents into his sack. He cut open all of the sacks of flour, sugar, other grains, and other baking ingredients. When Mika heard the commotion, she came scurrying out of the back room in a fit. When she saw what was happening, she started chattering.

When Juda saw Mika, he laughed at the fit she was throwing. Grabbing her by the scruff of her neck and holding a knife to her throat, he said to George, "Hey, George, what do you think? Do you think we could get a few coins for this one's pelt?"

"Uh, yeah. Sure, boss."

Then Nori started to weep and plead for her pet's life. "Please, I beg of you, don't hurt her. Take anything you want, but please don't hurt her."

"Fine. She is probably filthy anyway," said Juda as he threw the raccoon back to Nori, who caught her and held her tight.

With the damage to the shop done, Juda, walking back to the other side of the counter, backhanded Nori across the cheek. As the two men started to leave, Juda shared one last thought with Nori. "Let that be a warning to you, baker girl, preacher's daughter. Next time you don't have the money, you will be joining your father in the jail. We will be back tomorrow to finish what we did today."

Later that night, Nori tried her best to use flour to cover up the bruise that she now had on her cheek thanks to those tax-collecting thugs. Gathering up all her things, she, along with Mika said good-bye to the shop and their home. Then they made their way to the inn where the girls were staying. They went inside, asked where Princess Estrella and her friends were eating, and were pointed to a table near the back. Nori and Mika made their way to the table. When Estrella noticed them approaching, she offered Nori a seat. The girl accepted and sat down.

"So have you made your decision? Would you like to come with us?" asked Sloan.

"*Yes!* I mean, yes, I would like to come with you very much. I was wondering if I might share a room with one of you girls tonight?"

"Of course," replied Estella. She noticed that the girl seemed a bit frantic. She also noticed the slightest trace of a bruise concealed under some flour, but she thought that it would be best not to pry now. She would ask about it tomorrow, once they were out of the town.

"You can share my room, Nori," offered Karmina.

"Thank you very much," Nori said.

"All right, now that we have our newest member, let us continue with our backstories. Sloan, I believe it is your turn to share," Estrella said.

"All right. Well, back in my hometown, my father was a very well-known and renowned blacksmith. If someone wanted the best weapons and shields, they would travel all the way to my father's shop. He was a very kind and compassionate man. To his children he seemed invincible. There wasn't anything he couldn't do, and nothing that could stop him. He was very passionate about his work. All along, however, he knew something was wrong, but he hid it from us and put up a strong front so we wouldn't be worried. When I was twelve, he brought me into the shop and started to teach me about the trade. He may have convinced my sister that he was invincible and that everything was all right, but I had a feeling that something was wrong. He was moving slower and seemed to be very tired. Then he lost the use of his most valuable tools of the trade. He could no longer feel his arms or move them. That it when I picked up the work for him. Soon he got sicker, and lay in bed all the time. He started throwing up bile and was very feverish. He would break out into cold sweats and have night terrors. We knew he wasn't going to get any better, so we sent for the minister to pray over him and say his last rites. And then we had a doctor give him an elixir that helped him slip away. We buried him the next day at the church cemetery.

"From then on, I was in charge of the shop. I passed that responsibility on to my sister when Estrella and Karmina came into the shop and invited me to join the quest. Since then, I have been with them all the way." Sloan finished her story, wiping away a tear. Remembering her father's death had made her cry. When she looked up, she saw that all the girls were in tears.

"Sloan, I am so sorry to hear about your father's passing," offered Lena.

"It is all right. I have this new family with you girls now, and I couldn't feel happier," Sloan answered.

While they were chatting, Estrella could not help but think, *At least they had good and happy relationships with their fathers. I wish I'd had that.* Keeping these thoughts to herself, she said, "Well, now that we have eaten and have had our story for the night, I say we adjourn to our rooms and rest up for the trip tomorrow. Nori, we are very happy to have you with us." After that, they all rose from their seats and went upstairs to their rooms.

CHAPTER 13

Estrella Meets the Order of the Lion

In her room, Estrella laid out her night shift. She decided to write some letters home before she changed, starting with a letter to her Maia.

Dear Maia,

Did we ever live somewhere before...

That was the farthest she got, because she was startled by the sound of flapping wings at her window. She knew it couldn't be her Merlin, as he was silently perched and sleeping.

The sound woke Merlin though. It startled Estrella so much that she almost knocked over her inkwell; luckily she caught it before it spilled over onto her page. She looked about herself and was shocked to see an owl sitting on her desk with a message clutched in its talons, but she was even more taken aback when she heard it speak. "Don't just sit there and gawk with your mouth wide open like a fish, Estrella. It's not becoming."

"Excuse me, how do you know my name?" she asked, not sure how an owl could be talking to her, in plain English.

"Estrella, we know a lot about you. But you probably don't remember much about me. You might, however, remember my master, Merlyn Emrys."

"What?! Merlyn is your master? What happened to Shea?" she asked.

Merlin added, {"Yes, what about my mother?"}

"Shea is getting very old; she is not getting younger. Merlyn keeps her home, as she is sick. Do not be sad, Merlin. She would be proud to see her son grown up and protecting the princess. By the way, I forgot to introduce myself. My name is Archimedes. I am here because Merlyn would like to see you, my dear. He has this message for you, Princess," the owl said.

Then he handed her the note, which read, "Meet me at the willow twenty paces out of town. There are some people I would like you to meet, and a proposition I would like to offer you. ~Merlyn"

Estrella finished reading and asked, "He is here?!"

"Yes, and he is waiting for you, so you better hurry to meet him. It is not good to keep a wizard waiting," replied Archimedes. Then he flew out the window.

Estrella put on her cloak, pulled up her hood, took the sheets off her bed, knotted them, threw them out the window, and shimmied down them. Then she followed the directions to the spot. Merlin followed closely behind her, being her ever-vigilant protector. Arriving at the willow tree, she saw the white-cloaked elders standing around; they all had their hoods on as well. Estrella decided that if she wanted to avoid punishment for failing to show respect, she had best bow in front them. She dropped down to her knees, put her head down low, and held out one arm for Merlin to perch on. She kept her head down until she heard one of the elders speak.

"Rise, Princess. There is no judgment in our secret circle. You have indeed proven yourself worthy. Rise and take off your hood so that we may see you."

Estrella stood up on shaky legs. The figures before her were very intimidating. She could not see their faces, but she felt a slight twinge of fear in her heart, which made her respect them more.

She stood before them, removing her hood but keeping her head bowed out of respect. She did not feel worthy enough to make eye contact with the mysterious figures.

One of them spoke. "Do not fear, Estrella. You are safe with us. We would never harm you. Hold your chin high and see who has asked you here on this night."

She looked up. One of elders stepped forth and removed his hood; it was Merlyn Emrys, the wizard. Estrella remembered first meeting him when she was a little girl growing up in Faylin. Merlyn was the reason she had her Merlin. She was about to bow again but was stopped short by his response.

"Yes, my dear Estrella. It is I, Merlyn Emrys, your old friend. And you might want to hold that bow until after you meet my companions."

Estrella thought, *They must all be wizards, or royalty, if they are companions to Merlyn.* But she kept silent, knowing that to speak out of turn or without permission to do so would be disrespectful and dishonorable, and bring shame upon her.

✦❖"On my right, Estrella, are two people I would like you to meet, Arthur Pendragon and his queen, Guinevere." And with that, two more of the figures stepped forward into the light and removed their hoods. Estrella could not believe that standing before her was not only the most respected and feared wizard but also the high king and queen who ruled over the whole realm. She was finding it hard to keep her balance. Her legs, which had gone numb on account of being in the presence of these esteemed individuals, wanted to give out. Judging by the appearance of the high king, Estrella thought he couldn't have been more than ten years older than she. He looked just like her father had described him: young and well-built, with sandy hair and a kind face. The queen seemed the same age as Arthur, with brilliant fiery red hair. She was indeed as lovely as legend told. Estrella snapped herself out her evaluations; she had no right to be thinking about them in such a way. Here she was a lowly princess dressed in her warrior guise, dirty and poorly kept as of late, and these people were the highest of royalty. They should be the ones evaluating her and judging her based on her appearance, but they were not doing so. Instead, they stood there and smiled at her. Then, amid her daydreaming, she heard Merlyn clear his throat to bring her back to reality. She sheepishly looked at him and saw his skeptical expression and raised eyebrow.

"Forgive your humble servant, Merlyn. I mean no disrespect. I was only musing to myself. I promise, it won't happen again. Please have mercy, Your Majesties."

"My dear, you are forgiven. I know that this is quite a lot for one of your age to take in, in one night, especially at this hour, but if you can hold your focus for just a little longer, I assure you it will be well worth it," said Arthur.

"Estrella, we won't judge you by how you are dressed or by how well you can focus your attention. You are welcome among us. Let me finish with the introductions, and then we will tell you why we have asked you here tonight," added Merlyn. Then he continued, "Also on my right is the well-renowned knight of the Round Table Sir Lancelot." The third figure on the wizard's right side stepped forward and removed his hood. He was rather dashing, despite the rumors that he felt ashamed of his appearance.

Continued with the introductions, Merlyn said, "And here on my left is the knavish rogue Robin Hood, along with two of his trusted Merry Men, Little John and Will Scarlet, and his true love, the lady Maid Marian." With that, the four cloaked figures on the wizard's left stepped forward and tossed off their hoods. Estrella was again taken aback with surprise; this was quite an interesting group of people. On Merlyn's right were the most influential and most well-known of the higher upper class, and on his left were the most well-known of thieves. Estrella tried to process all that was going on, but it made her head swim and she started to feel faint. She fell to her knees and bowed her head in respect.

"My dear, what seems to be the problem? What brings you to your knees and makes you bow your head?" asked Merlyn.

"I am not worthy enough to stand in the presence of these people. I am only a young princess of seventeen years from a small fief. I do not deserve to be among such people as the high king and Robin of the Wood. My father told me that you had to be wealthy and worthy to come before the king. I am neither wealthy nor worthy. I have done nothing to deserve this honor," she responded pleadingly.

Merlyn addressed her in a very kind, calm voice, saying, "Princess Estrella, daughter of Queen Althea and King Indra, princess of the kingdom of Faylin, you were called here tonight before the ancient Order of the Lion. This order was established many years ago to establish leadership and uphold justice. I, Merlyn Emrys, handpick the members of the order. Everyone here has proven themselves worthy, and respectful toward each other in the group. You are no less important than Arthur. Your friend Kasim informed us of your quest and your abilities. We have been watching you, and we have discerned that you are indeed worthy of the honor. We would like to invite you to join the order. You may decline, but know that this is a high honor. In the order, we see to it that everyone we are in charge of is treated fairly and that justice is carried out. We have seen your skills, but you will have to go through initiation trials to prove that you have what it takes to become a good leader and someday maybe a great ruler. You will start off as an apprentice, who wears a navy blue cloak. So, Princess Estrella, will you accept the invitation and join us?"

She gave it some thought. This was a great honor to be counted as a member along with Arthur and the others. Soon she responded with her decision. "I accept; I will join the Order of the Lion."

"Then come forth, Princess Estrella, as the newest apprentice of the Order of the Lion, and take your new navy blue cloak," said Merlyn.

Estrella walked forward on now steadfast, stable legs, as at this point she had more confidence in herself. She removed the cloak she had on, accepted the new cloak from Maid Marian, and put on the fresh blue cloak.

Robin Hood stepped forward. "Not all of your trials will happen in one night, but they all will take place at night. You will know when your first trial will be when we send word. Your first teacher will be Master Arthur."

Then Arthur spoke, saying, "Once you complete all your trials, you will become an official member of the order and will receive your white robe. Each trial completed will get you a new cloak."

"We look forward to seeing you again, Lady Estrella," said Lady Guinevere. Then they all bowed. The order turned and left.

Estrella looked up into the sky. It was getting late. She still needed to get some rest for the journey ahead of her tomorrow. It would be embarrassing to fall off her horse in exhaustion. So she hurried back to the inn, climbed back in through the window, untied and the sheets, rolled up the unfinished letter, threw off her clothes, carefully folded her new cloak, put on her night shrift, climbed into bed, and fell asleep the second her head touched the pillow.

CHAPTER 14

Leaving Aveline

The next morning; the girls awoke, washed up, changed their clothes, packed up, and headed downstairs for breakfast. When they sat down to eat, they could see the people staring and hear them whispering.

"What are they staring at?" asked Nori.

"I do not know. What do you think they are whispering, Estrella?" asked Karmina.

"Probably just gossip. Just ignore them and brush it off, girls," she replied.

So they just brushed it off, although it was still bothering Sloan. Unable to leave some things unsaid, Sloan always spoke her mind. When the waitress walked over to their table to take their order for breakfast and was eyeing Estrella suspiciously, Sloan decided she would ask her what was going on. "Excuse me, miss, but what is everyone whispering about, and why are you looking at our friend that way?"

"Sloan, it is okay. Really, it is not important. Just leave it alone," said Estrella, trying to get her friend to hold her tongue and stay out of the gossip.

"No, I would like to know what's going on," she said stubbornly.

"Well, the word is that our town drunk saw your friend there sneak out of her window and meet some strangers out by the old willow tree. Now everyone is suspicious that she may be part of a coven, or in league with tax collectors."

"That is preposterous! Estrella would have nothing to do with witches and dark forces. Nor would she have anything to do with tax collectors. We just arrived here," shouted Karmina, standing up from the table and making a scene.

Estrella hid her reddening cheeks behind a menu; she was very embarrassed by the way her girls were acting in public. At their next stop, she would have to give her girls a lesson on manners and how one should act in public. She shot a look in Karmina's direction. "Karmina, sit down, please."

Karmina, catching the disapproving look and the stern yet loving tone of Estrella's voice, took her seat.

Then Estrella ordered breakfast for the girls.

"We will have five bowls of hot oat cereal with cream and honey on the side, along with a small bowl of fruit. And we will have five glasses of milk to drink. Thank you." She handed the menu back to the waitress.

"Ugh, Estrella. I wanted a pastry for breakfast and an orange juice," said Sloan, sulking from not getting to order what she wanted.

"Pastries are just sweets. We need a healthy breakfast to give energy and strength for our journey ahead," Estrella said.

"And why didn't you stand up for yourself and defend yourself against the rumors they are spreading about you? You didn't even get upset about it," said Karmina, shocked by how well Estrella had reacted to the rumors.

"This is not the time or the place to speak about this matter. We will discuss it later," Estrella replied coolly.

Within a few minutes, the girls' food arrived. They ate their breakfast in silence. When they finished, Estrella paid the bill. As they were heading to the door, Nori caught Estrella by her sleeve, pulled her aside, and asked her in a hushed voice, "Estrella, would you happen to have an extra hooded mantle I may borrow? It looks like it is going to be a little chilly outside. I don't have a cloak to wear."

"Of course. I just happen to have an extra one," said Estrella, she went back into her room and came out with her old cloak, and handed it to Nori. Nori, after gratefully taking the cloak from Estrella, draped it around herself, put up the hood, and headed out the door to catch up with the others at the stables. Estrella could see in Nori the signs of someone on the run. She had a bruise on her cheek that she was hiding, and she expressed a need for a cloak even though it was sunny and warm outside. She had flipped up the hood quickly and then rushed outside to join up with the others. Estrella knew that she would find out what was going on with Nori sooner or later, so she just threw on her new cloak, carried her things out to the stable, and went to meet up with the other girls. When she arrived at the stable, she found that all the pack mules were loaded with the girls' belongings. Nori had chosen the black Friesian horse and had already saddled the horse and loaded her belongings into a cart tied to her pack mule. Estrella smiled, got all her things loaded into her cart, and tied the cart to her pack mule. When she went to saddle Chesnutt, she found that one of her girls had already saddled her horse for her, so she swung up into the saddle and mounted. Before nudging Chesnutt on, she waited for the rest of her girls to mount. Once she turned around and saw that everyone was ready and waiting, she decided to speak to Nori before they left the stable.

"Have you chosen a name for your horse, Nori?"

"Yes, I have given her the name Agape. It means 'love,'" replied Nori.

"That's a beautiful name," said Sloan.

"Beautiful names aside, can we go now, Estrella? The stable really smells, and it is not exactly a pretty sight from the back of the line," complained Lena.

Estrella laughed. "Yes, Lena, we can go now." And then she nudged Chesnutt and whispered something in his ear. The horse whinnied, tossed his head proudly, and started to trot of the stable.

When Estrella and Chesnutt were out of the stable, Nori turned to the other girls and whispered, "Did she just talk to the horse?"

"Yes. Apparently she did," replied Karmina.

"What did she say to him that made him act the way he did?"

"I have absolutely no idea," said Sloan.

"Hmm," said Nori.

"Don't worry, we will find out more about her soon," said Lena.

As the girls rode through the town, they saw that Nori's bakery was on fire. The group started to panic. This was terrible!

"Oh my gosh! Nori, your bakery is on fire," said Karmina.

"Hurry, girls. We need to stop the horses and help put out the fire," said Lena.

Then Nori, holding her arm out to stop them, surprised them with her stern reply. "No. It's all right. Let's just keep going."

"But, Nori, that's your home," said Lena.

"No, that *was* my home. My new home is with you girls."

So the girls kept moving on. They rode out of the town in silence, mourning the loss of Nori's bakery and home. They all had left their homes, but at least most of them had a home to go back if they chose to leave the group. Nori no longer had a home to return to. Karmina knew the feeling of loss; she too had lost her home, along with her family and her fiancé. The feeling of loss was not something new to the group of girls.

Once they were out of the town, Estrella decided that they needed to hear another story to help them feel better.

"Lena, I believe it is your turn to share your story. And start from the beginning."

"All right. I and my family lived in a small town on the border of Spain and France, where we owned a small farmhouse with nice stables, where we raised our horses. We were a simple family who bred horses and earned honest wages. We bred the best horses in Spain and made quite a profit from taking our horses to town to sell. Well, one day, one of the don's stallions got loose and ended up in our stable along with the wild horses. We were going to return the stallion and breed the wild ones, but when the don found out that his stallion was in our stable, he accused us of being horse thieves. His officials seized our small ranch, our home, and our horses, and drove us out of Spain and into exile. We thought we might try to rebuild our lives in France, but the lord of the province we were hoping to live in was an ally of the don of Spain. The people of that province spread the rumor around all of Europe that we were horse thieves, so we traveled around in a wagon as gypsies. We had oxen that pulled the wagon. Our own personal horses, which we managed to save from the don's greedy hands by riding away on them, were led behind our wagon. After wandering a long time, we finally found the small town of Willow Creek, where we settled down and opened our inn and tavern. And the rest of the story you've heard—family business, disgusting thugs. Estrella and you girls saved my life, and now I am here. I have pledged my life and my alliance to Princess Estrella." Lena had concluded her story.

The girls were silent for a few minutes, taking it all in. And then Sloan spoke up, saying, "That's a very interesting story, Lena. It appears that ignorance and bigotry are quite common."

"Sloan, I'm afraid to say this, but as long as there is evil in the world, and as long as the Prince of the Air reigns over the world, there will always be ignorance, intolerance, and the like in the world," said Estrella.

The girls continued on their way until they came to a small clearing, where they decided to set up for their lunch. Lena stretched out the blanket, Karmina got out the salted ham, Sloan pulled out her dagger and began slicing it into little pieces, and Estrella pulled out the plates, the cups, her waterskin, and the baguette she had bought earlier. She broke the break into five pieces and placed the pieces on the plates. Sloan put the ham on top of the slices of bread, and then Estrella passed out the plates and the cups of water. She handed the heel of the baguette to Mika. The girls then all bowed their heads and asked the Lord to bless their food, after which they started to eat. This time, Sloan made sure she finished her lunch first so that Estrella wouldn't do the dishes. She put down her empty plate and waited to see if Estrella noticed.

Estrella looked up from the cup she was drinking from and noticed that Sloan was watching her and waiting for her approval. She put down her cup and sighed deeply.

"I understand that you don't want me to do the dishes. This doesn't not mean, however, that you can rush through your meals. And if you are done, then take the 'children' down to the stream with you to catch their lunch." After saying this, Estrella whistled to Merlin. He flew to her and landed on her outstretched arm. She said to him, "Merlin, go with Sloan down to the steam and see if you are able to catch yourself any fish. If not, I will have some dried fish ready for you."

{"Thank you, my lady,"} he replied. And with that, the blacksmith's daughter picked up the empty plates and cups, and was followed down to a stream not too far away by the fox, the otter, the raccoon, and the falcon.

Before Estrella stood up to feed the horses, she turned to Nori. "When Sloan gets back and I finish feeding the horses and mules and we are all ready to go, I think we all would like to hear your story, Nori—that is, if you are comfortable enough to share it with us."

"Of course, Your Majesty," replied Nori.

Estrella giggled and said, "Nori, out here I am only Estrella, so you can call me Estrella, or even Esy."

"All right. Esy it is, then," said Nori.

Estrella rose from her spot on the blanket, grabbed the bag of apples and the bag of oats, walked over to the place where the horses were tied up along with the mules, and began to talk to them and feed them, which she enjoyed.

The horses were very gentle and enjoyed someone talking to them. Having the ability to sense if someone was a good person with a good heart, they could tell that Estrella was gentle, kind, and compassionate. If the horses could talk to the other girls, they would tell them what they sensed about Estrella, but none of the others girls could speak or understand the horse's language. As a result, they just whinnied and tossed their manes, which made Estrella laugh.

When Estrella arrived back at the picnic spot, she saw that Sloan had returned with the clean dishes. The "children" looked as if they had all eaten. The girls took their things back to the horses and mules, loaded the possessions into the carts, and mounted the horses.

As they were riding down the dirt road, Estrella said, "Nori, I believe it is your turn to share with us your story." ✳

"Oh, okay then. Well, I lived with my mother, my father, my older brother, and my twin brother. My father was the reverend of our little town of Aveline. We built the little church ourselves and were very proud of it. My father and brothers even built me my little bakery. We were very happy and content with our lives and what we had.

Then about two months ago, the tax collector's thugs showed up at our little church and demanded that my father give them eleven hundred and forty silver shillings for taxes. Father told them we didn't have that much money. Saying that his lack of money wasn't their problem, they started to tear apart and deface our little church. We loved that church. We were heartbroken. Mother tried to beg for them to stop, saying that it would take longer for us to get the money if they destroyed our church, because we would need to raise the money for repairs. And then we would still not have enough for the taxes. My brothers wanted to fight the thugs. I was afraid of what the thugs might do. Father calmly and quietly reassured us that the thugs were only things and that the church was only a building—that the church was the individuals who make up the body of Christ. Well, after doing the damage, the thugs said that that was our first warning. After they left, we cleaned up the mess they had made. Before my mother, my brothers, and I went home, Father said that he was going to stay at the church and pray in his office, but I believe he stayed in order to count the money from the offering box, to see if he had enough to pay the thugs.

"When he came home, very weary and distraught, he called a family meeting. After dinner was eaten and the dishes were taken care of, we met him in the living room. He said that there wasn't enough money for either the repairs or the taxes, so in order to protect the family, tomorrow we would have to go stay with our aunt, Mother's sister, while he stayed behind to give the tax collectors what was in the offering box. The boys and I refused, saying we would stay with Father, but he was adamant: everyone had to flee. I reasoned with him, saying that I had my bakery to look after, so he said he would let me stay behind, but the boys would have to leave with Mother in the morning and watch over her. Then we all prayed. We thanked God for all of our blessings, and then we asked him for protection over the family. After saying that we knew he had a plan for all of us, we finished by saying, 'Amen.' Then we all hugged each other and went to bed. At dawn we went our separate ways. The boys left to go to

Aunt Martha's house with Mother; Father packed his things to stay at the church; and I packed my things to stay at the bakery.

"It couldn't have been more than a few weeks later when the thugs came back to the church and demanded the taxes. When Father couldn't pay them, they arrested him and burned down our precious little church. Yesterday, while you girls were eating your lunches, they showed up at the bakery and demanded I pay nine hundred and fifty shillings in revenue for taxes. When I told them that I didn't have enough money, one of them started destroying my bakery. He smashed the window, the tables, the chairs, the glass case, and all my baked goods. And then the other thug took all the money in my coin box. The two of them cut open all my bags of ingredients, pouring them out on the floor. Then one of them threatened Mika. On his way out, he slapped me across the cheek with the back of his hand as a warning.

"The reason I wanted to sleep with one of you girls last night was because I knew the bakery wasn't safe anymore. And this morning on our way out of town, the reason why I didn't want to stop was because I knew that those two thugs were the ones who had set it on fire. I am with you now because I don't have a home. My mother and brothers are out of town, and my father is in jail. I knew that I would have a new family with you—and protection," Nori concluded. She looked for the other girls, not knowing that they were a little ways behind her because they had reined in their horses, stunned by her story. They remained in shock for a few moments after Nori had finished speaking. Then they snapped out of it and caught up to her.

"That is just terrible," replied Lena.

"Oooh, people like that just make me so mad!" said Sloan.

"Well, all that matters now is that you are with us now. We will keep you safe," Estrella said.

The group rode on for a while until they came to another clearing just a little ways ahead. The sun was beginning to set in the sky. Thinking to take advantage of the time it was still up, Estrella put Lena in charge of setting up the tents, Karmina in charge of tethering the horses, and Nori in charge of gathering wood and starting a fire. Then Sloan and Estrella went off to catch something for their dinner. Within a half hour, the tents were up, the horses were secured, a small fire was going, and Sloan and Estrella had returned with three grouse and two rabbits.

Nori prepared the food, broke her special loaf of bread, plated the food, poured the water, and said a blessing. After the blessing, the girls all ate their food in silence. Mealtime was not usually a time for them to say much; it was a quiet time to reflect on the day and relax.

When the girls were finished eating, they scraped the leftovers off their plates for the "children" and set the plates aside to be washed in the morning. Then they went to their tents to sleep for the night. Karmina and Nori shared a tent, Lena and Sloan shared a tent, and Estrella had her own tent.

CHAPTER 15

Estrella's First Trial, Officiated by Arthur

Estrella had just laid her head down on her pillow when a dove flew into her tent with a message strapped to its leg. She propped herself up, heaved a heavy sigh, and thought, *My teachers have an impeccable sense of timing. Right when I'm either getting ready for bed or writing a letter, they want to see me.* Then she unrolled the note, which read, "Meet me about a mile west of your location, at the large barn at the farmhouse. ~ A"

"How do they know where I am? Oh yeah, I remember now. They have spies in the group," she said, pulling on her new cloak.

After pulling her boots back on, Estrella quietly crept out to where the horses were tethered. She found Chesnutt, untied his guide rope from the tree, and whispered in his ear, "Shh. Tread lightly and stay quiet until we are out of earshot from the camp." Then she quietly led him away from camp, swinging up on his bare back to ride him quietly out of camp. Once Estrella and Chesnutt were out of earshot, she nudged him in the ribs with her knees, which made him pick up his pace.

✦ When they reached a small farm that appeared to be deserted, Estrella led Chesnutt into the barn and secured him in a stall. Merlin, catching up with them, flew into the barn and perched in the loft. Estrella observed that the barn was fairly empty. Present were her horse, Chesnutt; her falcon, Merlin; a white-cloaked figure; and what seemed to be the figure's steed. Estrella slowly approached her teacher and kneeled before him.

"Sir Arthur, Your Majesty, I am ready for my first trial," she acknowledged.

"Very good, my young pupil. Rise. Your first trial is to test how well you handle pressure. I will ask you questions about scenarios and simultaneously add heavy objects to buckets set on a plank placed across your shoulders," said Sir Arthur.

"Yes, Master," Estrella said as she rose to her feet. Then she firmly planted her feet and squared her shoulders.

Arthur stepped forward into the light and removed his hood. Then he approached Estrella and placed a large plank of wood across her shoulders. Next, he placed an empty bucket on each end of the plank.

"Let's begin. I will start by adding rocks to the buckets to see how much you can hold. Once the buckets are heavily weighted on both ends of the plank, I will ask you questions to test your faith and your loyalty. For every right answer you give, I will remove a rock. Wait too long to answer or answer wrong and I will add to the weight. Are we understood?" said Sir Arthur.

"Yes, Master," replied the student.

Arthur began adding rocks to each bucket. Little by little, Estella felt the weight of the buckets increasing. She thought, *This is really heavy, but it can't be anywhere as heavy as having the weight of the world on one's shoulders, like the Christ had.* Soon both of the buckets were full. She could feel herself giving under the pressure, but she held her ground.

"You now have fifty pounds of rocks in the bucket at each of your shoulders. Now the test begins. Estrella, have you ever told a lie and broken the commandment demanding 'Thou shall not bear false witness'?"

"No, Master."

"Is that a lie?"

"No, Master."

"Would you ever tell a lie?"

"No, Master."

"Not even to save your skin or your friends' lives?"

"No, Master."

"What if you caught yourself slipping and telling a little white lie, thinking that it was harmless?"

"All lies have hidden harm. If I ever caught myself telling a lie, I would ask the Lord for his forgiveness."

"Well spoken," said Arthur, as he removed a rock from each bucket. "All right, next question: have you ever taken the Lord's name in vain?"

"No, Master."

"Have you spoken a curse against anyone in anger?"

"No, Master."

"Not even when a person wronged you and made you lose your temper?"

"No, Master."

"Have you ever used profane language?"

"No, Master. I was brought up to be better than to use such unclean and unladylike language."

"Well done," he remarked, and then he removed another rock from each bucket. "Estrella, have you ever made a graven image or an idol for yourself?"

"No, Master."

"Have you remembered to keep the Sabbath?"

There was a brief pause and hesitation before Estrella replied, "Sadly, I have not remembered the Sabbath day, Master. I have no good excuse for not observing the Sabbath. We have been traveling, and although it is easy to lose track of the days when one is not near a calendar, I could have marked down how many days we have been traveling."

"Well, you did hesitate to answer. You made no effort to defend your case or make excuses for your actions. You did, however, take responsibility for your actions. Therefore, I will only remove one rock from one bucket," he said. Then he removed one rock from the bucket on Estrella's right shoulder. "Estrella, do you honor your father and mother?"

"Yes, I do, Master."

"Estrella, do you serve any other god besides the Lord Almighty?"

"No, never, Master. The Lord Most High is the only God there is."

"Very good," he remarked as he removed a rock from each bucket. "Estrella, have you ever taken a life?"

"No, Master."

"Not even in self-defense?"

"I have not taken any lives in my battles, Master."

"Very good. Next question: have you ever stolen something that did not belong to you?"

Once again there was a hesitation. Estrella thought back to her encounter with the pirates. At the time, stealing from them had felt like the right thing to do. After all, the riches and money did not belong to them. They had stolen it first from someone else, so stealing from them seemed just. But thinking over it now, Estrella knew that stealing was wrong, even if she was stealing from pirates.

"Yes, Master. I am afraid to admit that I have stolen before. I stole riches from pirates. At the time, I didn't think I was doing wrong. I thought that stealing from those who had stolen would justify itself. But stealing is still stealing, and it is still wrong. I stole from them and gave half of what I took to my people. I kept some for myself. In fact, I've already used some of the money to buy horses for myself and my new friends. And I gave my friends some money just two days ago to buy supplies and pay for room and board for the night. My intention was good, but the deed I did was wrong. I did not repent of my actions, so I would like your permission to take a small break from the trial to pray to God and ask his forgiveness."

"Permission granted. And for admitting your wrong and seeing the error of your deed, I will remove one rock from the bucket on your left shoulder once you finish your prayer."

Estrella bowed her head, trying to keep it level to avoid getting dizzy.

"Dear Heavenly Father, I come before you today to confess my sin. In the past I have stolen plunder from pirates, and although my intention was good, the deed was wrong. I ask you today for your forgiveness. In Jesus's name, amen."

"Very well done, my student," Arthur said as he removed a rock from the bucket on Estrella's left shoulder. "Estrella, have you ever been with a man?"

"No, Master. I have never been alone intimately with a man; I have taken a vow of purity, committing to wait until my wedding night."

"Very good, very good. Purity is a high priority in the order," he said as he removed a rock from the bucket on Estrella's right shoulder. "Now follow the last few questions, which are about your faith. And then I will begin to test your loyalty, all right?"

"Yes, Master."

"Estrella, have you ever been envious of another person's belongings or possessions?"

"I have not felt any envious feelings about another's possessions. I have, however, felt a slight bit of envy when learning of the relationship my friends had with their fathers."

"I understand. I have met the king of Faylin. Indra is a very good leader. He is very driven to have the best and to be known as the best. But I have heard about his many long trips and the time he spends away from his family and his kingdom."

"He was only a father in the sense that he helped make my siblings and me. He was known as the absent king. He was more concerned about war campaigns and councils than he was about his family. I rarely saw him."

"I can understand your hurt, but you have to let the pain go and live for yourself. Do not let the pain, anger, and resentment make you a bitter person."

"I am trying, Master."

"That is all we ask of you, and all the Lord Almighty asks of you.

"Here is your last question of faith. Estrella, would you ever deny the Christ if it meant that by denying him, your life would be spared?"

"No, never, Master. For if you deny the Christ, he will deny you in front of the Father."

"Well put, my student," Arthur said. Then he removed a rock from each bucket. "Now to test your loyalty, I will ask only three questions. The time is getting late, and you should get some sleep. I can tell that you are very tired."

"Thank you, Master."

"Now, Estrella, would you ever betray your people, that is, the people of Faylin and your family?"

"Never, Master. I am a loyal daughter of Faylin; my people are kind and have always been good people. I would rather give up my own life than sell them out to an enemy."

"Very good, my student. Next question: would you ever betray your country and your high king by selling military secrets to an invading country if it meant that you would receive money and ensure the safety of you and your friends?"

"Never, Master. No amount of money is worth selling out my country and my high king. I am and always will be faithful and loyal to my England, and to my liege High King Arthur Pendragon."

"Very well done, my student. Answer this last question correctly and you will pass. Then you will receive an indigo cloak. You know that this is a secret order; no one outside the circle knows that we exist beyond what we are already known for. On your word, would you ever tell anyone outside the circle about what we say and what goes on inside the order?"

"No, Master. On my word, I will take this secret to heart. No one will know of the order."

"Very good. And if you have any recommendations of other people whom you believe would be valuable members, please bring them to our attention. Master Merlyn will consider your recommendations and give you permission to bring any candidates forward. Anyone you bring to stand before the members of the order must be blindfolded so as not to know our location. Am I understood, Estrella?"

"Yes, Master," she replied.

"Excellent. You have proven yourself faithful and devout to the Lord Almighty, and you have proven yourself loyal and devoted to your home, your country, your king, and the order," he said as he removed the buckets and took the plank of wood from her shoulders.

Her legs gave out; she had no strength left. She fell to her knees, shaking from exhaustion and the weight, which she could still feel on her shoulders. Arthur knelt down and lifted her chin.

"You have passed, my child; the trial is over." He untied the old cloak and removed it. In its place, he draped an indigo cloak over her shoulders. She managed to smile before collapsing from lack of sleep. Then she fell into a dreamless sleep. Arthur, in all his compassion, lifted up the sleeping princess, placed her on his steed, and then led Estrella's horse out of his stall. Arthur then swung up into his saddle behind Estrella. Whistling for Merlin to follow, he nudged his horse, who began trotting back to Estrella's campsite, Chesnutt following right behind. Once they reached the campsite, Arthur dismounted, removed Estrella from the horse, carried her into her tent, and covered her up, brushing the hair from her face and kissing her forehead. Then, before leaving the camp, he tied up Chesnutt. After mounting his horse, he rode out of the campsite. As he rode on, he thought about the girl. *The poor thing; she is only a child. Her father is absent, and her brother is sworn to me as a knight of the Round Table. And here she is on this quest of her own, very far away from her home. She is very strong and brave for one so young. Merlyn was right: she definitely has the makings of a great queen. I can see the spark. She will make a great member of the order, and she will be a great queen when the time is right. I will look forward to the day when I can be her ally and close friend.* And with that, Arthur continued making his way back to Merlyn to tell him of Estrella's progress.

CHAPTER 16

Anna-Mika

With the rise of the sun came a new dawn, a new day, and a glorious morning, but surprisingly, Estrella was not the first one up to enjoy it. She was still asleep once the others had awakened. They had torn down their tents, had begun making breakfast, and were starting to get worried.

"Does she usually sleep this late?" asked Nori, having known Estrella for only a day.

"No, she is usually the first one up with the sun," replied Sloan.

"This is most peculiar then," said Nori.

"It is most definitely not like her," Karmina said.

"Should we check in on her and see if she is okay? Maybe she is ill and needs her rest," said Lena.

"No, she is all right. I am sure of it. She will wake up when she is ready," replied Karmina.

"I can hear you," came a groggy muffled voice from inside the tent. Estrella's response startled them, as they were unaware that their voices had carried, or even their whispers were audible. "You should work on your whispers," she said.

"We are sorry to have awakened you, Estrella. Would like to sleep some more? We can leave later if you want," said Lena.

"No, it is all right. I am up now, and we need to keep moving anyway," said Estrella from inside her tent. The others could hear her rustling around.

"Is everything all right in there? Would you like some help packing things up?" asked Sloan.

"We saved you breakfast," said Nori.

"Everything is just fine. I am just getting changed and getting things packed up. I don't need any help, thank you. And thank you all for waiting patiently for me and saving me breakfast. I will be right out," said Estrella. Carefully packing away her new cloak, she remembered the night before and the strenuous trial to see how well she could handle pressure. Thinking about it made her shoulders ache. The last thing she remembered was Arthur holding her chin up and changing her cloak. Then nothing; she had passed out. She thought that he must have taken her back to camp and put her in her tent. *Wow, to have the high king care enough about me to bring me all the way back to camp. There must be something the elders know about me that I don't know yet. Or they just really care about me.* She snapped herself out of her daydream, finished packing, and emerged from her tent. She smiled and stretched, and then turned to tear down her tent. Her girls stopped her.

"Estrella, eat your breakfast. We will take care of your tent and your bags," offered Sloan.

"Thank you, everyone," Estrella said. Once she had sat down by the slowly dying fire, Nori handed her a plate of food.

Karmina went into her tent to bring out Estrella's bags, Lena went to untie the horses and bring Chesnutt over, and Sloan was waiting to tear down the tent. Estrella just sat and enjoyed the day. The sun was so warm that she found it nice to sit and relax for a bit. Usually when her servants were helping her at home, she was rushed and pushed and pulled. She liked to relax; she quite enjoyed the peace of the day.

Karmina emerged from the tent carrying Estrella's bags and Merlin's perch. She took them over to Estrella's cart, secured the tent to her pack mule. Then Sloan tore down the tent, packed it up, and it put in the cart along with the other things. Estrella set aside half of her breakfast to give it to the "children." When the animals finished eating, she put aside the plate and rose from her position at the campfire.

"Have the horses been fed and watered? They are probably thirsty. I can see that you took care of all of the dishes except for mine. So after I feed the horses and pack mules, I will take them with me to look for a stream. While I wash my plate, the horses and the mules can get a drink of water before we move on. So unhitch the pack mules and secure a bridle to their heads. We don't have to saddle the horses just yet, but keep their bridles on so I may lead them."

"Yes, Estrella. Would you like someone to help you take the horses and mules to the stream?" asked Karmina.

"You know, normally I can I do this on my own, but it would be nice to have some help today. It is eight horses and mules, by the way, and there is only one me. So, yes, it would be appreciated. Thank you. Once I finish feeding them, I would very much like it if one of you girls did accompany me," she replied. "But it is still a lot of animals to take care of, so let's leave the pack mules and take them in shifts. That way, someone can stay behind and watch the camp and the mules to make sure they don't run off or get stolen while the rest of us are away."

"That's a great idea, Estrella. I would not mind staying behind to watch the camp," said Nori.

"No. I believe that you will come with me to take the horses. You are the newest one to the group, so you should come with me. You and I will take the first shift, leaving the other girls behind. Then we'll switch off. This way, at least three of us will stay behind at a time. Then on our last shift, the four you can go down the river together while I stay behind and watch the camp. The first shift will be Nori and me, the second shift will be Karmina, and Sloan, and then the last shift will be Karmina, Sloan, Lena, and Nori. When you return from your shift, you should also bring back a bucket of water for the mules. On the last shift, the four of you should each bring back a bucket. I know that some of you already would have brought back a bucket, but you should keep in mind that there are eight pack mules, each of them needing water. Is everyone okay with their shifts?" she said.

"Yes, Estrella," the four girls replied in unison.

"Very good. Now, Karmina, could you unhitch the mules from the carts and tie them back up? I will feed them, and then we'll start our shifts."

"Yes, Estrella," replied Karmina. She set to work unhitching the mules and tying them back up. Then she unsaddled the horses, leaving their bridles on.

Estrella went to the feed barrels, grabbed a sack of apples and a sack of grain, and went over to the horses and mules. She started with one horse at a time, holding an apple in her hand for a horse to eat. When a horse finished eating, it would whisper to the others. Estrella would stroke its manes, and it would toss its head and whinny. She would laugh. When another horse became impatient, whinnied at her, and stomped its feet, she would turn to it and kindly say, "Be patient. I'm getting to you."

And it would toss its heads, and whinny back, almost as if saying, {"You care for that one more than you care for me."}

And as if she could speak and understand horse language, she would reply, "That is not true, and you know it. I care for all of you the same, even the mules." Then she would move onto another horse and feed it an apple, and going through the same routine. The horse would eat out of her hand and then whisper to the other horses, and she would laugh before moving on and do the same thing again.

When Estrella reached Juniper, she fed her a nice shiny green apple. Afterward, she pulled a small rag from her belt and polished Juniper's horn. The two of them would talk.

When Estrella finished with the horses, she moved onto the mules. She attached their feedbags, picked up a brush, and brushed their shaggy manes. She complimented them on how clean they kept their coats, saying they were the prettiest mules she had ever seen. You could almost swear that the mules held their heads higher after hearing such praise, and that the horses snickered to hear such things said about mules. Everyone knows that horses think themselves to be superior to beasts of burden such as donkeys and mules. Estrella would shoot the horses a stern look and hush them, and then she would comfort the mules.

When the horses and mules were all fed, Estrella took Chesnutt's lead, the Lusitano's lead, and Agape's lead. Grabbing two buckets, she led the three horses over to Nori. Handing Nori Agape's lead, Estrella said, "Let's get going. It will be midday soon. When the sun is directly overhead, it will be hotter. A thirsty horse doesn't have as much energy as one who has a full belly and has quenched its thirst." And with that, the two girls and the three horses started on their way to find water. As they were walking, Estrella bent Chesnutt's head down just a bit and whispered something in his ear. He whinnied, put his nose to the ground, and started sniffing around like a dog.

This was certainly a sight to see, as it is unusual to find a horse sniffing the ground like a dog following a scent trail. Nori asked, "Estrella?"

"Yes, Nori?"

"What did you just say to your horse?"

"I told him he should see if he can sniff out water."

"And what did he say?"

"He laughed. He thought it was pretty funny, but he did it anyway."

"What did you tell him back in Aveline, in the stable?"

"I told him that he was a pretty boy and that he should be very proud of himself. Sometimes you need to be kind to your pets and animals. They are just like us in that they need to be complimented every now and then."

"Oh, I see. That makes a lot of sense."

"If you treat them with kindness, they will be more loyal to you. Just like people."

Then there came a whinny from the Lusitano and from Agape. The Lusitano stomped her hooves. Estrella whispered into both of their ears in turn They tossed their heads and nudged her.

"What did they say?" asked Nori.

"They still think they are superior to the mules, so I told them that they were too proud and should behave better."

"Really?"

"Oh yes, horses think themselves to be far superior to and better than pack mules and donkeys."

"How do you know this?"

"Have you ever seen the difference in the way horses, donkeys, and mules behave and act? Horses always hold their heads high and prance about, because they think they are better. Donkeys keep their heads up, but they don't prance about; they just walk. But pack mules keep their heads down and kind of trudge about. This is because the mule doesn't feel loved or proud of what it is. You wouldn't either if you knew that you were the result of a breeding between a donkey and a horse, and if you spent your days in the barn watching the horses prance by while whinnying their insults at you and mocking you."

"Wow, I never really thought of it that way," Nori remarked. Then she turned to her horse. "You need to be nicer to our mule." Agape hung his head down, whinnied, and nudged her.

"What did he say?"

"I believe he apologized. Give it time and you will be able to understand the animals too. You should forgive him, and praise and compliment him now to make him feel better."

"Okay, I forgive you, Agape. You are a beautiful horse, and you are a very good boy." With that, Agape tossed his head, whinnied playfully, and nudged Nori.

Then Chesnutt began to pull forward on his lead. Nudging Estrella, he pulled forward again.

"What is he doing?" asked Nori.

"I believe that he is trying to tell me he can smell the water just ahead."

They walked forward a few yards, and sure enough there was a small stream. Estrella led her two horses there, and Nori guided Agape to the water. Estrella bent down, rinsed off her plate, and filled up her bucket while the horses drank. Nori filled up her bucket as well. When the horses had drunk their fill, the girls picked up the leads and the buckets, and began walking back to the campsite. Now that they knew where the stream was, they could tell the others. Once they arrived back at camp, Estrella gave Karmina and Sloan the directions.

"There is a small stream probably about five miles away from camp, Karmina, you should take Juniper and the Knabstrup. Sloan, you should take Fletcher along with the Lipizzaner. This way, on the last shift, Lena will only have to take Sage."

"All right, Estrella," said Karmina as she went to grab Juniper's lead and the lead of the Knabstrup. Then she grabbed a bucket and waited for Sloan. Sloan followed suit, grabbing her horse, Fletcher; the Lipizzaner's lead; and a bucket. She then made her way toward Karmina. The two of them with their four horses went off toward the stream.

While Sloan and Karmina were gone, Estrella and Nori took their buckets over to the mules and let them drink. Then they saddled up their two horses and the Lusitano.

"I think we should name the pack mules," suggested Nori.

"I think that is a great idea. What do you think, Lena? Should the mules have names too, or should we just keep calling them 'mule'?" said Estrella.

"I think that naming the mules is an excellent idea. I think they would enjoy having names," replied Lena.

"Great. My mule's name shall be Charlie," said Estrella.

"Charlie? I like it. He looks like a Charlie to me. Mine will be Abner," said Nori.

"I think I will name my mule Jasper," suggested Lena.

"I like Jasper. And I think our mules will be happier now that they have names," said Estrella.

By the time Nori and Estrella were done saddling their horses and had finished packing up and naming their mules, Sloan and Karmina had returned with the other horses—just in time for Nori, Karmina, and Sloan to return to the stream with Lena, and for Nori to take Sage to the stream and fill up more buckets. Sloan and Karmina set down their buckets in front of the two mules. Before they turned back around to pick up two more buckets, Estrella told them, "All right, before you go, those two mules are yours. You have to name them. Nori, Lena, and I already named our mules, Charlie, Abner, and Jasper."

"Oh, all right," said Karmina. As she looked over her mule, she smiled. Then she said, "My mule looks like a George, so his name will be George."

"Very good. And how about you, Sloan? What are you going to name your mule?" asked Estrella.

"Give me a minute. I have to think of a really good name for this poor, sad-looking fellow," responded Sloan. After looking at him for a while, she smiled and snapped her head up. "His name is Clyde. It is a very good name for a mule, one he will be proud to be called."

"I agree; Clyde suits him just fine. Now, the four of you head off to the stream with your buckets. Get Sage watered and talk amongst yourselves. I will get the rest of the horses saddled up for you," said Estrella.

And with that, Sloan, Karmina, and Nori picked up their buckets. Lena picked up her bucket and took Sage's lead. Then the four of them headed off to the stream. While they were gone, Estrella saddled the rest of the horses, brushed them down to make sure they were looking their best, and packed up the food and the empty buckets.

Once the four girls had reached the stream and were filling up their buckets, Sloan asked Nori, "So what did you talk about when you were out here with Estrella?"

"Horses, surprisingly enough."

"Did she tell you what she told her horse when we were leaving the stables?" asked Karmina.

"Yes. She told him he was pretty boy and that he should be proud."

"That's what she told him?" asked Lena.

"Yes. She said that they need to be treated with kindness and complimented. She also said that the horses think they were superior to donkeys and mules."

"Really?" asked Karmina.

"Yes. She said that is why the horses hold their heads high and prance around."

"Wow, I never really thought of it like that," said Sloan.

"Well, to change subject, our buckets are full and Sage has had enough to drink, so I think we should take our buckets and head back to the camp," suggested Lena.

They each picked up their buckets. Once Lena had grabbed Sage's lead, the four girls started back to the camp. When they arrived back at camp, the other horses and mules were waiting for them. They gave the buckets of water to the mules that hadn't yet had a drink. Lena saddled up Sage. When the mules were done drinking, the girls packed up the empty buckets, mounted their horses, and started to ride.

Having ridden west for a time, they came to a sign that read, "Wrong way!"

This seemed very peculiar. Sloan, always being the first one to speak her mind, said, "Well, that seems odd."

"Yes, very odd," agreed Estrella.

"Maybe it's a warning or a bad omen. Maybe we should turn around and head east?" said a cautious Nori.

"I don't believe in bad omens," said Estrella.

"Yeah. Where is your sense of adventure, Nori?" asked an eager Karmina.

"Back at camp, asleep under the covers," replied Nori.

"Let's keep going, girls," said Estrella, nudging her horse forward.

As they rode on, they passed more signs. Some warned them to turn back; others said that they were going in the wrong direction; and still others stated that they were trespassing.

"Estrella, please, can't we turn around and go back? We are obviously not wanted here," begged Nori.

"'Do not be afraid. Take courage. I am here.' Matthew 14:27," said Estrella, quoting the Bible again. "If we have Jesus, then why should we fear? If God is on our side, whom then shall we fear?"

"But—" Nori objected.

Sloan heaved an exasperated sigh and cut her off. "Nori, give it a rest. There is no arguing with her when she starts quoting scripture. Once she starts whipping out Bible verses, there is no further discussion. The Bible is truth, and nothing you say can sway her from it."

"How does she know the Bible that well? I am a preacher's daughter and I don't know the Bible that well by heart," said Nori.

"It's like a second language to her," said Karmina.

"Actually, I can speak quite a few languages. French is my second language," Estrella said.

"Then how do you know the Bible so well?" asked Nori.

"Well, it was part of my studies. But I am not quite sure how I can recite it on the spot. It just comes to me naturally, I guess," replied Estrella.

The Lord led the girls to a small fief. When they approached the town, it seemed to be deserted. As they scanned the town, they concluded that it looked as if no one had lived there for decades. All the doors and windows on the shops and homes were either smashed in or boarded up.

"See, Estrella, there's no one here. Let's turn back now and look somewhere else," suggested Nori.

"As much as I hate to agree with Nori, she is right. Why would the Spirit lead us to an empty abandoned town? There is no one here to join us," said Sloan.

"No! The Spirit led us here for a reason. You four, split up and check the houses and shops for any survivors of this town. I will go on ahead and look inside the stores at the end of the road," said Estrella.

Karmina and Sloan checked all the shops on the east side of the road, and Lena and Nori checked all the houses on the west side of the road. Estrella rode on ahead. She was about to check the old fortress when she noticed the flicker of a small candle and the slightest movement inside the whitesmith's shop. She tied Chesnutt up outside and quietly walked toward the shop's entrance.

The other girls were wondering why they had entered this empty town, but Estrella felt the pull of the Spirit. She felt it grow stronger as she came closer to a small jewelry shop.

Well, that seems strange, thought Estrella. *I swear I saw something inside move.* Then she let out a small whistle to signal the girls to come over. They came at the signal. Estrella found a gap in the boards and climbed in, the girls cautiously following behind her.

"This is bad, very bad. We shouldn't be in here, Estrella. Clearly someone wanted to keep people out of here if they boarded up the windows and the door," said Nori.

"Nori, don't be such a nervous Nellie," said Sloan.

"Yeah, Nori, don't be a scaredy-cat. Estrella knows what she is doing," added Karmina.

"Shh, girls, quiet. We are not alone in here. There is someone else in here with us," said Estrella.

"What?! We aren't alone? Now I am scared," said a visibly frightened Nori.

"Shush!" snapped Estrella. Having silenced the loud outburst, she turned back around and searched the room. While Nori was trying to keep from crying, Lena held her hand. Karmina and Sloan were right behind Estrella. Everyone was holding as still as possible and being silent as the winter. Estrella held her hand up to signal not to make any sudden movements after she heard the sound of big padded feet on the wooden floors. Something very large was approaching them in the dimly lit shop. Estrella maintained the signal to hold still, hoping that someone would keep Nori quiet and keep her from freaking out. A small gap in the roofing allowed the sun to shine dimly into the room, illuminating the area in front of the girls. In that lit space, they saw a great black lioness approaching them. Her eyes glowed like golden embers in a refining furnace. Nori would have screamed if it hadn't been for Karmina's hand over her mouth. Sloan stepped up next to Estrella with her bow drawn and an arrow nocked already, but Estrella held her arm out to push her back, quietly whispering, "No." That was when they heard a cry come from behind the counter.

"No! Please don't hurt her. You can take whatever I have left, but please, I beg you, don't hurt her. She is just protective." Then the girl stepped into the light, kneeled down next to the lioness, and wrapped her arms around the beast's neck.

The Lord whispered to Estrella, "She is your fifth. She has gone through loss and hardship; she needs your light to shine through her fear."

✦ The girl was very lovely. She had fair yet almost tan skin, with dazzling, almost mesmerizing, sapphire blue eyes. Her hair was as light and fair as the moon; it seemed to be white or silver. Her dress seemed to be of the richest velvet and the deepest purple. But her face was smudged with ashes and dirt, and her arms were scratched up and slightly burned. Her hair was all tangled up and frizzy, looking like it hadn't been combed in months. Her poor dress was ripped, torn, and dirty. Estrella, seeing how frightened the girl was, knew that she needed their help. This she was the reason the Spirit had led them here.

Estrella got down on her knees and held out her hand. "We won't hurt her, and we won't hurt you or take your things. My name is Princess Estrella, and these are my friends. We are here to help you." Then Estrella held out her hand, gently placed it on the lioness's muzzle, and stroked it. The beast relaxed and purred quietly. Then Estrella extended her other hand to the girl in friendship and trust. The girl considered it. Realizing that Estrella had calmed the lioness, she took the hand. When the two girls stood up, the other four smiled and cheered.

Estrella smiled at the disheveled girl and said, "Let's get out of this dark and dirty store and into the light. We can get you all cleaned up and looking better than new. And then, if you feel up to it, you can tell us about yourself."

"I would like that," replied the girl. With that, the group of girls stepped outside, followed by the lioness.

Once out in the light, the girl had to shield her eyes from the sun. It had been many years since she had left her shop. The group of five took the new girl and cleaned her up. Estrella gave her one of her own gowns to wear while Lena stitched, hemmed, and otherwise repaired the dress the girl had been found in. Sloan brushed the girl's hair for her, and Karmina handed her a wet cloth to wash herself off. When the new girl was all clean, Nori handed her some bread, which the newcomer hungrily accepted and ate quickly. The girl greatly appreciated all that Estrella's group had done for her, especially the food. She had existed on hardly anything for a very long time.

"So what is your name?" asked Sloan.

"My name is Anna-Mika, and this is my faithful and protective companion, Cleo," the girl replied.

"I already introduced myself as Princess Estrella. These are my friends and their companions, or, as we call them, our children: Karmina and her unicorn companion, Juniper; Sloan and her otter companion, Odell; Lena and her companion, Tokala the fox; and Nori with Mika the raccoon. Then there is my trusty falcon companion, Merlin," said Estrella, introducing the group.

"It is very nice to meet all of you, and thank you very much for everything."

"Anna-Mika, can you tell us what happened here?" asked Estrella.

Anna-Mika stood up, took a deep breath, and let out a deep sigh. "It's a long and tragic story." She started walking to the head of the town, where the girls had entered. The group followed her. "Let me begin by giving you the tour of what my little fief used to be. My little town used to be called Sima of the Neona, which means 'Treasure of the New Moon.' We were once a peaceful, prosperous people. On the east side of the road were all of our shops. As you can see, we had the usual kind of shops—the butcher's, the baker's, the tanner's, and so on. We also had a blacksmith shop and a whitesmith shop. I was trained in the whitesmith trade and art when I was eleven years old. I made this circlet that I am wearing. On the west side of the road is where the other inhabitants lived."

When the girls reached the end of the road, they were standing before the ruins of an old manor. The windows were boarded, the doors were broken or missing, and the steps were smashed. It was clear that the manor had once been a great pillar in better days, but now it was just a reminder of disaster. "This is where I lived with my family: my father, Lord Koen; my mother, Lady Fiona; and my sisters, Deserai and Faith. We lived here for many happy years with our pets: my mother's lioness, Leona; my father's lion, Haydar; and the pair's first litter of cubs, which included my Cleo, Des's Bayhas, and Faith's

Layth. Everything was perfect until five years ago. One perfectly normal and peaceful day, the town sentry sounded three blasts from his horn, which meant invaders from the sea were approaching. Everyone rushed and panicked. Father took charge, instructing everyone to hurry inside, lock their doors, close their shutters, and hide until the threat was neutralized. Father, who had the gift of grace under pressure, commanded respect and was seen as an authority. Well, everyone did as he instructed them. Once everyone was hidden away, it looked as if no one lived in our town at all. They were all too afraid to make any sound. Father told our nursemaids to take me, Des, and Faith inside and hide us in the secret passage behind the wall, where we could see glimpses of what was going on. He waited for the intruders to come. Within hours, they arrived, Vikings, big, smelly, sweaty, loud, and rude. They broke down all the doors and crashed through all the windows; they sacked and looted all the shops; and they plundered and pillaged all the houses, taking all of our goods and possessions. And as if that wasn't enough, they took our women and children as slaves. Then they called out our father and mocked him and our town. To get him to emerge from hiding, one of them said, 'If ye be the lord of this fief, then present yeself and fight us like a man. If not, then ye must be a wee babe and a coward to let this happen to your town and ye townspeople.' Well, Father couldn't let that challenge or the insults about our town go unresponded to, and Mother wouldn't let him go out alone, so they suited up in their armor, suited up their war lions, and kissed each other, knowing that this could very well be their last stand. Then they emerged into the sunlight and faced off against the invaders. Father tried to reason with the leader while brandishing his sword. 'Take what you will, but you will not be taking our people with you. Take our things, and then leave our people and our town in peace.'

"The leader of the invaders spoke up, saying, 'I do not think so. I am leader here. My men listen and answer to me. You are outnumbered, two dozen Vikings to two puny little town leaders. So surrender your puny, pathetic lives to us, or else we will have to take them from you.' When Father refused to surrender, they swarmed him and cut him down, along with Haydar. Then, taking mother and Leona with them as slaves, they left. When the invaders were gone, my sisters and I rushed out. That is when we discovered that Father was dead. We couldn't stay in the manor any longer. It was not our home without Father and Mother, and we felt it was no longer safe, as invaders could show up and destroy us and the manor. So we moved into the abandoned whitesmith's shop.

"Those who had survived the first attack were smart enough to leave our town. Two years ago, my sisters told me about their plan to sail the seas and search for our mother and Leona, I begged them not go. I tried to reason with them, warning them of the dangers, but they refused to listen to me. They left and found a small vessel of sailors to sail with. I haven't heard from them since. Too afraid to leave my whitesmith shop, let alone this town, I stayed behind and hid inside my shop. The sentry of the other town will alert me if there is another invasion so that I will have time to hide." Anna-Mika concluded her story.

"That is terrible. So what is your town called now?" asked Sloan.

"It's called Rune, because all that is left of this town is ruins," said Anna-Mika.

CHAPTER 17

The Plan

As Estrella thought about this girl's story, a voice called to her in her head, "Estrella, I have a plan!" It was Alyia, the warrior spirit.

"All right, I'm listening."

"Yes, let's play!"

"But you have to play nice with the other girls."

"I will. I promise. Let me out!"

"All right."

A silver glint appeared in Estrella's eye as the wicked grin spread across her face. The girls groaned, knowing that Alyia had emerged with a plan.

"I am so sorry to hear about your family. That truly is a tragedy. But I have been thinking, how would you like to prevent any more Viking attacks? I have a plan, but it could take a few days to put together the bigger elements," said Estrella, with a sly eyebrow raised.

"Uh-oh, I don't like that look," remarked Sloan.

"What look?" asked Anna-Mika.

"She gets this look when she has a mischievous, slightly dangerous plan she wants to put into action. That's when her warrior spirit, Alyia, comes out," said Karmina.

"Just look at her," said Lena. They all turned to look at their leader. She had a sly smile stretching across her face, her eyebrows were raised, and she was wringing her hands together. "See, nothing good can come from a look like that."

★ "I have a plan. It's a little-known fact that Vikings are superstitious. We need to create scare-witches, fake witches, and fake ghosts to give those invaders a fright they will never forget. My plan is this: We lure the Vikings to the old manor and scare them with the ghost of Lord Koen, played by yours truly, since Anna-Mika looks more like her mother. Once we scare them out of the manor, we can scare them out of the town for good with the scare-witches," Estrella explained

"But, Estrella, how are we going to draw them to the manor? And how are we going to make you look like my father? And how are we going to scare them out?" asked Anna-Mika.

"So many questions. I will explain everything in time. But first, Sloan and Karmina, I need you two to gather supplies to build the scare-witches, one for each of you. Gather what you can from the abandoned shops: burlap sacks for the bodies and heads, straw for the hair, paint for the faces, and dresses for the outfits. Make sure the dresses are black or dark colored. Nori and Lena, I need you two to begin making signs to draw the Vikings to the town. The signs should make the town look desirable and inviting. Next, you girls are going to make the bait for the Vikings to fall for: fake jewels, fake bread, fake meat, and fake ale. All these things are going to be booby traps. Anna-Mika, I need you to go back to the manor and find me an old portrait of your father, some of his old clothes, anything that smells dead or rotten, plus some really old pale makeup," Estrella instructed her followers.

"Yes, Estrella," responded the girls as they spilt up to go gather their materials. While they were busying themselves, Estrella went to back the manor and started putting together her plan. At the foyer's halfway point, she marked off where a booby trap would go, and about two feet behind that, she marked off where her secret fire trap would go. She picked out her hiding spot, and the spot where Anna-Mika would hide to work all the booby traps. When she was finished, she left the manor to meet with girls and give them instructions about what they were to do next. When she reached the center of the town, she saw that all the girls were waiting for her.

"All right, Sloan and Karmina, you two start by stuffing the burlap sacks with hay, wood chips, and anything else like that you can find. When they are stuffed, sew them shut. Then make the head, arms, legs, and bodies. You will also need some parchment rolled into cones to amplify your witchy howls and shrieks. Nori and Lena, to make your fake jewels will take a while. Find broken glass, sand down the sharp edges, and paint it bright colors. To make the fake bread, get old stale loaves and cut out the centers to make bread hollow. The Vikings will see only see the outer crust. To make the fake meat, grab some old mutton bones, wrap them in wool and leather, and paint the leather with honey so it glistens. For the fake ale, fill a barrel with vinegar. And paint the inside of the treasure chest with gold to make it look like it's full of gold. Anna-Mika, your first task is to help me look as much like your father as possible. I will wear his old clothes over my own, filling them with straw to make my body look bigger and fuller. Then I will need help pulling back my hair and pinning it up. I'll wear the pale makeup, and I'll fashion some wool into a fake beard. The dead and rotten things will make smell as if I am deceased. Once I look and smell like a dead person, I will show you what your next task will be: to work all the booby traps from inside the manor with me," she instructed.

With that, the girls set about their jobs. Karmina and Sloan went to work assembling their scare-witches, stuffing and assembling the bodies, dressing them, and then painting the faces. It took Nori and Lena a little longer to complete their jobs. Once they found the treasure chest, Lena painted the inside gold. Nori found all the broken glass she could, sanded the pieces down to the size of jewels, and painted them bright colors.

Once the decoy treasures were assembled and the chest filled up, the girls started putting together the fake food. Finding two old empty wine barrels, they used one as a table and one as the barrel of fake ale. They found the jugs of vinegar to use for filling up the barrel. Then they searched the garbage and found old stale bread and mutton bones, which they made look fresh and delicious.

When the girls were finished carrying out their tasks, they met back up with Estrella in front of the manor, where they awaited their next set of instructions.

"Here is my simply complicated plan. Sloan and Karmina, you are to set up two scare-witches on the sides of two buildings, not directly across from each other, but on a diagonal. The four of you will be on the rooftops pulling strings to make your witches fly up. Nori and Lena, you two will set up the signs at the entrance to the town. Then you will set up the bait in the manor where I have marked out the spots. Anna-Mika, you are going to set up mirrors around the bounty tables and place wood in the fireplaces.

"Here is what is going to happen when my plan comes together: The Vikings, presumably after their long journey, will be drawn to the empty town by the new signs promising free treasure, liquor, and food. The food will be rotten, and the 'liquor' will be vinegar. Once they reach the town and find it empty, they will head for the manor, where they will find our bait waiting for them. When they get disgusted with the food and drink, they will become discouraged and will want to return to their vessel, but their leader will not be so easily moved. He will keep them here to inspect the treasure. They will all be forced to stay, because they cannot disobey their leader. Once the leader opens the lid to the treasure chest, Anna-Mika, you will light the fires in the fireplaces and pull on a rope to raise a disgusting skeleton over the chest. I will be in the background coming toward the Vikings. I will be dressed like the late Lord Koen, giving them my warning that they should leave immediately. Seeing that the chances that they will be the same Vikings who killed your father are very slim, they probably won't even know what he looked like and won't know the difference.

"If that plan doesn't work, I have a plan B in place. While the Vikings are distracted, Anna-Mika, you are going to throw some rocks, round stones, and marbles behind them, and then I am going to step forward into a ring of fire and issue my last warning. If they still don't heed my warning, I will lunge at them, swinging my sword and forcing them to step back and trip on the stones, which will make them crash through the manors doors. Nori, Karmina, Sloan, and Lena, once you see them crash through, start raising your scare-witches and begin howling to push them back. Anna-Mika and I will pursue them to the edge of town," Estrella instructed.

"Exactly how is that a simple plan?" asked Nori.

"Yeah, I don't understand how all of this is supposed to be simple. And how is it that you know so much about Vikings in the first place?" added Sloan.

"If my plan works out accordingly, it will go over very simply. To answer your other question, I know so much about Vikings because I was taught these kinds of things from the many tutors my father hired," she explained. "Now, everyone, go set up your stations," she instructed.

So the girls ran off with their supplies and materials, and started to set up their booby traps. When everything was set up and ready for the plan to work, they met back up with Estrella for the rest of the preparations. They wanted to be ready at a moment's notice for the impending raid.

"All right then, our next plan of action is this: First of all, you girls need to pack up your belongings. Karmina, you are going to take all the horses, mules, and carts and hide them in the forest. Nori, I need you to hide all of the pets in the forest. Anna-Mika, I need you to pack up your belongings and your inventory, and then help me to get dressed in your father's clothing, which includes helping me with my hair. Tomorrow morning after we eat, we need to get into our positions and be ready. Anna-Mika, I will need you to help me with the final touches to get ready. If everything works out, this town will never be bothered by Viking invaders ever again," she instructed.

"Yes, of course. Right away, Estrella," replied Karmina, with Nori nodding her agreement. Then the two girls set about their tasks.

As the girls were packing and taking care of the animals, Anna-Mika was packing up what little belongings she had left, along with all the jewels and pieces she had hidden in her inventory. Once she was done and had everything packed up, Karmina took Anna-Mika's belongings and hid them with everyone else's and the horses. When that was finished, Anna-Mika helped Estrella into her father's old tunic, trousers, and boots. They were rather big on her, but in the morning they would be stuffed full of straw and wool to fill them out and make her appear broader. And she would have to be made to look taller so as to convince the Vikings she was the late lord. To do this, she would fill up the shoes with wooden blocks and then create stilts to stand on.

When everyone had completed their jobs, they took the remainder of the evening to rest. Nori prepared a light meal for them. When they all finished eating, Lena stood and went to wash everyone's dishes. Then they all set up their cots in the old whitesmith's shop to sleep. While the rest of them were sleeping, Estrella lit a small lantern and set up her parchment, ink bottle, and quill to write a letter home. When she was finished writing, she rolled up the letter, sealed it, and set it to the side for the night. Then she blew out her lantern, laid her head down, smiled while thinking of the blessings the Lord had given her and of how her plan was going to work, and fell asleep. In the morning, Estrella would dispatch Merlin to take the letter to her home.

When the sun rose, all the girls awoke. Lena made the breakfast. It was simple—bowls of oatmeal and cups of water. When they finished eating, most of the girls took their positions. Anna-Mika helped Estrella with the rest of her costume, stuffing her tunic with straw, hay, and wool. Then she painted her face sickly green, and coated her with the smelly rotten food to make her truly smell dead. After slashing though the tunic in the same place where the Vikings had run the good lord through with a sword, Anna-Mike placed the fake beard and mustache on Estrella and then helped her into the boots and onto the stilts. After that, Estrella helped Anna-Mika put on her ghostly white makeup to make her look like a banshee. When Anna-Mika left to get into position, Estrella whistled for Merlin. Once he arrived, she handed him the letter, stroked his head, and sent him on his way. Then she went to get into her position and wait for the invaders.

Nearly two hours had passed when they heard the blast of a horn coming from the town nearby, 30 minutes away.

"Anna-Mika, how far away is the town that the horn blast came from?" whispered Estrella from the shadows.

"It's about three hours away from us. The first blast means that the invaders have reached the edge of the town. They will send off another one once they leave that town and head for ours," responded Anna-Mika.

"Good. And when they get here, they will be in for quite a surprise."

"Estrella, do you really think this plan will work?" asked Anna-Mika.

"I know that with the Lord on our side, it's sure to work!"

"But how do you know? How are you so sure? There are only six of us, and probably a lot more of them than there are of us," questioned Anna-Mika.

"Because I have faith in our Lord. King David encountered this same kind of scenario when he was just a young shepherd boy. He was sent to the Israelite soldier's camp to take food to his brothers.

When he heard that the Philistine giant Goliath was mocking his God, he became angry and told King Saul that he would fight him. Now, both King Saul and the Israelite soldiers thought that he was crazy; they wondered how a little guy like David could successfully fight a towering giant like Goliath. But David knew that he had a bigger giant on his side: he had God. King Saul agreed and lent David his armor, his shield, and his sword. But when David tried on the armor, he found that it was too big. Plus, the shield and the sword were unwieldly. So David faced Goliath with only five small smooth stones and his sling. When David faced off against Goliath, the giant laughed at him and called him a dog. David called out to the giant, saying that he had come in the name of the God of the Israelites. He placed a stone in the sling and swung it around and around. When David let it go, the Lord propelled that little rock with so much force that when the stone hit Goliath's head, it killed him dead. With the giant dead, young David rushed over and cut off his head. So, you see, if the Lord can help a shepherd boy defeat a giant, he can help six maidens scare away some Viking invaders," explained Estrella.

Just then, the girls heard the second trumpet blast. They had three hours before the Vikings would arrive.

Within three hours, the Vikings were at the entrance of the town. They saw the new signs boasting about the abounding wealth.

"Aye, Olaf, look there. These signs are just asking us to pillage this village. Must be a good omen," piped one member of the raiding party.

"Yah, Sven. Looks like the gods are in our favor," said the one named Olaf.

"Look lively, boys! This reeks of Loki's doing to me!" yelled the raiding party's first mate.

"Oh, Lothar, you worry too much. Can you not see that they are handing this town to us on a silver platter?" remarked Olaf.

"Yah, Lothar. Better this town on a platter than our heads on a silver platter," said Sven.

"We go in," barked their superior jarl.

"But, Rolf," replied Lothar.

"We go in. End of discussion, Lothar," barked Rolf.

"Yah, Lothar. Don't be such a sissy girl," mocked Olaf.

"Yah, maybe you should have stayed back home with the women," taunted Sven.

"I am still your superior, Sven. Don't you forget that. I can easily put you back on rowing duty or even have you demoted to karl!" snapped Lothar.

"Sven and Lothar, that's enough of this bickering like girls. Let's get this job done!" barked Rolf.

"Yes, Rolf," whimpered Sven and Lothar sheepishly, like children. If there was something they both knew, it was that you don't mess with Rolf.

The looting party entered the town and looked around.

"Looks like the town is empty," said Igor, one of the drangs, or young warriors.

"I can see that, Igor. You, Ivan, and Arne, check the shops on the left, and Leif, Olaf, and Sven, check the buildings on the right," ordered Rolf. The looting party checked all the buildings and still couldn't find anything to pillage.

"Rolf, I don't like this. It's too empty. It just reeks of Loki's handiwork," complained Lothar.

"We are not going back empty-handed. The first town didn't have anything worth taking but furniture. They were dirt-poor. We are not going back to the chief empty-handed," snarled Rolf.

While the looting party was searching the town, the girls were on the rooftops watching and waiting for the signal. The Vikings were very noisy, but the girls stayed as still and quiet as they could, which was very difficult seeing how they had been up there a very long time. They were thirsty, and the air was so dry that they wanted to sneeze. But they stuck to the plan.

One of the drangs approached their jarl. "Rolf, why don't we see what's in that old empty manor up ahead?" suggested Arne.

"That's a great idea, Arne. In fact, that's the best idea I have heard today." Turning to Lothar, Rolf snapped, "I don't see you coming up with any good ideas. Maybe I should promote Arne to subjarl instead of you and send you back to the vessel."

Lothar kept his head down and walked forward. He had shamed his name and shamed his jarl by acting like a chicken.

When the Vikings entered the old manor, Anna-Mika was waiting for them. As soon as they stepped inside, she pulled the rope that was tied to the door, causing the door to slam behind them. When the Vikings saw the bounty, they ran straight for it without a second thought. They were so ravenously hungry that they just started eating and filling cups of the 'ale.' They didn't think to check if the food and drink was fresh or if it was really food at all. They grabbed the fake bread and the fake leg of lamb and started taking large ravenous bites like starving animals, but as soon as they put the fake food into their mouths, they dropped it to the floor in horror.

"What manner of trickery is this? This meat is not meat at all, but leather and wool on old bones," spat Olav.

"And this bread is empty, as if hollowed out. How can this be?" said Sven.

"I warned that this was Loki's doing," remarked Lothar.

"I don't care about the food. All I want is the treasure!" barked Rolf, reaching for the treasure chest. When the Viking jarl opened up the treasure chest, Anna-Mika lit the fires in the fireplaces so that Estrella's ghostly appearance surrounded the men in all the mirrored reflections. Then Anna-Mika pulled on the rope that triggered the skeleton to spring up from behind the treasure chest.

"You are trespassing on cursed ground. I am the tortured soul of Lord Koen, cursed to remain in this empty manor to keep invaders from desecrating my home! Your people invaded my home and took my life! This whole village is cursed since I have not been able to rest in peace. Leave now or forever be cursed," moaned Estrella in a most ghostly voice.

"Rolf, let's go. I told you this place was bad," said a whimpering Lothar.

"Not without our treasure," growled Rolf, as he lifted up a fake gem to inspect it in the light.

When Estrella saw the Viking jarl lift the glass gem to inspect it, she unsheathed her sword and flashed the signal for the backup plan to Anna-Mika. If scaring the Vikings away wouldn't work, she would have to resort to fighting them back and pushing them into the booby traps. Anna-Mika, seeing the signal, spilled some oil and loose pebbles, rocks, and marbles on the floor behind the Vikings so that when Estrella pushed them back, they would trip on them. Then she set to work stoking the fires.

Estrella brandished her sword and stepped forward into the special fire pit she had made for plan B. It was a circular pattern with a small opening in the back for her to step through, with a small platform in the middle, which she stepped onto. Once Estrella was in the center, Anna-Mika lit coals and pitch wood, which ignited around her friend. With the fire burning around her, Estrella barked out her last warning. "I warned you that if you didn't leave, you would be cursed. Ignorant and stubborn, you didn't heed my warnings. Now you will face my wrath." And with that, she leapt forward out of the fire pit and, with a flick of her sword, knocked the fake jewel out of the Viking jarl's weathered hands. Then she began swinging her sword back and forth before the old Viking had a chance to react and unsheathe his own weapon. The Vikings were taken aback by this aberration coming at them and threatening them. They had previously assumed it was only an angry spirit or one of Loki's tricks. They had not expected this thing to come out of the fire toward them, let to swing a sword while pushing them back. This thing was swinging a sword like it was flicking away flies! The Vikings drew their swords and weapons to fight back. The angry aberration started pushing them back toward the door. Before they knew it, they were slipping and sliding. Then they went crashing through the doors.

When the girls on the rooftops saw the Vikings crash through the doors, they knew it was time to start the second phase of the scare. As soon as the Vikings passed the first house, Sloan pulled up her scare-witch, which flew into the air. The Vikings were so surprised and scared that they stumbled backwards. When they stepped back, they knocked over the trigger that signaled Karmina to pull up her scare-witch. When that lifted into the air, Karmina grabbed her rolled parchment, raised it to her mouth, and started making ungodly noises: shrieks, cackles, hoots, and screams. That sent the Viking raiders reeling in a frightened frenzy. When they started scattering and running, they stepped on the signals for the other girls to raise their scare-witches. Once all the witches were up, Karmina, Sloan, and Lena, following Karmina's lead, picked up their pieces of rolled up parchment and started cackling and shrieking through them. To scare the Vikings out of the town, Estrella and Anna-Mika followed close behind them, the former still dressed as the ghost and the latter dressed as a banshee. They chased the Vikings all the way to the north entrance of the town, bellowing, shouting, shrieking, and yelling. Once the Vikings were out of the town and on their way back to their vessel, the girls threw rocks after them.

When the Vikings were out of sight, the girls wanted to celebrate. Karmina, Sloan, Nori, and Lena climbed down off the roofs and joined Estrella and Anna-Mika in the town square, where they all started cheering and laughing.

"Excuse me for a minute, everyone. I have to wash up. I still smell like the dead," said Estrella. Then she left the group to go take a well-deserved bath. She walked for some ways, leading her horse, and then found a small pond. She took off the late king's trousers and tunic, removed the shoes and stilts, and stepped into the water. Very cold, it made goose bumps rise up on her skin and caused shivers to run up her spine, but it felt good on a hot day. It refreshed her to wash all the stink off. She scrubbed off all of the dead fish, rotten food, mud, and makeup. Once she was all clean and fresh, she stepped out of the water, walked over to her horse, grabbed the blanket, and dried off. As soon as she was certain that she was completely dry, she put on one of her clean outfits and then walked back to where the girls were waiting for her.

Back at the town square, the girls were still giggling and laughing about their little act.

"That was the most fun I have had in many years," remarked Anna-Mika.

"Did you see those Vikings run? I thought I might lose my senses watching them trip over each other," said Sloan.

"I don't think I have ever seen men that big and heavy run that fast," Lena said, giggling.

"I don't think I have heard men that big and brave scream like that. They sounded like scared little girls," Karmina added, laughing.

"I don't think they will be coming back any time soon," Nori said.

"So, Anna-Mika, now that we have rid your village of those vermin, do you want to stay here or join us and become part of our little family?" asked Estrella.

"Well, having been by myself for so long, I have grown somewhat accustomed to it," Anna-Mika began.

All eyes were on her, waiting for her response.

"Well... of course I'm coming with you. Did you really think I would give up the chance to be part of a family again?" Anna-Mika concluded, beaming and smiling from ear to ear.

"Yay! Another sister!" The other girls cheered.

"Welcome to our family, Anna. Glad to have you with us," said Estrella, who then warmly embraced Anna-Mika.

"I'm glad to be with you guys," Anna-Mika said.

"All right, first things first. Before we head out, you have to pick out your horse and your mule," said Estrella.

"I get my own horse?" asked Anna-Mika.

"Of course you do, silly. What did you think we were going to do, make you walk or ride with one of us? Not that we would mind sharing. But Estrella thought ahead and bought horses for everyone who might need one," said Karmina.

"Have you had your own horse before?" asked Sloan.

"Well, yes, I have had my own horse before. My first horse was taken as plunder by the Vikings during the first raid," said Anna-Mika.

"Well now. You get to keep this one as long as you want. It will be well cared for and protected, and you get to name it yourself," said Estrella.

"You mean it? I can name it and keep it forever?" asked Anna-Mika.

"However long forever takes," replied Estrella, beaming with pride for blessing her new sister.

"Oh, thank you so much, Estrella," exclaimed Anna-Mika with glee.

"Bring out the horses, please, Sloan," instructed Estrella.

As Sloan brought out the horses that had not yet been claimed, Anna-Mika's face lit up like a full moon on a chilly December night. She beamed and almost wept. After taking a long stride toward the beautiful steeds, she ran her hands along all of the horses' coats and inspected all of them. They all looked stunning, but the one that caught her eye was the sweet and loving gray Lusitano stallion. Standing in front of the stallion, holding his head in her hands, and nuzzling his forehead with hers, she felt a very strong connection.

"This is the one. I know it," she said after a long moment.

"I am glad. What will you name him?" asked Estrella, who began loading Anna's things onto her cart.

"His name is Apollo. I felt a connection, a wonderful connection, between our two spirits, like we have been needing each other our whole lives. And although we are opposites—he is the sun and I am the moon—now that we have each other, we can never be apart," explained Anna-Mika poetically.

"Wow, Anna-Mika, that was beautiful. I pity the suitor who has to compete with your horse, Apollo, for your affection," quipped Lena.

"Well, now that you and your horse have finally met each other, strap on your saddle, mount up, and take the reins of your mule and cart, because we are leaving now," instructed Estrella.

Anna-Mika smiled, strapped on Apollo's saddle, swung up into the seat, and grabbed her mule's reins. Then, taking one last look at her past, she smiled at the memories, turned toward her future, spurred on her beautiful stallion, and joined the girls. Thus began a new chapter in her life. She followed after her new family, with her companion Cleo following close behind her Cleo like the other companions was focused on protecting, it's person, and had a shared purpose with the others and respected for them.

CHAPTER 18

Estrella's Second Trial, Officiated by Will Scarlet

After the girls left the town of Rune and Anna-Mika's past, they rode for about a ten miles and then came to a clearing in a meadow. There they set up camp for the night. Estrella set up the tents, Anna-Mika tended to the horses and mules, Sloan collected the wood for the fire, Lena cared for their pets, or "children," Nori caught and prepared their dinner, and Karmina filled their waterskins. Once they had all settled down for the night, Merlin flew into Estrella's tent with a reply letter from her mother, which read as follows:

> My Dearest Estrella,
>
> Why do you scare me like you do? It had been a while since I'd gotten your last letter, and then when I do receive one, you tell me you are facing off against Vikings! I nearly fainted.
>
> I miss you more with each passing of the moon. I look toward the heavens and remember the beautiful night when your father and I were blessed with such a beautiful baby girl. I remember that you are a gift to this world, someone to help those who are in need, to be a light in this darkened world, and to guide the lost back to the Savior. Please keep yourself safe out there. And write to your poor mother more often. Lord be with you, sweet one.

Your mother, Queen Althea

Estrella put down the letter and wiped away her tears. O how she missed her mother. Besides Kasim and Gideon, her mother was her truest and best friend. Being so far away for so long had made her heart ache.

Estrella was just about to lay her head down on her mat when a dagger came flying through her tent and landed in front of her. It scared Merlin half to death. The racket he made almost woke the other girls, but Estrella hushed him and pointed to the scarlet ribbon tied around the dagger's hilt. That could only come from one person, Will Scarlet, one of Robin Hood's Merry Men and a member of the secret Order of the Lion. Estrella had heard from the stories about Will Scarlet, that the scarlet ribbon wrapped around the hilt of a dagger was his calling card, his trademark. Estrella grabbed her indigo cloak, the one she had received after her last trial, and left her tent silently so as not to wake the others. She looked around. Seeing moonlight glinting off a knife blade, she made her way in that direction. When she reached the edge of the forest, some hands came out of the shadows and pulled her into the trees. She struggled and tried to pull away, but the hands pulled her faster and held her tighter. Soon she found herself in a clearing.

✑ The moon was shining all around the clearing, allowing her to see the half-hidden cloaked figures surrounding her. Then she saw Will Scarlet jump from a low tree branch and land just outside the circle. The others parted the circle and let their leader enter the clearing. Will stepped forward into the clearing and approached Estrella. She looked him over and sized him up, as he did her. She figured him to be around five feet ten inches in height, slender but not gangly, with a nice build, strong arms, and broad shoulders. He had slightly unkempt hair, but it was not dirty. He had a cocky but not overly confident smirk on his face, yet he somehow was able to project a boyish charm and maintain a soft gleam in his eyes. After assessing her new teacher's appearance, Estrella realized she had been staring at him and judging the way he looked. She blushed and hid her face in the hood of her cloak.

Will smiled as he realized the effect he had on the young lady.

"Stand up straight, young lady, so I may return the favor of assessing your traits."

Estrella instantly stood up straighter and put on a brave face. She didn't want to disappoint her new teacher. When she was younger, her father often got on her case about her poor posture, but he had been the cause of it.

Will Scarlet circled around Estrella, looking her up and down, closely examining her every aspect.

"Well, my dear, from my assessment, you appear to be around the age of seventeen years. Judging by your clothes, you are of royal blood, but I knew that bit already from our first introduction. By your hands, I can see that you have done hard work while you have been out in the wilderness. You are about five feet two inches in height, and you enjoy the outdoors as much as the indoors. Since you have been out on your own, you have tried to keep up your appearance," he said, making her nervous.

"Can I—" she said, but he held up a hand and cut her off, indicating that he wasn't quite done.

Then he smiled and said, "All right, you have permission to speak now."

"First of all, Mister Scarlet—"

"Just Will."

"All right, Will. First of all, I apologize for judging your appearance as I did. It was rude of me. I picked up the habit in the palace. Secondly, I am not sure what kind of a lady you take me for, but I do not take kindly to being so roughly handled and yarded in a place with which I am not familiar."

"You are forgiven. I understood what you were doing. I was only having a bit of fun at your expense. And you have my apology, my lady Estrella. My boys meant you no harm. We just needed to get you into the clearing as soon as we could in case there was any present danger."

"I thank you for your concern, but I can handle myself, thank you."

"I can see that. You know the order has been watching you?"

"Oh, great. What have you seen? Do you watch the way I eat, how I sleep, and which royal habits I engage in?" she remarked sarcastically.

"No, not at all, Your Highness. We have seen you get ready to sleep, which is when we send your trial alerts. We observed how you handled those Vikings back in Sima of the Neona. There were some of us who had our doubts about your being in the order because of your age and personality, but the way you took charge and came up with a plan and strategy on the spot like that proves even more that you belong with us. Many people would have just saved Anna-Mika and left, but you decided to send a message. That was very cunning of you."

"I thank you, Will. I couldn't let their kind take advantage of that town again. I wanted to make sure it would stay protected for future generations and people to repopulate it. And send the message that they can't take what they want."

"We could see that very clearly and are very impressed. Now let's get down to the reason why we brought you here. It's time for your second trial, to test your skills."

"And what skills would those be, exactly?"

"Knife skills, mostly throwing"

"Knife throwing?! But I don't have any knives. And what will I be throwing at?" she exclaimed.

"Don't worry, I will provide the throwing knives for you. And after your test, if you pass, you may keep them with you. As for the target, well..." he said, trailing off. Then he called for one of the figures who was standing in the circle to come forward. "This is Troy; he is going to be your target." The young boy stood there before her, unflinching with his leader's hand on his shoulder.

"What?! I can't throw knives at this poor boy."

"Do you harbor any malice in your heart? Would you wish any harm upon him?"

"No, never. I don't know the lad well enough to wish anything upon him."

"Do you trust yourself enough not to harm him?"

"Well, not that much. I have never thrown knives before, let alone at a living, breathing target."

"Well, first, he will be in front of a plank of wood. You will be aiming around him. Second, my boys have learned blind faith and trust; they put their trust in the person throwing. I would never put my boys in danger if I knew the thrower had ill will. And third, all you have to do is pray for the Lord to guide your blades, trust yourself to hit only the wood, and have trust in your heart that you can do this."

"But I'm not sure.... I don't know if I can." She started to doubt herself.

"Estrella, listen to me. You just planned a scheme to scare a group of Vikings twice your height and three times your size around. You had faith in yourself and in the Lord that you could get them out. You can trust yourself to throw with accuracy and not harm the lad."

"I'm too young to handle this much pressure. I... I..." She hesitated.

Estrella shook her head. Tears dripped down her cheeks. She stepped back and sunk down against a tree. Her body was shaking from having held her doubts and fears inside for so long. Now she was finally giving in and believing the lies. Will felt deep sympathy for the princess, who was young and so far away from home. But he knew that these doubts and fears were not coming from her heart or mind. No, those were the tools of the Prince of Lies himself. Satan's best tools were fear and self-doubt. Will sent the young lad off to the target board and then crouched down next to the poor distraught princess.

"Estrella, listen to me. This is not who you are. You have more confidence than anyone I have ever met. Do you think that King Josiah was afraid and thought he was too young when they made him king of Israel at age eight? Probably, but he became one of the best kings they ever had—after the long line of terrible kings. When your brother left you in charge of your home and family, did you for one second think that you were too young, or doubt that you had what it took to take on the responsibility?"

"N-n-n-no.... I knew it was my duty to take care of our Maia and our people since Father was never home long enough to take care of either. Gideon took over Father's business at home. When Gideon was called away, I knew it was my responsibility to care for those they left behind."

"And what about this self-proclaimed quest of yours? Did you think that you were too young, or did you think twice about leaving your home and going off on your own? Did anyone tell you were too young or too foolish, or tell you to stay home?"

"No. I knew that the task laid out before me to take care of the kingdom was too big for me to do on my own, so I went in search of friends to help me. I wanted the kingdom to have someone else to help Mother. In return, the Lord came with me and is using me to find those who need my help."

"And when you were offered a place in the Order of the Lion, did you turn us down saying you were too young, or cry when we told you that you had to go through trials?"

"No, sir, I did not. I accepted the position. I also accepted whatever it would take to join the order."

"And when you thought of this plan to scare away the Vikings and your new friends were doubting that they could go carry out the plan, or that it would even work, did you agree with them and flee, or did you stand up to the challenge like a David and slay your Goliath, with a few resources and five girls?"

"You know very well that we scared those invaders back to their vessel. And we sent them packing with their tails between their legs, like cowards!"

"Estrella, you are a strong, brave, confident young leader. You have the will of the Lord on your side. The Enemy of your soul wants you to doubt your fire, but instead he just added to it to ignite an inferno with your holy anger. Use your confidence to trust in yourself."

She turned and looked Will dead in the eye, with a glint of determination and a smirk to prove the Enemy wrong.

"Master Will Scarlet, hand me those knives. I am ready to silence the naysayers."

"That's the spirit," he said as he handed her a kit with seven knives in it. And then he led her over to the area where Troy was waiting.

Estrella closed her eyes and prayed, "Dear Heavenly Father, please direct my aim. Make my blades fly sure and true so that no harm comes to the young boy. My hands are in your hands. Guide my aim. In Jesus's name, I pray. Amen."

She opened her eyes, felt the weight of the blade, and determined the balance level. Then she turned her gaze to her target, narrowed her eyes, took a deep breath, and let the knife fly as she exhaled.

There was a silence as the blade flew through the air. Then with a thud, the blade hit the outline, right under the boy's left arm. When Estrella saw that she had hit only the outline, she sighed with relief. Then she picked up her next blade and got ready for her next throw.

She took a deep breath and let go with the exhale. When she let the blade fly, she closed her eyes. When she heard the sound of the blade hit the board, she opened her eyes to see that this one hit under the boy's right arm. She smiled.

"Very good, Estrella. See, when you focus on your desired target, the outline around Troy, you hit the mark. Now just focus on where you want the next two blades to go—and then make it happen."

Estrella smiled. She had faith that she could pass this half of her trial. With the Lord's help, she could do anything. Nothing is impossible when you trust in him. She picked up her third blade and then pictured it flying through the air with accuracy, hitting the board just beyond the lad's left thigh. She threw the third blade, which hitting the area just outside Troy's left thigh. Her confident smirk came back. Now that she knew what she was capable of doing, who was going to stand in her way and tell her she couldn't do on account of her being young, female, and privileged. If her God was for her, then who could ever stop her? And if her God was with her, then what could ever stand against her? She picked up her fourth blade and pictured the location where it would land, just outside Troy's right thigh. Then she opened her eyes, inhaled, exhaled, and threw the knife through the air. It hit the board with a resounding thwack right outside Troy's right thigh. Estrella smiled again. She had only three blades left.

As she bent down to pick up the fifth blade, Will whispered different instructions into her ear. "With the last three blades, I want you to surprise us and show us what you can do based on instinct. Don't picture the throw in your head, don't plan it out, don't overthink it, and don't analyze it. Just trust your instincts. Go on what your heart is telling you to do. These skills will come in handy someday, as in future scenarios you won't have time to picture your target and plan out your knife throws. You will just have to focus on your instincts and go with them."

"All right. I will try," she said. She took a deep breath and closed her eyes. When she opened them, the silver glint appeared in her eye. Alyia smiled, raising the blade and quickly flicking it through the air like it was nothing. The tension was so thick you could cut it with a blade. Everyone held their breath watching the knife spin through the air. Each person, even Estrella, let out a gasp once they saw the knife hit the board to the left of Troy's chin. Where had that come from? Estrella had no idea she had that in her. It must have been Alyia, her warrior side, coming out in her instincts. She picked up her sixth blade and thought to herself, *All right, if this is what you can do, then please at least don't let it get too close.*

She sighed and flicked the knife. This one spun through the air and hit the board on the right side of the boy's chin.

"All right then. Estrella, now you have only one blade left. Trust your instincts and try not to hit the boy. Those last two were a pretty close shave." Will laughed as he instructed her.

She picked up her last blade, flipped it in her hand a couple of times, tossed it from hand to hand, and then flicked it just like the last two. This time, every eye was on the blade to see where it would hit. When it finally hit the board, there was gasps from everyone in the circle. It had hit just below the boy's crotch.

"Okay, who is this new girl, and where was she before we started? This is definitely not the same girl who was letting her fears drive her to tears," remarked Will. He sent another boy over to retrieve the blades and to help Troy down from the target.

Estrella took a deep breath and sighed, sending Alyia back inside.

"Well, this is my warrior side. I like to call her Alyia. Using the alternative name protects my family. She was kind of drowned out by the lies, but she is back now. Will if I may permission to go back to camp, I am exhausted and would like to go back to my camp now?"

"Yes, Lady Estrella. You may be dismissed. You have passed you second trial. Your reward is the set of throwing knives and a new cloak," Will said, handing her the kit. Then he her helped her with her new cloak, a crimson one, and handed back her old cloak, folded up.

"Thank you, Master Will," she said sleepily. Then she whistled for Merlin. The two of them headed back to camp.

When the boy rejoined his leader, the two of them watched the young princess head back to her camp. Troy said, "Master Will, that young woman has deadly aim."

"Aye, that she does."

"She would make a great asset to Master Robin's Merry Men."

"That she would. But Merlyn has even bigger plans for her."

Estrella sleepily stumbled the rest of the way to her campsite. Once she finally made it inside her tent, her head hit her mat. She slept soundly for about three hours.

CHAPTER 19

The Next Morning

When the sun started to rise with the dawning of a new day, the girls had already awakened, all except Estrella, who was still sleeping after her late-night trial with Will Scarlet. A few hours later, the girls gathered outside Estrella's tent.

"Should we wake her?" whispered Anna-Mika.

"No, let's let her sleep just a little while longer," replied Lena.

"Being a light sleeper, I heard her leave her tent sometime after we went off to bed. Then later last night, I heard her stumbling back to camp," said Sloan.

"Where do you think she goes off to at night? What do you think she does?" asked Nori.

"Whatever it is, it is none of our business," retorted Karmina.

Then there was a stirring sound from inside the tent. Estrella was waking up. Slowly awaking, she stretched and ran her fingers through her hair, somehow managing to get them stuck in the messy knots. When she was able to get her fingers unstuck, she stretched her arms again, this time knocking over her quill and ink bottle, spilling ink everywhere. Her startled reaction and jerky body movements caused her tent to collapse on top of her. She was very embarrassed by her less than graceful morning that she just sat under her fallen-down tent.

The girls just stood there outside the tent, confused by what they had just seen.

"Estrella, are you okay?" asked Anna-Mika.

"Is everything all right in there?" asked Karmina.

"Um... yes. Yes. I'm fine. Just an off morning, I suppose," Estrella replied from inside the tent.

"Would you like some help getting ready?" asked Nori.

"Um... hmm, no. No, I don't think so, just give me a few minutes. And think of it this way: I just saved us the trouble of tearing the tent down later." Estrella giggled.

"Estrella, you silly girl. You should have packed up your things and cleared out of the tent before tearing it down," teased Lena.

Estrella somehow managed to change her clothes inside her collapsed tent. Once changed, she emerged. The girls tried to conceal their laughter once they beheld the princess's appearance.

"Um, Estrella, did crawling out of your tent mess up your hair a bit?" asked Karmina.

"A bit?! Look it at! It's a complete disaster, like a bird made a nest of it," said Sloan.

"Sloan, it's not polite to make fun of the princess," scolded Lena.

"No, no, Lena, it's all right. Sloan was just being honest. Honesty is what I look for in my friends and new sisters. You wouldn't believe all the lies and brownnosing that one hears in court—a lot of gossip, bickering, and backstabbing. And believe it or not, even a princess wakes up with messy hair," she said with a smile.

"Well, now that you're out, I insist you let us help you get ready, and help you clean up and pack up your things," Karmina insisted, tapping her foot with her arms crossed, like an impatient mother waiting on her child. Estrella peered up from the ground where she sat, looking like a little girl trying her mother's patience. This situation reminded her of her youth in the palace; however, it was always her nursemaids who had waited on her during the day. Her parents had to take care of the kingdom's business and such, but every evening her mother made time for all her children.

Estrella looked up and smiled. "Okay, Mommy," she teased back

"All right then. Sloan and Nori, I want you two to move her collapsed tent and pack it up, along with her belongings, for her. Anna-Mika and Lena, could you two help her with her hair, please? I will help her with her horse," Karmina instructed.

"Yes, Mommy," they teased, before starting their tasks. It had become apparent that although Estrella was the group leader, Karmina was the group mother. Karmina rolled her eyes as she walked over to Estrella's collapsed tent. She retrieved Chesnutt's saddle and brush and then walked over to Chesnutt. Sloan and Nori moved the collapsed tent off of Estrella's things. Sloan folded and wrapped up the tent and poles and then packed the bundle onto the cart. Nori cleaned up Estrella's spilled ink bottle, packed up her bedding, her clothes, and her belongings, and put it all onto her cart. Lena and Anna-Mika had a harder task, namely, taming the bird's nest of hair on Estrella's head. Lena, using her own hairbrush, tried to pull it through Estrella's hair.

"Er, grr, ugh.... Sheesh, Estrella, when was the last time you brushed this mane of hair of yours?" Lena grunted.

"I can't—ouch!—remember," Estrella said in pain.

"Here, use this hair oil and some soap. We will have to wash it first and then try to brush it. When did you last wash it?" asked Anna-Mika, who began gathering the washbasin, soap, and hair oil.

"I washed it yesterday after we scared away the Vikings, remember? I excused myself to wash off the stench and dirt of pretending to be dead."

"Oh yes, that's right," Anna-Mika said. "All right, if you move forward a bit, we can put the washbasin behind you, and then you can lie down and we can wash your hair," she explained.

"All right then," replied Estrella. She moved forward about two feet. Anna-Mika placed the washbasin behind Estrella, and Lena filled it with water. Then Estrella lay back and let her messy raven locks fall into the basin. Lena ran her fingers through the wet strands and pulled out leaves, twigs, and such.

"Um, Estrella, what exactly were you doing last night?" asked Lena.

"First of all, I can't tell you. It's a secret. And even if I did tell you, you wouldn't believe me," Estrella explained.

"Come on, please tell us, Estrella. We want to know, and we promise not to tell," begged Anna-Mika.

"Nope. I'm sorry, but I can't, not now at least. Maybe one of these days. But for now it's my little secret. Besides, it gives you guys something to wonder about," explained Estrella.

"All right, I guess you're right," said Lena as she washed Estrella's hair. Once Lena finished rinsing out the soap, Estrella sat up. Then Lena left to empty the washbasin. Anna-Mika sat down behind Estrella and used a towel to remove water from her hair. Then she applied the hair oil to Estrella's scalp and worked it down to the hair tips. She took out her hairbrush and started brushing Estrella's hair from the scalp down with long slow strokes, ten strokes on each side. It felt good to Estrella to have someone brush through her hair slow and steady. When she brushed it herself, she hurried and did not even do very much with it. When her handmaidens did it for her, it was painful, as they rushed and fussed, and pulled and pinned her hair until it no longer even resembled her own hair. But this, having someone with nimble fingers and a gentle touch take her time to slowly brush her hair, made her feel so much lighter.

When Anna-Mika was done brushing Estrella's hair, she took out separate strands, picked up a long red ribbon, and started plaiting Estrella's hair. When she finished the long braid, she used another ribbon to tie it at the bottom. Then she stood up and smiled as she began to put her hair accessories away. Estrella stood up and grinned, and then spun to feel the braid whip around.

"Thank you so much, my friends, for all your help. This morning may have been slow and rough, but the rest of the day should go smoothly." She grinned. Then they all mounted their horses and rode off.

CHAPTER 20

Harpies Attack!

Having ridden only two miles down the road, the girls noticed some strange shadowy figures circling overhead.

"Hey, Estrella, are those vultures circling overhead?" asked Sloan.

"I wouldn't' think so. We don't have any dead meat with us," replied Karmina.

Estrella looked up at the figures and felt dread in the pit of her stomach. They were definitely not vultures. When Merlin swooped down and screeched a warning, her fears were confirmed. ✳

{"Harpies. Harpies! They are here, Estrella."}

"Oh, dear Lord, protect us," she prayed.

"What was that, Estrella? What is the problem?" asked Nori.

"They're Harpies, unholy spawn of the Devil. Hurry, everyone, arm yourselves and turn back," she yelled. But she soon realized that it was easier said than done to turn around horses, mules, and carts. When they couldn't turn and run, the girls tried to cover themselves for protection.

"Dear Lord, what have I done? I have just found my new sisters, but I have already led them into danger. I must do whatever I can to keep them and protect them. I will not lose them now. Give me strength to save them," Estrella prayed. Turning to the girls, she gave them her orders: "Quick, leave your things with me and run for cover. I see a cluster of rocks about forty paces behind us. Hide yourselves behind those rocks. I shall protect you."

"We can't just leave you behind, Estrella," yelled Karmina.

"Go! Now! That's an order," she shouted. She didn't like to order her companions around like that, but it was for their own protection. Not wanting to disobey, they dismounted and ran for the rocks. Once there, they kept their heads down and watched. Estrella, seeing that her girls were safe, breathed a sigh of relief before catching her breath again. When she saw that one of those flying things was swooping toward them, she instantly opened her knife case, in one fluid motion whipped out a dagger, and flicked it at her target. The Harpy let out a bloodcurdling shriek as the dagger hit it in the back. Behind the rocks, the girls had no idea of what had just happened. All they saw was a flying beast coming toward them. Then they heard a shriek and saw the creature fall to the ground.

When the other Harpies saw what had happened to their friend, they turned and swooped down toward Estrella. She looked up in horror as they dived at her. She was about to reach down for another blade, when she heard the swooping of wings above her. Merlin was trying his best to distract the Harpies and lead them away from Estrella. With the Harpies drawing closer, Estrella lost her edge and her confidence. She reached for another dagger and threw it, but it didn't fly far enough, only hitting one in the shoulder. Then she jumped off her horse and ran. She knew she could ride faster than she could run, but she wanted to get the heartless Harpies away from her and the girls' horses. She ran as fast as she could, but the Harpies caught up to her. Two of them swooped down, grabbed her by the arms, and carried her into the air. Her girls watched helplessly from the cluster of boulders as their leader was being taken away. Karmina was about to open her mouth to cry out for her dear friend, when Sloan clamped a hand over it. Pointing toward the Harpies in the sky and then to the girls' horses, she whispered in a hushed tone, "Shh.

One loud noise and we are all goners. And we are no use to Estrella dead. I will silently sneak over to my horse and grab my quiver. Then, when the moment is right, being careful to hurt only those beasts and not Estrella, I will shoot them down."

"What about us? We want to help too," said Lena.

"You guys can gather up all of our bedding and blankets to make a cushion in case Estrella falls," explained Sloan.

"That doesn't seem like a very big part in your plan," retorted Anna-Mika.

"There are no small parts. We all have a part in ensuring her safety. Would you rather have her fall and hurt herself? But the longer we argue about it, the longer they have to finish her. I for one don't want to lose our leader and our new sister, or have to tell her parents that we lost her. Now let's get to work," said Sloan.

The Harpies carried Estrella higher into the air. One was pulling on her arms, another was pulling on her legs, and still others were ripping at her clothes and pulling her hair. They started hissing and screeching at one another, fighting over who would get which part of the princess. Then Estrella heard them hissing at each other. Their argument went like this:

"I want her blood; it should be mine."

"No, no, no. You have lived long enough, longer than most. I should get it."

"No, it should be mine. I should drink it."

"There should be enough for everyone to get some."

While these Harpies were arguing and fighting over who would get to drink Estrella's blood, they let go of her, at which point three younger Harpies swooped in, grabbed Estrella, and flew away with her. When the older ones noticed that their prey was missing, they flew after the younger ones, who by that time had Estrella pinned against a tree ten yards away. The older Harpies flew to the tree and were about to reach Estrella, but one of the younger ones stopped them.

"Listen, the princess must die. That is certain. Master's orders. As for her blood, there should be enough for everyone to have a cup and refrain from getting drunk from it. But she must die, and we must bring back her heart."

Estrella had never been more afraid in her life. If she didn't have faith in her Lord, God Almighty, and in her girls for her rescue, then she would most definitely fear that this would be the end of her life.

When the Harpies were flying to the tree, Sloan took the opportunity to sneak over to her horse, Fletcher, and grab her quiver. Once she had slung her quiver and bow over her shoulder, she signaled for the girls to rush to their carts and grab as many blankets as they could. When the Harpies were talking over how they were going to kill Estrella, Sloan was getting into position. Once the girls had their blankets and other things, they signaled to Sloan to shoot her arrows. Receiving their signal, Sloan readied her arrow and, with perfect ease, loosed it right into the back of the oldest Harpy, which shrieked in pain and fell to the ground like a rock. With the cry from their sister, the others turned around and started to fly toward her assailant. Sloan grabbed another arrow, nocked it, pulled back, and fired into the heart of another one, which fell to the ground instantly.

While the Harpies were distracted with Sloan, the girls rode their mules as fast as they could to the tree and set up their cushion for Estrella's fall. Two of the Harpies had stayed behind to keep a hold of Estrella when the others went Sloan. As the creatures were flying toward Sloan, she fired arrow after arrow at them, hitting all the vital areas to ensure a quick demise. Some were hit in the head, heart, and chest. Others were hit in the stomach, others in the wing, and still others in the neck. This last group had an agonizing death as they fell to the ground.

There were no actual accuracy shots. Sloan, like Estrella, was just firing on instinct. Inside everyone there is the instinct to protect oneself and one's loved ones by any means necessary.

When most of the Harpies had been shot down, two of the younger ones flew back to the tree to finish their unholy mission. Once the girls had set up their cushion, they rode their mules back to safety to hide. The two Harpies were about to rip apart Estrella when Sloan spotted them. She adjusted her position to get a clear shot at both of them. With one in her sights, she reached for an arrow, nocked it, brought up her bow, pulled it back, and fired it. It hit one of the Harpies in the arm, causing it to release Estrella. Sloan turned her attention to the other side of the tree, repeated her actions, and shot the other Harpy in the arm, causing it to fall backwards and release Estrella, who also fell.

CHAPTER 21

The Girls' Rescue of Their Leader

When Karmina, Nori, Anna-Mika, and Lena saw Estrella start to fall, they rushed to the tree and held up a large blanket to try to catch her. She fell quite a ways, getting scratched on the way down by branches, twigs, and leaves. She bumped her head on one of the branches, but there was no real damage. Luckily the Harpies had held her on the side of the tree that had the least number of branches. ✶ When Estrella finally made it down, the girls caught her in the large blanket and gently lowered her onto the cushion. When she was lying down, they all started to crowd her to see if she was all right.

Karmina spoke up, saying, "Girls, give her some space to breathe. I will see to her wounds."

"No. First we need to send those fiends back to where they came from," objected Estrella.

As the girls were talking, Sloan made their way toward them, pleased with her success at fending off the Harpy attack.

"But, Estrella, you have been through a lot today. You need to rest," said Karmina.

"I will rest later. Right now we need to finish the job. Sloan, bring me my sword, please," Estrella instructed.

"But, Estrella, you could be hurt. Let me finish them off for you," urged Sloan.

"No, I need to do this. You girls, gather material and brush for a big burn fire," she said, slowly rising to her feet.

"As you wish, Estrella," replied Sloan, who went over to Estrella's horse, retrieved Estrella's sword for her, returned to her leader, and helped her finish standing up.

While the other girls were gathering up fire material, Sloan was helping Estrella go from Harpy to Harpy and do what had to be done. Estrella took her sword and cut each Harpy's throat. When the Harpies were all slain and the fire pile was built, Sloan dragged the bodies over to the pile one by one and threw them on top. When the putrid, smelly bodies were all on top of the fire pile, Estrella leaned on Sloan's shoulder and addressed the girls, saying, "All right, girls, I need you all to mount up and ride on ahead. The smell of burning flesh and feathers stinks to high heaven. Sloan and I will follow behind after we light the fire."

"But, Estrella," Lena said back.

"No buts. Do you really want to stay behind and watch this? It's not pretty, and it's going to stink really awful. Trust me, we will be right behind you. Karmina, you take the lead on this one. We will ride until you find us a town to stay in for the night," Estrella instructed.

"Yes, Estrella. Come on, girls, let's mount up." Turning to Sloan and Estrella, she said, "We will wait for the two of you a mile ahead on the road." Karmina then mounted and started riding ahead, with the other girls mounting up and following close behind her.

Sloan and Estrella threw some more dry wood on the pile. When they were sure that the last cart was out of sight, Estrella lit a torch, threw it on the pile, stepped back a couple of paces with Sloan, and watched it blaze before she collapsed on the ground.

After watching the unholy creatures catch fire on the burn pile, Sloan caught sight of Estrella falling down.

"Estrella, are you all right?"

"No, I am not all right. Sloan, I really do need your help. I am hurt badly and am in a lot more pain than I said I was. Please, I need your help," she pleaded. Sloan began helping her to stand back up.

"Yes, of course. You can rest in the back of my cart. I will move my things to your cart, set up the bedding and blankets the back of my cart, and lead your horse with mine," Sloan stammered. Then she started rushing around to get things ready.

"Sloan, please just stop and help me. Just prop me up next to my horse as you get things ready," Estrella insisted. Sloan helped Estrella limp over to her horse and then leaned her against. Once that was finished, she set to work making a small cot in the back of her cart and moving things around. When she finished making the bed and moving things around, she gently picked up Estrella, carried her over to the cart, laid her down, and made sure she was comfortable. When she was sure that Estrella was supported and comfortable, she tied Estrella's horse to the back of her cart, and Estrella's cart to the back of her own horse's saddle. Then she mounted up and rode on carefully, being sure not to jar or bump Estrella and cause her any more pain.

When Sloan and Estrella caught sight of the others, it was past midday and getting colder. The other girls were worried when they did not see Estrella riding with Sloan. Also, it concerned them that it had taken Sloan and Estrella a while to catch up with the group.

"Sloan, where is Estrella? I don't see her on Chesnutt," asked Karmina, her voice rising a little in volume and pitch. She was obviously worried.

"Hush, please. Estrella is resting in the back of my cart. I moved my things to her cart to make a bed for her in mine. She really is in a lot pain. She felt the need to get rid of the corpses first and act strong for the rest of us, but she is in pain and needs to rest. So, Nori and Lena, the two of you ride ahead and scout out the nearest town for us to rest at. Karmina and Anna-Mika, the two of you can stay here and wait with me to take care of Estrella. Lena, I will need you to stay in the town you find and wait for us. Find an inn and get us any rooms you can. Nori, once you find the town, ride back and get us. Are we all clear on the plan?" Sloan said.

"Yes, ma'am," replied Lena and Nori in unison as they turned their horses and rode off.

It was clear to see after that that Sloan had found her position in the group. Estrella was the leader, Karmina was the mom, and now Sloan had asserted herself and proven that she could take charge when she needed to. Sloan had found her place as Estrella's right hand, as second in command.

Lena and Nori rode for two hours before they finally found a small town. They rode in to the town as quietly as they could. Their carts were a little noisy and it was getting late; they didn't want to wake the whole town up. The town had small cottages, a chapel, a schoolhouse, a merchant's shop, a tailor, a doctor, a boardinghouse, and an inn. Nori left her mule and cart with Lena and rode back to alert the others of their good find.

Back at the carts, Karmina and Anna-Mika were caring for Estrella's needs. They were helping her drink some water to keep hydrated, and they fed her some pieces of bread to get her to keep her strength up. Also, they were doing their best to keep her awake in the event that she had a concussion.

"Estrella, Estrella? Can you hear me? Where are you hurt?" asked Karmina.

"Ugh. My chest hurts, and my arms and legs hurt. I think I bumped my head. I am very weary. Can't I just close my eyes for just a little bit, please, Mom?" she said feebly.

"No, Estrella. You need to stay awake for me, please. Do you think you could do that for me, please?" Karmina asked in a soothing voice.

"I will try my best," Estrella responded in a small voice.

Anna-Mika gave Estrella another drink of water. Karmina walked over to her horse, Juniper, and tied her and the mule cart to the back of Anna-Mika's cart, explaining why to the unicorn.

"Juni, I won't be riding you. Estrella needs me to be with her, to make sure she is okay."

{"I understand,"} Juniper replied.

Karmina passed by Sloan on her way back to Estrella's side.

"How is she doing back there?" Sloan asked.

"I am not a physician; I am only a very good friend," replied Karmina.

"Hopefully, we can find a physician for her in the town," said Sloan.

"Hopefully. Until we reach the town, I will ride in the cart with her to keep her awake—if you don't mind," said Karmina.

"Of course I don't mind. Anything to help her," remarked Sloan.

Karmina walked around to the back of the cart and climbed in behind Estrella, where she sat holding up her leader's head to keep her awake.

"Estrella, tell me a story, please. I want to hear a story."

"I don't know if I can remember any stories, Kar. I'm so tired."

"Please? Just try to remember one for me. I need you to stay awake. You can't fall asleep yet."

"All right, I will try. Let me see if I can remember one," Estrella managed to say, trying to remember some story to tell in order to stay awake.

Nori returned to the group with the good news that they had found a town with a physician. Upon hearing the great news, Anna-Mika mounted her horse, Sloan nudged her horse forward, and they followed behind Nori at a cantered steady pace. Estrella managed to remember the story of the archangel Michael and the great war to tell to Karmina so as to keep herself awake. She remembered this and other stories from the Bible from the time when she was small and her mother, the queen, would read them to her.

By the time the group of girls reached the town, Lena had found them a good-size stable and barn for their horses and things.

"The inn was full, but I was able to talk the owner of a boardinghouse into letting us stay there for a few nights. She had only three rooms available, but I convinced her that we could sleep two to a bed," reported Lena.

"Good job. Lena, could you please direct us to the boardinghouse? And take the horses and mules for us," instructed Sloan, as she dismounted, along with Anna-Mika.

"Of course. The boardinghouse is on the right, two buildings down," replied Lena, who began to see to the horses.

"Thank you," said Sloan. She picked up Estrella from the cart and carried her to the boardinghouse, with Karmina and the others following close behind.

"Estrella, sing me a song please?" asked Karmina, trying to keep her awake.

"But, Karmina, you are the songstress. Could you sing one for me?" she asked feebly.

"I don't know any new songs. I want to hear you sing one, please. Please, Estrella, just try to sing one to me," Karmina encouraged.

"Okay," Estrella said. Finally remembering a song, she started to sing, "Tu-ra-lu-ra-lu-ra..."

They entered the boardinghouse. Sloan asked the woman at the front desk, "Ma'am, could I please have the keys to our lodgings, and could you please send for a lad to help one of my girls with our bags?"

"Yes, my lady," replied the owner. "James, please help these ladies with their belongings," she instructed. The boy came forward and then hurried out.

"Nori, go out with the boy and help bring in our belongings, please," instructed Sloan.

"Yes, Sloan," replied Nori, heading out after the boy.

Sloan and Karmina rushed upstairs. Karmina called downstairs to Anna-Mika, "Quickly, Anna, go find the physician." Then she whispered to Estrella, "Estrella, can you recite the alphabet for me?"

"Which one?" came her reply.

"Whichever ones you can remember, and however many you can recite to keep you awake."

"All right. A, B, C, D, E, F, G..."

"Very good. Keep going."

Anna-Mika turned to the owner and asked, "Please, could you tell me where I might find the physician?"

"He is just across the road, my lady. His name, Doctor Morgan, is on the door. I wish you the best of luck, my lady. Your friend looks in bad shape," she directed.

Anna-Mika rushed out the door, passed Nori and the young man with their bags, crossed the road to the physician's house, and banged on his door.

"Doctor Morgan, O Doctor Morgan. Please come. Please, we need your help," she begged.

An older gentleman came to the door. With long light brown hair tied back into a ponytail, tan skin, and hazel eyes, he looked to be in his midtwenties. He had a kind face and a gentle demeanor, looking down at the young girl while drying his hands. He saw that she was just about out of breath and shaking like a leaf. She nearly fainted; he managed to catch her by the elbow.

"Please, please, sir. We, we need—" she said, trying to explain the situation.

"Hush now, young lady. What seems to be the problem? Try to catch your breath, and then tell me what is wrong."

Anna-Mika took a breath and reported, "Our friend Princess Estrella from the far kingdom of Faylin is badly injured. We were attacked by something. We need you to come quickly and see to her."

"Yes, of course. You rest here while I grab my bag. Then we will head over to your friend. Where might you and your friends be staying?" he asked.

"We are staying in the boardinghouse. I'm sure that if we ask the owner, she can direct us to their room," Anna-Mika replied.

"Good. I know the owner. She will tell us which room your friends are staying in," he said. After heading back into his house to retrieve his bag, Doctor Morgan reemerged. Then he and Anna-Mika hurried over to the boardinghouse.

Arriving within minutes, they burst through the door.

"Martha, which room is the injured young lady in?" the doctor asked frantically.

"Upstairs, room four, on the left," she replied.

Doctor Morgan and Anna-Mika rushed up the stairs and ran to the room. When they arrived, they found that the other girls were gathered around Estrella's bedside. She was muttering something, but it was barely audible. "Ah, Be, Ke, De, E, Ef, Ge, Ha..."

"I am Doctor Morgan. How have you been keeping her awake?" he asked the girls.

Karmina stood up. "My name is Karmina, but they all call me Mom. I have been trying to keep her awake by having her recite things for me, like stories and songs. Since we entered the room, I had her recite any alphabets she could remember, starting with the English one. Now she is on the Latin one, after reciting the French, German, Gaelic, and Greek alphabets."

"Good job. I see you care very much for her. But now I am going to have to ask you ladies to go to your rooms so I may examine her privately," he instructed.

"But... but she needs us," protested Nori.

"And I'm going to be sharing the room with her," argued Sloan.

"I thought I would stay with her," Karmina said.

"Wait a minute, now. Maybe I wanted to stay with her," argued Lena.

The girls continued bickering over who would stay in Estrella's room with her. Estrella stopped in the middle of her Welsh alphabet, the one she was currently reciting, and tried to prop herself up.

"Enough already. Here are your room assignments for tonight: Lena and Nori, room two; Anna-Mika and Sloan, room six; and Karmina will share with me tonight. Now please go to your room and relax. Karmina, just wait outside our room while the good physician sees to my wounds. You did your best. Let's let the doctor do his job," she ordered, using most of her strength to do so.

"All right, ladies, you heard her. Don't worry, she is in good hands," reassured Doctor Morgan.

Reluctantly, the other girls left the room. Estrella fell back on the bed, exhausted from having exerted herself to speak. Doctor Morgan smiled seeing the girls' loyalty to their princess. But noticing Estrella's strength waver, his face clouded with concern.

"Hush now, Your Highness. You're going to be all right. Save your energy and strength," he said to calm her, propping her up with pillows. "May I have your permission to remove your outer garments to check for broken bones?"

"Yes, Doctor Morgan, you have my permission. Just be gentle with me."

"Your Highness, I am always gentle with my patients, but I will be extra gentle and discreet just for you," he reassured her gently. "First let's check your head for a concussion."

He had her look straight ahead so he could check her vision.

"Your eyes both look to be beautifully normal, Your Highness. Clear as a pool, and shimmering like stars."

"Do you flirt with all your patients, Doctor Morgan?" she quipped.

"Only the beautiful princess ones," he joked, "And so far, you are my first royal patient."

"I hope I don't disappoint you."

"Not at all. You are a very good patient. Now, can you tell me how many fingers I am holding up?" he asked, with four fingers of his left hand raised.

"Four," she replied.

"Good, your vision seems okay. And you seem to be concentrating well. Can you tell me what happened to you while I check for broken bones?" he asked her, concerned. He gently and carefully removed her blankets and helped her out of her outer garments.

"Well, you see, we were traveling down the road, when these Harpies descended on us." She recounted all that had happened, leaving out the part about the Harpies' wanting her blood and claiming that she would die, because she did not even understand that part herself.

When Doctor Morgan finished, he looked up. He appeared to be pensive and concerned, perhaps a bit troubled. Then he said, "I will spare you the lecture of staying out of Harpy Valley."

"I thank you. We don't know the land. We are just travelers on a holy quest. I will spare you my backstory and all the details and just say this: I set out on this quest not knowing where to go or what to find, yet I found myself where I was needed and found those who needed me," she said.

"Well, your quest is most noble indeed. As for your physical condition, nothing seems to be badly broken, just bruised bones. And you have a good-sized bump on your head but no concussion. I suggest you get plenty of sleep and rest yourself tomorrow," he said with a smile. Then he covered her up.

Estrella said, "Thank you, Doctor Morgan," before finally resting.

Doctor Morgan quietly left the room. Outside, he told Karmina his diagnosis and his instructions for Estrella. When Karmina reached for her coin purse for payment, he declined, saying that it was not needed. Then he left. Karmina quietly entered the room, changed into her night shrift, and climbed in bed next to the sleeping Estrella. They slept peacefully through the night.

CHAPTER 22

Estrella's Recovery

The next morning, Estrella awoke feeling rested and refreshed, yet her body was still sore. She tried to sit up, but Karmina, feeling her stirring and shifting around, was determined to stop her from rising.

"What are you doing?" asked Karmina, rolling over and shooting her friend a stern look.

"Um, I was just... you know, getting up, to get dressed." Estrella hesitated, trying to find an excuse to get up and do something.

"Do you not remember your instructions from Doctor Morgan last night?"

"Well, I was a little sleepy when he was done. But I remember something about sleep," Estrella said, trying to avoid the subject.

"Well, I remember. He said for you to rest today, so whatever you had planned for the day, let the other girls and me take care of it," Karmina said, getting out of bed.

"I don't know if I can rest. Since our quest, I have been finally getting used to doing things for myself," Estrella remarked, falling back against her pillows.

"Well, let's start by picking out your clothes for the day. What do you want to wear?" Karmina asked, walking over to their bags of clothes.

"Does it matter? I'm not going to be able to leave my bed or room with you girls in charge," said Estrella, pouting and crossing her arms.

"Come. Come now, Estrella. You are acting like a child. You're a royal princess. Act like one," responded Karmina with a stern look. Estrella drew up her knees, and shrunk back with a sad, cowering look.

Karmina looked at her with a softer gaze. "Estrella, what's wrong?" she asked, coming over to her.

"You sounded like my mother at first, but then... then you sounded like my father," Estrella responded with a voice shaky from emotion. Karmina sat down next to her and gave her a gentle hug.

"I'm sorry, Estrella. I didn't mean to sound so harsh," Karmina apologized.

"It's okay. I understand that you care and want the best for me. Let's start over. Could you bring me my trousers and tunic, please? And my parchment and quills, please, to make a shopping list?"

"Of course," replied Karmina, fetching Estrella's outfit for her and then retrieving the parchment and quill.

Estrella took her parchment and quill with the little ink that was left and started making her list.

"Shopping list: bottle of ink, quill, parchment, blanket, hairbrush, fresh mint leaves, and anything you girls would like to get for yourselves." When she finished her list, she set it aside and gently pushed her covers off her body. "Karmina, could you please help me get my outfit on?"

"Of course, Estrella," replied Karmina, who then carefully helped Estrella off with her night shrift and helped put on her trousers and tunic. When Estrella was all dressed, Karmina pulled the covers back over her.

"Thank you, Karmina. Could you please send the girls in now, and go downstairs and get me something to eat?" Estrella asked kindly.

"Are you sure you want to be alone?"

"Yes, I'm sure. With you girls hovering over me and worrying about me, it makes it hard for me to breathe, let alone be by myself."

"I'm sorry if I've been crowding you, Estrella. We have just been worried about you."

"It's all right. I just need some room for a while."

"All right. I will send in the other girls and go get you a plate of food," said Karmina. She opened the door. The other girls fell into the room.

"Um, we weren't listening to you through the door," said Sloan.

"That's all right. I was hoping to see you girls. I need you to run some errands for me."

"Really? You want us to do your shopping for you?" asked Lena.

"I just need a few things. I have a list" replied Estrella, handing over the list. "Your spending allowance is in the small chest. Take the medium-sized bag of coins."

The girls went over to the chest, and looked in awe at all the gold.

"Where? How?" asked Nori.

"It is only a small fortune, covering about three months of my allowance. Now I have explained where it came from. Take the medium-sized bag—and use my list, please," she explained.

"All right, Estrella. We will be back as soon as we can," said Nori, who grabbed their shopping allowance and the list. On their way out, they all stopped at Estrella's bed to give her a kiss on the forehead.

The girls left the boardinghouse and walked out into the little town. Down the road a little ways, they found the merchant's shop. Once inside, they looked around and split up to find the things on Estrella's list.

Nori walked up to the counter to ask for stationery. "Excuse me, sir, but I need some stationery supplies."

"Of course, miss. What kind of supplies do ye need?"

"I need a bottle of ink, a quill pen, and some parchment. Could you also add to my order the past and current month's calendar, please?"

"Certainly, miss," replied the merchant, who began gathering the items.

Sloan searched the shelves and found a beautiful deep purple quilt with detailed stitching. "This will make a lovely blanket for Estrella. It will keep her warm, and it is beautiful like she is."

Lena went to the counter to get the merchant's attention. "Excuse me. I know you are busy, sir, but could you please tell me where I can find soap, privy supplies and mint leaves? We are trying to buy things for our friend. She is not feeling well."

"Well, miss, our toiletries are against the back wall there, and mint leaves are behind the counter. I respect you ladies doing something nice for your friend; I hope she feels better soon. How many mint leaves?"

"Five ounces, and just hold onto them for me. We'll pay for all our items together."

"Sure thing, miss."

Lena went to the back wall and grabbed six bars of soap, six towels, and a hairbrush for Estrella.

Anna-Mika looked around the small store, locating the spices and teas. She grabbed a few cinnamon sticks to suck and chew on, and then she selected a few pouches of tea leaves.

When the girls had all their purchases together at the counter, the clerk measured and weighed what needed measuring and weighing. Then he calculated their total.

"Well, ladies, the total cost comes to one hundred and thirty-five coins."

"Is all of this really that much?" asked Lena.

"Yes, miss, all of your purchases come to one hundred and thirty-five coins."

"That seems fair to me," said Anna-Mika, reaching into the coin purse, bringing out a handful of coins, and counting out the right number.

Back in the room, Estrella was trying to get some sort of exercise. She had just maneuvered her legs out of the bed and sat up. Her next challenge was to get up out of the bed and try to walk. She grabbed hold of the bedposts and pulled herself up. Then, grabbing hold of the chair next to her bed, she stood up and took a few steps. With every step, she felt the pain in her chest and sides from the fall. She went about ten steps before the chair snagged on the rug and she fell down with a crash. While lying on the floor holding her sides, she could hear voices in her head. She thought she was going crazy or that it was a symptom from her fall out of the tree. This is what she heard:

"Don't bother getting up. You are far too weak and helpless to do anything," said the first voice in a harsh cruel tone.

"Get up, sweet girl. You are strong! I know because I made you that way. You are not helpless; you can do all things in my name," said a softer, kinder voice.

"Lord, is that you?" she asked to the air.

"I am here, Estrella. I have been with you the whole time. Get up, my child, and try again. You are not a victim, you are not helpless, and you can do it," replied the Lord. Estrella remembered everything the Lord had brought her through. Mustering up all her strength, she was able to pull herself back up and take a few more steps.

Meanwhile, Karmina was downstairs fetching a plate of breakfast for Estrella. The cook was putting a small plate of food on a tray when Karmina heard the footsteps and chair scrape across the floor. Concerned, she grabbed the of food tray and rushed up the stairs. Hearing Estrella crash upon reaching the door to the room, she dropped the tray of food and felt around in her pockets for the room key. While she was searching for it, she could hear Estrella talking. She couldn't hear any other voices, but it sounded like Estrella was talking to someone. By the time Karmina was able to find her key and get the door open, Estrella was already at the other side of the room, sitting down at the little desk.

Estrella looked up and smiled when she saw Karmina open the door. Then when she looked out into the hall, she saw her plate of food on the floor. Pouting, she teased her friend. "Kar, was that my food?"

"I'm sorry, Estrella. Hearing you crash, I dropped the plate so I could reach for my key. Were you talking to yourself in here?"

"Aw, but I was looking forward to eating something today."

"We will find something later." After a pause, she added, "You did not answer my question. Were you talking to yourself?"

"No, I was talking to the Lord. I probably sounded a little crazy. When I fell down, I heard voices in my head and thought I was crazy, but one of the voices was the Lord encouraging me to get back up, so I did."

"Well, next time you feel like walking after an injury, let us know so we can help you."

"I don't want help, though. I got up to work on my own strength. If I let you girls help me every time I get hurt, I wouldn't learn to do anything on my own. And you girls will just be coddling me."

"All right, but next time just let me know what you are going to be doing so I don't worry."

"All right then," Estrella said with a smile. There was a soft knock on the door. Once it opened, the girls peeked in.

"May I ask what happened with the breakfast plate?" asked Sloan.

"I dropped it to find my key, because I thought I heard Estrella crash, turns out she was just practicing walking again." Karmina explained.

"May we come in?" asked Lena.

"Of course. Everything is fine now. Did you girls get what I requested from the shop?" asked Estrella.

"Yes, we did. Plus a few extra items," replied Nori. The girls all walked in with their purchases. Estrella got up to walk over to the bed. Sloan went over to her to help, but Karmina stopped her.

"She wants to do it on her own," explained Karmina.

"Thank you." Estrella smiled. Then she turned around, pushed her chair back to the bed, and sat down. Nori was the first to come over and hand her the purchases, except for the calendars.

"Here is your new bottle of ink, your quill pen, and your parchment."

"Thank you very much. Now I can write letters home again," said Estrella.

Then Lena stepped forward with her purchases. "Here is a hairbrush for you, a towel, and a bar of soap."

"Good, now I can keep clean. And I won't have messy hair anymore." She smiled.

Sloan was next to come over to the bed with her purchase. "I bought you this blanket to keep you warm. It's beautiful, just like you are."

"Oh, Sloan, thank you very much. It's so thoughtful of you."

And then finally, Anna-Mika, after putting the rest of the money back into the chest, came forward with her purchases. "I bought some tea for you to drink to help with your healing, and some cinnamon sticks for us to suck on to keep our breath fresh."

"Thank you all very much. These purchases are all going to be very helpful." Estrella smiled.

Later that evening, they all shared a meal in Estrella's room. Once they had finished and put their dirty dishes aside, Estrella handed out their new room assignments.

"All right, here are your new room assignments for the night. And there will be no arguing over it. Room two will be Lena and Anna; room six will be Karmina and Nori; and Sloan will be staying with me tonight."

"Okay, Estrella, that seems fair," replied Karmina. "Come on, girls, let's get our things situated into our new rooms." She got up and ushered the girls out to collect and rearrange their things.

The girls set about moving their things around. When everyone was ready and settled, Sloan helped Estrella get ready for bed and then helped her lie down comfortably. Then she got herself ready, turned down the light, got into bed next to Estrella, and settled in for the night.

CHAPTER 23

Estrella's Third Trial, Officiated by Arthur

That night, Estrella, finally feeling peaceful and in the mood to rest, had just fallen asleep when she heard a soft tapping sound at the window. She was too tired and sore to get up and open the window, so she sent Merlin over to open it and see what was making the noise. He flew over and gently pulled open the window. Receiving a note from a small carrier pigeon, he closed the window and flew the note over to Estrella. She was able to turn up the lamp on her side of the bed just enough to read the note. It read, "Come to the old schoolhouse for your third trial. ~Arthur." Estrella's eyes grew wide. This was her third trial already, and Arthur was going to administer it, just like the first one. Not just that, but also he was in the same town waiting for her. Her head began to swim with thoughts. *If he is here, then why isn't the whole town abuzz with excitement? Do they know it is him? If they had known the high king was coming to town, they would have made preparations for his arrival. And if he is here, is Queen Guinevere here as well?*

Merlin broke Estrella's train of thought by gently nipping at her hand and whispering, {"You should get going now."}

"You're right," she whispered back. As she carefully maneuvered herself out of bed, she disturbed Sloan next to her.

"Where do you think you're going at this hour, young lady?" Sloan asked sarcastically.

"I have to go somewhere tonight."

"You don't *have* to go anywhere. You *need* to stay right here and get some rest," countered Sloan, sitting up in bed.

"I have to. This is important," Estrella retorted, changing out of her night shrift.

"If it is so important, then take me with you this time," Sloan negotiated, getting out of bed and standing in front of the door.

"I don't know." Estrella hesitated, pulling on her trousers and tunic.

"You are not going anywhere without me," Sloan insisted.

"Fine, but you can't tell me what to do, and you mustn't say anything about what you see or hear tonight. You have to promise me that," Estrella instructed, as she tied her hair back.

"All right, I promise. Now take me with you," Sloan said, walking over to the wardrobe and hastily changing into her clothes.

"Fine," replied Estrella, putting on her slippers. Then she pulled on her newest cloak, tied her bedsheets together, anchored one end to the bed's headboard, and threw the other end out the window.

"Why are you doing that? Why can't we just go out the door?" asked Sloan, pulling her hair back. Then she put on her slippers and her cloak.

"We would wake the others," explained Estrella. With a day of rest and exercise Estrella was able to climb out the window and down the bedsheets.

After Estrella reached the ground, Sloan climbed down after her. "All right then, can I know where we are going?" she asked.

"No, I can't tell you that. You will just have to trust me, and follow," Estrella answered.

The two girls started walking toward the schoolhouse. Once they reached it, they saw King Arthur's royal steed tied up outside. Sloan's eyes grew to the size of dinner plates in shock. She was about to gasp in surprise, but Estrella shushed her. Upon entering the schoolhouse, Estrella gestured for Sloan to take a seat in the back, but Arthur spotted them and motioned for both of them to come forward. They made their way. Both curtsied once they were in front of the high king. "Forgive my timing, sire. But after an encounter in Harpy Valley I had two days ago, my friends wouldn't let me out of their sight. Sloan insisted on coming with me," Estrella said, pleading her case.

"Your Majesty, I hope I am not interrupting or intruding on anything, but I couldn't leave her alone after what she went through. Please understand my concern for my friend. I promise I won't interfere or interrupt," Sloan said, making her case.

"I understand, and I honor your loyalty to your friend. I have heard of your bravery and courage in Harpy Valley. I actually have a use for you, Sloan, during this trial," said Arthur.

"Me?! How can I help, sire? I don't even know what's going on," Sloan said, perplexed.

"You have not told your new friends why you have been sneaking out at night?" asked Arthur.

"Well, I assumed that our meetings and trials were a secret since we met at night. And you told me at our first meeting that I was not to tell anyone," Estrella explained.

Arthur turned to Sloan and solemnly said, "Sloan, you are witnessing Estrella's third trial in a series of trials to discover whether she will gain membership in a secret group known as the Order of the Lion. You are to keep what you hear and see here a secret until such time that we permit Estrella to reveal her secret. Do you understand everything I have explained to you?"

Sloan stepped out into the aisle and knelt before the high king. "I understand, and I swear on my life and arrows to keep your secrets, Your Highness."

"Very good. I commend you on your loyalty. In this trial, we are going to test Estrella on her leadership skills. We'll also be determining how well she does as your group's leader. But instead of asking Estrella my questions, I will ask you questions about her. You are to remain completely honest and truthful, and not let your friendship with her get in the way of your answers," he explained.

"I swear on my steel, Your Majesty, I will answer with full honesty," Sloan answered.

"Very well. Estrella, you are to sit here," he instructed, pointing to a seat at the front. "Sloan, you will stand to her right. I will stand here to her left. Estrella, you are to remain silent throughout the proceedings, sort of like an inverse court trial."

"Yes, Your Highness," replied both girls, taking their positions. Arthur stood to Estrella's left, opened a scroll, and began to read from it.

"There are seven traits of a good leader and for good leadership: vision, humility, integrity, loyalty, charity, mercy, and patience. A good leader must have good vision, and I am not referring to eyesight. To have vision means that a leader has the ability to see potential, to create in her mind what she cannot at present see with her eyes. Sloan, would you say that as a leader Estrella has good vision, that she can see the potential for a circumstance and then act on it? And if so, will you give an example of a time she made use of her vision?"

"Yes, Your Highness, I believe that Estrella has excellent vision. Take for example the time we scared off the Vikings. We all could have abandoned the empty town without looking back, but Estrella envisioned an opportunity for us to send a message to any and all invaders never to come back," Sloan defended.

"Very good. Second, a good leader must have humility. To have humility means to seek first to understand and then to be understood, and to be humble. Sloan, has Estrella ever pulled rank over you or the others? Has she ever delegated other tasks or chores to you or the others because she felt entitled on account of the fact that she is royalty? Or has she held her nobility over you?" Arthur questioned.

"No, sire."

"No what exactly, Sloan? No, she doesn't have humility, or no, she doesn't hold her status over you?" he inferred.

"Sire, I may not know many royals, but Estrella is not like any I have seen. She shows grace along with humility. Along our journey, every girl has a choice and every girl is humble. I have seen Estrella doing the dishes for us after our meals and then going to feed our animals after that. She is the most humble princess I have ever known," Sloan explained with a smile.

"Well done. That covers two traits out of the seven traits. Five more to go over. Next, a good leader should have integrity. To have integrity means to show continuous improvement, to be levelheaded, to be controlled and calm, and to have devotion and piety. Has Estrella shown continuous improvement since you have known her? Has she been levelheaded, or has she been rash and acted in haste based on emotion? Has she remained calm and in control when a situation seemed out of hand? Where does her devotion lie? Is she pious for the Lord?" King Arthur questioned.

"My lord king, I have not known Estrella very long, so I cannot truthfully say that I know of any improvements. As far as her being levelheaded goes, I can assuredly say that she has proven herself to be very levelheaded. She always remains calm and in control, even when the rest of us are in panic. She is very devoted to the Lord God Almighty, which speaks to her piety," replied Sloan.

"Good, very good. That covers vision, humility, and integrity. The next trait is loyalty. This question should be fairly easy to answer. Does Estrella show teamwork and team-building skills? Does she tend to be aloof and do things on her own, or does she include the rest of the group? Does she develop the unity and creativity of the others? Does she keep her word, and remain loyal to her friends?"

"Sire, Estrella is the most loyal person you could ever meet. Her loyalty to us, her new friends whom she has only just met, astounds me. Back in Rune when dealing with the Vikings, we all worked as a team at our different positions. The only time Estrella is aloof is when she sneaks off to her secret meetings, sir. But she is definitely loyal," Sloan replied.

"From what I have heard about her, she is most loyal. The fifth trait of a great leader is charity. Does Estrella protect others, rather than accuse them of faults?"

"Estrella protects everyone she meets. She stands against injustice and fights for those who have been oppressed. She would never accuse the innocent of faults. She looks past mistakes and accepts people for who they are. The only person Estrella would accuse of failures, sadly, is herself, sire," Sloan said, making Estrella's case.

"That is a flaw most leaders possess, self-accusation. But her charity is very commendable. Well done. All right, I believe this next question goes along with charity and should be very easy to answer. The sixth trait is mercy. Does Estrella treat the defeated with respect and dignity?"

Sloan hesitated for a minute to compose her thoughts before speaking. "Sire, I will speak with utmost certainty. In the time I have come to know her, Estrella has not encountered very many enemy attacks. The only time she does not show an enemy respect is when she is making an example out of the enemy's humiliation, when the enemy doesn't deserve respect, or when she is teaching the enemy a lesson. When we first found our friend Lena, she was a captive stolen from her home. When we fought her captors, Estrella sent them home in their undergarments to humiliate them." Estrella blushed, remembering her lack of mercy for those thugs. That was not a very good example of her past dealings with oppressors, she thought.

Sloan continued to explain, saying, "Another situation was when we scared the Vikings out of Rune. We were only teaching them the lesson that they should not mess with that town any longer. The last situation was when we were leaving Harpy Valley. Estrella finished them all off and sent them back to the abyss. Those *creatures* did not deserve mercy."

"I see. Well, mercy is a trait Estrella will just have to work on. Finally we come to the last trait a good leader should have: patience. Does she have good patience? Does she act in desperation? Does she keep calm?"

"Sire, she has the patience of a priest. When we first saw Lena and her captors, our friend Karmina and I were the ones who wanted to charge in and save her. It was Estrella who had us wait patiently for the right moment and a better plan. So in conclusion, sire, Estrella shows the best leadership of anyone I have ever known or heard of," Sloan finished with assurance.

Arthur smiled and motioned for Estrella to leave her seat and kneel before him. He took out a green cloak from his satchel. Estrella kneeled before the high king.

"Estrella, I have found you in possession of six traits of good leadership. You will need to work on showing mercy to your enemies, even if some are undeserving. Remember that the Lord above shows mercy to us even if we don't deserve it. But considering all the traits you do possess, you have passed your third trial. Arise and exchange your cloak, Princess Estrella," Arthur instructed. Estrella stood to her feet and bowed her head as she unclasped her crimson cloak, which she had received upon passing her second trial, and handed it to Sloan. Then Arthur draped the new cloak around her shoulders and fastened the clasp for her. Estrella lifted her head, looked into the kind eyes of her high king, and smiled.

"Thank you, my lord. It is an honor to have found favor in one such as you. May I ask if I will be having you as my instructor for any more trials?" she said.

"I am sorry, Estrella, but this is the last trial you will see me. I must return to Camelot in the morning. Your next teacher is Maid Marian, but that is all I can tell you," he replied soulfully.

"Excuse me, my lord. I know I am not part of the order, or even going to be, but may I ask a few questions?" Sloan inquired.

"You are permitted two questions," Arthur replied.

"My lord, how many trials does she need to complete to be in the order?"

"Estrella needs to complete nine trials to be a member. She has passed three."

"All right. My last question is, who are all the teachers or members of the order?"

"Me, my queen, Guinevere, Sir Lancelot, Merlyn Emrys, Robin Hood, Maid Marian, Little John, and Will Scarlet. Now, ladies, I must be going if I am to get on the road to Camelot by midday. And you have to get some sleep." With that, Arthur Pendragon, high king over all the realm, leaned his head down and kissed both girls on the forehead. Then he flipped the cowl of his cloak up, slipped on his satchel, spun around, walked out of the schoolhouse to his horse, and rode out of town.

Sloan stood there with her mouth open in shock, while Estrella just blushed.

"Let's head back so we can get some rest before we have to leave in the morning," said Estrella.

"Wait, Estrella. What are you going to do with your old cloak now that you have the new green one?" asked Sloan.

"You can keep it, Sloan. After each trial, I get a new cloak that is a different color. You can have the crimson one."

"Thank you, Estrella," replied Sloan, as she put on the cloak. Then she followed Estrella out of the schoolhouse. The two made their way back to the boardinghouse. Once they were in their room, they picked out their outfits for the next day and packed up their belongings. Then they climbed into bed for some well-deserved sleep.

CHAPTER 24

Indra's Return

Back in Faylin, Queen Althea was sitting down at the table, about to write her next letter to Estrella, having received no word from her. King Indra, just arriving home from a campaign, came through the main entrance door.

"My queen, I am home," he called out as he came in.

Althea put her quill pen down and came out to the foyer. "Where have you been, Indra?" she asked.

"Is that any way to welcome your king? I have been engaged in war campaigns for our high king."

"The realm has been in peace for at least seven years."

"Then obviously I have been in conferences to keep the peace. Where are my children?" Indra said, changing the subject.

"Kylia and Keena are at lessons. Gideon has been called to join King Arthur's Round Table, and Estrella left home on her own quest.

"That's impossible. Gideon is only twelve years old. And Estrella is only ten. They are too young to be going off on any kind of adventure."

"Gideon is a young adult at nineteen years of age, and he was summoned. You of all people know you can't refuse a summons. And

Estrella is seventeen years old. She left on a quest to find her friends of her own. Maybe if you were home more, you would have known."

"Are you saying I don't know my own children, Althea?"

"You gave up the role of being their father when you decided you wanted to be on war campaigns more than you wanted to be with your family and watch your children grow up into the independent young adults they are," she snapped back, on the brink of tears. "And since the realm has been in peace, where have you really been, Indra? Because it hasn't been here."

"You really want to know, my queen? I have met another woman. I just found her two months ago. I am not cheating on you, or an adulterer. She is a widowed baroness whose children have grown and moved out. I plan to pursue this relationship with her after you and I go before Arthur and petition for a divorce," Indra confessed.

Indra's words cut Althea to the heart. Her husband, her king, was going to leave her. She couldn't believe it! She could hardly remain standing from the impact of his words.

"But... Indra," she said, trying to reply.

"Althea, we both knew that our marriage had lost its love years ago."

"But if you met her two months ago, and given that there haven't been any wars in years, then where have you been going?"

"I have been getting counsel from some other lords and barons, and attending conferences with generals and soldiers to keep myself busy."

"I just can't believe it; you're actually leaving your family."

"Another thing, Althea. I would like to have Faylin and the castle. Arthur gave us the kingdom, but I think I should have it."

Althea lost her temper when she heard that he wanted the kingdom that he never stayed in.

"No! You can't have it! These are my subjects more than they are yours. And you can't kick us out of our home. You moved us out of our first home; you can't move us out again. Where will Gideon and Estrella come home to when they finally return? It's not that easy for someone to find a new place to live," she fired back at him. "I am not leaving; I won't move my family again. You can move out. I'm sure that with your being a king, someone will let you stay with them until you have your own estate. You can stay here for the night, but tomorrow I want you to leave," she reasoned.

"I understand. We can settle the rest of this matter later in court. I will have my things packed tonight to leave, my queen."

"I am no longer your queen, sire. You have made that clear. We may still be married according to the law and the Lord, but I am no longer your queen," Althea replied coolly, keeping her emotions under control. Turning to walk away, she stopped herself and added, "Oh, and Indra, when our children do return home, I expect you to be here to welcome them. Not for me, but for them." She turned on her heels and walked away with all the dignity of a queen. She didn't look back and kept her chin up. Once she reached her study, she picked up her quill and began writing her letters to her children.

> Dear Gideon,
>
> It has been a long time since I last heard from you. I have missed you, my son. The kingdom is not the same without your warm and charming laugh ringing through the halls. I can't wait for your homecoming, when I will meet your beautiful Bliss. Please write to me more often. I love you very much.
>
> Your Maia, Althea

There were many other things she wanted to say to him, but she didn't want to tell him about his father just yet, as it would upset him. So she kept her letters brief. She rolled up her first letter and then set about composing her second, which read as follows:

> Dear Estrella,
>
> My dearest daughter, why haven't you sent me more letters? Your dear mother is worried about you. Please write me as soon as you can, so I can at least know you are safe and not in any danger. I pray the Lord keeps you well and in safe hands. I wait anxiously for your safe return to my warm embrace.
>
> Your loving mother,
>
> Althea

When she had finished, she called for her page boys, who brought in two carrier pigeons to deliver her letters to her children. She went out to her balcony and released the birds.

Later that night, Althea retired to her bedchamber early, had her dinner in her chambers, and then fell asleep. King Indra stayed in one of the guest chambers, and in the morning he packed his things and left Faylin.

CHAPTER 25

Luanna

The morning after her third trial, while Estrella was packing her belongings, she heard a tap at the window.

"I wonder who *this* letter is from," Estrella said sarcastically.

"Well, open the window and find out, silly." Sloan laughed.

Estrella went to the window, opened it, took the letter from the bird, and then sent the messenger away.

"Who's it from?" asked Sloan.

"I wouldn't know. I haven't opened it yet," replied Estella.

"Maybe it's a secret admirer?" Sloan teased.

"I highly doubt it. No one knows us out here," replied Estrella as she opened the letter.

It was from her mother, Althea. Feeling the emotion and worry in every word, Estrella longed to see her mother. It had been a long time since she left home. Reading the letter, she remembered that it had been a while since she had written her mother.

"So, who's it from?" asked Sloan.

"My mother," replied Estrella.

"Oh. You miss your home, don't you?"

"Yes, I do, but my quest is not finished, so I can't go back home yet. Anyway, there is a lot I haven't told her yet. Do you think I should tell her about my trials?"

"Of course. Arthur would allow you to share that with you mother. However, I suggest not mentioning the Harpies."

"I agree. The last letter I sent told her about the Vikings, and that didn't make her too happy. Once we stop at another town or village, I will write her back," said Estrella, who rolled up the letter and packed it away.

When everyone was packed up and their belongings were loaded in the carts, the girls sat down for one last meal at the boardinghouse. Sitting to chat with each other a bit, they then got up to leave, leaving money on the table for their meals and then stopping at the desk to pay for their two nights' stay. From the dining hall, they took their leftovers for their animal companions. After going to the stable and mounting up, they began to ride.

Estrella wanted to stop by the doctor's house to pay him for his aid. She dismounted and knocked on his door. He answered it. Upon seeing the young princess, he smiled.

"Good to see you are better, my dear."

"Thank you again, Doctor Morgan. I am much better thanks to your help." She smiled and handed him a small pouch of coins.

"Oh, Princess, I can't accept that. Seeing you well is all I need."

"I insist on compensating you for your trouble, so please take it. My girls and I are on our way. We have places to see, so we must go."

"I will accept it, not because I need it, but because you gave it to me. Please be careful out there. I would hate to hear that my new favorite patient is in trouble again," he said, taking the small pouch.

"No promises," she said. Then she returned to her horse and swung back into her saddle.

Doctor Morgan smiled and waved as the girls rode off. Then he went back into his house.

The girls rode for hours, stopping once for a few minutes to eat a meal and feed and water the animals before mounting again. Once it had gotten late, they decided it was best to make camp rather than ride in the dark. Anna fed and cared for their animal companions, Lena took care of the horses and mules, Karmina set up the camp, Nori made a fire, Sloan caught their dinner, and Estrella filled their waterskins for the night. After they ate dinner, they all went to their tents. Estrella lit a small candle next to her mat, got out her parchment and quill, and began to write home.

She sealed the letter to her mother and placed it aside for the morning, and then she began to write to her brother, as follows:

> Dear Gideon,
>
> It has come to my attention that I have forgotten to write Mother lately. I am assuming that the same is true for you. I also assume that you have received the same letter from Maia requesting more letters. She worries about us so. We should try to keep better in touch with her. I hate to hear Mother worried in the letters she sends me.
>
> Yours truly,
>
> Estrella

She rolled and sealed that letter and placed it aside with the first one. Then she blew out her candle and lay down to sleep for the night.

The next morning when Estrella awoke to the first rays of sunlight, she sent Merlin off to deliver her letters. After the girls had finished their breakfast meal, Estrella left to wash the dishes. She felt the stir of her spirit again when she noticed a lovely young woman sitting down by the water with a palette of paints and an easel. Estrella set down her dishes and sat down to watch the beautiful young painter work. She heard the Lord whisper, "She is your sixth. She needs your joy and adventure as her inspiration."

Estrella smiled.

When Estrella did not return to camp with the dishes, the girls became worried and went searching for her. They found her hiding behind a bush and spying on someone.

"Estrella, what are you doing? You had us worried," said Karmina.

"Hush and get down here. She might see you," whispered Estrella.

"Who might see us?" asked Anna, crouching down.

"That lovely young artist over there," mentioned Estrella.

"Oh my, she is lovely," agreed Lena.

"Look at her hair. It's the same color as the sunlight. It even looks like it has some pink and blue in it," Estrella remarked.

"Do you think she is the next member of our group?" asked Sloan.

"I believe so. Why else would the Lord make us stop where and when we did? But joining us is her choice, remember. Maybe now we should introduce ourselves, slowly and one at a time, before she notices us or leaves," Estrella replied. Then she stood up from behind the bush, collected the dishes, and made her way to the stream. She knelt down and started to rinse the dishes, calmly speaking to the painter, "You're quite the artist."

"Thank you," the girl replied, not looking away from her canvas.

"May I ask your name?"

"It's Luanna Daley."

"It's very nice to meet you, Luanna. My name is Princess Estrella. May I ask what it is you are painting?"

"It was the stream and fish, but then I started painting a young princess hiding behind the bushes watching me. Now it's a young princess washing dishes in front of me, so please stop moving so much," Luanna remarked with a laugh.

"You were painting me?" Estrella asked, shocked.

"You were in my line of sight, and you are most beautiful to paint."

"Thank you. You are quite lovely as well. Would you like to meet my friends? They are waiting behind that bush to meet you."

"Once I finish. I would go a lot faster if you would stop talking, please. And you don't need to reply."

Estrella just smiled as Luanna finished with her painting. Then she placed it aside, with the other two.

"You can call your friends over now," she said with a smile.

Estrella sat back up and motioned for the others to come over. The other girls saw that Estrella had made sure it was okay to come, so they calmly approached.

"Luanna, these are my friends. First is Karmina Algur."

"Nice to meet you," said Karmina.

"Next is Sloan Ailes," Estrella said, motioning toward Sloan.

"How do you do?" said Sloan.

"Next up are Lena Acosta, Anna-Mika Barnett, and Nori Becker."

"It's a pleasure to meet you all. Would you like to see my paintings?" Luanna said as she stood up.

"Yes, please. Will you show us what you were working on?" asked Karmina. Luanna showed them the three paintings. In the first one, of the stream, it seemed as if the fish were jumping right off the canvas. In the second one, they could see Estrella peeking innocently over the bush. And the third one really captured the princess's beauty, with a glow behind her as she looked down at the dishes in the stream.

"Luanna, those are amazing paintings. You have quite a gift," remarked Estrella.

"Thank you, Your Highness."

"Please call me Estrella. Do you know of a town we can stay in?" Estrella asked.

"Of course. You can stay with me in my village. My little house might be a bit small for all of us, but I believe we can make something work," she replied. "Oh, wait, I forgot to call for my dog. She is out for a run around. Let me call her.

"Kiva!"

"What kind of a dog is Kiva?" asked Estrella.

"Well, she is somewhat of a misfit. I will explain more once she gets here," Luanna said, looking around. "Where could that little creature be?" Then a pair of pointed ears appeared over the top of a small glen. Luanna smiled. "Kiva Daley, get over here. We have guests, and it's time to head home."

The "dog" Kiva ran over to the group, wagging her tail with a fish in her mouth.

"She is very pretty," remarked Anna-Mika.

"Now that you can see her, I will explain what she is. She is a coywolf. Her mother was a coyote and her father was a wolf, so she is a bit of a misfit. She is half coyote. Her father, being a wolf, didn't like coyotes much, so he killed most of the pups of Kiva's litter. Kiva's mother was able to save her. She ran off to hide Kiva and raise her until she was able to take care of herself. I found her about four years ago, when we bonded. She catches my dinner for me, and I give her a home," explained Luanna.

"Wow, she is very beautiful, and rare. You are very lucky and blessed to have each other," said Estrella. "May we fetch our companions and horses before we head out?"

"Of course. Kiva and I will wait for you here," Luanna replied.

The girls returned to camp. After an hour, they returned to the stream with their horses, carts, and extras.

"How far is your village?" asked Karmina.

"Not far, really. Just over the next hill. You will know you are there when you see it," she explained. As they walked, the girls looked down in wonder at the coywolf's steps in front of them. With every step she took, little white flowers sprang up behind her and made a trail that looked like snow.

"Lu, do you know about Kiva's special ability?" asked Estrella.

Luanna looked back at the trail her companion was making behind them, and smiled. "Yes, I have known about Kiva's 'flowers' for quite some time. I realized it when I found her. She was lying in a bed of those little white flowers. At the time I thought she had found the flowers to lie in. When she followed me and I saw the trail behind her, I knew there was something more about her that drew me to her."

"Well, she is quite special and rare," remarked Karmina.

"Much like her lovely owner," added Anna-Mika.

"You guys are very nice." Luanna blushed.

They had just crested the hill when they saw the colorful town in front of them. It was glowing brightly with many colors.

"Is that your home?" asked Sloan.

"Yes, that is my village."

"Wow, it's gorgeous," remarked Lena.

"Thank you. It's even prettier up close. Shall we go, then?"

"Of course. Lead the way," replied Estrella. The girls followed behind Luanna to her home village.

CHAPTER 26

Celebration of Color

Estrella, Sloan, Karmina, Lena, Nori, and Anna-Mika followed Luanna down the little hill to the brightly colored village with little cottages. The path in front of them looked like it was painted as well, but it was only covered in petals from the flowers planted along the roadside. When they came to a town sign, Luanna introduced them to the town.

"Welcome, my friends, to Itzel!" She beamed with pride in her home.

"Itzel? What does that mean?" asked Nori.

"*Itzel* means 'rainbow.' You can see why."

"Oh, it's very beautiful," remarked Karmina.

"Let me just warn you, the people of Itzel may look strange to you, but to us it is normal. And to my people, you outsiders are the strange ones for being so plain. And today we are celebrating our town holiday. We call it the Celebration of Color. You are welcome to attend if you like," Luanna explained.

"I think it would be a great idea to attend your celebration. It would be an opportunity to see what others celebrate," offered Estrella.

"Oh, I'm so glad. Follow me. We will put your horses away in our barn and then get the rest of you situated," said Luanna, leading them through town. She hadn't been joking when she said that the people of Itzel were strange-looking. Their faces were painted like flowers, rainbows, and sunshine. Bright colors were painted into their hair, and they were wearing flashy and flamboyant colorful outfits. They all smiled when they saw Luanna coming, but their expressions turned quizzical and perplexed when they saw the other girls following behind her.

"I feel like a fish out of water," remarked Lena.

"I feel the same, so out of place—and underdressed," added Anna-Mika.

"I feel like some strange, rare creature," Sloan said, concurring.

"Trust me, once they meet you, they will welcome you with open arms and you will feel like a local," said Luanna. She led them to a barn and helped them put away their horses, mules, and carts.

After that, she led them to her own house. Luanna's cottage was painted like a daisy; the roof was painted yellow and the walls were painted white. It was quite the quaint little house. On the inside it had two bedrooms, a kitchen, a sitting room, and an art room. And every room had a window. Estrella wondered who else lived there. There were two rooms but she saw only Luanna, and Kiva.

"Luanna, who else lives here with you?" she asked.

"It's just Kiva and me. I lived in this house with my mother and father many years ago. My mother was also a great artist, and a seamstress here in Itzel. My father was a visiting prince who fell in love with my mother and married her. We lived here for ten years, and then my mother became ill and passed away. My father wanted me to come with him when he returned to his home kingdom, but I said that I wanted to stay with my own people and that I could take care of myself. So I stayed. And I have lived here on my own since," Luanna shared with them.

"I am sorry to hear about your mother," said Nori.

"It's all right. We all pass away sometime. It was just her time, I suppose. She loved me and taught me so much that I can still feel her near, in my heart."

"That is beautiful," said Sloan, wiping tears from her eyes.

"Thank you. You may share my old room on the left, and you are welcome to spread out in the sitting room—if you don't mind sleeping on the dirt. All the houses have dirt floors."

"You are very kind just to open your house to us," Estrella said in gratitude.

"It's not a problem at all. I am just showing the love of the Lord Almighty by welcoming strangers. I'm sure you would do the same for me if I came to your homes," replied Luanna kindly.

"I am certain we would," Estrella said.

"So, Lu, tell us about your Celebration of Color What exactly does it celebrate? What do you do?" asked Karmina.

"The Celebration of Color celebrates two things. First, it celebrates the third day of creation, when God made vegetation—the trees and flowers. And the second part of it celebrates the last day of the great forty-day flood, when Noah sent out the dove and it came back with the olive leaf, and then the Lord promised with a rainbow never to flood the earth again. We celebrate with a performance of those days, and we finish with dancing and by throwing flower seeds and petals," Luanna explained.

The door opened. A young girl with green in her hair and vines painted on her arms and face came in.

"Peony where have you been? Brenin was wondering if you forgot your part in the celebration this year," said the girl.

"I did not forget. What did Aerowyn say?" Luanna said to the girl.

"She knew you wouldn't have forgotten. She said that you were busy refreshing you soul."

"She always speaks poetically."

"That she does."

The girls just stood there staring at the two girls chatting, until Luanna noticed and smiled.

"This is my friend Ivy. And this is what I was talking about: everybody gets painted up for the celebration," she explained.

"I see. Why did she call you Peony? I thought your name was Luanna," said Estrella.

"It is. In Itzel, everyone has a name that indicates a plant or a color. Luanna is the name my father gave me; Peony is the name that the people of Itzel gave me."

"I see. That's very interesting. Well, we will set up our things and let you and Ivy get ready. Would you mind if I took a walk around for a bit?" Estrella said.

"Of course. Ivy will come get you when it's time to get ready for the celebration. Don't wander off too far." Luanna smiled.

After setting up her mat on the sitting room floor, Estrella, despite the girls' protests, went outside for a short walk around and to get a good look at the beautiful village and surroundings. She was sitting down on a small hill enjoying the clouds and open sky when she saw a welcome sight, her falcon Merlin flying over. Then another familiar sight crossed her field of vision and intercepted Merlin in flight. It was the beautiful eagle Elder that belonged to her brother, Gideon. Her brother's eagle flew over with a message in his beak as he locked talons with her falcon. He always picked fights with Merlin, seeing himself as the superior. Estrella smiled at the sight of the two, and whistled for their attention. They heard the whistle and flew down to her.

"Elder, old friend, it's good to see you. How is Gideon?" She smiled, striking up a conversation with the beautiful bird of prey. If anyone from the village had seen her, they first would have thought she was being attacked by the birds, and then that she was crazy for talking to them.

{"It is good to see you as well, Estrella. Gideon is just fine; he sends you this letter,"} replied the eagle, reaching for the parchment and handing it to her.

Estrella took the rolled scroll from the bird and thanked him. Then she read as follows:

> Dear Sister,
>
> I have no doubt that you have received a letter from Mother just as I have. She has not worried about us this much before. I have a feeling that there is something or someone at home that is upsetting her, news that she doesn't want to trouble us with. I think you know who it is. We should write home to let her know we are safe and to keep her from worrying so much. She has enough to worry about as it is what with running the kingdom on her own, our being absent, and Kylia and Keena growing up. I pray that our letters of reassurance will bring her some peace. I think about you out on your own, and I remember how strong and independent you can be. Please keep safe. After you write to Mother, write me back. I would love to hear how your adventure is going.
>
> Sincerely yours,
>
> Gideon

Estrella smiled, placing the letter next to her. "Did he write Mother back?" she asked Elder.

{"He did, right after he wrote your letter. He will be waiting for my return to send the letter home to your mother,"} replied Elder.

"Very well. You best return to him quickly so you don't keep Mother waiting for the reply. Let Gideon know that I received his letter. I will send Merlin back with my reply."

{"Thank you, Estrella. I hope you stay safe,"} Elder replied. Then he flew off, heading back to his master. Estrella sighed. Knowing that her mother was upset and didn't want her upset made her upset. There was one person who could make her mother upset like that, and Estrella didn't care for him.

Merlin decided it would be best to break his mistress's frustration by whining, {"I... I think he hurt my wing."}

"He barely touched your wing. If anything, he gently scratched your leg when he locked talons with you."

{"Then he broke my leg..."}

"He did not break your leg. It's not even bleeding. You complain too much for a bird of prey."

{"He hates me; he has had it out for me ever since I hatched."}

"Nonsense. He loves you as Gideon loves me, as a brother. Brothers play rough with you when they love you."

{"He doesn't have to love me so rough, though."}

"Are you really hurt? Can you still fly?"

{"I'm fine. I just needed to get your mind off of *him*."}

"I know; *he* has always been an issue with me."

{"Then forget about *him*. Put him out of your mind. You are far away from him, on your own and finding the lost for the Savior. Get up and join the others."}

"How did you become my encourager?"

{"I learned from you."} They were smiling—if it was possible for a bird to smile—and talking when a young girl with long green-painted hair and brown bark-like clothes approached them.

"Are you Estrella?" the girl asked.

"I am. What's your name?" Estrella said in return.

"My name is Willow. Peony sent me out here to find you so I could bring you back and get you ready for the celebration."

"Well then, lead the way. I wouldn't want to be late for my first Celebration of Color festival," Estrella said, tucking the letter in her tunic and getting off the ground. Merlin followed as she walked.

"Tell me, Estrella, do all girls look like you do where you're from?" asked Willow, glancing at the princess's tunic and trousers.

"No. The place where I am from is a kingdom. I am a princess. So I am more used to wearing long beautiful gowns."

"If you are a princess, then what brings you all the way out here to Itzel?"

"The Lord's will. I heard the Lord calling me to find new friends and to find the lost. And the Lord prompted me to find and meet your Peony. I am hoping she will consider coming with my friends and me to become our new friend and sister."

"As much as we would hate to lose our best artist, and Holly's daughter, a new family is just what Peony needs."

"Well, I hope you can help us persuade her tomorrow to follow us."

Estrella followed Willow back to the Luanna's home, where the other girls were getting painted and put into colorful costumes by other girls with wild makeup on.

"I found Estrella. What did you have in mind for her, Peony?" asked Willow.

"I see her as more of a Jasmine. Her costume and paints are ready by her cot, Willow, if you want to get her ready," instructed Luanna, who was painting maple leaves on Sloan.

"May I ask who you are going to be?" Estrella asked Sloan.

"She is going to be Autumn. She can't speak while I paint her, as it will mess up her leaves. I will get to your face paint once I finish up with Anna's, or Rose's. I have already painted Karmina's, who is now Poppy, and Lena's, who is now Heather. Next I will paint Nori as Cherry," Luanna said.

"I see. Well, I won't disturb the master at her work any longer. Willow, will you help me fit into this beautiful costume?"

"Of course," replied Willow, helping Estrella out of her current outfit. When Willow saw the leather sleeve that Estrella was wearing under her tunic, she was dismayed again. "What is this?" she asked.

"Oh, please do keep that on. That's my protection. I hold my companion Merlin on that arm."

"And who is Merlin?" asked Willow.

"He is her falcon; he follows her everywhere," replied Poppy/Karmina.

"Oh, I see. Well, I will leave it on then," said Willow, helping Estrella put on the rest of her costume. When she was finished, Estrella was in a frilly green gown with little white flowers popping up all over it. And when Luanna had finished with the other girls and had completed Estrella's face paint, they were all ready for the festival, looking like a beautiful flower garden.

All dressed up and painted, the group of girls left for the town square, where they would wait for the play to begin.

The play started out with five small children playing the part of the seeds that the Lord planted. Once they sprouted and blossomed into flowers and trees, the scene changed. There was now water all around and a big ark. A man stepped out of the ark and looked around for land. Then Luanna came out dressed as a dove. She "flew" off and came back with a leaf. Then seven girls dressed in rainbow colors and trailing silk scarves behind them came out and cartwheeled across the square.

After the demonstrations, Estrella decided that now, before the rest of the festivities started, would be a good time to ask Luanna to join her and her group. Seeing Luanna go into her house, she decided to follow her. She went up to the door and knocked. "Uh, Peony? It's me, Peony."

"Come in, Estrella. I'm just changing into my dance costume."

Estrella pushed the door open and stepped inside. "You did quite well out there. Then again, it was my first Celebration of Color show. I bet you do well every year."

"Thank you. It's quite an honor to be picked to play the part of the dove."

"Lu, I have something I have been meaning to ask you," Estrella said in a more serious tone.

"Oh?" asked Luanna, sitting down to lace up her slippers.

"I know that Itzel is your home. It is where you grew up, and you know everyone here. But you live alone. I know you are probably used to it, but it must get awfully lonely. So what I am trying to ask you is if you would consider starting a new adventure in your life with us and joining us as our new sister. We'd like you to become part of our family, follow us, and stay with us. Take tonight to think it over. Tomorrow when we are packing up, you can give us your answer," said Estrella. Then she made for the door.

When she was about to open the door, it seemed to open on its own. On the other side stood a tall young man painted completely in gold. He was smiling at her.

"Oh!" remarked Estrella.

"Well, hello there. Judging by what you are dressed as, I would say you must be Jasmine," he said.

"I suppose I am," Estrella replied, still dismayed by the golden young man in front of her.

"Then you are exactly whom I was hoping to dance with. Peony, would you mind if I borrowed this flower from your garden?" he asked.

"No, of course not. Go right ahead. I will see you later, Jasmine. Go enjoy the festival," said Luanna.

The young man held out his hand to escort Estrella back outside. She accepted his hand and started walking with him.

"I'm sorry, I didn't quite catch your name," she said.

"Of course not. That's my fault, as I forgot to give it to you. Please don't tell my mother I forgot my manners and didn't introduce myself. My name is Orel," he said.

"I won't tell your mother, Orel. What did you mean when you said that I was exactly the person you were looking for?"

"I saw you follow Peony out of her house for the show. You caught my eye. So when you followed her back to her house, I felt compelled to follow you so I could meet you."

"Really, I caught your eye?"

"Yes. Is it true that you are a princess?" he asked her.

She pulled back, almost disgusted. "Is that the only reason why you wanted to dance with me, because I am a princess?"

"No, of course not. You are also very beautiful."

"Oh, so it's about beauty and title. Well, I'm sorry, Orel, but I'm going to pass on this dance. Besides, I can't dance. I will only slow you down," Estrella said, letting go of Orel's hand and walking away.

"You're making a big mistake, Jasmine. My family is the wealthiest in this town. We would have made a good dancing couple!" he yelled after her, indignant.

Once Estrella was some distance away, she sat down by herself, feeling very hurt and used. Five minutes later, another young man, this one half painted in black, walked up to her.

"My lady, my name is Cole. I was hoping to have the honor of being your escort for the rest of the festivities," he said with a smile.

"Please tell me you don't want to dance with me just because I am princess."

"Of course not, my lady. Your title makes no difference to me. Orel thinks that because he comes from money, he can have anything he wants. I saw how hurt you looked when you were with him. I know how to treat a lady such as you with respect. We don't even have to dance if you don't want to."

"Thank you, Cole. That's very kind of you." She smiled, standing up to follow him.

"May I ask for your real name, my lady?" he said, offering his arm.

"Estrella Sela of Faylin." she replied, accepting his arm, and interlocking hers with his.

"Well, Estrella, let me be your guide to Itzel." He smiled as he began to show her around, explaining their traditions and festivities while walking her through town. At the end of the day, they returned to Luanna's house.

"You are quite captivating, my lady Estella Sela of Faylin."

"And you have been such a wonderful escort and gentleman, Cole of Itzel."

"I wanted to show you the real Itzel, and that not all the young men here are like Orel."

"You proved that well, but you know that I can't stay here. My girls and I are leaving tomorrow."

"I know. I will remember the beautiful, captivating princess. Please try to write me and remember me."

"I will. Thank you for the lovely day," she said. Then she slipped inside the house, went to her room, and changed into her nightclothes, ignoring the whispers from the other girls about her escort. When she was ready for bed, she crawled under her blanket, curled up, and slept well for the first time in days.

CHAPTER 27

Minotaur

The next day after they all awoke, the girls packed up their things and saddled up their horses. As they were about to leave, Luanna ran out to see them.

"Estrella! Estrella, wait. I thought it over last night. I would like to join you, if it's not too late."

"Not at all. If you have your belongings packed, we have a horse, a cart, and a mule all ready for you," Estrella said with a smile.

"You knew I was going to join you? What if I had declined?"

"She bought horses for any new girls who would join us. If you didn't join us, someone else would get the horse," remarked Anna.

"But... I had a feeling you wanted to join us. So pick out your horse and get your things together. Then we will be on our way," Estrella said.

Luanna walked over to where Lena stood with the last two horses, the gray Lusitano and the white Lipizzaner. They were both beautiful mares and lovely animals, but Luanna chose the Lusitano. After making her decision, she strapped the saddle to the horse. Then she got some help from some of the local boys, Cole included, to bring out her things and load them into the cart. The boys loaded her cart, hooked it up to the mule, and tied it to her saddle. Then they bid Luanna farewell. Cole smiled at Estrella, and then the girls rode out of town, leaving Itzel behind. Luanna looked back at her past, and rode forward to her future.

"It's not too late, Lu. If you change your mind and want to go back to your old life, you can go back. You don't have to come with us. It's still your choice. I won't make you stay with us if you don't want to," Estrella said, comforting her.

"No, it's all right. I have made my decision to join you. Besides, I can't start the new chapter of my life if I'm stuck on the last one. And you can't make a new piece of art if you keep painting on the first one. You need a new canvas. This journey is my canvas, and you girls are my new paints and colors, with which I'll make my most remembered masterpieces," Luanna said with a confident smile.

"That's the spirit," Estrella cheered.

They traveled for a few hours, the veterans talking about the adventures they'd already had, and the whole group imagining the adventures that would come.

Estrella spotted something about one mile away from them in an open field. It appeared to be two men on horseback carrying a large cage with some kind of animal inside. She couldn't tell what it was, but something in her told her that that the creature was not bad and had done nothing to deserve being caged up. She halted her horse, held very still, and thought of a plan.

Sloan, the first one to notice that their leader had stopped, halted the rest of the girls.

"What is she doing?" asked Luanna. Being the newest member, she wasn't yet aware of Estrella's quirks.

"She sees something," replied Sloan.

"Where? I can't see anything, or anyone else but us, out here."

Sloan, staring out in the direction Estrella was facing, saw the figures off in the distance. "I see two figures ahead of us. Not sure what or who they are," Sloan said.

"Two men on horseback," said Estrella to no one.

"How can she...?" whispered Luanna.

"You learn that it is best not to question Estrella. Some things she just knows, and some things she can just see better than others," replied Karmina.

"Oh," said Luanna in response.

"Are they a threat to us?" asked Sloan.

"No, but they are carrying something in a cage."

"Then they must be hunters with their game," said Nori.

"No, if it were game, it would be dead. This creature is alive—and it's not happy."

"What is your plan of action?" Sloan asked Estrella.

"Disable the captors and liberate the prisoner."

"What?! You just said that it wasn't happy, and you want to free whatever it is? Are you serious? What if it is dangerous?" exclaimed a frantic Luanna.

"You guys, focus on disabling the captors. Leave the prisoner to me. Sloan, do you think you can hit one from here?" said Estrella.

"I don't think so; we are too far away. If we hide the horses and carts and make our way through the forest, we can plan our attack strategy," Sloan suggested.

"Are we really going to attack some people we don't know, and set free some creature we don't know either?" asked Luanna.

"You learn to just go with her plans. They always work out," Karmina explained.

The girls hid their horses and carts behind some trees and then proceeded to make their way toward the captors.

Once they were about 12 feet away from them, Sloan inquired, "All right, what's your plan, Estrella?"

"We are going to stage a 'damsel in distress' scenario. Lena, you will be our damsel. We will have you pretend to be tied to a tree. Lu, I will need your art skills to paint a dragon approaching her. Anna, Nori, Karmina, and I will supply the dragon sounds and smells for our painted dragon."

"What do you want me to do?" asked Sloan.

"You are going to get the men's attention. When everyone is ready and they are close enough, fire two warning shots in front of their horses to catch their attention. Then let the show begin," Estrella explained with a smirk on her face and a silver glint in her eye.

"Oh no!" declared Karmina, noticing Estrella's smirk.

"Not again," said Lena.

"What do you mean?" asked Luanna.

"The last time she had that look, we had to scare Vikings out of my former hometown," explained Anna.

"You guys faced off against Vikings?!" Luanna asked, shocked.

"We will tell you all about it later, but for now know that her look means she has some kind of crazy idea. And right now we need to get into our positions," explained Karmina.

Lena ran ahead and leaned against a tree, while Luanna quickly set to work painting sections of a large dragon on different parts of trees to make the beast look real.

When the strangers were drawing close, Sloan shot two warning shots in front of them. When the shots caught the strangers' attention, the girls began to make noise and release odors that smelled like a dragon's. When the two riders caught sight of the "dragon" and the "damsel," their manly instincts kicked in. They rushed to the aid of the poor girl, dropping their cage. Once they drew closer to the "damsel," the other girls advanced on them from the trees and overtook them, surrounding them. Their companions also surrounded the captors.

The men didn't stand a chance.

It was only when they saw Estrella approach the cage that they spoke.

"No, miss! Don't go near him. He is dangerous!" said the first captor.

"What has he done?" asked Estrella, still approaching the cage.

"That monster terrorized our village and stole our princess," said the other.

"Did you see him leave the forest or be anywhere near your village or your princess?" she asked as she drew closer.

"No. Miss, you don't understand. He is a dangerous beast. Our village has had mysterious things occurring at night, and our princess has gone missing," said the first man.

"And because you knew there was this thing living in the woods, you just blamed it all on him? Have you ever thought that maybe the strange occurrences and damage could have been caused by children or some rival village? Did you think that maybe your princess ran off with someone?" she scolded them.

Estrella reached the cage. What she saw was not a horrible dangerous beast but a frightened creature of the Lord. It was a Minotaur, and he was scared and lost. She went to open the latch. The captors didn't know which they feared most, or which they should take a chance on, the young ladies and fierce animals surrounding them or the raging beast the crazy girl was going to unleash, which would surely pursue them for capturing him. So they took a chance on their escape.

After managing to get away from the girls, the men rode off.

"Estrella, they got away. Would you like me to take out their horses?" asked Sloan.

"No, those men are not our problem. Let's get our friend out of his prison," she replied, opening the cage.

The Minotaur jumped out of the cage and roared and growled. The other girls turned to scream and run away, but Estrella just stood there with a stern look on her face. She looked at the creature with her arms crossed, waiting for him to settle down a bit.

"What is she doing?!" whispered Luanna. "Isn't she terrified? That thing could kill her!"

"As long as we have known her, nothing has really scared her," replied Karmina.

"Are you quite finished?" Estrella asked the creature calmly, like a parent talking to a youngster after the latter threw a tantrum.

{"Y-you... you are not afraid of me?"} it asked her, which sounded a lot like grumbling to the others.

"No. Should I be? Did you steal the princess or terrorize that village?"

{"N-n-no, I d-didn't.... I... I d-don't leave my forest. And I only see the princess w-when she goes by my forest."}

"I thought you were innocent. There is no reason for me to be scared. Do you have a name?" she asked.

{"M-m-my n-name is Duce,"} he replied.

"Duce, why are you still stammering? Are you still scared? We won't hurt you. Can you speak clearly?"

{"I th-think so."}

"Try for me, please."

{"You are very beautiful,"} he complimented.

"Not only can you speak well, but also you flirt with me?"

{"It's not flirting. You are very beautiful. May I meet my beautiful saviors?"}

"Girls, come here, please. He is not dangerous. In fact, he is quite kind and friendly."

Luanna was very confused. She was witnessing her leader, her new friend, actually having a conversation with this creature, as if she could understand him and as if the two knew each other.

"Is she actually talking to it?"

"Yes. That's Estrella for you," replied Karmina.

"Does she always talk to animals—and understand them like that?"

"Yep. We can't explain it either, but there is something about her that makes her able to talk to and understand creatures," explained Sloan.

The girls noticed that Estrella and the beast had stopped talking and that Estrella was calling them over, so they all carefully and cautiously approached, their companions following behind very protectively.

"Girls, this is my new friend, Duce. He is very kind. Duce, my name is Princess Estrella, and these are my friends who helped me save you: Karmina, Sloan, Lena, Nori, Anna-Mika, and Luanna."

{"Princess, you and your friends are lovely beyond compare,"} he said, bowing graciously.

Once Estrella translated his remarks, the girls all blushed.

"Duce, you are too kind," replied Karmina.

"You are the nicest Minotaur I have ever met," replied Lena.

"He is the only Minotaur we have ever met," Sloan said.

"That doesn't mean that he is not the nicest. I am sure if we ever meet any other Minotaurs, he would still be the kindest," countered Nori.

{"Ladies, you have all been very kind to a lowly creature such as me. I am forever in your debt. If I can be of any assistance at any time, you have my vow that I will help you."}

Estrella explained what he had said, and they all nodded their approval.

"Thank you, Sir Duce. We are very grateful. I would give you a favor, but I am afraid they would think you stole it and come after you. So please kneel and accept this kiss as my token of appreciation. Then go and hide yourself well," Estrella said graciously.

Duce knelt down and bowed his head humbly. Estrella leaned down, placed a kiss on his big fuzzy bull head, and then asked him to rise.

{"Thank you, Princess. I will forever remember the brave princess and her warriors who saved the lowly Minotaur and treated him like a prince instead of a monster,"} said Duce. He gave a bow before departing.

"Why did you kiss him?" asked Luanna.

"All of God's creatures deserve love and kindness. Even those that others see as monsters have hearts. And a simple kiss is the greatest favor I could give him," she replied, walking back to her horse. They reached their horses.

"So, Luanna, I don't believe you shared with us what you named your horse," said Karmina.

"I completely forgot. I was so distracted and caught up in our mission that I forgot to share her name. I named her Artemis. She looks like a beautiful goddess," responded Luanna, as she mounted. Then the girls rode off, continuing their journey.

CHAPTER 28

Sera

The girls traveled for a distance until they came to a fork in the road. To the left was a bright delightful meadow; to the right, a dark and eerie twisted forest. It seemed that the meadow would be the clear and best choice, but something told Estrella that they were supposed to go right. This was the first time Estrella questioned the Spirit's leading.

"So, Estrella, are we going left?" asked Sloan.

"No, I think we go right."

"What?! Are you serious? Do you not see the same twisted forest that we all see?" asked Lena.

"I agree with Lena. Clearly we should go left. That forest looks dangerous. We can't go in there," said Anna.

"Estrella, we have faced trials and dangers, but do you really think we are supposed to go through that forest?" asked Karmina.

"I personally do not think so. I agree with you girls; the forest definitely looks scary and dangerous. But something is telling me that our path leads to the right. Why don't we just take a small break? You girls, talk among each other. I am going to pray about this decision," Estrella said, dismounting to go sit on the side of the road to pray. The girls dismounted as well, deciding to have a small meal while Estrella sat in silence to pray.

"Father, I have followed your lead and your prompting. I have trusted your Holy Spirit the whole journey. But, Lord, I have to agree with my girls. Why would you lead us to a dark, twisted forest? There is definitely a dark and evil presence in there. Why would you lead us into such a place?" After she had prayed, Estrella sat in silence to hear the voice of the Lord.

"My child, who put this fear and doubt in your heart? Surely I say to you, it is not from your Heavenly Father. Your path does not lead to the right. If you follow that which seems more pleasant, you will not be following the plan I have set for you. There is someone lost to the dark in those woods. She is your seventh. It has been many years since she has seen my light. You are her only chance at freedom. If you don't go, she is lost to me. Have no fear, for the will of God will not lead you where the grace of God cannot protect you. Did not my Son's disciples doubt his power and sanity when he freed the man from the demon Legion? Did not David the psalmist write, 'Even though I walk through the Valley of the Shadow of Death, I will fear no evil, for you are with me'? Now then, my child, tell me: if I am with you, what do you fear?" spoke the Lord to her heart.

And her heart spoke without her mouth even moving. "Nothing!" Smiling, she felt the sun come upon her, which filled her with love. She stood up, brushed herself off, and called out to her "disciples." Once they had gathered, she said, "Mount up, everyone. Our journey leads to the right, so we go right."

"You are sure of this, Estrella?" asked Sloan.

"Yes. It is the Lord's will."

"The Lord wouldn't send us someplace where we could be in danger," said Nori.

"The will of God would not send us where the grace of God could not protect us."

"But, Estrella—" Lena started to protest.

"'Even though I walk through the Valley of the Shadow of Death, I will fear no evil, for my Lord is with me!' David the king, and writer of the psalms, said our Lord God Almighty is greater that he who is in these woods. He who is with us is greater. If the Lord is in you, what do you fear? So I say to you, is the Lord in you?" Estrella asked of her disciples.

The girls gave out a collective sigh, knowing that when Estrella quoted scripture, any further arguments were futile.

Knowing that the girls would not have followed her this far if the Lord was not in them, again Estrella asked, "Is the Lord in you?"

"Yes!" they said together.

"What do you fear?"

"Nothing!" they shouted, their confidence growing.

"Who is with me?"

"I am!" they each answered. Then they all mounted their horses and followed Estrella boldly into the woods.

As they entered the woods, their loyalty didn't change, but their courage did waver as their surroundings changed drastically. Once they went from bright blissful day to the dark, twisted, and marred woods, where the trees seemed to have twisted and split in pain, the girls became uneasy. Their dread increased the farther they traveled. The woods got darker and darker and more twisted. They had to light lanterns to guide their way.

The group came to a stop when they saw a sign that read, "Trespassers will be imprisoned, and traitors will be punished."

"Estrella, we fully trust you and the Lord, but don't you think that if an actual sign is telling us not to enter, we should take it as a warning?" asked Anna.

"She is right. Signs usually tell you the truth," said a small voice from somewhere in the trees. The girls looked around nervously, but Estrella just shrugged it off.

"If we heeded warning signs, Anna, you wouldn't be with us, remember," remarked Estrella.

"Oh, she has a point there," chimed another voice.

"They shouldn't be here; it is too dangerous," commented a third voice.

"But what if she is the one, the one to free us?" said a fourth.

"The prophecy is just an old legend made up by an old man who was too crazy for his own good," grumbled a fifth voice.

"You are an old man," said the fourth.

"I *was* an old man. Now I am an old tree man," said the fifth.

"The prophecy said this would happen, but no one listened to it—and now look at us," said the second voice.

"But the prophecy spoke of a savior who would bring back the light, break the curse, free the captives, and save the princess," said the hopeful fourth.

"She is too young; she can't be older than our princess. She can't be the one," quipped the skeptical fifth.

"You have not even given her a chance yet. We have lost too many to wait for another chance. The others have been locked up, turned to stone, or possessed with the desire to kill us," said the troubled second.

There were so many voices around them arguing and talking that the girls became scared and confused, but Estrella kept her composure. She smiled and answered the voices. "I might be the savior, but I would have to know what happened first. Why don't you come out of hiding and tell the story, please?"

"Silence. She has heard us. Now we are in trouble," snapped the fifth.

"We cannot come out, miss," said the compassionate fourth.

"Why not? What has you so scared that you won't come out?" she asked kindly.

"Lift your lantern a little higher and you will find out why we can't come out. Then maybe I will share our story," said the second.

So Estrella and the girls lifted their lanterns. The girls gasped. Estrella was saddened when she saw faces in all the trees surrounding them. No wonder the trees were in pain: there were people imprisoned inside the trees themselves. "What happened to you?" asked Estrella.

"It was four years ago, at our daughter's thirteenth birthday. The celebration was beautiful. All our townspeople came to celebrate. Seeing as our daughter was well loved, there were many presents. Some shadowed figure showed up once all the presents had already been opened. He presented our daughter with a strange box, telling her it would make her wildest dreams come true. I did not trust it; it was dark and decorated with bones. But she was so excited about her birthday and caught up in the lie, that her wildest dreams would come true, that she opened it. Once she did, it released all kinds of demons and spirits. She became possessed by them after looking into it. Her father, her siblings, and I, her mother, fled from the castle. The ones who couldn't flee the village quickly enough became stone statues. The ones who escaped the village but not the forest became imprisoned in the trees. Only a very few escaped the forest," said the mother tree.

"You said that you lost some and that some of the saviors were possessed with the desire to kill. What did you mean by that?" Estrella asked.

This time it was the father tree who replied. He said, "Young men have come, found out the secret, and vowed to save us, but they failed. They were thrown into the dungeon, which she made them dig, or else were turned to stone. Others were possessed and made to chop down one of the trees. Last time we lost her brother. If you chop down a tree without us being released, we perish."

"That's terrible," said Sloan.

"What must I do?" asked Estrella. All the girls looked at her in shock.

"Are you crazy?! Didn't you just hear what happened to the others who tried to break the curse?" exclaimed Luanna.

"Yes, I heard."

"And you still want to go? You don't know what we are walking into!" said Anna.

"Yes, I want to go. We have to."

"What if you are not the savior?" asked the father tree.

"I am not the savior. The Savior of all people, if they accept him, is the Lord Jesus Christ. He died to take away our sins; He is the Way, the Truth, and the Life. He is the Light of the World. I was called by the Lord, the almighty Father in heaven, to show your daughter the way, to speak and bring forth the truth of her fallen nature, and to bring life back to this place. I am the one to bring the light back and to break through the dark," Estrella proclaimed confidently.

"Then you are the one. And if you say all that to her, you will prove you are the one," stated the mother tree.

"I will," Estrella replied. Then she turned to her girls. "It is your choice. It will be dangerous and risky to go where I am going, so you may stay and wait here. Or you may come with me and help me break this curse."

"I will go," pledged Sloan.

"'I will follow," said Luanna.

"I will go," vowed Karmina.

"Thank you, my friends. And you three, Lena, Nori, and Anna, what say you?"

"I will stay and wait," answered Lena.

"I will stay and wait," answered Nori.

"I will stay and wait," answered Anna.

"Very well. I honor your decision. It is not cowardly or weak," she reassured the three, placing her hand on each of their shoulders in turn. Then she turned to the who had agreed to follow her. "Let us go into the darkness to bring back the light." Addressing Lena, Nori, and Anna, she said, "You three watch our carts for us." And then the group of four rode off to the center of the woods.

Once they arrived, they instantly saw signs of the enemy's work. There were statues of the unfortunate ones who had tried to flee but had not been fast enough to get away. The buildings were marked with reverse crucifixes, and there were fire spouts where fountains used to be.

"Be of great courage, sisters, for the Lord of our faith goes before us as we walk bravely into the den of wolves."

The girls dismounted, and held hands as they walked into the manor. They saw more statues and a girl in a deep red dress sitting on a throne. There was a dark spirit surrounding her, and another dark figure was standing next to her. She had pale white skin with black paint on her face. Her hair was black and straight, and her eyes were a haunting yellow as she glared at the girls approaching her throne.

"I am Sera D'Aubigny, High Ruler of Alameda. Who are you, and why have you come here?" she hissed.

"My name is Estrella Sela. I come in the name of the Lord Jesus Christ to bring you to the light and save you from the dark."

"What makes you believe that *I* need to be saved or that *you* are the one who can save me?" she snarled back.

"Your family is worried about you, Sera."

"I should have chopped them all down years ago," she hissed.

"I was sent here by the Lord Almighty to bring the light back to this place and show you the truth."

"How dare you use that name here?" snapped the dark figure, going for a lunge.

Estrella's hand reached for her sword. "I and my friends request a *private* audience with Her Majesty the High Ruler," Estrella calmly requested.

"Your Highness, I strongly urge you to reconsider. You need me by your side," the figure said to Sera, sneering at Estrella.

"*I* don't need anyone! *I am* the high ruler! You are only my advisor, and I can easily terminate you, just like all the other useless weaklings of this village," Sera growled to the dark figure. Addressing Estrella and her three companions, Sera said, "I will have a brief meeting with you and your friends. You can have your audience with me in my chambers." She rose from her throne and led the way to her chambers. The girls followed her down a dark winding hallway to a door with dripping red paint on it. They all entered a dimly lit room. The bed was made. Beside the bed was a sculpture of a fierce-looking wolf in midlunge. Everything was painted in red and black or ripped to shreds.

"You have a lovely room, but it looks like you have not slept in your bed for a while, Your Highness," said Karmina.

"I never sleep. Sleeping gives one's enemies a chance to ensnare and take her," she hissed.

"I like you sculpture, Your Highness. Where did you get it?" asked Luanna.

"The wolf was my companion. When I gained my power, she lunged at my new advisor and thereby became the first one to feel my power," she snapped.

Estrella knew this would be her only chance to try to reach Sera, so she unsheathed her sword and slipped it through the door handles. She looked around and found a photograph covered in soot with an inscription at the bottom: "Sera D'Aubigny, age 13." When she wiped it off with her sleeve, she discovered a girl with wavy hair as red as a blaze, eyes as enchanting as emeralds, and a smile as white as pearls. She took the photograph and approached the girl.

"Your Highness, what happened to this girl?" she asked, showing her the photograph.

"Where did you find that? I thought I destroyed all the gifts I received that day," she hissed.

"What happened to her, Sera?"

"The day I opened that box and gained my power, she became imprisoned."

"Don't you think she has been imprisoned long enough? Don't you think it's time to release her?" Estrella asked, trying to reason with Sera.

"She was weak."

"She was loved."

"She was ugly."

"She was beautiful."

Estella walked over to a mirror, wiped it off, returned to Sera, and walked her over to it. Having her look into the mirror, she said, "This is not who you are. This is not who the Lord made you to be. The girl you were was his masterpiece. All you have done to that masterpiece, all you have become, is telling him that you think his most beautiful creation is dirt."

"How can he forgive the damage I have done?" she choked out.

"I can help you. But this spirit that has control over you that gave you power won't let you go without a fight. If you want to restore the masterpiece, it's going to be hard," Estrella said encouragingly.

"If it brings me forgiveness that I don't deserve, then I will do what it takes," she feebly agreed.

Estrella led the girl to a chair and had her sit down.

"It may seem like I am acting against you. The spirit will fight against what I am about to say. But if I do what I intend to do, then when the spirit comes out, it won't hurt you in the fight," Estrella explained.

"Whatever you have to do," Sera agreed.

Estrella took strips of fabric and tied Sera's hands to the armrests.

"Girls, I need you to start praying for this place, asking that the light of the Lord sweep through to cleanse it," Estrella instructed. The girls sat down and bowed their heads in prayer. Then Estrella said, "Sera, the Savior of all people, Jesus Christ, died for the sins of all humankind, both old and young, to make them new. Jesus is the way to the Father. The only way to eternal life is through acceptance of Jesus Christ as your Savior. Do you accept him?"

The spirit thrashed and wrestled Sera, but she looked up and whispered, "Yes."

"Jesus is the Truth. The truth is that some other spirit has taken control of you and filled you with lies. He has filled you with darkness, whereas Jesus is the Light of the World. In the name of Jesus Christ, the Savior, Prince of Peace, Messiah, and Holy Lamb of God, I cast out the dark spirits that lay hold of this place, and stake claim on this girl, who is solely the possession of Jesus Christ. You no longer own this girl. Come out of her, and be gone back to your abyss," Estrella commanded in the name of the Lord.

The spirit thrashed and shook, and threw Sera around in the chair. Then the girls heard the dark advisor shriek. Suddenly there was a bright light coming from the center of the room. It fell on Sera, and the dark veil of the spirit evaporated as the one true Holy Spirit descended on her. The light filled the room and spread through the whole manor, transforming the room to its former glory and loveliness. It broke the stone statues, releasing the prisoners and changing them back into the form of people. It released the family and other prisoners from the trees. Those who were newly freed jumped out and ran to the town, taking Lena, Nori, and Anna with them. The stone wolf changed back and ran to Sera playfully like a puppy, kissing her owner all over. When the light dimmed, the girls saw the real Sera D'Aubigny, the one who was in the photograph. She had tears streaming down her face from the happiness of being freed.

"Thank you very much for freeing me from the curse. It has been many years since I have seen the light of Lord," she thanked the girls, her pet in her lap.

"It was my pleasure. It was my mission to save you. The Lord led me to you," Estrella said. The girls untied Sera from the chair. Estrella took her sword from the door handles.

The family came filtering into the room as soon as Estrella removed her sword. They rushed over to Sera, embracing the daughter and sister they had lost. There was so much love it was heartwarming. For the rest of the day, there was celebrating. The whole town was overjoyed to have their princess back as the person she was meant to be. The ceremony started with honoring the ones the townspeople had lost, and then there was a grand party with dancing, singing, and laughter. The day ended with a grand feast, with Estrella and her friends as the guests of honor. When the feast was over, the food all eaten and the tables cleared, the evening moved into a comfortable pace. The townspeople talked with the girls, and Estrella talked privately with Sera's parents.

"I know your joy upon getting your daughter back. But I believe that it is my mission, now that I have found your daughter, to invite her to be my friend and disciple and follow me back to my home. I will make sure she stays on the path of righteousness. It is her choice whether to go or stay, but I would very much like your blessing."

The lord and lady smiled as they considered the proposal. They had seen this young woman risk her life and prove herself to be of great courage by saving their daughter and restoring their home.

"You have our blessing to allow Sera to accompany you. We will talk with her tonight. You will have her decision by morning," replied Lord D'Aubigny.

That night, Sera's parents sat down with her before she went to sleep. They told her how much they loved her, how glad they were to have her back, and that their home would always be her home. Then they shared Estrella's offer, saying that it was her choice to stay with them or to go and follow Estrella. Sera said she would sleep on it and give her decision in the morning. Her parents kissed her good night and left the room. After they were gone, she started packing her things. Estrella had saved her from the curse, so Sera would follow her to eternity.

What happened with Estrella that night was that she fashioned some makeshift coin purses in the hopes of preventing any thieves from stealing the girls' coins.

In the morning, Estrella and the girls stood by the door with all their gear plus some extra items packed, waiting for Sera to come out and give her decision. When Sera emerged from her room and stood in the main hall with her knapsack on, Estrella smiled, because she knew her answer. Sera kissed her parents good-bye, hugged her siblings, and smiled at her new friends as she followed Estrella out with them. Estrella led Sera to the last stall in the stable, to the beautiful white Lipizzaner.

"She is very beautiful; I don't think I could ever imagine a name worthy enough for such a beautiful horse."

"Whatever you name her, it will be worthy enough." Estrella smiled.

Sera thought about it. She wanted a name that would suit her mare. Finally deciding upon the best name, she smiled. "I know; her name will be Zeda."

"Perfect. And what about your mule? What is his name?"

"Hmm, I think it should be Bailey."

"Bailey it is! Mount up and we will be on our way."

With her belongings packed and her companion in tow, Sera D'Aubigny mounted her horse and rode away from home with her new friends.

CHAPTER 29

Robbed on the Road

The girls were now on their journey to Estrella's home. Estrella halted them halfway through the forest.

"Why did we stop?" asked Sera.

"Is there something in front of us blocking our path?" asked Anna.

"No. We stopped because we need to change our clothes," explained Estrella.

"Here?! In the middle of the forest?" asked Lena.

"We need to change our appearance. In case we come across bandits and thieves, we need to look not like young ladies with any money but like laundry maids. We will put our nice clothes and money in the bottom of our trunks and then place false bottoms atop our stuff," Estrella explained. She dismounted and started undressing.

"I have a few questions to ask," said Sera.

"All right, ask," remarked Estrella, as she was changing.

"First, when did you come up with this plan?"

"Last night."

"Last night? Really? Wow. All right, second question: where did you get the rags and the maids' outfits?"

"I asked for them from your servants," replied Estrella. She tossed the others their clothes. "We will ride our mules from here and leave our horses behind. No one would believe that laundry maids would have horses like these. When we need them, we will come back for them."

The girls dismounted their horses and then put on their new outfits.

"Here, you will need these coin purses. Don't reach inside them. Just tie them to your aprons. And just follow my lead," Estrella instructed.

The girls, leaving their horses tethered to trees, mounted their mules and rode out of the forest. Not far down the road, a band of thieves rode up to them and blocked their path by encircling them.

"Where are you girls headed?" asked one of the bandits.

"We be just a small group of laundry wenches off to the closest creek," replied Estrella.

"Where did ye come from, lasses?" asked another bandit.

"Alameda, sir. The princess ordered us off to wash her robes and gowns," answered Sera.

"Alameda? Isn't that place haunted? What would eight maidens be doing in that horrible place?"

"She keeps us around to do her chores and shopping, sir," replied Sloan.

"Well, you don't mind if we just check your loads to see what valuables she trusted you with, do you?" asked one of them, circling closer to the carts.

"Oh, please, sir, if we lose any of her things, she will turn us to shadows," whimpered Karmina.

They drew closer to the girls, and open their trunks.

"What, just rags?! You said you had her robes and gowns," growled one of them.

"We did, sir. We have them, but they got snagged by the trees," replied Lena.

"What do you girls have in those coin purses?" asked the bandits' leader, riding up to Estrella.

"Oh, please, sir, we need these pouches. They are our spending allowances for the princess's food and luxuries," begged Estrella.

But the thieves closed in on the girls and swiped the coin purses off their sashes. What the thieves did not know was that the pouches were booby-trapped. The first one pulled open the pouch, reached his hand inside, and yelled while trying to pull it out.

"Ouch! What is this?" asked the leader, pulling his hand out and discovering that it was scratched and cut up, with grains of salt in the wounds. The other thieves were in shock, but to find out what was in their stolen pouches, they had to search. After reaching into their pouches, they all yelled pulling out their scratched and cut-up hands. Their leader called them away, and they rode off.

Estrella smiled to herself. Her plan had worked perfectly.

"Estrella, how did you know?" asked Nori, giggling.

"I figured that eight beautiful young ladies would be an easy target, even if we looked like laundry maids. If we got robbed, like we just did, our assailants would find out not to mess with us."

"You truly are a great leader," said Anna.

"Just a very cunning and clever one." Estrella smiled. "Now, let's head back to our horses, change, and start our real journey back."

They turned their carts around and rode back to the forest to claim their horses and companions. Once they arrived, they dismounted their mules, retrieved their good clothes from the trunks, changed back, and mounted their horses.

"So, Sera, what is your companion's name?" asked Sloan.

"Her name is Sita." She smiled. "She has been by my side as my best friend and guardian for years, since before the curse."

"I am happy you have each other. We all have our companions. What is it that you like to do, Sera?" asked Estrella.

"I like books, reading, and writing."

"You write books?" asked Lena.

"No, not yet. Someday I would like to write my own book, but for the moment I just write poetry and journal entries," replied Sera.

"That's a nice talent. I hope one day you will let us read your first book," Estrella said with a smile.

"I promise that you will be the first to read anything new I write," responded Sera, as they all rode off and out of the forest.

CHAPTER 30

Estrella's Fourth Trial, Officiated by Marian

It had been a day since the girls had broken the curse on Alameda, saved the princess Sera, and left the forest. Their journey was coming to an end, but their adventure was far from over. They finally had all the members of their group, but they still faced the long journey to Faylin. The day was coming to an end when Estrella decided the area they were in was good enough to camp for that night. Each girl set up her own tent and took care of her own companion, horse, and mule. But they all chipped in on building the fire and getting dinner ready. When the food was all eaten, the dishes cleared and cleaned, and the fire put out, the girls retired to their tents. Some fell asleep fast, whereas others had lit their candles and were reflecting on the day and their journey. Karmina was working on a ballad telling of all Estrella's heroic feats, Sera was writing of the heroic rescue in a poem, and Luanna was painting a portrait of Estrella. Estrella, going through her things to write a letter home, came across the letter she had been writing when she got the invitation to join the Order of the Lion. She sighed at the memory of Faylin in spring, and then another image flashed to mind. It was a little fuzzy, but she could make out rolling green hills, a gray manor, and a happy family. Then all of a sudden she saw a place of bright light, love, and happiness, and the shining, radiant face of man. He was the most beautiful man she had ever seen. And then as suddenly as the vision had come, she was pulled back forcefully into the present, which left her with a terrible headache. "Whoa. That was weird," she whispered to Merlin.

{"What was?"} asked Merlin.

"I just had a flashback to experiences I don't even remember having had."

{"Like a past life?"}

"That's ridiculous. There is no such thing as..."

Estrella was just about to continue her sentence, when she caught the sound of her name in the wind.

"Did you hear that?" she asked.

{"Hear what?"}

Then she heard it again, but it sounded like the flapping of bat wings this time, not the wind.

"There it is again. What is it?"

{"I don't know, but maybe..."}

And then they both heard it, but now it was the cooing of a dove. This time it said, "Estrella.... Merlin.... It's... time."

"It must be Maid Marian, for my fourth trial." Estrella gasped. "Come on, Merlin, we can't be late."

Estrella pulled on her green cloak and quietly slipped out of the tent. She crept forward to the forest nearby, from which she could hear the animal calls coming, but when she reached the forest she couldn't see anyone there.

"Hello, Marian? Are you there?" she asked as she looked around.

From the shadows, she saw the glint of the moon off the eyes of a tall slender figure leaning against a tree.

"Marian? Is that you?" she asked cautiously.

"Well, it's not Robin Wood, dearie," said the figure with a sly smile, stepping into the moonlight. She was tall, maybe around five feet eleven inches, and had a beautiful slender build and stunning features, with long, kind of rusty-looking, copper-colored hair.

"Ahem," came Marian's voice, breaking Estrella's focus.

"Oh. I'm sorry, Lady Marian, was I doing it again?" Estrella blushed.

"Yes, dearie, you were."

"I'm sorry. I tend to analyze others I just meet."

"I understand, but it's time to start your trial, my dear."

"What is my fourth trial, Maid Marian?"

"Your fourth trial is on cunning; you will learn how to blend into your surroundings, to call like the animals on the wind, and to use their night vision."

"Sounds interesting. Let's get started," Estrella replied, getting excited.

"Settle yourself, young lady. You can't become one with your surroundings if you're full of energy. You need to be calm," she scolded.

"But I am excited to start, my lady."

"I understand, but if you want to pass this trial, you need to calm your spirit."

"How do I do that?"

"Start by leaning against the tree, closing your eyes, and taking slow, deep breaths."

Estrella leaned against a tree and focused on calming her spirit. When she was at peace, she could feel the wind in her face and hear the forest around her. Marian smiled as she watched her pupil go through the calming phases of the trial.

"All right, Estrella, tell me, what do you hear?"

"I hear, I hear..." Estrella scrunched up her eyebrows to concentrate. "I hear the rustling of leaves caused by the scampering of small animals. I hear the hoot of an owl and the growl of a predatory cat. Perhaps the latter is my friend Anna's lion, Cleo, on the prowl."

"Very good. Now concentrate. Focus on one creature. You can slow it down in your mind and hear every move it makes," explained Marian.

Estrella closed her eyes tighter, opened her mind and her ears, and woke the spirit inside her.

"I can hear every heartbeat inside Merlin, every flap of his wings, every pulse of blood through his veins."

"That is impressive—very intense. Now for your next phase, you are going to use night vision. You are going to focus on a predator, and when you open your eyes, you will see through the eyes of that predator. Your eyes will even physically change to look like that animal's eyes. It will feel weird, but you will get used to it. You can change your vision by closing your eyes for five seconds then opening them again," Marian instructed her.

"All right, I will try," Estrella replied. She kept her eyes closed for five more seconds and then opened them.

"What do you see?" asked Marian.

"I see bright reds and yellows. It's a toad. I'm getting closer and closer and—oh gross!"

"What? What happened?" asked Marian.

"The python I became ate the toad. I don't think I like being a python anymore."

"Close your eyes for ten seconds. You can tap into other animal's night vision without the animal being there. However, your eyes will change. When you're done, blink your eyes twice to return to your normal vision."

"All right, I will give it a try. I don't want to be a snake anymore," said Estrella. She closed her eyes for ten seconds and then opened them again.

"What animal's sight have you tapped into, Estrella?"

"Wolf."

"Very good. Now I want you to bring your own vision back, although you won't need to have your eyes open for this. You can change your sight back," instructed Marian.

"All right, I will." Estrella closed her eyes and blinked twice, and her vision returned. "What is my last phase, my lady?"

"The next phase is wind calling. Take a deep breath. On the exhale, whisper what you want to say. Use a long breath for longer messages and a short breath for names and short messages," she instructed.

Estrella closed her eyes, took a deep breath, and whispered, "Karmina."

Back at camp, Karmina stirred after writing her twelfth stanza. It seemed strange to her, but she thought she heard her name. She looked around, shrugged, put away her scrolls, and settled in to go to sleep. Back in the woods, Estrella smiled and readied to do it again. She closed her eyes and took a long deep breath. When she felt the wind blow through her hair, she whispered, "Good night, girls. Sleep well tonight. You are blessed." When finished, she almost fainted because it was such a long message. "That one almost knocked me out. Are we finished tonight, Lady Marian?"

"Yes, my dear, you have finished your trial tonight. Kneel and I will present you with your new cloak."

Estrella turned around and kneeled in front of her teacher.

"Estrella Sela, you have finished your fourth trial for membership into the Order of the Lion. For completing your trial of cunning, you have earned the pale rose cloak," Lady Marian said.

Estrella unclasped her green cloak, which she had gotten after her third trial, and pulled it off. As Lady Marian dropped the new cloak over her shoulders, she said, "Congratulations, young princess. You have passed the first four trials. You still have five trials left before you finish and are officially inducted into the order."

"Thank you, my lady. May I ask a question?"

"You may."

"I actually have a couple of questions. Am I the only one being tested? And will I have you as my teacher again?"

"We are also training others. I cannot say who, but there are others. And, no, this is the only trial I teach. I cannot say if we will meet again, but I have hope."

"Thank you, my lady. I look forward to the day I get to see you again. And thank you for your teaching," said Estrella graciously as she rose, holding her old cloak in her hand. She bowed before her teacher, took her leave, and started her journey back to the camp.

CHAPTER 31

Attack of the Basilisk

Using Merlin's night vision, Estrella had made it back to camp. Safely back in her tent, she readied herself for sleep while thinking about all she had learned.

Four. Four out of nine trials. I have gone through four out of nine trials to get into this order. And somehow I have passed all four already. I must have; I received four cloaks—five if I count the one I received after accepting the invitation. I have five trials left, and I am not the only one going through these trials. There are more students. I have seen many things on this journey. I have met unicorns and a Minotaur, and I have encountered Vikings and Harpies. And, having finally found my seven followers, I am finally—here she yawns—on my way home. Who knows what creature awaits us, what battle challenges us, what foe is plotting against us? I know this: we will be ready for it.

She blew out her candle, closed her eyes, and dreamt of a distant place with green hills, a small manor, love and laughter, and a family that looked so familiar, she thought somehow they were her own.

The next morning before the girls awoke, Estrella snuck quietly out of her tent and tiptoed to the little wooded spot she had gone to for her fourth trial, having taken with her, her sword, her dagger, and the cloak from her third trial. She hacked at the tree limbs and the grass, cut the cloak into strips, and then took her dagger and sharpened the limbs into spears. When she was satisfied with her preparations, she started to walk back to camp. Once she arrived, she saw the girls sitting around the fire cooking something what they had found for breakfast. Obviously they had thought that Estrella was sleeping in again.

"Should we wake her?" asked Sera.

"It is time to eat. We should get moving if we want to depart before it gets too hot," said Lu.

"Hey, did you guys hear something strange on the wind last night, like it was talking to you?" asked Karmina.

"Yeah, I heard something like that," replied Sera.

Estrella smiled as she quietly snuck up behind the group.

"Good morning, my sisters! What's for breakfast?" she said in a loud voice.

"Ack!" yelled Karmina.

"Estrella whatever-your-middle-name-is Sela, in that castle you grew up in, didn't they teach you anything about sneaking up on people?" scolded Sloan.

"Celeste. My full name is Estrella Celeste Sela. And, yes, my brother actually taught me the best ways to sneak up on people. We were quite the little troublemakers when we were younger." She smiled, giggling at the memories.

"Why do you have those spears and blindfolds?" asked Lu, giving her a suspicious look.

"And why do you have that sly smile on your face?" asked Sera.

"Oh no!" said the others in unison. "She has an idea!"

"Oh yes, my dear sisters, I have an idea. You see, in our battles, we have relied too often on our eyes to behold the creatures we can see. I want us to train to fight creatures we can't see," she explained.

"Can't see? You mean they are too fast to see, or they are invisible?" asked Lu.

"Both, in a way."

"What do you mean by 'both'?" asked Lena.

"There is a creature out there I want us to be prepared to fight. It's called the basilisk. It's a snake about ten feet long, and it's almost invisible. Its scales reflect the surroundings, making it hard to see it, except for a faint outline around it. And its eyes... Its eyes are blazing red, and if you make direct eye contact with it, you become paralyzed. It moves very fast and strikes like lightning; you don't know you've been struck until it's too late. I want us to be prepared to fight it if we ever cross paths with it. We need to fight with our other senses," she explained, handing out the blindfolds and spears. "Follow me to a clearing to train."

The girls took the spears and followed her. "And how do you know so much about these kind of creatures, Harpies, the Minotaur, basilisks, and such?" asked Lu.

"I got the information from a restricted book in our library. My father tried to keep me from learning the truth about things that are out there, but I read about a different being or creature every night for at least seven years."

"How many creatures are listed in the book?" asked Sloan.

"Countless."

"And you have read about a different creature each night since you were ten? How big is this book?" asked Karmina.

"About four volumes."

"How did the author of these books find out these things about these creatures without meeting an untimely demise?" asked Lena.

"It is mentioned in the first volume that he did research by speaking with sources, such as people who survived their encounters with these creatures. Now, enough talk. We need to train. Blindfolds on, girls," Estrella instructed once they reached the clearing.

The girls held their spears in one hand as they wrapped and tied the blindfolds around their heads. Then they stood there wondering what was going to happen next.

"Stand ready, girls. Be alert. Use your ears to listen to what's around you. When you hear me walk behind you pulling my staff behind me and sounding like a snake's slither, stab with your spears in the direction of the sound," she instructed. Then she began their training, circling the girls and "slithering" around them, which caused them to stab in her direction, either in front of or behind her. "Very good, girls. Another sense you will use is smell. Basilisks burn the ground around them, so you will smell sulfur and brimstone."

"Estrella, what about our horses? Won't the basilisk kill them?" asked Karmina.

"We will leave them outside the forest where the basilisk is reported to dwell. We will have to walk inside the forest ourselves and take care of the basilisk alone."

"Wait, we have to go in by ourselves and kill this monster on our own?!" asked Lu.

"I have faith in us. I believe that with the Lord on our side, being our sight, we will make it through," Estrella said reassuringly.

"Estrella, we are not warriors. We are not even fighters. We are just a small group of girls. We are not trained for this," said Nori.

"Sloan, did you think the same thought when you shot down the Harpies?" Estrella asked.

"No. I just knew I had to save you and protect you. You're my sister," Sloan replied.

"Right. We have faced dangers and challenges that no one would believe we could triumph over." We are all sisters now, and we all have the instinct to save and protect each other. So we can handle this. I have faith," said Estrella, boosting everyone's confidence.

Karmina removed her blindfold and smiled. "All right, everyone, we make our choice now. If you are with us, I want to hear a battle cry. If not, turn back now and return to the lives you left to join in this adventure. I know we are more than halfway through our journey and that it's late to make this decision, but here is where we separate the women from the girls. So who is with me? For Estrella!" Karmina cheered.

One by one each girl took off her blindfold and cheered, "For Estrella!"

It filled Estrella's heart to hear her girls cheering her name. "All right, then, I believe we are ready to continue." Estrella smiled.

After returning to camp, finishing their breakfast, cleaning the dishes, feeding and watering the animals, and packing up their gear, the girls started riding again. They rode for hours until they came to a dark forest, where a voice spoke to Estrella, saying, "Here. Dismount."

"Guys, we dismount here," she instructed, swinging down from Chesnutt.

"Are you sure?" asked Sera.

"Yes," Estrella replied, grabbing a length of rope.

"What is the rope for?" asked Lu.

"We go in together as pairs, each tied to each other, so we don't get lost or separated. We will also keep in constant contact. Karmina is with me, Sloan is with Lena, Nori is with Anna, and Luanna is with Sera," she instructed, passing out the cords of rope. "Tie it to your waist, and then tie on your blindfolds."

The girls did as they were instructed and then began to follow behind Estrella holding hands. At the halfway point through the forest, they realized they were lost. Estrella began to worry. First she pulled on her own rope to feel it tug, making sure Karmina was on the other end. Then she called out the names of the other girls. "Sloan and Lena, are you there?" She listened for their response.

"Yeah, Estrella, we are still here," Sloan called back.

"Nori and Anna, you girls still there?"

"Yes, we are here," replied Nori.

"What about you, Luanna and Sera? Are you girls still there and okay?"

"Yeah, Estrella, we are still here, and we are okay," Luanna called back.

"Good. Stay with your partners, everyone. And keep quiet and alert so we can hear the basilisk."

They walked on in silence. The forest itself refused to make any noise. The wind didn't blow, the leaves didn't rustle, and the birds didn't chirp. It was as if the whole forest was afraid of the beast that lurked in the shadows. The girls had gone about ten yards when Luanna and Sera finally sensed the creature.

"I smell sulfur," whispered Sera.

"Yeah, and I hear it slither," offered Lu. "Stab at the sound like Estrella taught us." She stabbed to the left, from where she heard it slither. Sera followed with a stab to her left. The basilisk hissed as their spears hit its sides, and then it slithered on. It went passed Sloan and Lena, who hit it with their spears. Then, coming closer to its intended target, it slithered faster, trying to get even closer to Estrella.

{"I can ssmell your blood, Princesss. It's running cold as iccce. Could it be you are already frozen with fright?"} the basilisk hissed in her thoughts.

"I am not scared. I am prepared to fight you," she answered inside her head.

{"Deny it all you want, to convincce yoursself you are brave. But deep insside you are jusst a little girl sscared of a ssnake,"} it hissed back, weaving its way toward her. It wove its way around Karmina, where it took a hit with a spear, only to continue its mission to abduct the princess. Slithering between Karmina and Estrella, it cut through the tether between them with its razor-sharp fangs, causing a sharp snap. Then it slithered around Estrella's ankles and, with a flick of its tail, knocked her down and pulled her away.

Karmina had a sinking feeling that something was wrong. Her suspicions were confirmed when she felt the tether go slack.

"Estrella!" she called out, receiving no answer. Then to her relief, she heard her leader.

"Kar...!" Estrella called out, but the sound was muffled.

Estrella was being pulled away from her friends again. First the Harpies, and now this giant snake, wanted her. She still couldn't figure out why she was a target. The basilisk pulled her away steadily, the end of its tail tightly coiled around her legs. When Estrella was about six miles away from her friends, the basilisk let go of her briefly. Then it coiled around her, tighter this time, working its way to her head, the tighter squeeze cutting off her airflow.

{"Remove your blindfold, Princesss. Look deep into my eyesss,"} the basilisk hissed.

"Nooo," Estrella managed to mutter, slowly losing consciousness.

{"Now, I'm not really that terrible. Basilisks are actually quite beautiful, but everyone is afraid to look at us. So no one really knows."} It squeezed tighter until Estrella passed out. {"Now how shall I finish you? I am supposed to bring back your heart, but I want to devour you. I am very hungry. You would make a good meal. But I can't eat it. If I bite you, then you will be paralyzed and shatter, making it easier for me to steal your heart."}

While the serpent was contemplating how best to finish Estrella, the girls, having followed the trail left behind, reached the place where it was holding her. They were twenty yards away, but the smell of sulfur was so strong that they knew they were close enough.

"Quickly, I need a mirror to see where the beast is and check on Estrella's condition. Then I'm going to fire a warning shot to startle it and get it to release her. Once it lets go, I will shoot a flaming arrow at it, hoping to set it ablaze," Sloan explained.

"How will you be able to do all that without looking?" asked Nori.

"I won't be able to without removing my blindfold," replied Sloan.

"But it will paralyze you," remarked Karmina.

"No it won't. Estrella said you would get paralyzed if it made eye contact with you or bit you. If I use a mirror, I won't be looking at it directly. Besides, we won't even be able to see it very well. She said its scales reflect its surroundings, remember? Now hurry. The more time we waste talking, the less time she has," Sloan instructed. The girls slipped off their blindfolds. Lena reached into her pouch, pulled out a small mirror, and handed it to Sloan, ignoring the skeptical glances from the other girls.

"Good," Sloan said. She angled the mirror so she could see behind herself. "I see Estrella. She is not moving and doesn't look good. I can barely make out the outline of the snake. It's wrapped really tight around her, squeezing her." Sloan reached behind her to her quiver, drew out an arrow, and nocked it. "Shh, I need quiet to concentrate." She turned on her heel and shot ten yards beyond Estrella, hitting some branches and making noise. The snake, in midbite, turned its head in that direction and slithered off to investigate, leaving Estrella lying on the ground.

"All right, you guys grab her. I will fire the flaming shot. And if that doesn't get the basilisk, I will take it down myself," Sloan instructed.

At Sloan's command, the girls rushed to Estrella's side to retrieve her. Once they had brought her back, Sloan wrapped a piece of her torn dress around the tip of an arrow, coated it in pitch, and nocked it.

"Sera, light me," she instructed. Once the arrow was lit, Sloan sent it flying. Right after she released it, she dropped her bow and grabbed her dagger. The arrow hit the basilisk's tail and the fire spread a bit over its body, but it soon extinguished. However, it made the basilisk mad enough to turn back and begin charging Sloan. Sloan pulled her blindfold on and ran at it, relying on her other senses. The girl and the snake collided. Sloan jumped away in time to miss a strike. She leaped up using the spear as a makeshift pole vault and, purely by luck, landed on the snake behind its head. She took her dagger and drove it into its eyes. With a final strike, she drove the spear through the creature's head killing it. When it was all done and over, she peeled off a scale using her dagger, broke out a fang for a trophy, and walked back to the girls as the exhausted champion.

When she returned, the girls had revived Estrella and everyone was cheering.

"All hail the champion, Sloan Ailes, the Harpy harpooner and basilisk banisher!"

Estrella stood up on wobbly legs and smiled. "That's twice, two times, you saved my life, and I am forever grateful. I hope one day I won't have to return the favor, but I will gladly come to your aid as you have come to mine."

"Let's hope you won't have to. That would mean my life would be in danger as well, but thank you, sister." Sloan smiled in response.

"Come on, girls, let's get our horses and ride on," Estrella said.

They turned back to the way they had come. Emerging from the forest, they retrieved horses, mounted them, and rode through the forest without fear of attack. With the basilisk slain, the forest was happier. The trees blew in the wind, the birds sang a cheerful tune, and the sun shone. With the sun shining upon the dead serpent, the creature soon ignited, the fire turning it into a pile of ash. As the girls rode past, Sloan collected the rest of its fangs and recovered her spear back. She put the fangs into her saddlebag.

"What are you going to do with those?" asked Lena.

"Chip them into arrowheads. Think of the weapon they could be. They could neutralize the enemy in one shot," she replied.

"That's a good idea, but remember not to let the power get to your head," warned Estrella.

"I won't," answered Sloan.

Riding on, the girls eventually made their way out of the forest, getting ever closer to the end of their journey, which would end in Faylin, Estrella's home.

CHAPTER 32

The Girls Write Letters

The day after defeating the basilisk, Estrella decided, once that she and the girls had set up camp, that all of them who had a family should write a letter home.

Estrella's first letter read as follows:

> Dear Maia,
>
> I have happy news. I have found all my friends and we are on our way back home! We have become so close that we are now sisters. Oh, Mother, the Lord has truly blessed me with this group of exceptional young women! I feel like Jesus did upon picking his disciples, except I definitely hope none of them betray me and sell me out like Judas did Jesus. I am very happy to report to you that I am finally on my way home. I long to run into your arms and live in Faylin forever. I miss you very much.
>
> Your loving daughter,
>
> Estrella

Then she added the note she was going to write before, the one asking about a place they might have lived before. She rolled up the letter and put it in Merlin's satchel.

Sloan had also busied herself with writing home, as had Lena. Sloan's letter read as follows:

> Dear Skylar,
>
> I miss you, brother. I have made many amazing new friends and had many unbelievable adventures. The stories I could tell you about the things I have seen and done! You would think I made them up. I am no longer the faceless little blacksmith's daughter, Sloan Ailes, the nobody. She is gone! Sloan the fighter has been born, replacing the old me.
>
> Thank you for all the years you made me feel important. You are and always will be my best friend. You will always have a special place in my heart. I could never replace you.
>
> I am on my way to Estrella's home. I am going to stay with her to the end, no matter where we go. I promise to write you every chance I get.
>
> Your best friend(s),
>
> Sloan and Odell

Lena's letter home read as follows:

> Dear Mama and Papa,
>
> I miss you all very much. Give my love to Marco. Tell him that his big sister, Lena, says to keep his innocence, smile often, laugh a lot, dream big, and hold onto his imagination. Tell Lorelie that her little sister has grown up in many ways out in the big world.
>
> We girls are getting closer to the end of our journey, Estrella's home in the kingdom of Faylin. You guys will always be *mi familia* and I will always have a

home with you, but I am loyal to Estrella and will follow her wherever she leads.

Your lovely and beautiful daughter,

Lena Acosta

After Lena and Sloan had rolled up their letters, they snuck over to Sera's tent. She was composing a letter to Estrella's family to find out her birthday so they could throw her a surprise party. Sera wrote the following:

Your Majesty, Queen Althea,

You have not met us yet. We are Estrella's new friends. She has done so much for us that we would like to do something special for her in return. Will you write us back and let us know when her birthday is? We would like to have a small party for her out here. We lose track of the days when we travel, and Estrella has probably forgotten her own birthday— or would she never tell us, being too humble to admit it or to take any attention away from our needs.

Your daughter is an amazing young woman. She has shown us much love, care, and kindness. You should be very proud of her. Being out on her own, far away from her home and loved ones, she has been very brave and happy. An ordinary princess would have given up on her first day away without her attendants or after getting dirty, but Estrella isn't an ordinary princess, is she? We can feel there is something special about her, something that is perhaps a secret that she isn't ready to learn of yet. She really is an incredible young woman. Throwing her a party would help us to show her how much we appreciate all she has done for us.

Sincerely yours,

Karmina Algur, orphaned songstress, welcomed by Estrella

Sloan Ailes, blacksmith nobody, found and given new courage by Estrella

Lena Acosta, innkeeper and dancer, rescued from thugs by Estrella's cunning and bravery

Nori Becker, previously a lonely baker and imprisoned preacher's daughter, saved from devastation by Estrella's gracious kindness and good timing

Anna-Mika Barnett, orphaned and lost princess and whitesmith, given new hope and courage thanks to Estrella's resourcefulness and imagination

Luanna Daley, artist and misfit, given a new perspective by Estrella's insights

Sera D'Aubigny, rescued from dark possession by Estrella's kind heart and faith

Sera rolled up the letter and gave it to Nori, who put the three letters together and placed them inside Merlin's satchel. Estrella then sent him off. He flew to Willow Creek first to deliver Lena's letter. Her family was filled with joy upon receiving the letter from the daughter they had said good-bye to long ago. Next he flew to Travelers Way and delivered Sloan's letter to her brother, Skylar, who smiled, and chuckled with joy knowing that his sister had made a friends and found her place in this world. Finally, Merlin flew home to Faylin to deliver the last two letters in his satchel to the queen.

Althea was speechless upon hearing from her daughter, one of the loves of her life. She was a little surprised by the letter's attachment, but she more surprised by the second letter. Once she reached the bottom half of the second letter, her surprise tuned to shock and alarm, which then turned to relief and pride once she saw the signatures. When she finished reading, she began writing three letters back. The first one was to Estrella, which read as follows:

Dearest Lovely Daughter,

Nothing makes me happier than to hear you have finally finished your quest and are returning home to me and your sisters. I am certain your friends are wonderful girls and that none of them would dream of betraying you like Judas. To answer your question about our former home, yes, my lovely girl, we long ago lived somewhere else, in a place called Lennox Manor, which is in the hills of Scotland. You were just a small child, barely even two years, when we moved to Castle Faylin and started a kingdom for the high king, Arthur. I don't see how you can remember that place, as you were so young when we lived there. I didn't want to move you so soon, but your father insisted, so we packed up all our things and servants and moved. That is all there is to know about Lennox Manor.

My dear sweet little angel, I can't wait to see my baby girl and embrace you in my arms once again. I am going to throw you the biggest and best welcome-home party with all your favorite foods and all the family.

Your loving and overjoyed mother,

Raine Maia Althea

Althea rolled the letter, dripped wax on it, sealed it, and set it aside. Then she started on her second letter, this one to Estrella's new friends. It read as follows:

Dear Ladies,

This is Estrella's mother, Raine Maia Althea. I am very happy to hear she has made such a wonderful impact on your lives. I had no doubts that she would find such lovely girls to be her friends and sisters. She is quite special indeed. We her family have known this about her for quite a while, but it's a family secret how special she is.

As to when her birthday is: We are now in the last days of March. Her birthday is in a few days, the fifth of April. She would love a party from her new friends.

I look forward to meeting each of you in person.

Sincerely,

Queen Althea of Faylin

Althea rolled up that letter, tied it with a ribbon, set it aside, and started her last letter, this one a bit more urgent, It was to her son, Gideon, and it went like this:

Dearest Gideon,

I am afraid it is happening. Estrella's identity is being shown. Her new friends are catching hints of it. She has reached the age for her true identity to mature and show through. This means that what the Lord told us in the prophecy about her is manifesting."

Althea flashed back to the time she was given the news she was pregnant with Estrella and learned of the prophesy of the weight placed on her unborn daughter. *"An angel would be born to you as a mortal. She will be known as a halfling, born of both heaven and earth. And when she reached seventeen, her nature would show to those around her, to those she helped. But it would also awaken the dark, which wishes to destroy her spark"*

Then she continued her letter. ". All our years of trying to protect her and keep her safe and sheltered have come to this. There is nothing we can do. She has reached the age of maturity. All we can do is trust her to stay safe, and to learn the truth when she is ready.

Your dear and worried mother,

Raine Maia Althea

Althea rolled up the final message. Placing all three missives in Merlin's satchel, she prepared to send him off. "You know where to go. Remember that we trusted you with Estrella's safety. Protect her, Merlin."

Merlin nodded and flew off. He delivered the first letter to Gideon, who was on his way home.

Once Gideon received the letter, he dismissed the falcon. Dismounting, he sat on a rock, opened the seal of the letter, and then read in shock and alarm the news his mother had sent him. Soon he began writing his response. When he finished writing, he rolled up the letter and gave it to his eagle, Elder, to fly to his mother.

Merlin flew all the way back to Estrella's camp with his two letters. He gave the first to Estrella, who accepted it joyfully. Then he secretly delivered the second to the other girls.

Estrella carefully peeled the seal off and unrolled the letter. She grinned upon reading the news. Her grin soon turned into a frown, and the frown then twisted into a half smile.

"What did your mother have to say, Estrella?" asked Karmina.

"What? Oh... um, she said that she is very happy that I am finished with my quest and returning home. She will be throwing me a big welcome-home party."

"Oh, a big party. That sounds like lots of fun. I bet she is going to be very glad to have you home," said Lena.

"She is. She has missed me very much, probably more than I've missed her. I can't wait to be home again."

"You have been away from your home for a very long time. I am proud of you for doing what no one would think of doing, leaving your home and starting out on a quest. No girl our age would ever think of doing this." Karmina smiled as she started to applaud Estrella. The other girls joined in.

Estrella blushed and bowed gracefully. "Thank you, sisters. Thank you. But I can't take all the credit. The Lord sent me on this quest and guided me to find you girls. It is the Lord who gave me skills, and the knowledge of what do to and where to go." She smiled back. "What did you guys get in the mail?"

"Oh, uh... just a letter from my parents back home, that's all," replied Sera nervously.

"Well, don't let me keep you. Go read it," said Estrella. She turned and walked back to her tent, still thinking about what her mother had said about Lennox Manor, and Scotland, and her father.

The girls hurried into Sera's tent and waited for her to open the letter. Once she had removed the seal, Sera read the words out loud.

"So it's in a few days?" asked Lu.

"It is. At least that's what her mother says," replied Sera.

"So when we get the chance, we need to buy her presents," said Karmina.

"When we stop for the night, we can throw her a party. We will have to keep her busy while we make our preparations," added Sloan.

"Not when we camp though, right?" asked Nori.

"No. We have a few days before her birthday. So by then we will have found a town to stay in for the night. We can send her around to collect and shop for things, like a scavenger hunt, so we can prepare for the party," said Sloan.

"That's a great idea, Sloan," remarked Lu.

"Then it is agreed. Estrella's party plan is in action," concluded Sera.

They all packed up their things, including the letter, and got ready to head out.

CHAPTER 33

The Marketplace

After packing up their camp, the girls mounted their horses to continue their journey to Faylin. Out of earshot from Estrella, Karmina, Lena, Sloan, Nori, Anna-Mika, Luanna, and Sera started discussing their plan for her surprise party.

"Okay, girls, what are we going to do to set up for this surprise?" Sloan whispered.

"Well, if I can find the ingredients and the tools I need, I will make her a large cake," suggested Nori.

"That's a great idea. She will enjoy the treat. What about you, Luanna? Any ideas about what you can do to help?" Sera asked.

"I can make decorations."

"All right, that takes care of the cake and decorations. What else do we need?"

"We should probably have something to eat first, before the cake—some sort of small meal," suggested Anna.

"Good idea. We definitely need a meal, a large dinner. I will prepare it," said Sloan. "I volunteer to hunt for pheasant and put together a salad of wild greens.

"Now for the biggest job. We need someone to distract Estrella and keep her busy while we get everything ready for the party. Who wants that job?"

"I will. I volunteer to send her on a wild-goose chase," offered Karmina.

"That's great. The only thing we need now are gifts, and to find a place to stay for the night," Sera added.

"I agree, but how are we going to pay for presents? We don't have any money," said Lena.

"We will worry about that when we get to where we're going," remarked Sloan.

"What do you get a princess who most likely has everything or doesn't want anything?" asked Luanna.

"I'm sure she would be happy with anything," replied Karmina. "I wrote a ballad for her. I might buy her something nice to go with it."

It had become strangely quiet behind Estrella. She could tell the girls were talking behind her back. "What are you girls whispering about back there?" she called over her shoulder.

"Oh... um, we were just discussing what we wanted to eat for lunch," Sloan replied quickly, covering for them.

"Well, I think there is a small marketplace coming up over this hill. There will be all kinds of food vendors there. You will probably be able to find something new to try," Estrella suggested.

"Really? How can you tell from here?" asked Nori.

"Because I can smell the sweet aromas of the food already." Estrella laughed.

"Good cover, Sloan, telling her we were thinking of lunch," whispered Sera.

"Yeah, good job coming up with that on the spot." Lena giggled.

"No, I really was thinking of lunch, you guys. It's been hours since we had breakfast. I'm very hungry," Sloan complained.

"Well, while we get lunch, we can find things to get Estrella for her birthday," Sera suggested.

They rode up the hill and looked down at the marketplace. Estrella hadn't been kidding. about all the delicious smells. It made the girls' stomachs growl and their mouths water.

"All right, ladies, I have something for you girls before we go," Estrella remarked. She reached into the saddlebag and pulled out seven medium-sized coin purses.

"What's this?" asked Sera, receiving her coin purse.

"Your spending money, for your lunches and anything else you want to get for yourselves."

"How many coins are in these purses?" asked Luanna.

"Don't you worry about that; they are for you to spend."

"But don't you need some to spend yourself?" asked Karmina.

"Don't worry, I still have some left. I want you to have some to spend on yourselves. Go on, take your allowances and shop."

"Thank you very much, Estrella." Sloan smiled.

The seven girls, their coin purses in hand, rode down the hill to the market. They were very excited as they hurriedly dismounted their horses and ran toward the vendors. Sloan, thinking of her hunger, ran right to a food vendor and ordered a mutton sandwich: a slice of rye bread, a thick slice of mutton, crisp lettuce, tomato, and mustard relish. The second she bit into it, her hunger pangs subsided and she forgot about all the other foods she had eaten on their journey, except for maybe that breakfast feast they had in Avalon.

After eating her lunch, Sloan looked over the rest of the vendors' wares, in search of her gift for Estrella. Not knowing what Estrella might like for her birthday, she decided on a pair of beautiful crystal earrings.

Karmina went right to a seller of musical instruments and purchased a small harp. Then she looked around at the other booths, finding a vendor that sold stuffed toys. Deciding on a little blue dragon, she paid the seller for it and then went back to her cart. Lena went to a fabric vendor and bought eight medium-size pieces of fabric, a backing piece, a smaller piece of fabric, a bag of wool, some thread, and a needle. She was going to make Estrella a lovely quilt that represented each of the girls, and a nice soft pillow.

Nori went to a booth selling kitchen wares and asked to purchase a sack of flour, a sack of sugar, a large wooden mixing bowl, two smaller bowls, a wooden spoon, and a sifter. After that, she looked around and found the booth of an herbalist specializing in essential oils. Nori thought that after all Estrella had gone through, and done for them, she would need a little help falling asleep, so she bought her a little bottle of lavender oil. As an added gift, she purchased a small bottle of rose oil perfume.

Anna-Mika went over to a jeweler's booth. Thinking that she could have made everything there on offer if she were still in her whitesmith shop, she picked out a silver filigree circlet with a dazzling sapphire in the middle. On top of that, she chose a sparkling aquamarine ring.

Luanna went to a craft vendor's booth, where she bought a dozen glass bowls, two bags of sand, a dozen small candles, and one large candle for a cake topper. Then she found a lovely stained glass picture of a glowing angel. It looked exactly like Estrella. Luanna thought it would make the perfect gift.

Sera was the last one to find a gift. She looked at all the booths and thought about what to get Estrella. She hadn't known Estrella very long, so she didn't have much to go on. One of the vendors was selling lovely cloaks and mantles in the most beautiful colors, some of them lined in fur. They all looked gorgeous. Deciding against one lined with fur, she picked out a deep purple cloak with a teal-colored lining. After paying the seller, she went back to her cart.

Now that everyone had bought their gifts and the materials they needed for the party, they met up at the food vendors' area for lunch. Sera bought a salad, Karmina chose a meat pie, Lena selected a bowl of pasta, Nori bought a bowl of fava bean and squash soup, Luanna purchased some dried cod, and Anna-Mika got a fruit plate. Sloan was in the midst of talking shop with another blacksmith when Sera waved her over.

"Sloan, get over here. We're having lunch. I thought you were hungry and wanted something to eat?" Sera called out.

"I already ate. I grabbed something to eat first, and then I bought the gift." She smiled back at the girls.

"Of course. Leave it to Sloan to eat before the rest of us." Karmina laughed. "Go ahead and enjoy the rest of the afternoon, Sloan."

Sloan smiled and went back to talking shop with the vendor. The other girls resumed eating their lunch.

Estrella was at the jeweler's booth looking at all the beautiful pieces. She wanted to make her new sisters feel beautiful and royal, wanting them to know they were princesses now. She picked out seven silver circlets; a ruby for Sloan, an amethyst for Karmina, a garnet for Lena, a peridot stone for Luanna, an emerald for Sera, an alexandrite stone for Anna-Mika, and a topaz for Nori. She also bought them each a ring to match the circlet. Then she went over to the cloaks and bought seven beautiful mantles. When she was finished shopping, she took all her gifts back to her cart and tucked them away. Then she joined her friends for lunch.

When they had all finished their lunches and, rejoining Sloan, had packed up their things, they mounted their horses and rode onto their next stop. They found a nice clearing on the side of a road and set up their camp for the night. When they finished with dinner, the seven girls went into their tents and secretly started to put together Estrella's gifts and decorations.

CHAPTER 34

Estrella's Surprise

The next morning, the girls packed up their gifts and decorations along with all their other things. They decided to start Estrella's birthday by letting her sleep in while they made her breakfast. Nori started a pot of oats cooking over a fire, and Anna scouted and found some eggs. Meanwhile, Lena and Sloan hunted some good-sized game to feed the animal companions, Karmina and Luanna fed and saddled the horses, and Sera packed up the carts and hooked up the mules. Then they all sat around the fire and waited for Estrella to arise. When Estrella awoke, she could smell the food cooking wafting into her tent. She smiled, rolled over, and whispered to Merlin, "I smell breakfast, Merlin."

{"I smell it too,"} he replied.

She wrapped up in her newest cloak and peeked out of the tent with a sleepy smile and messy hair. What she heard was a chorus of cheers and applause.

"What is all this for?" she asked, a bit bewildered.

"Three cheers for our beautiful brave leader," Sloan sang out.

"Hip, hip, hooray! Hip, hip, hooray! Hip, hip, hooray!" all the girls cheered.

Estrella smiled and teared up a little. "I... I don't know what to say. This is the best wake-up I have ever had—and I owe everything I am to you, my sisters. A great leader would be nothing without her equally brave and loyal followers. Thank you all very much."

"Come on out here, sit down, and have something to eat. Then you can get dressed. Lena will help with your hair, and then we'll be off to our next rest stop," Karmina said.

Estrella stifled a giggle and covered her smile with her hand as she tried to look very serious. "Yes, Mom!"

Six of the girls burst out laughing. Karmina rolled her eyes. Estrella emerged from her tent and sat down. Nori handed her a bowl of cooked oats with a boiled egg mixed in. The other girls sat down and joined her. Everyone was smiling and giggling, enjoying each other's company. Those who were going to Faylin for the first time were chatting about what it would be like staying in the castle and being pampered like princesses. Estrella, looking around at her circle of friends, smiled to herself, thinking, *Only the Lord. Only the Lord could use a lonely princess as his instrument to bring together such a diverse group of girls from every corner of England, which doesn't really have any corners actually, but that's not the point. These girls would have never met each other and become united if the Lord had not used me.*

They smiled and ate their breakfast cheerfully, happy to be all together and to be on their way home. When they had finished their meal, Karmina cleaned up the bowls and fed the rest of the food to the animals. Estrella went to her cart and carefully opened her trunk so as not to let any part of her gift for the girls show. She pulled out a blue dress. Taking the dress into her tent, she removed her cloak and shrift and slipped into the dress.

When she was dressed, she went back to her cart, packed away her clothes and other things, and took out some mint leaves, some cinnamon sticks, and her hairbrush. Then she walked back to the camp, where she found that the girls were already taking care of the fire and her tent. She handed out the mint and cinnamon sticks to her girls and kept some for herself. Then she sat down in her breakfast spot. She handed Lena her brush and sat patiently as Lena brushed her hair straight and then braided it.

Now that they were all dressed, cleaned up, and packed up, they mounted their horses and rode on to their next spot. Estrella took up the lead, with the girls hanging back to go over the party plans.

"All right, Lu, do you have all the decorations ready?"

"Yep, all ready and packed."

"Excellent. Nori, do you have everything ready for Estrella's cake?"

"All the ingredients and the utensils, yes. What I need is the oven to bake it in. But as soon as we reach a place to stay for the night and convince our hosts to let us take over the kitchen, that shouldn't be a problem."

"Perfect. Karmina, what do you have in mind for the distraction?"

"I think I will send Estrella on a wild-goose hunt, as I said before. I need a list of some random items you guys might want. Searching for those things will keep her busy and running around. But you should get things ready fast, because she will probably try to get her errands done quickly. So as soon as we reach the town, we should split up and get ready quickly."

Sera said, "Perfect plan. For now let's get this errand list made. We'll tell her I would like, let's say, forty sheets of parchment. And it has to be forty exactly—and a peacock feather quill." Sera laughed.

"Oh, I want slippers, purple silk ones with gold trim," Sloan chimed in.

"I want a bouquet of flowers, all different kinds and colors. Oh, and they have to be handpicked," Luanna added.

"I want a silver ring with a citrine gemstone," Anna suggested.

"I want a green cloak with gold trim and purple lining. And if they don't have one with the trim, she has to ask them to add it there." Lena smiled.

"I want a set of six wooden mixing spoons: one with a long handle, a short small one, one with slots in it, one with nobs on the end, one with notches in the handle, and one painted pink," added Nori.

"Great. And I will send her to find me a six-stringed harp. There. I think everyone is taken care of. This should be fun. She is going to love it." Karmina smiled.

After riding for a while, the girls saw a small town just ahead. The seven conspirators could hardly keep a straight face or contain their excitement. As soon as they entered the town six of them left to find house to stay in and set up, while Karmina stayed behind with Estrella, to distract her.

"What's going on, Karmina? Why did everyone split up like that?" asked Estrella.

"Oh, we already made the plan to split up and find something to eat and a place to stay," replied Karmina.

"Oh! Well, what can I do then? I feel different not helping this time."

"The girls gave me some errands they want you to run for them." Karmina smiled.

"Well, okay then. What's my first errand?"

"Sera wants you to buy her forty pieces of parchment and a peacock feather quill. And it has to be forty pieces."

"Forty pieces? Really? All right then. Should I dismount?" Estrella asked.

"I think it would be easier than pulling your horse, cart, and mule all through the town."

"Okay. Will you watch my things then?"

"Of course. I will watch them and wait here for you," replied Karmina.

Estrella dismounted and rushed into the town. Finding a basket outside a shop, she went inside and searched the shelves and cases for the parchment and the peacock quill. Lena and the other girls, rode their horses while leading the mules with their supplies, and went to the residents' houses, knocking on doors and asking if anyone had room for eight travelers. After being turned down time and time again, they found a small farmhouse with a barn. Sera walked up to the door of the farmhouse and knocked. The farmer and his wife answered the door. "Yes, can I help you?"

"I'm sorry to bother you, sir, but would you happen to have a place for eight travelers to stay for the night? My friends and I will sleep anywhere you have room. We just need shelter for the night, and to use your house for a party for our friend."

"Well, we don't have much room in our house, but we do have a barn. It's not very warm, but it has plenty of space. You can stay there."

"Please come in, ladies. My name is Martha, and this is my husband, Mark. You are free to use whatever we have," the wife said as she invited the girls in.

"Thank you very much. We will try not to be too much in your way. My name is Sera, and these are a few of my friends, Lena, Luanna, Anna-Mika, and Nori. Two of our other friends are out busy. Sloan is hunting our supper, and Karmina is keeping our birthday friend busy," Sera said.

"Where is your friend on her birthday?" asked Martha.

"We sent her off on some long errands. We want her party to be a surprise for her, so we gave her things to keep her busy while we get everything ready. She doesn't even know that it's her birthday," explained Lena.

"How can she not know of her own birthday?" asked Mark.

"She has been so busy on our journey, and done so much for us, that she has lost track of the days, even the special ones," replied Luanna, who then began setting up her decorations.

"Your friend sounds selfless. What can we do to help you ladies?" asked Martha.

"You are already doing a lot for us by giving us a place to stay and letting us use your house. May I use your kitchen to bake her cake please? I promise to clean up when I am done." Asked Nori, Looking around for the kitchen.

"Of course it's just through there." Replied Martha

The girls were getting started on the preparations. Meanwhile, Estrella was running all around the town searching for the unusual items her friends had requested.

Returning to her cart with the slippers Sloan had asked for, Estrella said, "All right, I found the purple silk slippers with gold trim. Don't ask me how, but I found them. And I was able to talk the merchant down from the high price without having to state my higher status to get it."

Karmina smiled and giggled. "I'm glad. Sloan will be very happy to hear that."

"What does she need these for anyway?" Estrella asked, placing the slippers in the cart, along with the parchment and quill.

"To keep her feet warm at night, of course."

"Oh, of course, how silly of me. She deserves nice shoes after everything. What's the next thing?"

"Lu wants you to handpick her some flowers, of all kinds and all colors."

Estrella sighed. "Very well, I will be back." And she walked off.

Back at the farmhouse, the girls were getting everything put together. Nori was in the kitchen mixing up the cake and getting the oven fires burning. Sloan had returned with two pheasants and a basket of wild greens, and was outside the house plucking the birds. Anna-Mika and Lena were setting up the small dining area and the dishes. Sera was setting up the presents.

"Do you think she will like her gifts?" asked Sera.

"Oh, I'm sure she will. She will be thrilled we did this party for her in the first place," Sloan called from outside, where she was prepping the birds.

"I just don't know her as well as you do. I was the last one to be found and the last one to join the group, so I haven't been with her long enough to know her well."

"Trust us, it only takes a day with her to know her well enough," said Lena.

"I guess you're right." Sera smiled.

Estrella returned a bit dirty, carrying a bouquet of flowers. She had a tired smile on her face. "Okay, I picked as many as I could, but I could only find a few different colors. I hope Luanna likes them," Estrella remarked as she placed the flowers in her cart.

"I am sure she will," said Karmina, smiling.

"All right, what's next on my list?"

"Anna wants a silver ring with a citrine stone, Lena wants a green cloak with purple lining and gold trim, and Nori wants six different mixing spoons."

"This is turning into quite a bunch of chores, but if that is what my friends want, then I will gladly fetch their gifts." Estrella smiled with a sigh. Her poor feet were tired, but she didn't care.

She walked off back to the shops to collect the other items. Karmina watched her go, thinking of all that Estrella had done for her and the other girls. She deserved this surprise party.

Back at the farmhouse, the girls were making the final preparations for their party. The cake was baking in the oven, the pheasants, having been plucked and cleaned, were roasting over a fire, the salad was tossed, and the table was prepared. They were just waiting for their guest of honor to arrive.

"So how old is your friend going to be?" asked Martha.

"Well, we are not exactly sure of that," replied Luanna.

"What do you mean?"

"Well, some of us have not been friends with her long enough to tell," replied Sera.

"She will be eighteen years old, ma'am," replied Sloan.

"You girls look very young to be on your own," Mark remarked.

"It's quite all right, sir. We chose to be on our own, and we can take care of ourselves. Our friend, the one we are throwing this party for, is a great leader. She has taught us how to be independent and shown us great ways we can help others," replied Lena.

"How will your friend know where to find us?" asked Mark.

"Oh! You're right, we forgot to think of that!" Nori called from the kitchen.

"No, we didn't. I already though of that. Sir, if you could help me move the pheasants to the oven to keep them warm, we can send a message using the smoke from the fire and my horse blanket," said

Sloan, taking a pheasant off the spit, placing it in a pot, and then going outside to get her horse blanket.

"That's a very smart idea," said Mark, taking off the second pheasant, which he put in the pot. Then he carried the pot to the kitchen to put the pheasants in the oven while the cake cooled.

"That's why Sloan is second in command," the other girls answered in unison. Then they all started laughing.

Estrella had finally returned to her cart with the last items the girls wanted. When Karmina saw the random-looking smoke clouds, she figured that it must be some kind of signal the others had thought of to let her know they were ready and where they were.

"All right, Estrella, we can head to our destination now. The girls have found us a place to stay."

"But, Karmina, I haven't found your gift yet. You didn't tell me what you wanted."

"It's all right. I don't want anything. Trust me, you will give me my gift soon enough." Karmina smiled as she helped Estrella put the last of her things into the cart and mount her horse.

"What do—" Estrella started to ask.

"Shush, you will see. Let's get going. The girls are waiting for us at the place where you see those smoke clouds."

"Oh, that was a good idea. Otherwise we would be lost looking for them."

"No doubt it was Sloan's idea."

"Of course it was. Sloan has many good ideas. She could be a great leader someday."

"Just like you."

"I don't know. I'm not that great of a leader."

"You must be joking. You're a great leader! We wouldn't be here without your great leadership. Don't sell yourself short. You are a princess, and that already makes you a good leader. You went off on this quest on your own, which means you have what it takes to be independent and solve things on your own. You brought together seven different girls and made them sisters, and that means you have a great gift for making a family. One day you will be a great queen and a wonderful mother."

"I don't know about the mother and queen part, but thank you. Karmina, you are a great friend."

The two rode in happy silence all the way to the farmhouse.

"Are you sure this is the place?" Estrella asked, looking around confused. "I don't see the others or their horses."

"The horses are probably in the barn, and the girls are likely in the house waiting for us. Now let's go in." Karmina nudged her.

Estrella dismounted her horse and walked up to the door and knocked politely. When the door was opened, She was blown back in surprise when she saw before her a table spread with a delicious-looking meal, presents stacked in a corner, beautiful decorations, and all her friends shouting, "Surprise! Happy birthday, Estrella!"

And that was when it hit her: she had forgotten her own birthday! All this time on her journey, she had been too busy to think about her own birthday. She started shaking and sobbing with emotion on account of the gift the girls had blessed her with.

"It's m-my b-bir... birth...?"

"Yes, Estrella, it's your birthday. The other girls and I wanted to bless you with this wonderful surprise for all you have done for us," replied Karmina, who was standing behind her.

"But how? How did you know, when I forgot it myself?"

"We asked your mother. When you sent her a letter, we sent her one as well. After we received her reply, we planned this whole thing for you," replied Sera.

"You guys, this just so wonderful. I don't know what to say!"

"I do. Let's eat!" said Sloan as she laughed. Everyone else laughed as they headed to the table.

As Estrella was walking to the table, Mark and Martha approached her and stopped her. Mark politely pulled off his hat and said, "Excuse me, but did your friends say you were Estrella, as in the princess of Faylin?"

"Yes, that's me."

Mark bowed and Martha curtsied.

"It is an honor to have you in our home, Your Highness," said Martha.

"Please, you don't have to treat me any different than you would anyone else. I am just a normal girl." She smiled.

Estrella then sat down at the head of the table. Karmina gave the blessing over the meal and the special birthday girl, and thanked the Lord for Mark and Martha, for giving the girls a place to stay. She thanked the Lord for everyone at the table and asked for blessing over everyone. Then they all shared and enjoyed the meal, happily savoring each bite of the special treats Nori and Sloan had made for the occasion.

At the end of the meal and after dessert, the girls retired to the fireplace and waited for Estrella to open her presents. Karmina, choosing to be first, handed Estrella a small pouch, from which the latter pulled the little blue dragon.

"Oh, Karmina, it's adorable! I will name him Hamilton, Hamy for short."

"I'm so glad you like it. I thought you would like something to snuggle with at night."

Next, Estrella opened her gift from Lena, a small pillow wrapped up in a large blanket.

"Oh my word, Lena. This is very soft and nice. Thank you."

"Each square of the quilt is a different color, for each girl. And I thought you deserved a decent pillow to rest your head on, even though we are close to returning to your home."

"Well, I love them both. Thank you."

Nori handed her two small pouches. Estrella opened them and pulled out the bottles.

Nori explained, "The smaller bottle is lavender oil for your pillow, to help you sleep. And the bigger one is rose perfume, because you deserve a good night's sleep, and to feel pretty."

"Thank you very much. I love it."

Estrella finished opening her other gifts, thanked her friends for such a wonderful birthday, and then excused herself to go to her cart to fetch something. Upon her return, she was carrying the things that girls had asked her to buy for them. She handed out the items. The girls all enjoyed the gifts. Each of them gave Estrella a hug. Then the seven of them headed out to the barn, with candles to guide them, to sleep for the night. Mark and Martha had offered Estrella their bed to sleep in, but Estrella happily refused. Instead, she set up her bed in front of the fire. After a while, she realized she couldn't sleep without her friends around her. She got up, lit a small candle, took her things out to the barn, lay down with her friends, and fell into a sweet and peaceful sleep.

CHAPTER 35

Phoenix

The next morning at dawn, Mark and Martha had a surprise visit. A group of knights of the Round Table had stopped by on their journey to their respective homes. Martha stopped in to the barn on her way to collect eggs to wake their overnight guests.

"Pardon the wakeup call, my ladies. You might want to get yourselves ready. We have some important guests who just stopped by."

"Guests? Who are they, Martha?" asked Estrella sleepily.

"Knights of the Round Table on their journey home, my lady."

"What?! There are knights here?!" exclaimed Sloan, sitting up with a jolt.

"Quickly, girls, get up, grab some mint and cinnamon sticks, and put your nicest dress on. We have to look our best for these gentlemen," Karmina cheered.

Martha collected the eggs as the girls got busy. They popped mint leaves into their mouths as they pulled on their dresses. Karmina, Sloan, and Estrella were lucky enough to still have gowns from Avalon, but they didn't have any that fit the other girls. The others didn't mind, though. Estrella decided that as soon as they arrived in Faylin, she would see to it that everyone would have a lovely dress to wear whenever they wanted to feel beautiful.

When they were all dressed, they did each other's hair. It took all of them to convince Estrella that she should wear her beautiful gifts; after all, she was the princess. She finally caved in and let Lena plait her hair back and carefully place the circlet from Anna-Mika on her head. Then she put on the crystal earrings Sloan had given her, and finished by slipping on the ring and the cloak. When the girls were ready, they left the barn together and headed to the house.

When Estrella pushed open the door, she looked around at the knights gathered inside. Then her eyes met with Gideon's. At the far end of the table, he saw her standing in the doorway and stood up in awe.

"Gideon?" she whispered, tears welling up in her eyes.

"Estrella? Is it you, little sister?" he replied with a smile, tears in his own eyes. She rushed in, and he met her in the middle of the room, where he caught her up in an embrace, held her, and kissed her forehead. Tears of joy ran down both of their faces.

"Who is this beautiful young woman in my arms? And what happened to the sweet young child I left at home, the one who left herself and accomplished this amazing quest?" He smiled and kissed her head.

"She made new friends, who became her family. She had many great adventures. She turned eighteen yesterday, and she is the young woman you see now," Estrella replied, beaming.

"Tell me then, Princess, in this glorious quest to find your new family, did you forget about your real family, the one you left behind?"

"No, never! Not a day went by that I didn't think about you, Maia, or our sisters at home. I missed you all. I love my family. No could take your place. It's just that that place grew bigger to hold more love for new family, to whom the Lord led me."

"I am glad. I have missed you, my dear little sister."

"I missed you very much, Brother. You are the sun in my sky."

"And you are my stars." He held her tight, kissing her head again. Then came a polite interruption.

"Excuse me. I don't mean to break up this beautiful reunion, but I think we should at least have introductions," Karmina said, kindly cutting in.

They both laughed, realizing they weren't the only ones in the room. Gideon smiled and released Estrella from his clasp. Estrella, wiping away her happy tears, smiled at her friends.

"Gideon of Faylin, these are my friends Karmina, Sloan, Lena, Nori, Anna, Luanna, and Sera. My friends, this is my brother and best friend, Prince Gideon of Faylin."

The girls curtsied, and Gideon bowed.

"It's an honor to meet you, Your Highness. We have heard wonderful things about you from your sister," Karmina said in greeting on behalf of all the girls.

"Likewise, lovely Karmina. My sister told me wonderful things about you girls in her letters. I am very pleased to finally see the lovely faces that go with the names she mentioned," he said, flashing his best smile. Then, addressing his men, he said, "Gentlemen, bow before a princess. This is my sister, Princess Estrella of Faylin, and her friends. Estrella and ladies, meet the returning knights of the Round Table: Sir Vincent, Sir Charles, Sir Jeffery, Sir Gavin, Sir David, Sir Christopher, and Sir Christian."

The men bowed; the girls curtsied and blushed.

"It's an honor to see the princess and her ladies we keep hearing about," greeted Sir Vincent.

"You are lovelier by far than Gideon gives you credit for," said a grinning Sir Jeffery.

Estrella blushed at the compliments; the girls giggled.

Sir Christian smiled. Addressing Estrella, he asked, "Did I hear right? You had a birthday yesterday?"

"Yes, my birthday was yesterday. I turned eighteen years old."

"Well then, I say this calls for celebrating. Father, if you don't mind, would you play your fiddle to give us some lively dancing music?"

"It would be my pleasure. I haven't played my old fiddle for quite a while, and this is just the occasion for it," replied Mark, picking up his dusty fiddle. He blew off the dust, pulled his bow across the strings a few times for warm-up, and then played a giddy little tune.

Gideon smiled and bowed to Estrella. "May I have this dance, Princess?"

"Of course you may, sir." Estrella smiled as she took his hand. They danced and twirled. The other knights took the hands of the girls and danced. When the dance was over, they laughed.

"Are you heading home, Gideon?" Estrella asked, once she caught her breath.

"I am. We stopped to stay for breakfast. We are returning the knights to their families. Mark and Martha are Sir Christian's parents."

"I picked up on that."

"We must be going, but before I forget, I brought you this." He reached into his bag and pulled out a necklace with golden star pendant studded in gems.

"Gideon its beautiful. I will wear it always."

"Happy birthday, Estrella. Oh, and Bliss wanted you to have this," he said, handing her a diamond cross necklace.

She teared up and threw her arms around him. "The best gift you gave me was seeing you the day after my birthday."

"I love you very much, Estrella. I will see you at home." Gideon smiled and kissed her forehead. He bowed to the ladies, and motioned for the rest of the men to head out. They thanked their hosts, said good-bye to Sir Christian, bowed to the ladies, and kissed their hands before leaving.

By afternoon, the girls were all packed up. They thanked Mark and Martha for their hospitality before heading out and resuming their journey.

After riding for a time, Estrella thought she heard something. She ignored it at first, but when they got closer to the sound and it got louder, she stopped her horse and signaled to the other girls, who were riding behind her, to halt.

Sloan and Karmina rode up to her. Sloan asked, "Estrella, what is it?"

"Shh, I hear something."

"What do you hear, Esy?" asked Karmina.

"I don't know, but it almost sounded like someone calling for help."

"Really? I didn't hear anything or anyone," said Sloan.

"You guys stay here. I'm going to check things out." Estrella dismounted and went off toward a wooded area, following the sound she heard. She went deeper into the forest and got closer to the sound. When she saw the source of the sound, she couldn't believe it. It was an elderly-looking man caught in a net and struggling to get out while calling for help.

"Help! Oh, help me. Please, anyone, help me."

Estrella approached him carefully. "Sir? Sir, are you all right? How did this happen to you?" she asked.

He turned his head and looked at her with sad eyes. "You can see me, young lady?" he asked, a bit bewildered.

"Of course I can," she answered. "What happened to you?" she asked him, trying to lift the net off.

"I was hunted," he replied.

"Who would hunt a poor old man like you?"

"I am not a real man, though."

"What do you mean? You look like a real man to me."

"I am a phoenix, a type of bird. Only the divinely gifted can see my spirit, and they do so with spiritual eyes. To the rest of the world, I am only a rare bird that bursts into flames. You must have the gift," he explained.

"I'm just a princess on her way home. The only gift I could possibly have is kindness and compassion," she said, still in shock but finally pulling the net off the man.

"But how did you know I was in trouble if you don't have the gift?"

"Well, I heard you call for help."

"As a bird or as a man?"

"Well, uh, as a man."

"Then you have a gift, but the Lord has not revealed it to you yet. Tell me, has anything happened to you on this trip you're on, anything you can't explain?"

Estrella thought back to the Harpies, the Minotaur, and the basilisk. And once she really thought about it, there was no way she could explain those encounters.

"I was attacked by Harpies. They were saying things about their master wanting my heart and my blood. I also met a Minotaur. He was trapped. I helped him escape. Then not too long ago, I was attacked by a basilisk snake."

The phoenix listened carefully and then replied, "When you first saw the Minotaur, what was your reaction?"

"I felt sorry for him. He was scared and upset but not dangerous."

"You see, right there, others would have seen an angry horrible beast and run, but you didn't and that says something. As for the Harpies and basilisk, they are messengers and minions of a dark power that must have seen the gift in you and sent those creatures to take it from you."

"But I don't even know what it is."

"When you are ready, the Lord will reveal it to you. I thank you very much for saving me, Miss..."

"I am Princess Estrella," she said, introducing herself.

"Thank you, Princess, for saving me. Don't worry, you will know your gift someday. I must leave you now. I have lived my lifetime. It is time for me to be reborn."

"You're leaving me? But I just met you and I don't even know your name. Does it hurt when you burst into flames?"

"My name is Elwyn. I must leave you. It's time for the next generation to be born and live its life. It does not hurt. It's like a healing. The old passes away in the flames, and the new is born from the ashes," Elwyn explained as he started to spark. Before he caught fire, he left Estrella with a message: "Be warned, Princess Estrella. The fears you have faced are only a warning. You will face greater fears, and beings who will hunt you and hurt you. When you need help, call for me.

My descendents will remember me and the princess who saved me." Then Elwyn burst into flames. From the ashes left behind, Estrella heard a baby cheeping. She dug it out and cradled it.

"Hush now, little one. You are safe now. You are precious and new. It's all right, you're okay. I knew your father before you were born. His name was Elwyn, and he was a good creature. My name is Estrella. I know some part of Elwyn will live on in you, and you will remember me. I will name you Ilya." She smiled at the babe.

When the babe settled down, Estrella looked at its peaceful innocent face and fell in love with the sweet tiny creature. She knew she couldn't leave the poor thing alone to fend for itself. It wouldn't last a night on its own, it was so defenseless. She cradled the tiny thing close to her heart.

"I will care for you, Ilya. You won't be alone. I will be your mother. I will feed you and raise you. One day you will be old enough to care for yourself. When your descendents are born, my memory will pass on to them," she whispered to the tiny creature. Then she wrapped it in her cloak and walked back to her friends.

"Estrella, you're back. Did you find what you heard?" asked Sloan.

Estrella smiled, remembering Elwyn and the chick. "I did."

"What is that you have in your cloak?" asked Karmina.

Estrella smiled and opened her cloak, revealing her little chick. The girls stared at it in surprise.

"What is it?" asked Sloan.

"This is a phoenix chick. What I heard was the older phoenix caught in a trap. I saved him before he burst into flames, and then this little one was born."

"You saw it catch flame? Are they supposed to do that?" asked Lena.

"Yes. Once a phoenix reaches the end of its life, it catches on fire. And from the ashes the next one is born."

"Is this one going to be okay?" asked Anna.

"I think it will be. I'm keeping it with us until it is old enough to take care of itself."

"What did you name it?" asked Nori.

"Ilya. It's name is Ilya."

"Ilya? I like it," said Sera.

"I like it too. Let's head out, girls." Estrella smiled. Then she carefully swung into the saddle and nudged her horse on. The girls continued their journey, each day coming closer to Faylin.

CHAPTER 36

The Journey and the Dream

Having traveled for half a day, the girls found a good clearing in a forest to set up camp. Sloan and Karmina dismounted and then helped Estrella down from her horse so she wouldn't bump the chick. While the others were setting up the camp, Estrella was getting the chick nestled and digging for mealworms to feed it.

{"What is that?"} asked a surly Merlin.

"It's a baby. What does it look like?" Estrella called over her shoulder to her falcon.

{"Why do you have it? Where is its mother?"}

"I'm its mother. I couldn't just leave it."

{"No, you are *my* mother, not that thing's mother."} He was getting quite upset.

"Merlin, that is enough! He is a baby phoenix; he has no one to care for him. And you are going to be nice," she yelled at him. The chick started cheeping. "Look, now it's crying. Merlin, I don't want to be mad at you. I will always be your momma, always, but he needs me too." She calmed down, stood up, fetched a few mealworms, ground them into a paste, returned to Ilya, and fed him the mealworms.

{"I'm sorry, Mom. I didn't mean to make the poor thing cry."}

"I know. You will always be my baby bird, but I have to care for whomever the Lord leads me to, and now that's this one."

{"Does my brother have a name?"} he asked, perching close to her.

She smiled. "Yes, his name is Ilya."

{"Well, don't expect me to feed Ilya like a mother bird. I'm not spitting worms into his mouth."}

"That's okay, I can take care of the worms. When he gets bigger, you might have to catch prey for two, or teach him how."

{"I can do that."}

Estrella happily fed her little chick while talking with her falcon friend. Someone seeing this for the first time might think she was rather odd and lock her away in a tower somewhere. But her friends understood that she had an unexplainable deep connection with animals. She certainly wasn't like most princesses.

The girls, having finished setting up camp, ate dinner. Then they began settling down for the night with their companions; Karmina was brushing Juniper's mane and polishing her horn, Anna was combing through Cleo's fur, and Sloan was brushing moss out of Odell's coat. Everyone was enjoying their evening after a long journey.

"Well, everyone, here we are, coming to the end of our journey, I can't say for sure if tomorrow we will be home—my home, your new home. But we are coming to an end. And I can say with utmost pleasure that through it all, I couldn't have been happier. I love all you girls and am very glad you're my new sisters," said Estrella, addressing her friends.

"We love you too, Estrella. If it weren't for you, we wouldn't be where we are now. We wouldn't be together." Karmina smiled.

"Go get some rest, Estrella. Tomorrow is a big day for you. You need to be rested," instructed Sloan.

Karmina prayed over everyone before they went to sleep.

Estrella smiled and yawned. Carrying Ilya with her, she walked into her tent and held open the flap for Merlin to fly inside. She kept her necklace on, and opened her music box as she settled into her cot. She opened her Bible to read a few passages before she went to sleep. After a while, the others went to sleep as well.

Sloan decided to take up guard and watch over the camp. But after a while she fell asleep—but even she wouldn't have been able to protect Estrella from a threat she did not have the ability to see coming. A dark cloud drifted into their camp. Something dark and evil was there to cast a nightmare spell over the sleeping princess in her tent. The cloud drifted through the camp seeking Estrella. It crept into each tent and searched for her pure heart and glowing aura. When it reached her tent, it descended onto her head, encasing it in a fog.

In Estrella's dream, things were playing out just like a memory, but it wasn't like she was reliving something: she was watching it. She rewatched herself giving the speech she had given before bedtime, watched herself go to sleep, and saw the others go to bed. She watched Sloan stand guard, but as soon as Sloan fell asleep, a serpent the color of tar slithered into her tent. Estrella started to panic.

"Sloan! Sloan, wake up. There's a snake in my tent. Sloan, you have to wake up and save me!" she called out.

Sloan didn't hear her, but another being did. It crooned behind her, its voice dripping with sweet poison.

"She can't hear you, Estrella. You are not really there; you are just watching *my* dream come true."

She spun around and came face-to-face with a figure that looked like an angel of light, but it was distorted.

"Who are you?! Why are you doing this? How is this your dream come true?" she demanded.

"Because it's your nightmare. And your nightmares are always my favorite dreams," he crowed.

"Who are you?!" she yelled, beating on the image until it shattered like glass, revealing a foul dark creature smiling like the cat that ate the canary.

"Silence, petulant child. This is my favorite part," he snarled, spinning her around, restraining her with black cords, and holding her fast to watch.

The serpent turned into a man, as dark as night with eyes as yellow as the moon and fangs like a serpent. He kneeled next to Estrella. When she stirred, he hissed and recoiled, but she stayed asleep. He leaned over her and bit into her neck. She winced but went still, paralyzed by the toxin he had released into her veins, which traveled through her bloodstream and stopped her heart. He took her dagger—holding the hilt with a cloth so it wouldn't burn him—stabbed her in the chest, and pulled out her heart, which he put in a pouch. Then he stabbed Merlin so he wouldn't wake the others. For a snack, he ate Ilya, the baby phoenix, in one bite. Then he turned back into a snake and slithered out.

"No! No! No!" Estrella cried out.

"Oh yes! You see, I win. And it's just starting. The goody-goody princess lies dead. My messenger brought your death and brought me your heart."

"Who are you? Answer me! What do you want with me?" she begged.

"I want you to see what happens to your happy little world without you in it. Now watch what happens the next morning when your friends find out." He held her head up to watch as the night changed to morning, which turned to mourning.

315

Estrella watched as the girls awoke. Karmina walked into Estrella's tent and screamed, "No! Estrella, no! She's dead. No, this can't be happening."

Sloan woke up instantly, rushed in, and fell to her knees at the horrific sight. "No! This can't be happening. It's all my fault. Had I stayed awake, I could have saved her. It's my fault, all my fault." Sloan broke down and sobbed, curling up into the fetal position, blaming herself.

The other girls came in to see what was going on. They were all shocked at what they saw. Karmina knelt down, picked up the circlet and sword, and handed them to Sloan.

"Sloan, take these. We have to present them to Estrella's family. You were her second in command. She would want you to hold them for her."

Sloan looked in horror at what was being handed to her, as if Karmina was handing her Estrella's head on a platter. She got up and backed away.

"No, I can't. I'm not worthy to touch those possessions. I'm not worthy to tell her family. I killed her. I did, me. If I had stayed awake, she would be alive. I killed her with my mistake," Sloan sobbed. Then she ran out of the tent.

"Stop! Stop it! I don't want to watch my girls break apart and run away," Estrella cried.

"I'm not done yet. But I will give you this: I will show you pictures of your future. Sloan deserts the group and becomes a vigilante wanted by authorities. Karmina and the girls return to your home. The kingdom mourns your death for a month. Your mom visits your grave every day until she dies of a broken heart. Gideon joins the Crusades, and is captured and tortured until he dies. Your sisters have to marry and then leave the kingdom. They are never happy again. Shall I go on?"

"No, stop! Answer my question: who are you?"

"I can be anyone, anyone who ever hurt you—maybe your father?" He smiled and taunted her, changing his form into that of her father. "Estrella, what have you done? How could you let this happen?" he scolded.

"No! No, it wasn't my fault I died. I didn't want any of this to happen!"

While all this was going on in Estrella's head, in the real world she was struggling with this nightmare, muttering and tossing. Ilya, her phoenix chick, was screeching, crying, and carrying on, which woke Merlin. Merlin began pulling on Estrella to wake her. {"Estrella? Estrella, wake up. Wake up, Princess."}

Sloan woke up first to all the racket. She pushed into Estrella's tent to see what the fuss was about. She caught sight of Estrella's state and went to her side.

"Estrella. Estrella, it's okay. I'm here," she said, trying to comfort her.

When she couldn't comfort Estrella and didn't know else what to do, Sloan woke Karmina and the others. Karmina came into the tent, went to Estrella, and held her head. She instructed Sloan to hold Estrella's hand and then told the girls to start praying. Nori bowed her head, held the other girls' hands, and prayed, "Dear Heavenly Father, please protect our sister Estrella. In the name of Jesus Christ, we cast this demon out. Please bring Estrella back to us."

In the dream, Estrella was breaking down. "No, no, no. This can't be happening," she sobbed.

"Oh, but it is, my dear. Your happy little world is shattered and broken, all because of you."

"Lord, how? How could you let this happen? Where were you that you didn't protect me, didn't save me?" she yelled to the sky in frustration.

Amid the noise, whirling winds, and torment, Estrella heard a small whisper: "Be still and know that I am God. My angel, I have always been with you. You have just been blinded by the darkness around you. Don't look so long at the dark that you forget the light. None of what you are seeing has happened. It's not real. I could help you change this picture, but I want to show you the truth."

A fuzzy image appeared and replayed the night's events: Estrella giving her speech, the girls praying for her before bed, Estrella playing her music box, the fog creeping in, and her friends coming in to pray for her.

"Now, bow on your knees and pray. I will give you my sword so you can beat this enemy and return to your girls."

Estrella fell to her knees, bowed her head, and clenched her fists. The enemy danced circles around her, crowing in her ears.

"You are worthless. You are hopeless. You are useless. You are nothing," he mocked and taunted.

"The Lord's eyes on the sparrow, so also are his eyes on me. I am worth more than a dozen doves." The sword materialized in Estrella's hand.

"You are nothing. The Lord left you. He doesn't love you. He doomed you to fail."

""I know the plans I have for you," says the Lord, "plans to prosper you and not to harm you."' Jeremiah 29:11. I am a princess, a daughter of the King of Kings." The sword became stronger and solid. "I can do all things through Christ, who strengthens me!" she growled, standing and flashing a bolt of light at the enemy.

The enemy was hit. He shrank in size from the power of the Word and the blast of light. And Estrella saw her opportunity to have the upper hand and take down this monster.

"I am an overcomer." She stood up and directed another blast at him.

"What? What is happening?! You are weak and you died, remember? You sinned; you died. You belong to me!"

"No. 'The wages of sin is death, but the gift of God is eternal life in Christ Jesus, my Lord!' Romans 8:23!" Another blast of light. "I will never be yours. My Savior paid for my life and my sins with his life on the cross, once and for all."

"But I had you. I was winning."

"Christ wins every time. Love wins every time!" Another blast, another hit. "I am more than a conqueror, and I am loved. 'For God so loved the world'—that includes me—'that he gave his one and only Son, that whoever believes in him, shall not perish but have eternal life.' John 3:16! So my body may perish, but you have no claim on my spirit, which belongs to Christ. I may die, but I will be with Christ in heaven forever. I win!" She took one last swing at the now three-foot-tall enemy, knocking him down to three inches. She walked over to the bug he became, squeaking curses, insults, and foul language up at her, and she smiled. She even laughed.

"I shall crush you under my boot, and you will never interrupt my sleep again. Tell your master when you see him again that he can throw whatever he wants at me for whatever reason, as I will be ready." She crushed him. It was over. She was free; she had won!

The girls were praying fervently over Estrella. When they noticed the fog lift from Estrella's head, all of a sudden she glowed, shining brightly in the tent. The girls were surprised and stunned when a blast of light filled the tent.

Estrella gasped and sat bolt upright, with tears streaming down her cheeks. "It's over. It's finally over," she sobbed.

"What's over? What happened, Estella?" asked Sloan.

"I had the worst nightmare. It was horrible, I can't begin to describe it without reliving it and crying. All I can say is that I was in a battle with the enemy and I won."

"Oh, Estrella, I'm so sorry. I'm here now if you want me to be," said Karmina, comforting her friend.

"I'm okay now. The rest of you can go back to your tents. Thank you for your prayers."

The rest of the girls started to head back to their tents, when Estrella grabbed Karmina's sleeve.

"Karm, would you please sleep with me? I think I will sleep better with you beside me."

Karmina smiled, knowing how scared Estrella still was but not admitting it.

"Of course, Estrella, I will stay with you."

Karmina lay down next to Estrella. Soon they fell asleep. They remained peaceful through the night."

The next day, the girls awoke and began to prepare for their ride home. They tore down their tents and camp, ate breakfast, and then got themselves ready, looking as nice as they could. When they were done, they mounted their horses and rode out of the forest.

They had been traveling for a day when they came to the top of a hill. They could see the kingdom on the other side.

"There it is, girls, our home, Faylin. We reach it after going through the Enchanted Forest, where we'll stop to see the fairies."

The girls cheered, joyful that their journey was finally coming to an end. They kicked their horses into a gallop and rode on in excitement.

When they reached the Enchanted Forest, Estrella called them to a stop. Then she summoned her fairy friends, "Come out, my friends.

It is I, Estrella. I have returned from my quest and have brought my new friends. I was hoping you would give them something."

At first nothing happened, but then the forest was full of glowing twinkling lights, which appeared all around the girls. Estrella smiled as a tall glowing figure appeared. She was beautiful with long white hair, silver eyes, and bright yellow butterfly wings. Estrella dismounted and bowed.

"Girls, this is Bronwyn, Queen of the Fairies. She is a dear friend of mine—and she is ancient, being an immortal."

"Rise, Princess. You honor me enough with your visit," Bronwyn said. Greeting the phoenix chick, she added, "I'm glad to see you again, Zebulum."

"Excuse me, Your Highness, but the chick is named Ilya, not Zebulum," said Nori.

"I understand that is the name of the chick. But when I knew him, he was Zebulum. When I was young girl many, many years ago, I too found a phoenix chick and raised him like Estrella is doing. Zebulum is the ancestor of your Ilya. Phoenixes are immortals, just like fairies and some species of elves. Phoenix chicks pick their mothers to raise them. It takes a special person. You were chosen, Estrella. But that's not why you are here. You stopped here on your way home because you want your friends to be gifted, right?"

"Yes, please. If you don't mind, Bronwyn."

"Of course I don't mind. Please dismount and kneel, ladies." The girls dismounted and kneeled in front of the fairy queen.

"I, Bronwyn, Queen of the Fairies, bestow upon you, Karmina, the siren song. May your song enchant and entrance those who hear it. To you, Sloan, I grant you magic arrows that always hit their mark. To you, Lena, I give the gift of being a perfumer. May your scents and fragrances catch the hearts of those you lure. Nori, you shall receive the gift of herbalism. May your knowledge of oils and herbs heal the sick and harm the wrongdoers. To Anna goes the gift of alchemy. May you transform the simplest of objects into precious metals. To you, Luanna, I give a magical paintbrush and paint. May whatever you paint, with good intention, come to life. Your paint will never run out or change to any color. And finally to you, Sera, I give a magical quill pen and magical ink, to create whatever story your reader wishes. All your gifts are to be used for good and cannot be used for evil. They will cease to work in anyone else's hands. If someone takes your magical objects, they will stop working, but they will reassume their magical properties once they are returned to you."

The fairies sprinkled dust over the girls and bathed them in light now that the gifts and abilities had been bestowed upon them.

"Your friends have been bestowed with gifts of magic, Estrella. The next gifts are from the Lord." Bronwyn smiled and bowed, departing.

Estrella said, "Girls, while you are kneeling, let us pray. Dear Heavenly Father, we ask you to bless us as we arrive home. We ask you to bless us with gifts of the Holy Spirit, whichever gift you see fit to bestow upon us."

Then the Lord spoke all around them. "My daughters, I have watched you and heard you. I grant you my Holy Spirit, and to each of you I grant not only a spiritual gift but also a gift of ministry. Karmina, you are blessed with the gift of tongues. When deep in prayer, you will be able to speak the tongue of the angels. You will also be blessed with the ministry of being an encourager and comforter. This is because of your kind heart.

"Sloan, my daughter, I give you the gift of wisdom and the ministry of being an apostle. Lovely Lena, I give you the gift of knowledge and the ministry of being a helper. My sweet devoted Nori, your faith has been your gift this whole time. Your ministry is being a prophet. I shall give you visions and you shall send out my message.

Anna-Mika, you are given the gift of interpreting tongues. You will be able to understand other languages. Your ministry will be as an evangelist, spreading the good news of my Son's gospel to the lost. Luanna, you will have the gift of miraculous powers. In my Son's name, you will raise the dead in body as well as the dead in spirit, and heal the sick, which fits with your ministry as a miracle worker. Sera, you have come so far from your dark past that you will do great things through your testimony. I give you the gift of distinguishing spirits, to tell apart the spirit of the Lord and the spirits of evil. Your ministry will be as a teacher. You mold and be in charge of those young in age and spirit."

"Lord, what about me? What is my gift?" asked Estrella.

The Lord's voice became a gentle whisper, wrapping around her in a breeze. "You are not ready, my sweet child. You are already demonstrating your gift of leadership and administration. Be patient. When you are ready, your gift will be made known to you." And then all was quiet, and the sun shone around the girls.

Estrella smiled and said to her girls, "My turn to bestow gifts."

"But, Estrella, you have already given us so much. You gave us a home and made us a family. What else could you possibly give us that could be better?" asked Karmina.

"The gift of being princesses, being royals with me, and always feeling like the beautiful girls you are." She went to her cart and pulled out the cloaks, circlets, and rings. Then she asked the girls to kneel. "Stopping at each girl in turn, she said, I dub thee Princess Karmina, Princess Sloan, Princess Lena, Princess Nori, Princess Anna, Princess Luanna, and Princess Sera." Asking the girls to stand, and again walking the line, she draped their cloaks around their shoulders, placed the circlets on their heads, and slipped the signet rings onto their fingers. "You are now princesses, daughters of the one true king, the King of Kings, Jesus Christ." The girls all had tears in their eyes, moved by everything that had just happened to them.

They had a home, a family, and now magical as well as spiritual gifts. On top of this, they were now princesses. It was all amazing. Estrella smiled. She had found her sisters! And now her quest was over and she was home, finally home.

"Come on, my sisters, let's go home." Estrella smiled as she mounted up with Ilya.

The girls mounted up on their horses with new pride in themselves. Then as a group they rode out of the forest and up to the gates of Faylin.

CHAPTER 37

Homecoming Party

The girls arrived at the gate to Faylin. To Estrella's surprise, the gate was closed. She would have assumed that with Gideon arriving before her, he would have informed their Mother of when Estrella would be arriving and the gates would be opened to welcome her home.

"Estrella, didn't you tell your mother in your letter you would be home soon?" asked Karmina.

"Yes, I did," Estrella replied, raising an eyebrow in confusion. She looked around and saw a sentry atop the wall. "Hey, you!" she called up to him. He looked down in surprise to see who it was that had the nerve to talk to him like that.

"Oy, who said that?"

"I did, you blind fool. Open the gate and let me in," she called up to him.

"Estrella, shush! You shouldn't talk like that," Karmina corrected her.

"I can if I want."

"And who might you be, miss, that you think you can talk to me like that and that I should let you in?" he called back at her.

"The Royal Princess Estrella of Faylin. I have finished my quest and have returned home."

"And how can I be sure you are who you say you are and not an imposter?"

Estrella grunted in frustration. This guard was pushing her buttons, when all she wanted was to go inside and see her family. She threw off her hood and looked right at him. It was then that she recognized the young man toying with her.

"Gilbert Brown! You annoying little blackbird, you've known me since we were three years old. How in the kingdom did you become a sentry? You couldn't stay awake in class to save your life!" She laughed.

He laughed back, knowing that his game was over and that it really was Estrella. "Hard work, dedication, and rising through the ranks."

She raised an eyebrow. "You?!"

"Okay, fine, a lot of work. And my dad gave me the job, and threatened to tan my hide if I fell asleep on the job."

"That sounds like Francis. Now will you let me in, please? I really want to come inside." She smiled.

"Well, I guess since you said please," he teased her. Gilbert smiled and motioned for a soldier behind the gate to go alert the queen of the princess's arrival.

Althea was seeing to the menu, the guests, and the decorations. The head chef, Horace; his staff; and his daughter, Bertha, were busy cooking and preparing the feast—many wonderful foods.

"Pastries go on the right, next to the present table. Meats go on the third table to the left, next to the fire pit. Breads go on the second table, between salads and meats. The banner goes over the gazebo; the decorations go over there." Althea was frantic organizing everything.

"My queen, it is okay to take a break to breathe," Captain Francis, Gilbert's father, reassured her.

"But it has to be perfect, Captain. I want Estrella's welcome-home party to be wonderful."

"And it will be, just by having her home again and with her mother to welcome her into her joyful arms."

"But, Indra..."

"... is occupied and ordered to stay out of your way. Besides, he is no longer in charge here. You are. You can do whatever you like. Organize the party your way, and rule how you see fit.

"You are Queen. We follow your rule, my lady."

"You are right, I am Queen. I am in charge. And it will be wonderful to have my oldest daughter home."

The young soldier arrived at the courtyard. Bowing, he said, "My queen, the princess has returned."

"Thank you, Jensen. Go tell Gilbert to let her in and begin phase two," said Captain Francis.

"Yes, sir," replied the soldier, who then returned to the gate.

"All right, everyone, let's get ready. Gilbert will be here with Estrella and her girls soon," Althea announced joyfully with tears in her eyes.

Back at the gate, Gilbert was pestering the girls with his lame jokes. "All right, I have a good one. You there in the red," he said to Lena.

"Me?" she asked.

"Yes, you. You look like you could use a laugh. How about this one: When it rains, why don't the sheep shrink?"

Lena giggled. Estrella rolled her eyes.

"Oh, this one is sure to make you laugh, Princess. Of all the knights around King Arthur's Round Table, the largest was Sir Cumfrence. He got that way from eating too much pi."

Estrella yawned.

"Why did the king go to the dentist?" he asked.

"Why?" asked Lena.

"Don't encourage him. We will never get in," Estrella groaned.

"To get his teeth crowned."

Lena giggled.

"Gilbert, I swear, one more terrible joke and I am climbing the wall and tackling you," Estrella taunted him.

Then the young soldier rode back with two other young soldiers and Gilbert's horse.

"All right, Princess, I have a riddle for you to solve. Figure it out and you can come in. Oh, and Estrella, you have to call me by my nickname."

"No, it's too silly. You came up with all our nicknames when we were seven. You were full of yourself then, and you're full of yourself now," she said with a scoff.

"Come on, Estrella. Just this one riddle and I promise I will open the gate," Gilbert pleaded with her pathetically.

"All right, Gilbert the Great." She smiled.

"All right, here is your riddle: My life can be measured in hours. I serve by being devoured. Thin, I am quick; fat, I am slow. Wind is my foe. What am I?" Gilbert smiled, knowing it could take the girls a while to solve the riddle.

The girls thought for a time. Most of them were stumped. Estrella giggled when she figured out the answer.

"Sir Gilbert the Great, the answer is a candle. The life of a candle is measured by how many hours you use it. A thin candle is used faster than a fat candle, the latter of which is slower to burn down. And the wind blows a candle out."

Gilbert smiled and nodded. "Princess Proper, you may have solved my riddle, but I have won, for I have succeeded in making you laugh."

He hopped down off the wall and onto his horse on the other side of the gate. Then he the other young soldiers pulled the gate open. "Welcome home to Faylin, Princesses." He smiled.

The girls, with Estrella in the lead rode in. Gilbert rode next to Estrella, with the others at their sides and at the rear.

"So, Estrella, explain to me your nicknames," asked Sloan.

"I can explain that, my lady," replied the soldier next to her.

"And what are you called?" she asked.

"Jasper the Jester, my lady." He smiled.

"Jasper the Jester? I take it you get in trouble quite often, then?"

"Every day, my lady."

"You can call me Sloan. So explain the other names, Jasper."

"Well, Gilbert the Great is so named because he acted like a spoiled prince when he was younger. You know my nickname. Then we have Jensen the Joyful, because he always has a smile. And in the back we have Allan the Adorable."

"Allan the Adorable?"

"Yes, he had a cute, innocent face when younger. He could get away with any prank just because one wouldn't believe him capable of it judging by the look of innocence on his face."

"And, uh, Princess Proper?" asked Sloan.

"Well, that's our little joke. You see, in class Estrella was the perfect little princess, a teacher's pet and star student, but outside of class she was anything but proper. She would laugh loud, play rough, and get dirty and scraped up with the rest of us. It would drive her nannies crazy and her poor seamstress to tears. We would tease her and call her Princess Proper when we played. It annoyed her, so it stuck." Jasper laughed.

They took the long way to the courtyard, the boys showing the new girls the town square of the kingdom. When they reached the courtyard, Estrella could hardly keep from falling off her horse. There were lights and lanterns, delicious-looking food, and many gifts. And there, among all the joyful cheering people, was her mother! Estrella dismounted in a rush, handing her phoenix chick to Karmina once she landed. She pulled up her skirts and ran to her mother. They embraced in tears.

"Oh, Momma, I missed you so much!" Estrella sobbed.

"I missed you too, my baby girl. Welcome home, my sweet girl." Althea kissed her daughter's tears away and held her tight.

"I love you, Maia!" Estrella smiled.

"I love you too, my sweet angel, much more than you could even know. Why don't you introduce me to your friends?" Althea smiled, kissing Estrella's forehead.

Estrella, still smiling, wiped her eyes, turned around in her mother's arms, and motioned for the girls to dismount.

The girls dismounted and walked over to where Estrella and her mother were standing. They curtsied.

"Raine Maia Althea, I present to you my sisters, the newly crowned princesses: Karmina, Princess of the Song; Sloan, Princess of the Golden Arrow; Lena, Princess of Knowledge; Nori, Princess of Healing and Faith; Anna-Mika, Princess of Alchemy and Evangelism; Luanna, Princess of Paint and Miracles; and Sera, Princess of Books and Teaching. My sisters, I would like you to meet my mother and best friend, the Reina Maia, or Queen Mother Althea Sela."

"It's an honor to meet you, Your Majesty," said Karmina.

"You are absolutely beautiful, Your Majesty. I can see where Estrella gets her beauty from," complimented Lena.

"You are everything she said you were," remarked Sloan.

"You girls are too kind. Thank you, from a concerned mother, for taking such good care of my daughter." Althea smiled.

"Your Majesty, we thank you for the wonderful person your daughter is, in so many ways. If not for Estrella, some of us would be in danger and very bad places in our faith," Nori said in gratitude.

"It is true. Your daughter's devotion to her faith and her following the lead of the Holy Spirit has been an inspiration to us," Lena added.

"Your Majesty, I was under the spell and influence of darkness and dark spirits. Your daughter rescued my town and me and brought back the light of the Lord. I owe my salvation to her," Sera confessed.

Althea teared up at the beautiful stories she heard; her daughter was an exceptional person. "I don't doubt any of it. I knew she was special and would do great things the first time I held her in my arms." She beamed.

"I love..." Estrella was going to say something, when she heard, "Cheep, cheep, cheep."

"What was that?" asked Althea.

"That would be our newest member, and the little prince of group. Karmina, if you would hand him to me, please?" Estrella asked, holding her hands out. Karmina handed her the baby chick, and then Estrella turned around and presented it to her mother.

"Queen Althea, I would like you to meet Ilya, my phoenix chick." Estrella smiled.

Althea's eyes went wide in wonder. Ilya had triggered a memory of a chick from her youth.

"A phoenix?" she whispered.

"What is it, Maia?" asked Estrella.

"Nothing, my sweet girl. I will explain later. Are there any other creatures I should know about?" She smiled.

"Yes, we each have our own animal companions, like my Merlin, but they are staying with the horses. If they came forward, it might startle our guests. Some of them are quite intimidating."

"Well, you girls will have to tell me about them afterwards. Right now we have a party to celebrate. Go mingle and enjoy yourselves." Althea smiled and hugged Estrella tighter, before letting her go to enjoy the party.

Estrella went around and introduced all her new friends to her old friends and family members. King Liam and Queen Irinia were there with Lucian and Nolani. Gideon was there. He introduced Estrella and the girls to Bliss. Estrella's grandparents Lavina and Ambrose were there, as well as her aunt Grace and her uncle Duncan with her cousins Aidan and Keegan. All her princess friends, and of course her sisters, Kylia and Keena, were there. Kylia and Keena were happy to have their sister home.

The girls had a marvelous meal and ate until they were sleepy. The minstrels picked up and played a lovely song, at which time the girls caught a second wind. They danced until they were sure they couldn't go another step. Estrella opened her splendid presents. The party lasted into the early evening. It couldn't have been more wonderful or perfect, that is, until Althea delivered some stressful news at the end of the party. When the other guests and family had already left to return to their kingdoms before dark, Althea gathered Gideon and Estrella together.

"Your father is here. He has something he has to tell you."

"What?! Father is here?" asked Estrella in shock.

"Where is he, my queen?" asked Gideon a bit more calmly.

"He is over to the far left. You two should go see him and hear what he has to say, but remember that no matter what he has to tell you, he loves you both very much." Althea sighed as she watched Gideon and Estrella walk over to their father.

Indra was standing with his plate of pastries, a smile on his face.

"Welcome home, Estrella and Gideon. It's very good to have all of my children home." Indra set down his plate as he greeted them.

Estrella had her fists clenched. She faked a smile. "Thank you, Father."

"It's good to be home again, my king." Gideon bowed.

Estrella shot him a look, but she changed her expression upon looking back at Indra.

"I have gifts for the both of you." Indra smiled and turned around, pulling out a gift for each of them.

Gideon opened his package. It was an exquisite sword, light, intricate, and thin.

"Thank you, my king. It's beautiful."

Estrella opened her gift: all four volumes of *Mystical Beasts*. "Father, I don't know what to say."

"I know now that I can't protect you from the world, especially by hiding books that you found anyway. I have no use for them, but you do. Enjoy them, sweetheart."

"I will."

"The queen said you had something you wanted to tell us?" asked Gideon.

"I wanted to give you your nice gifts before I gave you the sad news."

"What is it, Father?" asked Estrella.

Indra took a deep breath. This would ruin their joyful party, but he had to tell them before he left.

"Estrella, Gideon, I am getting a divorce from your mother. We lost the love in our marriage years ago. It's not your fault. Your mother and I grew apart. I have found someone new to love, and I hope that someday, when you forgive me, you will come and meet her and visit with us. I will always love you, and I ask your forgiveness."

Estrella was in shock. She had so many emotions tossing around inside her, it was like a tempest sea. She was furious with her father. How could he do this to them? She was sad for her mother and for herself. She was confused, wondering how her father could have found someone else. All these emotions made her frustrated. She dropped her books and rushed off.

"Estrella?" Gideon called after her.

"Let her go. She is upset. I blame myself; my confession was the last straw that drove her away. I broke my baby girl's heart. She may never forgive me," Indra said with tears in his eyes.

Estrella continued to stormed off. She was furious. Her girls caught sight of her and were concerned.

The girls went after her to find out if she was okay, but Althea cut them off.

"Estrella, what's wrong?" called Karmina.

"She will be okay. She just received some upsetting news. Whenever she gets upset, she doesn't know how to control her emotions well, so she runs off to be alone. But she has always had a good friend and mentor to help her get through it," Althea told them.

"Who is that, my queen?" asked Sloan.

"His name is Kasim. He came here on his own when he was twelve years old. The Lord sent him here at just the right moment, when Estrella needed him most. They have always been very close," Althea explained.

Estrella continued running, tears blurring her vision, emotions clouding her mind. She didn't like the feeling of not being in control, which made her more upset. She was so upset that she almost ran into a wall, but a hand caught her by the elbow and pulled her close. She didn't know who it was at first, but she didn't care. She was so upset that she let her anger out on the stranger's chest, beating it with her fists.

"Are you all right, dear one?" asked the stranger, hugging her close.

"No, I'm mad and upset. And I just want to be alone. Please, let me go so I can be alone," she sobbed.

"I know you're upset. Can you tell me why?" he asked.

"He is leaving us for good. My father is leaving our family and our home. He found someone else he loves." She wept.

"Well, I am sorry to hear that, dear one. I can't make him stay or change his mind, but you don't have to be alone on this day. I can be your friend and teach you how to better let out your feelings," said the stranger.

Then it clicked: Estrella remembered that she'd heard those same words when she was six years old and running away from her feelings on her horse. A young boy had found her, took her back home, and soon became her best friend—the friend she had left months ago to go on her quest. She looked up.

"Kasim?"

"Aye heev meesed faloo, mee freend," he replied in their secret language, a smile on his face.

"Oh, Kasim! I missed you so very much. I am very sorry I didn't write you as often as I had hoped, but—"

"It's all right, little sister. I can see from your new friends over there that you were very busy on your mission and all your adventures. But I have the real Estrella here in my arms, not just the one whose words I can read in letters. I'm going to hold you until you feel better. I'm sorry to hear about your father, but he still loves you, doesn't he?" he said, holding her close to him.

"Yes. Mother even said that he loved us before she sent me and Gideon to him to hear the news. And then when he was telling us the news, he said that he loved us."

"Then that is good. I know you're hurt, and he has done a lot to hurt you, but give it time. Someday you will find it in your heart to forgive him, not for him but for yourself."

"You're right, Kasim. Thank you. I missed you very much. It seems I needed my old friend to tell me it's okay and help me let out my emotions. Will you join me at the party?"

"I would like to, but it is getting late, little sister. You should get back, go to the castle with your new friends, and get ready for the night. I hope to see you in the morning and meet your new friends. I will always be here for you, my little sister." He smiled, kissing her forehead and letting go of her.

She smiled, kissed his cheek, and turned to leave, wiping her tears as she returned to her friends. Althea had already had servants gather all the gifts and take them to the castle. The kitchen staff had cleaned up all the scraps of food to give to the pigs to eat, and the leftover good food was divided up into baskets to give to the townspeople. The horses and mules were put away in a stable, and the animal companions were housed in an empty barn. All the girls' things were brought into the castle and put into their rooms. When Estrella had finished taking a hot bath, washing off properly, soaking, and applying body oils, she changed into her night shrift, got Merlin and Ilya settled in, and got herself settled into bed with her new pillow and quilt, her toy dragon, and her old doll Bonnie. Then she heard a knock on the door, a sound she had not heard in quite a while.

"Come in," she said.

Althea peeked in and then entered the room. Even wearing her night robe, with her hair loose and with her makeup wiped off, she looked amazing. It made Estrella smile.

"Hello, my sweet girl." Althea smiled.

"Hello, Mommy!"

"Are you all comfy?"

"Yes, thank you. I had a wonderful homecoming party. Thank you so much, Maia." Estrella smiled.

"I'm so glad. I wanted it to be wonderful just for you." Althea smiled, and then she sighed. "I'm sorry you had to find out about your father at your party. He told me while you were on your quest. I didn't write you with the news because I didn't want you to be upset while away from home. I told him he had to be here when you and Gideon came home. I still don't want you to be upset."

"It's all right, Maia. I'm not upset anymore. Kasim helped me get out my feelings."

"That's good, dear."

"Maia? When I showed you my phoenix chick, you looked shocked, almost like you had seen it before," Estrella said.

"I can tell you why now, now that it's just us and quieter. Many years ago when I was your age, I also found a phoenix chick. When I brought him home, my mother had the same shocked look. I named him Christmas, because I had found him in December. I raised him until he was big enough to take care of himself.

"After I had brought him home, I asked my mother the same question you asked me. She said that when she was seventeen years old, she also found a phoenix chick, but she said she named hers Americus. So that was why I was surprised to see that you had found one too," Althea explained.

"You had a phoenix too? And if they become their own descendents, then it's possible we have the same phoenix." Estrella gasped.

Althea nodded.

"It's very possible."

"Wow." Estrella yawned.

Althea smiled and tucked her in.

"Good night, my sweet angel. I'm very glad you are home. Get a good night's sleep. I love you, my princess," Althea said with a kiss on Estrella's forehead. Then she blew out the candle.

Before Althea closed the door, Estrella yawned again. She said, "Good night, Maia. I love you too." And then she closed her eyes and went to sleep, dreaming of her adventures, her friends and her trials to come. Ready for whatever the world threw at her.

Printed in the United States
By Bookmasters